The Hidden Palace

Dinah Jefferies began her career with *The Separation*, followed by the No.1 *Sunday Times* and Richard and Judy bestseller, *The Tea Planter's Wife*. Born in Malaysia, she moved to England at the age of nine, and went on to study fashion design, work in Tuscany as an au pair for an Italian countess, and live with a rock band in a commune in Suffolk.

In 1985, a family tragedy changed everything, and she now draws on the experience of loss in her writing, infusing love, loss and danger with the seductive beauty of her locations. She is published in 29 languages in over 30 countries and lives close to her family in Gloucestershire.

To find out more about Dinah Jefferies:

www.dinahjefferies.com
 / dinahjefferiesbooks
 @DinahJefferies

DINAH
JEFFERIES

The Hidden Palace

HarperCollins*Publishers*

HarperCollins*Publishers* Ltd
1 London Bridge Street,
London SE1 9GF

www.harpercollins.co.uk

HarperCollins*Publishers*
1st Floor, Watermarque Building, Ringsend Road
Dublin 4, Ireland

First published by HarperCollins*Publishers* 2022
1

A catalogue record for this book is available from the British Library

ISBN: 978-0-00-842705-4 (PB)
ISBN: 978-0-00-845871-3 (TPB, AU, NZ, CA-only)
ISBN: 978-0-00-854465-2 (HB, US, CA-only)
ISBN: 978-0-00-854462-1 (PB, US-only)

This novel is entirely a work of fiction.
The names, characters and incidents portrayed in it are
the work of the author's imagination. Any resemblance to
actual persons, living or dead, events or localities is
entirely coincidental.

Set in Dante MT by Palimpsest Book Production Ltd, Falkirk, Stirlingshire

Printed and bound in the United States of America
by LSC Communications

For my family

'To honour her brave people, I award the George Cross to the Island Fortress of Malta to bear witness to a heroism and devotion that will long be famous in history.'

King George VI
15 April 1942

The British Crown Colony of Malta was a military and naval fortress, and the only Allied base between Gibraltar and Alexandria, Egypt. Between June 1940 and October 1942, the Maltese Islands endured over 3,000 air raids by Nazi Germany and Fascist Italy. Axis submarines also attacked British convoys, thereby denying food and other vital supplies to the islands. The Allied garrison and the people of Malta withstood these attempts to starve or bomb them into submission – consequently the Axis failed to strip the Allies of their key naval base in the Mediterranean. Despite the deprivation they suffered, the Maltese population courageously resisted the bombardment. For this reason, King George VI awarded the George Cross to Malta and its people in recognition of an entire nation's bravery.

PROLOGUE

ON BOARD AN ADRIA STEAMSHIP

The woman on the deck glanced up as a dozen bad-tempered seabirds yelled and hooted. *Fool! You fool. Fool,* they cackled, hurtling towards her. She ducked, raising a hand to ward them off, but it was the wind snatching at her hair not the birds. She swallowed, tasted the tang of salt on her tongue with a hint of seaweed. Was she safe? It had been a leap of faith to board this ship in Syracuse and the further she leapt, the further away safety seemed to be. She gazed at the shifting ocean. This was what she'd wanted, wasn't it?

The sun began to set and the ship edged towards land. She gripped the railings, leaning over as far as she dared, mesmerised by something moving in the violet water.

She closed her eyes, felt the breeze cooling her burning cheeks.

The seabirds shrieked again. She raised her head, opened her eyes, and straightened up. How long had she been clutching the railings, listening to the voices in the sea? Because now, as the sun finally sank into the ocean, the sky was darkening to a deep velvety indigo, with such a sweep of stars that it stole her breath. And right before her eyes, as the ship slid closer to the island, a glittering scene unfolded as if a curtain really had been raised on a fairy world. Spellbound by the sight of the waters in the Grand Harbour dancing with the reflected lights from hundreds of illuminated vessels, she hugged herself, then turned to her companion.

'It's going to be all right,' she whispered. '*I'm* going to be all right.'

CHAPTER 1

Florence

England, late August 1944

Jack cursed under his breath, wincing in pain as he attempted to force the window shut, and Florence coughed, her throat dry and sore. Completely jammed, the window resisted, and the acrid black smoke continued to billow in.

'There's no point,' she muttered. 'Save your strength.'

'It'll disperse when we're out of this damn tunnel,' he said.

She nodded, leant back against the carriage wall, and slid to the floor where she rested her forehead on drawn-up knees and wrapped her arms around her shins. Anything to escape the smell. Not just engine smoke, but the sour odour of unwashed bodies too, and the cheap tobacco that hung in blue-grey clouds throughout the train and clung to their hair and clothes. Sitting in the corridor like this, crumpled and dirty and trying not to breathe, Florence felt exhausted and not quite able to relinquish the fear lodged in the pit of her stomach.

They'd been stuck in the dim light of the tunnel for more than three quarters of an hour, and they still had another train to catch before they could even dream of arriving at Exeter station where she hoped Jack's father would still be waiting.

Eventually there was a bone-shaking jolt.

Florence lifted her head and caught Jack's eye. He nodded as they heard a shrill whistle and a muted cheer from the weary passengers as the wheels turned, clanking and rattling as the train awoke. A thin, uniformed guard climbed over three or four servicemen lying half asleep on the floor by the door, their heaps of kit blocking the corridor. Grumbling to himself, he elbowed his way around the tight group of civilians bunched up next to Jack and Florence and then tripped over Jack's large, booted feet.

'Westbury,' he yelled after he had righted himself and glared at them. 'All change for Exeter.'

Just as well he had such a loud voice. Not only was it a way to let off steam, but also all the station signs had been removed – so unless you were a local, you had no idea where you were.

Jack scowled when, very soon after that, the train pulled into Westbury station. 'Typical,' he said as he scrambled up from where he'd joined Florence on the floor. 'If I'd known we were this bloody close we could have just got out and walked.'

'Don't think I'll walk anywhere, ever again,' she said, and meant it.

He gave her a commiserating smile. It wasn't easy for him either. As they had made their escape across the Pyrenees mountains, they had both injured themselves. When she'd fallen badly, Jack had reached out to save her, seriously aggravating an old injury sustained when he'd made a bad parachute landing back in the Dordogne. Her legs felt like jelly; his arm was strapped up. Fine pair they were.

As they joined the crowd shuffling towards the open door people pushed and shoved, desperate to exit the hot train and get to wherever they were going. Fatigued soldiers longing to see their families again, no matter how briefly, had perked up, but the worn-out nurses still in their uniforms stared ahead with glazed eyes. Everyone was grey and drawn.

'Platform for Exeter?' Jack asked a red-faced platform guard and was told which way to go.

When the crowd were not too far from the waiting Exeter train, Florence heard two men behind her speaking in a foreign language. She froze and Jack, noticing her distress, took her elbow and propelled her forward.

'It's all right,' Jack said quietly, linking arms with her. 'Only Polish servicemen. Come on, we need to hurry.'

Florence knew the men hadn't been German but was so tired that logic and common sense had deserted her. She could never reveal her secret, not now, not back home in the Dordogne, nor in the Pyrenees as they dodged Nazi patrols, and not in Franco's Spain either. Slowly, oh so slowly, they had avoided capture as they made their way under a burning sun from the north to the south of Spain. In Gibraltar they boarded *The Stirling Castle* which, before the war, had been an ocean liner, but was now a troop ship sailing back and forth between Gibraltar and Southampton.

Jack firmly pushed her up the steps and onto the next train.

'Frome – Castle Cary – Langport – Taunton – Exeter,' another station guard yelled.

Florence had a splitting headache from the constant noise and wished she hadn't been forced to leave France. This dreary worn-out England wasn't the England she remembered. But it would have been unthinkable to stay in France. Unthinkable. Irrevocably altered by what had happened to her, she prayed that surely, *surely* she'd be safe here.

They traipsed along the corridor for what seemed like an age then, thank God, Florence spied two seats and, stumbling over her own feet, she hastily claimed them. Once settled in the carriage, she leant her head back in relief. She would survive this, she told herself. She had survived much worse. And then she fell asleep, vaguely aware of the station stops and only opening her eyes properly when Jack shook her and told her they were almost there. She glanced out of the window as the train pulled into Exeter station and then came to a shuddering, screeching, stop. She spotted a poster with a head and shoulder image of the British Prime Minister, Winston Churchill, and a quote from him, too. 'Let us go forward together' it proclaimed. Yes, she thought. We all need to go forward, and she would just have to find a way to stop herself from looking back.

She felt light-headed as she and Jack straightened up, then stood to stretch their legs and smooth down their crumpled clothes. Tired, hungry, filthy dirty, they were home.

Home, she sighed. Where was that now? It was Jack's home they were going to. They retrieved their bags from the luggage rack overhead, climbed down from the train and made their way out of the station.

Forty minutes later as Jack's father, Lionel, drove them downhill along a bumpy gravelled track, Florence caught her first glimpse of the Devonshire cottage. She gaped at it from the front passenger window, blinking rapidly and feeling she'd arrived in the borderlands between what was real and what was not. Thatched and tucked into a cosy space between green forested hills, it had surely grown out of the meadow that lay in front of it. A fairy-tale cottage. And, except for the suicidal scuttling pheasants attempting to escape the wheels it was completely silent. There could be no greater contrast between what they had been through than this and just the sight of it revived her.

'A place to restore the heart and soul,' Lionel said with a knowing look back at Jack as they drew closer. 'Glad to see you safely back in Blighty, son.'

'Two sides of the house are backed by hilly oak thickets,' Jack said, on a more practical note. 'A steep hill slopes down to the house on the third side and, as you can see, a brook and water meadow borders the approach. Magnificent walks in every direction.'

'Like a sanctuary,' Florence said, breathing properly for the first time in weeks. 'And the hills standing guard.'

'Hope it will be a sanctuary for you, my dear,' Lionel said and coughed awkwardly, as if that might have been a bit too personal for a first meeting.

Florence smiled at him.

'Can't drive across the brook in winter, mind. Have to park this side of it, but you can always cross by foot on the stone slabs over there when the water is flowing,' he added. 'Will be absolutely fine now though. Had a go at mowing the lawns myself, but the grass was too long and too thick. Needs a scythe, Jack.'

'I don't think I've seen a more romantic place in my whole life,' Florence said, glancing at the teeming wildflowers, the tangled rose bushes, and the clematis cascading over the front of the cottage. 'Mind you, the climbers need a good pruning.'

'Like to garden, do you, my dear?' Jack's father asked.

He was tall and solidly built, a bear of a man with a full head of grizzly salt-and-pepper hair and ruddy cheeks. Probably a little too fond of a glass of port, she thought privately. She did her best to resist the image of her garden at home in France as it flashed into her mind and almost stopped her breath. She swallowed. 'I adore gardening,' she managed to say.

'She's something of an expert, Dad,' Jack added.

Lionel drove over the shallow brook and pulled up outside the cobbled pathway to the house, near a massive horse chestnut tree. 'Well,' he said. 'Welcome to Meadowbrook. But for the farmer's wife, you won't see another soul. And the old boy up at the manor never comes down here.'

'I love it,' Florence said. 'Thank you so much for driving us. Sorry we're so filthy.'

'Not at all. The house has been well aired and there are a few basic supplies. Bread, milk, bacon, and so on.'

'Thanks Dad,' Jack said and clapped his father on the back. 'I don't know about Florence, but more than anything I need to sleep.'

Florence glanced down at the ingrained dirt in her nails. 'Me too and tomorrow a bath.'

Jack gave her a weary smile. 'I think that can be arranged. Come on. Ready to go inside?'

CHAPTER 2

Devonshire, 1944

The next morning

How could she be the person she was before? She couldn't, but still the past drew her back. All night, dreaming, Florence had longed to stumble upon a garden just like hers in the Dordogne. But it wasn't a garden she found; in her dream it was a cemetery with her name carved on a headstone, paper roses strewn before it. Torn between worlds, in that hazy state before the day opened properly, her mind felt clouded, her heart unsettled, but then she heard water running over stones. From her bedroom window the evening before, she had spotted that the garden briefly dipped downwards, so the water was a little deeper there before it vanished under shrubs and bushes. Things became clear again. England, the early morning light here more fragile than it was at home, diffused. And then tapping. She heard someone tapping on her door. Barely able to remember the strange dream now, she heard Jack's voice and rubbed the sleep from her eyes just as he poked his head around the door.

'Sorry to disturb. You all right?'

She pulled the sheets up to her chin, acutely aware she wasn't wearing a nightdress. Last night, Jack had dug out a long-sleeved winceyette nightie that had once belonged to his grandmother, but she hadn't liked to say how much she hated the horrible itchy thing.

Jack ran his fingers through his hair, leaving it tousled, and didn't quite meet her eyes.

'You didn't disturb me,' she said. 'I was half awake.'

'Good. I thought you might be hungry.'

'Might be? I'm famished!'

'There's eggs and sausages from the farm next door and a fresh loaf.'

She smiled. 'Give me fifteen minutes. No, ten.'

'Scrambled? Fried? Poached?'

'Up to you.'

'Good. Truth is, I can only really do fried.'

She laughed as he left the room. Then she splashed her face and gave herself a quick flannel wash with water from the china jug and bowl on the marble-topped washstand.

Then she put on the dressing gown Jack had given her and brushed her tangled blonde hair, tying it back in a low ponytail. She glanced in the small wall mirror, smiling at her own gunmetal grey-blue eyes, the ingrained dirt on her heart-shaped face and the annoying red spot on her chin. Too bad. She would have to do. Relief at being safe bubbled inside her and as she opened her bedroom door, she could smell the sausages frying in the kitchen. Mmmm. Delicious.

She hurried down the narrow stairs. There was a brick-built outdoor bathroom, a sort of add-on affair, complete with a lavatory, a huge Belfast sink, and an old bath, but no electricity. At night you had to use a torch or a candle. You reached it via the scullery, so at least you didn't have to go completely outside, and she dashed through before heading for the kitchen.

'Smells wonderful,' she said a little later as she joined Jack. 'I missed a good old British banger when I lived in France.'

He pulled a wry face. 'Sorry. Burnt them a bit.'

'The only way sausages are meant to be eaten.'

'You like them like that?'

'Absolutely.'

Dark blonde hair framed his strong face, clean-shaven now for the first time, with even his sandy moustache gone. This man who had come into their life so suddenly, who had been a friend to her sisters as well as to the Resistance, had been her way out of France, her means of escape. He smiled at her, his green eyes bright with life. 'Better?'

She nodded, her mouth full of sausage, then glanced around the oak-beamed kitchen. It was small but immaculate, with a cream-coloured Aga which Jack filled from a store of anthracite in one of the sheds. She'd take over that task when he was gone.

When he was gone.

She didn't dwell on what else she might do when he was gone. Jack had brought her here so she had somewhere quiet to recover before she made contact with her mother. He hadn't told her where he would be going, and she didn't want to think about him leaving, but he was still a member of the Special Operations Executive as far as she knew, albeit with an injured arm.

She forced her mind away from the unsettling subject and looked around her. In the kitchen there was also a built-in wooden dresser, latticed cupboards with wire netting on the inside, hooks hanging from beams, another Belfast sink, and four oil lamps, a nod to the cottage's fragile electricity supply. The deep window seat, on one side of the pine table, overlooked the water meadow in front of the house. From another window at the back all you could see was the green slope of the hill behind the house where Jack told her the pheasants ran about like lunatics. Even a shadow in the window would be enough to set them off. A massive open fireplace with an oak mantel and a bread oven at the side took up almost one wall and a heavy chopping block lay on a smaller table in the middle of the kitchen.

'It's lovely to be here,' she said.

'Can't swing a cat,' he replied.

'It's cosy, and anyway you haven't got a cat.'

'Would you like one? Gladys has kittens up at the farm.'

'Maybe,' she said. 'But I can't see my mother letting me take a kitten to her cottage.'

'Fair point. When Dad brings his dog over, do you fancy taking him for a walk?'

'Just as long as I can have a bath first.'

She could already feel the Devonshire landscape calling her. She loved the countryside – the animals she'd seen on the nearby farm, the brook, the water meadow, the wildlife. And from the moment she had arrived the day before, she'd loved the earthy green smell of it too. It helped revive her spirits and lessened the exhaustion, the homesickness, and the loneliness when she thought of her sisters still in France. It had been more than two months since she'd seen them or been in contact; England was still at war and Hitler was still wreaking destruction in Europe. It might be years before she saw Hélène and Élise again.

Later, after Florence had finished her bath and had scrubbed her body until it was pink and glowing, Lionel turned up, bright and jolly, waving aside offers of tea and saying he needed to get going.

Justin was a young, lolloping black Labrador with heart-melting chocolate eyes, so the three immediately prepared for their walk. There were boots, jackets, waterproofs, and wellingtons in the cottage, accumulated over the years, Jack said, and she could always find something to wear. He had inherited the cottage from his grandmother but had often stayed there in the past so had left plenty of his clothes stored in wardrobes and chests.

It helped to have the dog easing the edge between them and they laughed as he bounded off to bark at pheasants and imaginary rabbits.

After crossing the shallow brook at the front of the house, they were now walking up the bumpy gravelled track they had driven down the day before. There was a valley on the left where a stream meandered, and beyond that a bank of beech, elm, and oak trees that marched up another steep hill. Jack strode on ahead and, as she watched him, she couldn't help thinking about what they'd been through.

'Do you think about Biarritz?' she called out.

He twisted back to look at her and frowned.

'I was so frightened,' she said, as she caught up with him.

'I try not to think of it, Florence, and I wish you wouldn't. But I have to admit I thought we'd never find a *passeur*.'

'I can't help going over it in my head. What could have gone wrong.'

He nodded. 'I know.'

She remembered blindly following the man into the darkness and the narrow passes of the foothills of the Pyrenees with Jack coming up behind. She'd stumbled and tripped and cried out in fear, her heart pounding.

'It'll be all right. The Boche won't find us here,' Jack had said when they spent the first night in an abandoned shepherd's hut listening to gunfire. After everything that had happened, it was hard to even recall the girl she had been a year ago.

Now, as he tramped on calling to the Labrador, she picked up speed too.

'What's up?' Jack asked.

'Oh, I don't know.'

He ruffled her hair and smiled. 'What a funny one you

are, Florence Baudin.' And though he sometimes treated her like a kid sister, she liked it.

That night, after she closed the curtains at the three casement windows, she sat on the sofa, feet tucked beneath her. Larger than the kitchen, the beamed sitting room was rectangular, with a comforting smell of old books. Even though it was not cold, Jack had decided to light a fire. She watched as he layered the twisted paper, kindling, and smaller pieces of wood, and tried to work out what he was feeling but his face, as usual, was unfathomable. Occasionally she would catch his eyes upon her, glittering, intense, and he would seem almost on the point of speaking, but when she smiled to encourage him, he would frown and look away.

She knew she needed to write to her mother and get a message to her sisters to let them know she and Jack were safe in England. Hélène would be sick with worry. She tasted something acidic on her tongue and then smelt something too. Guilt maybe? Could you smell or taste guilt? She glanced toward Jack again. They had already lost so much of their lives to war. Didn't you just have to grasp each day and live it?

'The first fire of the season is always special,' Jack said, seemingly oblivious to what had been going on in her head. 'Although I know it's not really the season, but these cottage walls are thick and it can be cool at night.'

He was still squatting as the fire caught but spun round on his heels.

'Are you happy to be here?' he asked, gazing up at her. 'You do seem subdued.'

So, he has picked up on something, she thought as she watched the flickering flames casting shadows across his face. 'I don't mean to be. Thank you for bringing me here – I love it.'

'You don't have to stay. If you'd rather go to your mother in the Cotswolds straight away, I won't be offended.'

She frowned. 'It isn't that. I'm glad to be here.'

'Then?'

She turned the issue of Hélène over in her mind again but didn't have the courage or the will, so spoke of how strange it would be to see her mother after seven years.

Then she fell silent.

She inhaled the scent of wood smoke as they remained without speaking for a few minutes longer, the only sound the fire as it crackled and popped.

'Damn thing smokes,' he said, 'when the wind howls.' And then he laughed and spoke in a spooky voice. 'The windows rattle, and the ghosts come out to play. Whooo.'

'Stop it,' she said laughing.

He grinned. 'Well, it isn't windy now, of course, but when it is you just have to pull out these two knobs.' He pointed at them.

Again she thought of the Pyrenees.

The wind hadn't been howling there either, not at first.

On that first night they slept a little and when dawn came she could make out the distant peaks of the mountains, shocked by how high they were and how high the stakes were too. A skinny young Basque guide collected them from the hut but seemed too nervous to know what she was doing. If Jack had chosen the wrong person, his misplaced trust could have meant certain death for them both.

She shook the images away as she realised Jack had been asking her something and wished she didn't keep going over these dark thoughts. But no one else could understand, no one else had been with them on those wild mountains with the constant risk of death. Just her and Jack. And then Hélène came into her mind again and a feeling of shame inflamed her cheeks as her sister's face danced in the firelight.

CHAPTER 3

Two weeks later Florence was sitting at the kitchen table reading her mother's letter for a second time. She needn't have worried about how things would be after Jack had gone, because *she* was going to be the first one to leave, after all. Though he was being extremely mysterious about when he would be leaving and where he would be going. Both Florence and Claudette had been thrilled with the news that after the success of D-Day, Germany had surrendered Paris on 25 August. A knock at the door interrupted her thoughts. She smoothed down her hair and opened up to find a pint-sized woman wearing a faded grey jumper, baggy green corduroy trousers, and black wellington boots. She had dark, raisin-like eyes that crinkled as she smiled and her white hair hung in a thick plait down her back.

'Oh, you must be Gladys,' Florence said, 'from the farm.'

The woman bent down to pick up a basket, its contents covered by a tea towel displaying a Union Jack, the red and blue faded with age and the white rather grey. 'I am indeed, and this here . . . is Gregory,' she said and laughed, her eyes crinkling up.

Florence glanced down at the duck now waddling into the kitchen behind the woman.

'Comes everywhere with me. Hope you don't mind.'

'You are both most welcome. Jack told me you might be popping in.'

'Out, is he?'

Florence nodded.

Gladys glanced at the letter lying on the table. 'Don't want to disturb you if you're busy.'

'Oh, I'm not. It's just a letter from my mother. She's expecting me the day after tomorrow and she's sent directions about how to get to her place in the Cotswolds.'

'She'll be happy to see you. Jack said you have sisters still living in France.'

'Yes. Hélène and Élise. I've written to let them know I've arrived here, but you never know with the post. I haven't heard back so I just hope they received it.'

'I'm sure you do, love. It must be hard.'

'It is. I don't know how they are or what's happening over there now. Hélène is a nurse you know, for the local doctor, and Élise is expecting a baby. I worry about them.'

'And you've come all the way over here . . .' Gladys glanced at her with a question in her eyes. 'To be with your mother?'

Florence couldn't tell her the truth about why she'd

risked such a long and hazardous journey to England, so after a moment she simply said, 'It's rather a long story, but yes.'

Gladys seemed to catch her reluctance and changed the subject. 'Here, I've brought a couple of bits for Jack.'

She plonked the basket down on the table and whipped off the tea towel with a flourish.

Florence glanced down at a beautiful brown loaf nestling in the middle of the basket along with a bottle of something golden. She sniffed. 'You're very kind. The bread smells divine, and I can't wait to know what's in the bottle.'

Gladys smiled. 'Gooseberry wine.'

'How lovely. I used to make fruit wines in France.'

'Miss it, do you dear? It must feel strange for you coming here while we are all still fighting this terrible war and everyone so weary and plain.'

'It is. But it was worse in France.'

'Yes, at least we don't have the Nazis over here. But the fighting's gone on too long and everyone's worried for their menfolk over on the Continent or out in the East.'

Florence murmured that she understood.

'And people are hungry, them that's in town that is. Us, with the farm, we're all right. We grow veg to send to the hospitals here, you know.'

Florence nodded, noting the tone of pride in the older woman's voice.

'We all do our bit. I wanted to send food to the Red Cross to parcel up for our boys overseas, but they only need tinned food. You know, condensed milk, Spam, corned beef, processed cheese. Stuff that doesn't go off. The boys mostly want chocolate and tobacco. That sort of thing.'

For a moment Gladys looked terribly glum but then seemed to rally. 'Stay with your mother long, will you?'

Florence sighed. She had hardly any money and would have to search for work of some kind to earn her keep while at her mother's and eventually she'd need to find herself somewhere to live. She felt anxious just thinking about it. How was she going to be able to make a new life in England during a war?

'Everything is a bit up in the air,' she said.

As if picking up on her turmoil, Gladys patted her hand. 'One thing at a time love, that's what I always say. Now I'd better be off, or my old man will think the Hun have taken off with me.'

Florence smiled. 'Thank you for the bread and wine.'

'Not at all. You look tired, my dear, do look after yourself. Off we go, Gregory,' Gladys said and left the house with a little wave to Florence.

On the morning she was due to leave, Florence was feeling flustered as she finished ironing the green-and-white spotted dress she'd adapted from one of Jack's grandmother's. She heard him calling her and glanced up as he came into the kitchen.

'There you are,' he said, frowning as he scrutinised her face, 'and looking a bit overheated. Fancy a stroll in the garden before I take you to the station? There's time and it might cool you down.'

'I just need to finish this and get dressed. "Make do and mend" as the posters say. Must look reasonable to go to Maman's.'

'Bag all packed?'

She mumbled a reply, fighting tears. She didn't feel ready to leave Devon and couldn't bear the thought of saying goodbye to Jack.

'Chin up,' he said.

She gave him a half smile, grabbed the dress, and ran upstairs to slip into it. Maybe leaving here really would be for the best. She liked Jack, she really liked him, but her sister, Hélène . . . She couldn't complete the thought.

They trailed around the garden avoiding the shade cast by the hill behind the house and walked instead where sunlight slanted through the trees. Florence glanced at Jack and saw his face patterned with ribbons of light. Lionel's dog followed behind, sniffing the earth around the tangled rose bushes, the overgrown buddleia, and the red and yellow dahlias, all the time sending the pheasants scattering up the hill. She watched the dog, tasting the fullness of a late British summer on her lips, and imagining the autumnal fruit to come. Before long these warm days would end and, much more imminently, her time with Jack. Would she ever see him again?

The dog barked and she realised she'd missed something Jack had said.

'Sorry, what did you say?' she asked.

'I asked if you'd like to know how this cottage came to be in my family?'

'Of course,' she said, sensing from Jack's bright tone

that he was trying to focus on something other than her leaving. For both their sakes, she thought. Or maybe not. Perhaps he was only trying to lighten the moment to make *her* feel better.

Florence forced a smile.

He scratched the back of his neck. 'My little Meadowbrook cottage is on the estate of, and was once owned by, the family of eighty-five-year-old Lord Hambury.'

'The old boy up at the manor?'

'Yes. As a young man, the previous Lord Hambury had a secret "liaison" with the family's nanny, my great-grandmother, Esther.'

She nodded, listening to him, but also aware of the circus of thoughts going in her own mind.

'When Hambury's wife, Maud, discovered them in bed, there was a godawful scene. As the story goes, priceless crystal goblets were hurled at their heads. Esther was turned out without a reference, but Lord Hambury had fallen in love with her, so he ordered the renovation of Meadowbrook and gave the place to her, deeds and all.' Jack paused and looked at her. 'Florence, are you listening?'

She blinked rapidly. 'Yes, of course. I wouldn't have liked to have been his wife. She must have been spitting nails.'

'I'm sure she was livid but there was nothing she could do. Hambury supported Esther financially until she married and my grandmother was born, though nobody knows if she was the child of Lord Hambury or not.'

'Golly. So, you could be the illegitimate great-grandson of a lord.'

He laughed. 'Knew you'd like this story.'

And for a moment she imagined she could hear Hambury and Esther murmuring in the dark. But they would be friendly ghosts, those two. Perhaps not so his poor wife.

She sighed. It was time and she didn't want to prolong the pain of parting any longer.

'Right,' she said a bit too briskly. 'I suppose we'd better get weaving.'

He nodded and something twisted inside her as he gave her a look she couldn't decipher.

CHAPTER 4

Gloucestershire, mid-September 1944

Florence nervously brushed down her dress, glad she'd not worn anything long-sleeved. You couldn't be sure of the temperature in September, and her choice of outfit was perfect for a day like this. She wiped her brow and approached an elderly station porter to ask about catching an onward train to Toddington or Broadway.

'Sorry, miss, both gone,' the old boy said and began to turn away, bustling with self-importance.

'Wait . . . I mean, please. Could tell me when the next train is due?'

'Ah. That'll be tomorrow mornin'. Sorry, love. Taxi outside. Or hotel of course. We 'ave lots of 'em 'ere in Cheltenham.' He spoke with pride and a strong Gloucestershire accent. 'Carry your case?'

She shook her head. If she had to pay for a taxi, she'd

need every penny; anyway she had so little her case wasn't heavy.

'How far away is Stanton?' she asked. 'By road, I mean.'

'Couldn't rightly say. Twelve, thirteen miles. Never been there meself. They say it's pretty. Visiting someone?'

She nodded. 'My mother.' Thanking him, she picked up her case and headed for the exit.

The taxi was available and after agreeing the price she settled herself in the back. They set off, wending their way past the elegant buildings of the Regency town centre before reaching a road signposted, 'Winchcombe'.

'I thought all the signposts had been taken down,' she said.

'They have. Best to confuse the enemy, eh?'

'Why's that one still up?'

'Search me, love, we've all seen one or two been forgotten. My son's going round ripping them down hisself. You from round here?'

'I've just come up from Devon.'

She saw him glance in the mirror to look at her.

'Just you have, well . . . sort of an accent I suppose.' He shook his head. 'Maybe not an accent exactly. Perhaps just a look.'

'I see.' Florence was surprised. She didn't believe she had an accent at all, and nobody had ever mentioned it before.

'Sorry, love. Don't mean to offend. Can't be too careful these days.'

A little further from the town she wound down the window and, feeling the breeze on her cheeks, she glanced up and took in a lungful of fresh country air. The earlier mackerel sky had given way to a hazy blue wash, dotted only by thin wispy clouds and in the warmth, she let her mind wander. It was such a relief to be out of the noisy train. Two children had squealed with laughter as they raced out of the carriage and up and down the corridor, chased by a harassed mother. There hadn't been so many servicemen going home on leave this time, so at least it was less smoky than the train from Southampton. It still felt a bit odd hearing the unfamiliar English voices around her, and she couldn't quite get used to not having to look over her shoulder for the inevitable German soldiers. Nor the fact, as they passed a village of thatched cottages and half-timbered houses as well as some larger Victorian and Georgian ones, that it looked nothing like France.

'Prestbury,' the driver said, twisting round to glance at her.

She viewed the lush, still green countryside as they drove on. The road wound upwards, steadily climbing, the hedgerows bursting with berries and now she could see the early signs of autumnal red and gold dusting the trees.

'Warm for the time of year,' he added. 'Indian summer. Though I like it better when there's a bit of a nip in the air.'

He seemed to want to continue passing the time of day, but Florence didn't feel like talking any more. Her head was spinning as she went over what she was going to have to say to her mother, Claudette, about why she had come back to England. She hadn't seen her since well before the war. Hadn't even been to this cottage. Claudette had sold their old Richmond home after their father's death, saying they couldn't afford it. Their family holiday house in France was too small for all of them, she had said, so Florence, aged fifteen, along with her older sisters, had gone to live in France while Claudette had moved into the cottage in England. She had helped settle them in France to begin with and promised to visit occasionally but had never quite got round to it and then the war had kept them apart. But now the time had come.

The landscape turned flatter, more open, with the hay already stacked and cattle and sheep grazing contentedly in the fields, and before long they reached the first honey-coloured stone cottages of Stanton.

'That's the manor house,' the driver said, 'on your left. In 1543 it passed to Catherine Parr in her dowry. I've heard tell it's haunted.'

'By her?' she asked, and he chuckled. She pictured a croquet lawn, a walled garden and the ghost of Katherine Parr wandering around in a long white dress.

'What was the name of the cottage you wanted?' he added.

'Little Charity. And I don't think it's haunted. My mother said it's up the hill just after the post office.'

Each house and cottage flanking the quaint high street as it climbed the hill was constructed of the same golden stone, and many of them were swathed in climbing roses or the last of the year's honeysuckle. Some of the buildings were grand, others less so, but the entire place looked as if it had been forgotten, lost somewhere in a sleepy past. She imagined the people who must have once lived there: the women in their long dresses and bonnets, the laundress in her oversized apron, her bare arms muscular, the kids playing tag and marbles or rolling their hoops over the cobbles.

When the driver pulled up opposite a small village green just before the street climbed even higher, she paid him, got out, and surveyed her mother's cottage. Drenched in sunlight, there were three small-paned windows upstairs and two similar ones below. She'd been warned in the last letter that it was tiny, with two bedrooms and only an outside toilet. Florence found it impossible to imagine her poised and very fussy mother coping with that during a muddy English winter. There was a minuscule front garden with a low hedge and as she approached the pillared porch – framed by autumnal Virginia creeper – the front door swung open.

Claudette stood waiting in the doorway, a tight smile on her face, and to Florence it was as though her entire childhood had suddenly appeared there beside her.

'Chérie, you made it. Come on in. We're very simple here. I hope you understand.'

Her mother was speaking English, never usually her first choice, but Florence supposed after living in England for so long, especially on her own here, she'd got used to it. Her hair, with a few silver threads in it now, was neatly drawn into a chignon at the back and, elegant as ever, she wore a grey pencil skirt and pale pink twinset with a single row of pearls. Just as she had done when they lived in Richmond.

Florence went to her, pasting a smile on her face despite

feeling a huge distance between them. Her mother looked older, not quite like herself, and was she a little bit thinner too? Seven years was a long time.

After a brief hug, Claudette took her hand. 'Chérie, I don't understand why you would travel to England while the war is still going on. You didn't say anything in your letter. Why did you take such a risk?'

'It's a long story, I—'

'You weren't happy there?' her mother interjected. 'I thought you were happy.'

'Well . . .' Florence paused to think about how to reply. 'I was happy, Maman, up to a point.'

'So why come back?'

'The war changed things,' Florence said, dodging the question, not quite ready to tell her mother the truth. She spoke brightly as she carried on. 'I told you how I did all the gardening, baking, preserving, and so on? I really loved it.'

'Mmm.'

'You should have seen the garden. It was wonderful. I grew all kinds of vegetables, and we had chickens and goats and—'

Claudette hardly seemed to be listening. 'Heavens, what are we doing chatting like this and still in the hall?' she said, interrupting Florence. 'I've lit a fire in the living room. It is a bit cold today.'

Florence frowned. *She'd* been thinking how lovely it was to have such a warm sunny day, just when you thought the summer was fading.

As she put her case down, a simple hall mirror – or

looking glass as her mother would say – caught her eye, placed exactly opposite the front door. How like her mother, never known to bypass a chance to admire her own appearance. This time, however, Claudette didn't even glance at it, though Florence did, patting her unruly blonde curls.

In the tiny hall a large marmalade cat lay dozing on a chair beside a small table on one side and a grandfather clock on the other. The cat opened one green eye to scrutinise her for a moment and then, apparently satisfied, went back to sleep.

'You have a cat.'

'Not mine. Belongs to . . . well, *belonged* to an old dear who passed over.'

'She died?'

'Such an unpleasant word. Anyway, the cat just moved in. I like it.'

'What's it called?'

'Franklin Robinson,' she said. 'I call him Robby. Would you like tea?'

Florence raised her brows. Since when did her mother keep cats and drink tea? Through all the years they'd lived in England growing up, when her father was alive, her mother had been resolutely a Frenchwoman, even though she might have dressed like an English lady of the manor.

While Claudette clattered about in the kitchen, Florence looked around the sitting room. The low-ceilinged room was pretty, and she spotted some of the old familiar furniture from their English home: the yellow and blue needlepoint cushions on the two armchairs and a navy blue and white rug that used to be in her parents' bedroom. But with a roaring fire on the go, it was sweltering, and she longed to throw open a window. After a few moments, her mother returned carrying a tray of tea things.

'Where's the bathroom?' Florence asked, standing up.

Her mother placed the tray on a small side table and pointed towards the back of the house. Florence saw Claudette's hands were noticeably older.

When Florence returned, her mother was holding the teapot aloft. 'I'll be mother, shall I?' she said. They both laughed.

'Biscuit? Oat, of course, and there's never enough butter. I make them for the WI to sell. Raising money for the war effort you see.'

Florence wasn't sure how to respond. This was an odd version of her mother.

'And jam. Rhubarb and apple. I grow the rhubarb and there are two apple trees in the garden, though it's hard to get the sugar. I often use carrots or, in the summer, figs.'

Florence wondered if Claudette had missed their father when she moved up here, whether she missed them, her daughters. She'd never said anything about that in her letters and rarely mentioned their old life in Richmond except to tell them what she'd sold and what she'd kept. Florence wanted to ask how Claudette felt about those days, but her mother never discussed feelings so instead she just said, 'So, you're happy here.'

Claudette nodded but looked strained. 'The house is seventeenth century, you know.'

'Why did you choose to move here, to this village?'

'The Cotswolds remind me of the Dordogne.'

'But Maman, you could have joined us there. While travel was still possible. Then, at least, we could have been together during the war.'

'No. I could not. You know there was not enough room, not for any length of time. You and Élise would have had to share.'

'I wouldn't have minded.'

'It would have felt cramped. Anyway, you girls were better off being there without me.'

Florence couldn't help feeling Claudette was avoiding something. Had her mother wanted to be alone so she could see. . . . She paused. Surely not. There had been so many years since her mother had ripped up the red dress. The last time she had seen *him*. She lifted up her tea and took a sip. It was delicious – clearly her mother's impeccable taste had extended even to making English tea while rationing was in force.

'How are your sisters?' Claudette asked.

'They're well, I believe, or were when I left.' She hesitated. 'Did you already know Élise is expecting a baby?'

Claudette pursed her lips. 'Without a husband, as I understand it. But of course, that's Élise all over. Always was my wild child.'

'Maman, the baby's father was Victor. A brave man, whom the Nazis executed. It was terrible. I didn't think Élise would ever get over it. I'm not sure she has.'

Claudette sighed and shook her head sorrowfully, but Florence wasn't sure if it was over Victor's death or Élise's unmarried status.

'It was a dreadfully difficult time for all of us,' Florence said, and her voice shook at the thought of everything that had happened. She steadied her breathing and carried on. 'Really it was impossible for any of us *not* to become involved with the local Resistance. Even Hélène couldn't sit on the sidelines, and you know how cautious she can be. But in the end, well, you were either on one side or the other.'

Claudette nodded but didn't speak. Didn't comment about how awful it must have been for them. Didn't reach out a hand.

'You wouldn't believe how divided the village was. Old friends became enemies. It was horrible, although after Victor was executed a lot of people changed their minds. I think it was the last straw.'

Claudette didn't respond and Florence felt as if her words were falling into a vacuum. Energy was buzzing through her, not at all comfortably, as she fought for the courage to voice what she really needed to. She took a deep breath and then she spoke. 'Look, Maman, I know I have to tell you the truth about why I had to leave France and there is something I do have to tell you. Something about me. I—'

'Not now,' her mother interrupted curtly. 'Another time. Florence, I have no time for what happened in France at present.'

Florence felt as if she'd been winded and folded an arm around her middle. 'I want you to go somewhere for me, to find someone,' Claudette went on, not appearing to have noticed her daughter's discomfort. 'It's urgent.'

'I've only just got here. Can't it wait?'

'No. It really cannot.'

'But Maman,' Florence said, trying to remain calm when really she was beginning to panic that her mother might never listen to her, 'I do need to talk to you – about everything that's been happening – and about the past.'

But her mother seemed to have barely heard her. 'Well, the past will have to wait. As I said, I need you to go somewhere for me.'

Florence stared at her, jaw tightening. She'd waited such a long time to talk to her mother about this. But nothing had changed. She might have been her mother's favourite, according to the others, but Claudette had never allowed any of them to talk about difficult matters.

'Why have you hidden things from us?' Florence asked.

'I don't know what you mean. In any case it doesn't matter now. None of that matters. *This* is what matters.' And she got up stiffly, walked over to a bookshelf, and carried back a small wooden box which she handed to Florence.

'What is it?' Florence asked, biting back her anger.

'Open it.'

Florence lifted the lid and found inside a Catholic rosary with a Maltese cross attached, and a note.

'Rosalie sent me that.'

Florence frowned. 'Your sister? How did she know you were living here?'

'She didn't. They were lost in the post for ages but eventually turned up at the house in Richmond and were then forwarded to me here. Read the note . . . from Rosalie. She said she'd write again. There were problems, she said, and she needed my help urgently. But she never did write again.'

Claudette looked close to tears and Florence held out a hand, but her mother, looking terribly forlorn, didn't respond.

'How distressing for you,' Florence said. 'I'm so sorry. But now I'm here we'll have plenty of time to talk about what happened, won't we? And I can help you in other ways too.'

'No,' Claudette snapped. 'For God's sake, I'm not old and I don't need help.'

Unaccustomed to hearing such a harsh tone from her mother, Florence recoiled. Élise was used to Claudette's sharp tongue, cruelty even, but not Florence.

The room went silent for a few moments.

Florence was the first to speak. 'Do you miss her, your sister?' she asked.

Claudette sighed deeply and snapped back. 'Of course. What do you think I am? When she went, it left me in pieces.'

Florence wondered if Rosalie's disappearance accounted for a great deal about her mother.

'I think she may be in Malta.'

'Because of the cross she sent?'

'Yes. It's a tiny fortress island just south of Sicily and close to Africa.'

Florence nodded. 'How did your parents know she'd run away and hadn't been . . . well, hadn't been taken.'

'They knew. Oh yes. They knew and I did too.'

'And did they know why?'

'They did.'

'And you?'

'Yes. Now, that's enough,' Claudette snapped.

'Very well . . .' Florence said, on the verge of asking exactly what had happened. But seeing the distress in her mother's eyes her other questions were left to hang in the air. Except for one. 'All right, what is it you want me to do?'

Claudette looked lost for a moment, her eyes shining with unshed tears. 'I think Rosalie may be dead. But I want you to find out. Please. If she is alive, it might be my only chance to . . . well, to put right what happened in the past. I didn't help her when she needed me in Paris nor when she sent me that note.'

Florence blinked. 'But she didn't tell you where she was. And she ran away almost twenty years ago, didn't she? Nobody has seen her. Nobody knows where she is.'

Her mother's face crumpled. 'She was always in trouble, wild and independent, just like your sister. My parents couldn't cope.'

'Like Élise?'

Claudette nodded and with a shaking hand she swiped her tears away. 'And it's true nobody knows where she is, and I don't know anything for sure. All I have is this note and the rosary. But if you do find her, I need you to tell her how sorry I am,' she said. 'I have few regrets in my life . . .'

Florence wasn't sure that was true. Surely her mother had plenty to regret.

'But,' her mother continued. 'I know . . . well, the thing is . . . I know I let my sister down.'

'Do you have a photograph?' Florence asked.

'Only the one I stuck on the hall mirror in France. You remember?'

'Yes, I do. She had red hair, didn't she? The photo was only black and white, but I remember you saying about her hair,' Florence said, although she struggled to recall the girl's face.

'She had wonderful shiny red hair and beautiful deep blue eyes. Her hair curled way past her shoulders when she was young. Our mother always made her plait it. Said it was as uncontrollable as she was.'

Florence absently scratched the back of her neck, unsure what to think. For her mother – her mother! – to have made such a strange request. Her mother, who never apologised for anything, and who had only rarely mentioned her sister, never explained why she'd gone, had even made out it hadn't mattered. It had been the family mystery that no one would talk about, and Florence and her sisters had got used to it, accepted it. So, why now? After all this time. What had really happened to Rosalie and why was it so important to Claudette now?

CHAPTER 5

Florence spent an unsettled night in Claudette's spare bedroom, partly feeling sorry for her mother, partly worrying about what to say about the past, and partly feeling annoyed. Hélène and Élise had always accused Claudette of being unfeeling, but Florence hadn't really understood it until now.

She thought about Rosalie too, and her mother's request. Rosalie's disappearance was intriguing, but her mother hadn't seemed to realise that it was almost impossible to travel while there was a war on. She wished she could ask Jack what he thought about it.

She missed Devon and, thinking how much she longed for Jack's beautiful cottage, as well as Jack himself, her chest tightened. But she scolded herself, got out of bed and, deciding to brave the outdoor bathroom later, dressed in the clothes she'd worn the day before. This was to be her life now, and the sooner she forgot about Jack, the better.

When she got downstairs Claudette wasn't in the sitting room or the kitchen. She glanced out of the kitchen window and saw her mother halfway down the garden looking back at her with a blank expression. Florence waved, opened the back door, and went outside. There was nothing for it, she couldn't put off telling her what she'd discovered in France any longer.

'Chérie,' Claudette called. 'I didn't want to wake you. Thought you might need the sleep.'

Florence joined her where she was cutting creamy roses, softly flushed with pink.

'They're beautiful.'

'Alfred de Dalmas, I've been told, a very old variety and hard to get hold of. But this one was here when I moved in. I didn't plant it.'

Florence nodded. 'And where's your vegetable garden?'

Her mother pointed to the very back of the garden. 'Behind that hedge. It's not actually in my garden but in the field behind. The farmer gave me permission because of the war. You see the small gate?'

'Yes.'

'Go through, have a look.'

Florence took a step away to do as her mother said, but then turned back. She needed to grasp the nettle no matter how much it might sting. 'Maman, I wanted to talk to you about France,' she said.

'Did you, chérie?'

'You know I did.'

'Come and look at these,' Claudette carried on talking as she walked across to a bed of pink hollyhocks and blue cornflowers. 'Of course, they're past their best now but they thrive in the same growing conditions, you know, fertile soil.'

'In France I used mature compost,' Florence said, but determined to get on with what she really needed to say, she added, 'Could we maybe talk over a cup of tea?'

'All in good time. Come, let me show off my lettuces.'

Florence sighed and followed her through the gate.

'Here we are,' Claudette said gaily, completely ignoring Florence, who was growing increasingly frustrated.

But she held it in, and her voice took on a conciliatory tone as she said, 'You've done well, Maman. I never expected you to be interested in growing vegetables.'

Claudette bent down to pick a lettuce and then straightened up. 'Needs must, as they say over here. This lettuce will make a nice salad for lunch, don't you think? With some tomatoes from the greenhouse.'

'I grew tomatoes in France. Don't you miss it? France, I mean.'

Claudette frowned and brushed a few stray hairs behind her ears. 'Not especially.'

'What about when you were younger? When we were little and stayed there in the summer. Don't you miss those days?'

Claudette turned her back and answered curtly. 'I don't think about those days . . . Heavens, would you look at those weeds!' And she marched over to the shed as Florence sighed.

When Claudette came back with the weeding fork, she

began to prod at a patch that Florence could see didn't need weeding at all.

'Did Father ever come to France?' Florence asked, persevering. 'He was half French after all. I don't remember him there.'

Silence.

'Maman, will you come inside? Please.' She'd spoken cajolingly, hoping to encourage her mother.

'I need to do *this*.'

'No, for goodness' sake, Maman, you really don't,' she snapped, feeling the storm brewing inside her.

Her mother rose to her feet, standing erect, and with fury in her eyes she said, 'Do not speak to me in that tone of voice. I need to do the weeding.'

Florence felt something twist inside her. 'And I need to tell you I've met my real father. I know— the truth.'

She covered her mouth, instantly regretting blurting it out. She had wanted to raise the subject sensitively, tell the whole story about how it had transpired a little at a time, but now she had no option but to plough on.

'I've met Friedrich, Mother. My real father. I know he's German, that you and he had an affair, and I have a half-brother too, called Anton.' She tried to keep her voice steady, while her heart pounded.

Claudette didn't meet Florence's eyes.

'Maman? My German father is why I had to leave France. Hélène thought there would be trouble during the liberation, afterwards too. They're already punishing collaborators. It was terribly hard, having to leave. The journey was—'

Florence stopped, overcome as her tears began to fall. Her mother's face gave nothing away. She only raised a hand to her brow and shielded her eyes for a moment.

'I didn't mean to shock you like that. I'm sorry I . . . but why did you hide the truth from me?'

Claudette turned away, marched towards the house, and opened the back door. To Florence's astonishment she went inside without saying a word, the door closing behind her. Florence wiped her eyes with her fingers and followed.

She found her mother in the kitchen staring at the floor in silence, her face drained of colour. Then she raised her head and glared at Florence. 'How dare you come here and speak of such things. And in the garden, where anyone might be listening.'

'I'm sorry I didn't mean to. I asked you to come inside.'

Claudette hissed her reply. 'It was private. You do not speak of a German father in England. I did not expect you to talk of *that*.'

'I'm sorry. I'm really sorry, but I need to know what happened. Did you love Friedrich, Maman?' Florence spoke tentatively, not really sure what she wanted to hear.

Claudette turned her face away.

'Why are you being like this? I just want to know if you loved him.'

Florence heard what might have been a stifled sob and went to her mother, tried to touch her, reassure her, but Claudette pushed her away. Florence stepped back, hurt. 'Did you ever love Father? Were you unhappy in Richmond all that time? Unhappy with us?'

Her mother looked increasingly stiff and unyielding. 'You will desist with these questions,' she said.

'I don't understand. Why are you being so cold? Are you embarrassed that we found out? Is that it?'

The kitchen clock seemed to be ticking too loudly. Claudette did not reply but her fingers were twitching dangerously.

'Don't I have a right to know?'

Her mother raised a shaking hand as if to stop her speaking. 'The past is the past. You have no right.'

'But Maman, you lied. All these years you lied. How did my English father feel about it? How? And how could you do that to him if you didn't love Friedrich?'

'That is enough! You will not speak of this. You will never speak of this again!' Claudette's voice was harsh as she spoke through gritted teeth and then delivered such a flood of angry bitter words in French that Florence burst into tears.

'Stop it. Stop it. Don't speak like that. Please don't speak like that.'

Claudette raised a hand as if to strike her. Florence recoiled, stepping back and stumbling at the rage distorting her mother's face.

And then her mother, who still held the trowel in her other hand, threw it with all her force at the wall. It hit the kitchen clock and as the glass casing shattered and fell to the floor, she marched towards the back door.

'Please. Isn't it time we talked?' Florence called after her, but her mother had already left the room.

Florence ran up to her room where she picked up a

pile of her clothes and threw them into her case. Shattered by the depth of her mother's fury, tears streamed down her face but, angry and confused, she wiped them away with her hands. How could Claudette be like this? How had she never fully recognised her mother's capacity for rage before? And what did that make her, for not realising? She remembered Élise's arguments with Claudette. Once, she'd yelled at their mother, calling her a harpy, a hideous monster of Greek mythology. A terrifying bird woman. And Claudette had risen from the sofa as if to spread her wings and lunged at her daughter, wild with bitter laughter. But Florence had always blamed Élise for being so unkind to Maman. Now, for the first time in her life, she saw what her sister had been getting at and felt ashamed. She should not have judged Élise. And deep inside her now a little voice was whispering. Had her mother ever loved any of them?

One thing was clear – if Claudette would not allow her to speak about what she had found out, she, Florence, couldn't stay here. She felt too hurt and too upset. She flung her hairbrush on top of her clothes in the case, snapped it shut, then ran down the stairs, glancing into the sitting room for anything she may have left behind. The front window was open and everything was still but for the breeze lifting the corner of Rosalie's last note as it lay forgotten on the coffee table.

CHAPTER 6

Rosalie

Paris, 1925

Rosalie Delacroix hurried south-west of the Jardin du Luxembourg and down the shabby darkening streets of Montparnasse, glancing in at the bright windows of the Café du Dôme, as she passed. The glittering café, recently renovated with mirrored walls and accents of scarlet and gold, was the place where people went to see and be seen. She could smell the Gitanes cigarette smoke mixed with drains, gas from the few remaining gaslights, and hints of the animalistic scent of Shalimar drifting from the café.

She loved bohemian Montparnasse where the sound of jazz came flooding from the dark cafés and bars. *Le jazz-hot*, they called it. Raw, passionate, earthy; to Rosalie it spelt liberty.

When she arrived at her destination, she pushed open the smoked glass door and was met by the owner, Johnny Cooper.

'Okay,' he said in a bad American accent and grinned at her.

With awful teeth he didn't look a bit American, and she was sure his name was an affectation aimed at pulling in more American tourists in the fabulous 'City of Light'. Johnny was even serving a 'hamburger steak', something Americans were fond of apparently, and he had a waiter from London called Norman with whom Rosalie was planning to practise her English.

'Fine,' she replied to Johnny as she heard a girl calling her name.

'Took your time,' the girl said and took a last drag of a Gauloise before stubbing it out on the tiled floor. 'Come on.'

'Couldn't leave until they went to bed,' Rosalie said.

The other girl was dark-haired, dark-eyed Irène, who lived in one of the slums where there had been a flood of wartime refugees. 'You think it's hard for you, you should try my life,' she said.

Rosalie knew poorer Parisians were crowding into ever smaller living spaces, and while she longed to escape the constraints of her bourgeois background, Irène wanted to escape a harder one. Irène was one of the small troupe of young cabaret dancers whom Rosalie would be joining in the back room tonight, wearing a puff of pink flamingo feathers and not much else.

'You okay?' Irène asked. 'Your first time and all.'

Rosalie nodded, but in truth she felt almost delirious with nerves.

In the dim light of the tiny changing room, she revealed the golden costume she'd secretly made herself, copied from an outfit she'd spotted worn by movie star Marion Davies in her mother's latest *Vogue* magazine.

'Pretty good,' Irène said as she looked her up and down with narrowed eyes, 'but you need more make-up.'

Rosalie frowned but Irène pointed at a chair. 'Sit.' And she opened the box of communal make-up resting on a small table. 'Scarlet lipstick, chérie. And lots of it, with a perfect bow. Sensational with your red hair. And I'm giving you smoky eyes. You know you have amazing eyes, right?'

'Do I?'

'You know you do. Such a deep blue. Different colouring but you do look like Leila Hyams.'

'Who?'

'Movie actress. Incredibly pretty. Heart-shaped face and the cutest mouth. Just like you. You should cut your hair, like hers.' Irène rummaged in a pile of magazines on the floor and held one up to show her. 'Here. She's not that well-known yet, but she will be.'

Rosalie scrutinised the photograph of a woman with arresting eyes, her hair curly and cut short in a stylish bob.

'Glad to see you've plucked your brows. I'm going to make them darker though.'

'I don't want to look like a clown.'

Irène stared at her, hands on hips in mock offence. 'As if.'

Many others, older than her, had danced and had fun

since the end of the war in 1918. Now, Rosalie, at just nineteen, longed to let off steam too. Paris felt wild with the chance of frivolity and it was her turn, even if she had to keep it a secret. On her way here she'd hidden her skimpy golden costume beneath her father's old flapping greatcoat.

Paris adored the African American jazz musicians and a lovely man called Saul from New York would be playing for them tonight. He didn't say much but he was beautiful, with melancholy eyes and an engaging smile. From the changing room, Rosalie could hear him warming up, his sensual floating notes sending her spirits sky-high. He nodded at her as she hurried after Irène, make-up finished, into the wings behind the curtain that hung across the tiny stage.

But despite the fun, there was also danger. Alongside this feeling of liberation and surging optimism – this feeling that anything was possible – a new right-wing movement had formed.

'Watch out for them,' Irène had warned just before they went on. 'And scarper if any come in.'

'How will I know?'

'Oh, you'll know the bastards.'

Inspired by Mussolini's fascism, the 'bastards' called themselves Jeunesses Patriotes and hated communists. Most of the aspiring writers and painters who patronised Johnny's place were *not* communists but merely drinkers. They talked about writing and painting and devoured cheap plates of *saucisse de Toulouse* with mashed potatoes, but there *was* a bold and growing Communist Party too.

There had been clashes on the streets of Paris and Rosalie didn't want to be caught in the middle of one in a bar. She was taking enough risks without being arrested.

Her strictly conventional family lived in the residential 16th arrondissement, close to the parks. Their high-ceilinged seventeenth-century apartment with two wrought-iron balconies had a wonderful view of the Seine, but back there, where everything and everyone was sleepy, Rosalie felt trapped by her parents' expectations and false hopes. Here was buzz and colour and life to be lived. And she was determined to live it.

She listened for the music that would be their cue to begin.

'Not yet,' Irène whispered and gripped her elbow. 'Wait until I push you, then go.'

Tonight Rosalie was about to fulfil her destiny by finally becoming the rebellious daughter they'd always accused her of being. She'd learnt long ago that as much as she had disappointed her parents, *they* had disappointed her too. So now, full of nerves but also brimming with excitement, she was doing what she wanted to do.

She wanted to be somebody, whatever it took. She wanted to be different. She wanted to reach for a bigger, more exciting world. A vivid, electric world where dreams might come true.

Then, suddenly, Rosalie's heart raced as the music changed. This was it. Their cue to get on stage and begin the dance.

Irène nudged her. 'Go on,' she whispered.

CHAPTER 7

It was several weeks after Rosalie's first performance, and another Saturday night in Paris. Johnny's Bar was sizzling. In fact, everywhere was sparking with so much light and laughter that Rosalie was a little nervous. She felt as if the city might just take off into the air and leave her to be dragged back to her parents' home. She glanced around, her eyes darting from one face to another. Every single night, in the unlikely event that one of her parents' friends might be out for a good time, she had to establish that no one they knew was in the audience or bar. Tonight she couldn't identify anyone and she breathed a sigh of relief. Buzzing now with delicious energy, she felt as if she could soar above the clouds and float there forever. She saw Irène shake her head with such a superior – although not unkind – look that Rosalie bumped straight back down to earth.

'Away with the fairies again?'

'Was I?'

'Feet on the ground, girl. Johnny's Bar is where it's at.'

She was right. The bar was here. The bar was now. And it was good enough . . . for the time being.

Irène stubbed out her cigarette. 'Come on. Time to face the music.' And she laughed. 'Honestly, you and your big ideas.'

'What about you?'

'Me? No, I just take what I can get.'

As the dancers began their second routine of the evening, the smoke in the room stung the back of Rosalie's throat. But she managed to catch her breath and threw herself into twisting her body in rhythm with the music. Dancing was her love, her life, her passion. She smiled at Irène and the other three as they spun around, joyfully swinging their arms wide, reaching high then swooping low almost to the ground before rising with fantastically high kicks. Rosalie was the most balletic of the dancers, a result of a decade of ballet training. And she loved losing herself to the sound of Saul's beautiful playing when even the air seemed to be vibrating and you could feel the sound of it in your blood and in your bones.

As the routine ended, she heard raised voices and from Irène's expression could see that her friend had heard them too. Unease was sweeping right across the stage. There had been a feverish air about the night as if the desire for fun had surged; the kind of night when anything might happen. Rosalie had known something had been building although she hadn't identified it until now, and she wasn't surprised when a loud crash followed the shouting. Then another crash, like a table being tipped over and, in its wake, glass breaking. Saul stopped playing and signalled to the girls to grab their coats and cover up just as a tangle of men fell into the hall from the bar. The men picked themselves up and began snatching up chairs, raising them above their heads and hurling them against anyone who got in their way. Rosalie fled to the changing room to slip on her coat but when she came back out again, she saw one of the young thugs from Jeunesses Patriotes had Saul in a headlock. Everything was noise, confusion and smoke. So much smoke, although she couldn't see where it was coming from. Her heart thumped against her ribs, instinct telling her to run, but she could not. She had to do something to help and quickly. She ran towards Saul to try to release him, but Irène pulled her back, whispering furiously in her ear. 'It won't help. Save yourself.'

There was no way out except through the bar where all hell had broken loose. From among the melange of screaming women, shouting men and weeping girls, more and more people were piling into the little hall to join the fight. Rosalie shrugged Irène off and ran to Saul, grabbing hold of the other man's arm and trying to pull him off the musician. Just then someone's elbow caught her in the temple. It sent her reeling and she reached for something to break her fall. But there was nothing, and when she fell and hit her head on a step, she saw a last sliver of light and then blacked out.

By the time she came round again, dazed and trauma-tised, a huge number of police had arrived and were busily handcuffing an indignant Saul and several of the right-wing

Jeunesses Patriotes who swore and kicked at them. One of the policemen helped Rosalie to her feet. She was about to thank him but then he handcuffed her too.

'But I didn't do anything,' she protested.

'Then how come you have blood pouring down your face?'

Rosalie touched her cheeks and felt the sticky wet surface. She glanced at her hand. 'Oh God. I'm bleeding.'

He narrowed his eyes. 'Indeed. So, what's a nicely brought up girl like you doing in a place like this? How old are you?'

'Twenty-one,' she lied and touched her mouth, worrying that she might have broken a tooth too.

'Sure you are. And I'm the Lord Mayor of Paris. Come on, off to the station with you.'

She tried to pull the edges of her coat together, do her buttons up, hide her scanty costume.

'Don't worry, miss. Already seen what you got. Tasty little piece. Soliciting, were you?'

'Course not.'

'Well, you can explain yourself down the station unless you've got something else to offer me?'

He laughed and she kicked him in the shin. Another policeman took hold of her arm and dragged her outside to a waiting police van. And although she protested loudly, she was bundled into the back of the van, her objections unheeded.

At dawn the next morning, the door to the cell Rosalie shared with two other women – both of whom had

painful-looking bruised eyes – swung open and a policeman entered. She had used her coat to rub the blood and
as much of her make-up as she could from her face.
Certainly, the scarlet lipstick was gone, the rouge too,
she hoped, but the eye make-up . . . well, she wasn't so
sure. She had no mirror to check but she didn't want her
parents seeing her 'done up like a tart' – her mother's
habitual reaction at the sight of a vulgar 'fancy' woman.
The policeman pushed Rosalie through a long, rank corridor smelling of stale sweat and tobacco, and then up some
stairs which led to a small room at the back of the station.
There her father stood, rigid with anger.

'Thank you, Officer,' he said, so tight-lipped his voice
was almost a hiss. 'I can assure you this will never happen
again.'

'Very good, sir.'

'And I can trust you to keep this quiet?'

The man nodded and patted his pocket. Her father had
clearly paid him off.

Rosalie opened her mouth to speak.

Her father held up a hand. 'Not . . . one . . . word.' He
thrust her out through the door and followed behind.

She spent the silent car journey home trying to figure
out what to say. Her coat was tightly buttoned, and her
father hadn't seen what she was wearing beneath it, so
maybe she could say a friend had taken her to the bar for
a drink. It wasn't the best excuse, and they wouldn't like
it, but it was better than admitting she worked as a dancer
there. Her authoritarian father would have a fit. And as
for her mother, there was no way of guessing what she

might do, but it would certainly involve hysterics. Neither of them had the first idea about having fun.

Papa was a senior civil servant in the Ministry of Public Works. He was proud that during the turmoil between ministers he had been the spokesman on anything to do with the reconstruction of France. His career meant every-thing to him, and his wife and children only seemed to cause him barely concealed indifference.

Rosalie had only told her sister about her secret dancing job. Claudette was nine years older and promised not to say a word but had strongly advised against continuing with it. She had three children: Hélène, Élise, and little Florence, and they all lived in England. Her husband was half French, half English. She regularly came back to Paris to see her parents, and in between visits Rosalie missed her big sister terribly. For theirs was a home of little warmth, where keeping up appearances was everything, emotions were repressed, and it was Rosalie's duty to become a good wife and mother. Claudette was the only one Rosalie loved.

Back at home, her parents gave her a horrendously hard time, but she stuck to her story that she had been taken to Johnny's Bar for a drink by a friend who had led her astray.

'What is that black stuff round your eyes?' her mother demanded.

'I—'

'Who was the friend?' she interjected, not waiting for an answer. Her father, who was less interested in that, spoke up now.

'I'll not have you involved with the communists,' he said, true to form.

'I'm not,' Rosalie insisted. It was true, after all. She wasn't involved with communists.

Her father supported the Action française which was said to be financially underwritten by perfumier, businessman, and newspaper publisher, François Coty. The rumours spoke of his many mistresses and multiple illegitimate children, but her father turned a blind eye to that. What he cared about was that Coty had grown to become one of the wealthiest men in France during the war and had backed several of her father's reconstruction projects. Whatever was true about Coty or not, it was clear he and the rest of the right wing aimed to prevent the growth of French socialism by fanning the populist fear of communism.

Her mother was still demanding to know the name of the friend who'd led her astray.

'Just someone I met at ballet class,' Rosalie lied. 'Anyway, she's left now.'

'Well, you are never to see her again,' her mother replied. 'In fact, it's high time you stopped ballet. I will cancel your lessons and increase your typing classes.'

Rosalie quietly groaned.

'You're too tall to ever be a ballet dancer and far too . . .'

And there she stopped, but Rosalie knew what she meant. Rosalie was extremely curvaceous, which of course had been one of the reasons Johnny had been keen to take her on. The Americans enjoyed a woman with something they could grab hold of and were not interested in half-starved Parisian waifs.

'Time to find you a suitable husband,' her mother continued. 'Or you'll be left on the shelf. You can't remain under our roof for ever, doing just whatever you please.'

Rosalie turned away. When she found the man for her, she'd know it. Her heart would sing, and she'd feel such passion it would bowl her over. None of her mother's choices had caused even the slightest wobble.

CHAPTER 8

A bearded man with a bulbous nose, who could either have been an artist or a criminal, seemed to be studying Rosalie. She tried to meet his pale, guarded eyes but they were focused just shy of her left ear, unsettling her. Judging by the look of the network of broken veins on his cheeks, he was a drunk, but still Irène led her across to the bar to introduce them.

He frowned and something pulsed inside her. A warning maybe. Rosalie shot her friend a curious look. Why was she insisting on introducing them?

'This,' Irène said, ignoring the look, 'is Pierre.'

'Drink?' the man said.

She spotted he had two chipped teeth then looked down at his feet. You could tell a lot by a person's footwear and his shoes were expensive, Italian leather. When she glanced up, she smiled. 'Pernod, please.'

'Good choice,' the man said.

'Pierre has something for you,' Irène said.

'Really?' Rosalie said, tapping her fingers on the bar counter.

The man studied her face before speaking, and something about the way he did it made her feel wary. There was menace in his gaze. She saw it in the way the skin around his eyes tightened as if he were calculating.

'What would you say if I told you that your father has a secret?' he finally said.

Rosalie frowned. How did this man even know who her father was?

'I'd laugh at you,' she replied, already sensing that if she engaged with him there might be no turning back.

He tilted his head to one side and scrutinised her face again. 'You'd be wrong to do so.'

'How can someone like you know anything about my father?'

'I could take the information to the police.'

As well as a sickly-sweet cologne, danger came off this man in waves.

'What's it about?' she asked.

He scribbled something on a piece of paper, and she raised her brows.

'Well?' he said. 'Interested in saving your father's reputation?'

'You have proof?'

'I do.'

And what do you want in return?'

'Just a small payment.'

'How much is small?'

The door of the bar swung open and a group of wealthy young people swept in, older than her of course, laughing and teasing each other as they clamoured for champagne. High spirits, she thought, longing to be one of them.

The man whispered something in her ear.

She raised her brows. 'I don't have that kind of money.'

'I'm sure you can find a way.'

'In that case,' she said, turning to watch the newcomers and quickly deliberating before twisting back to the man, 'I will see you and your proof the evening after next.'

'No,' he said. 'Tomorrow.'

The next afternoon, while her mother was taking a nap on the chaise longue in the drawing room, Rosalie crept into her parents' bedroom, where heavily draped velvet curtains shut out the light. This was risky and she'd have preferred to wait until a time when her mother might be out enjoying her weekly luncheon with her cronies.

Would the man really go to the police? What information could he possibly have? Rosalie had lain awake all night going over it in her head. Now she withdrew the small key to the old jewellery box her mother kept on a shelf in her wardrobe. Her father had intended to install a safe in the apartment, but luckily for Rosalie, that hadn't happened yet. She unlocked the box, lifted the mother-of-pearl lid, and then pulled open the lowest of the satin-lined drawers where the very smallest pieces of jewellery were kept in velvet drawstring bags. Without her mother ever noticing, she'd been trying on these family heirlooms for years. Now she withdrew a pair of tiny glittering earrings, their absence least likely be noticed. She replaced them in their velvet bag and, hearing a sound from the drawing room, crept out and ran soundlessly to her own room.

That night she danced as she'd never danced before. More overtly sensually, and more dangerously. In the crowded, smoky room, the mirrors glittered with reflected light and, ramping her performance up, she swayed her pelvis, feeling like an enchantress. Then she turned her back and rotated her feather-clad bottom to jubilant yells from the audience. She kicked up her legs and twisted her body, the eroticism charging the already excited audience with an even headier thrill.

When it was over and the clamour had died down, she met with Pierre again. This time Irène did not stick around, perhaps knowing it was going to be a private exchange.

'You got what I wanted?' he asked when they were both settled in an alcove with drinks before them.

Discreetly, she showed him the earrings.

He whistled. 'Nice. But I said cash.'

'That wasn't possible. These are diamonds and worth far more.'

He pulled a disgruntled face. 'More traceable too.'

She smiled, beginning to enjoy the exchange. 'I'm sure you'll find a way. So, what have you got for me?'

He drew in his breath and then leant forward conspiratorially. 'It's complicated. The bottom line is that your father is using another name, not his own.'

'And?' she frowned. 'Why would he do that?'

'To defraud the government.'

Now she laughed. 'Don't be ridiculous. It's clear you know nothing about my father.'

He inclined his head and gave her an insincere smile. 'There was an article in which he was quoted and in which his photograph appeared.'

'In *Le Temps*. I saw it. He was talking about the success of French reconstruction since the war. It's the department he works for.'

'And you were proud of him?'

She sniffed. 'I don't have that kind of relationship with my father, not that it's any business of yours.'

'So, you wouldn't be interested in knowing he has set up a little construction company of his own?'

'I'd be extremely bored by that.'

He tilted his head. 'A company that does not really exist, into which considerable sums of governmental money have poured for work that has never been done.'

She laughed again. 'Where on earth are you getting all this?'

'I have my contacts.'

'So? Go to the police.'

He narrowed his eyes. 'The police do not pay for such information.'

'And you have proof with you now?'

He passed her a folder. 'You will find it there. My cousin, shall I call her, works at the bank where the money is paid in and from where your father draws it out. Like I said, he uses a false name, but my "cousin" recognised him from the photograph in *Le Temps*.'

'Where's the bank?'

'All in the folder. The bank is in a distant suburb where under normal circumstances nobody would be likely to recognise your father. Civil servants are usually grey, faceless men. Usually his image would not have been in the paper, but with no minister in post, it was.'

'But why would my father do this? It doesn't make sense.'

'You may not know it, but your father has another secret.'

She stared at him, feeling a strange fluttering in her chest. 'Not another family?'

He laughed. 'I can put your mind at rest about that. He gambles, my dear.'

She frowned. 'Where?'

'Private members' clubs. Secret clubs.'

'So why not go straight to him with this?'

He twisted his mouth to the side. 'Because he'd kick over the traces in moments and I'd likely be carted off as a blackmailer.'

'Which you are.'

'Maybe.' He lifted the earrings and smiled. 'But I'm not a greedy man. These will do nicely.'

'Who else knows?'

He sighed. 'Only my cousin knows about the bank. But I do have an associate who works in one of the private members' clubs. It was only I who put two and two together.'

The next day was Sunday and Rosalie was feeling jittery, her nerves completely on edge. She needed to decide whether to show the folder to her father or not. He would be outraged if he saw it, not least with her, and would undoubtedly deny everything, but if she didn't show it to him, what then? Pierre or his cousin might get greedier. Demand more, or even inform the police. If a scandal erupted, then everything would be lost and her father could go to prison. She wasn't his greatest fan, but she didn't hate him. At least if she gave him the folder, he might be able to ward off disgrace and humiliation.

After a long dreary lunch, during which she tapped her foot nervously and was scolded for it while her mother ate painstakingly slowly, she went to her room and then came back into the drawing room carrying the folder.

'You need to see this, Papa,' she said, holding it out.

He didn't look up. 'Put it down somewhere, I'm reading.'

'Papa, you have to see this now.'

Her mother raised her chin. 'Do not speak to your father like that, child. What are you thinking?'

'But Maman . . .'

Her father looked up now. 'Well give it to me then,' he said and reached out for the folder. Rosalie watched anxiously as he opened it and read the contents. His face turned pale.

'What is it?' her mother demanded and when he held it away from her, she snatched it from him.

Rosalie remained motionless, holding her breath. Her father was staring at the floor and breathing heavily.

There was a long, terrible silence.

Then her mother rose to her feet, her face pinched and

white. She marched over to Rosalie and slapped her hard across the face. 'How dare you?'

Rosalie gasped, took a step back and rubbed her stinging cheek.

Her father retrieved the folder from his wife and tried to hide it, but his hands were trembling and he looked truly awful. 'This is nonsense,' he said. 'How could you come here and show me such a thing?'

'I was given it. I thought you should know.'

'Ridiculous,' he said, but there was a hint of something else in his outrage. 'You actually believed this filth?'

'I . . . I didn't know what to believe.'

'Enough, I don't want to hear it,' he said.

Then, a strange look passed between her parents and Rosalie felt certain that her mother knew something about this.

Her mother spoke again, her voice vitriolic. 'You treacherous little madam. The sooner you leave home and make your own way in the real world the better. Then you'll find out how hard life really is.'

Rosalie fled the room in tears. Soon after she heard the front door slam as her father left the apartment. He never usually went out on a Sunday.

Smarting from the slap, she remained in her bedroom brooding and listening to her mother's heels click up and down the corridor and around the hall.

A few hours later Rosalie heard her father come home.

Her parents murmuring voices rose steadily until all she could hear were her mother's accusations and sobs and then her father slamming a door. She longed to know what was happening, but they would never tell her. It was bad though, and Rosalie knew she would take the blame.

Her eyes swam with tears. 'It isn't fair,' she muttered. 'It's not my fault.'

She'd been trying to help, give her father fair warning, but she knew her parents, and they would never forgive her. Her mother already resented her for being the late, unexpected, unwanted child, who'd always got in the way.

In a flash she knew what she would have to do. Whatever was going to happen here, it would happen whether she was around or not and if she *were* here, she'd be imprisoned in her own home. Her mother wouldn't let her out except to marry a suitable man, and how easy would that be if a family scandal erupted? In any case, her dancing life would be over. No. Her whole life would be over. She couldn't go to Claudette. Her sister's hands were already full enough looking after her three daughters.

It was frightening, but Rosalie prided herself on being independent, the kind of person who adapted easily, who could move on without a second thought.

Although that had never been put to the test.

Until now.

CHAPTER 9

Florence

Devonshire, 1944

Florence arrived back at Jack's cottage to find it locked and Jack absent, so she left her case and walked up to the farm to see if Gladys knew when he'd be back. When Gladys opened the peeling blue door, Florence blinked rapidly, taken aback by what she saw. The kitchen was a large and square, black-beamed, low-ceilinged room, smelling of bacon and cats. A jumble of crockery, magazines, old newspapers, mugs, cups, glasses, electrical equipment filled every surface and, amongst it all, she spotted three cats. A huge grey one with big round yellow eyes stared at her imperiously from a table covered in an orange and white checked oilcloth, a tabby was curled up fast asleep on a Windsor chair, and a black-and-white smaller one with only one ear was stretching itself inside a soup tureen, between a pressure cooker and a skillet on the dresser.

But what really caught her attention, what made her heart speed up, was Jack standing by the range, eyes wide, looking as startled to see her as she was to see him. Just for a second his face lit up, but a moment later his expression clouded over. Why? Was he not pleased to see her?

'You're back,' she said.

'Actually, I haven't left yet. I'll be off early tomorrow morning.'

Gladys clucked about, insisting that she looked pale and peaky and in need of feeding, before she shepherded Florence and Jack into the sitting room with cups of steaming tea and a plate of Bovril sandwiches and left them to it. There, in Gladys' cluttered room with a faint whiff of cats, Florence poured out her heart to Jack. Told him about her mother's coldness and complete lack of interest in anything about their lives in France. And, haltingly, almost in tears again, she told him about Claudette's rage.

After a few moments of silence he nodded, as if taking it all in.

'I'm so sorry to put you on the spot like this,' she added. I—'

But he stopped her. 'Florence, it's all right. I understand.'

'I need to find work, Jack, and somewhere I can begin my life properly here in England. I've got the ration book you obtained for me but nothing else.'

'The passport and papers I got hold of in Spain will be
fine here. They prove who you are, either for a job or a
place to rent.'

'You're sure?'

'The British Embassy in Madrid was already using fake
medical certificates to get hold of Franco's "sick" British
prisoners. With the false passports, they were then moved
to Gibraltar, as were you. From there they were repatriated to Britain and that's exactly what John Lyons, the
British diplomat with whom I was rather usefully at
school, eventually did for us.'

He gave her a quick grin and continued.

'Added to that, your grandmother was English, your
father half English, and with the record of his work in
the Home Office and your long residence in Richmond,
it shouldn't be difficult to obtain legal residency here, if
that's what you're going to need in the long term. It may
not even be necessary.'

'That does make me feel better.'

'Make Meadowbrook your home for now,' he said. 'I'm
going to be away much of the time anyway, so you'll have
the place to yourself. Take your time.'

And she had hoped that he was secretly as glad to see
her as she was to see him.

That had been over two weeks ago, and Florence had
settled back in while Jack had been away. He didn't tell
her what he was doing, or where he was, but she imagined
he must have been taken under the wing of a Special
Operations Branch in a government ministry of some

kind. She was no fool. He'd mentioned he was attending meetings and hinted that they were connected to his old architecture business, but something about his stiff tone of voice hadn't quite rung true. Florence doubted that he'd be sent back to France – his injured arm had healed, but it did still cause him pain and wasn't as strong as his other – so perhaps he was training new recruits or something like that.

Anyway, it was none of her business.

She had become accustomed to the sound of RAF aircraft flying over, no longer looking up every time, and now she was doing something she loved. Sufficient sugar was hard to come by, but she'd been lucky to find a tiny lemon growing in a pot in a dilapidated greenhouse, and half a bottle of sweet sherry lingering in the drinks cabinet. She opened the oven door and a tempting aroma of baking filled the air. Jack had sent a note to let her know when he hoped to be back and, all being well, that would be tomorrow, so she'd wanted to make something delicious to welcome him home. The combination of lemon, a smidgen of butter, and sherry sweetness was mouth-watering. After all, who could resist a cake?

She went over her final conversation with Jack after she'd returned from her mother's and before he left.

'Claudette asked me to do something for her,' she'd said. 'It's odd, but she wants me to find her sister, Rosalie, who ran away from Paris twenty years ago. No one has seen her since.'

'Where did she go?'

'Maman showed me a box with something Rosalie sent

her. A Maltese Cross attached to a rosary, so that's where my mother thinks she must be. Malta. Rosalie's note said nothing, only that she wanted her help. But as it's been quite a few years since then, I reckon she could be dead.'

'There isn't any way you can get to Malta now,' he'd said.

'The war. I know. But I don't even know where I would start to ask. People are missing all over the world.'

'Why has she asked you now?'

Florence had shaken her head, but whatever the reason, another trip was the last thing she needed. Her mother's request had made her feel uneasy and there had already been enough secrets. If she did go looking for Rosalie, she didn't know what she'd find and she was still coming to terms with the other terrible events of the year *and* who she was now. The landscape of the past had altered irrevocably with the revelation of who her real father was.

She sighed and turned away from the cake, now cooling on a wire rack. Most foods were covered by the rationing system – butter, bacon, cheese, sugar and so on – so a cake was a rare treat. They could get hold of fruit and vegetables, and they were fortunate to have Ronnie and Gladys's farm nearby. Florence could hear Gladys coming up the garden path right now.

'Coo-ee,' Gladys called. 'Anyone in?' and she pushed open the door.

'Hello,' Florence said. 'Please come on in.'

'My, that is a fine smell, dear. Dab hand you are at the baking. Jack's a lucky man.'

As her duck waddled in behind her, she lifted the striped tea towel covering the basket she was carrying and said, 'See what I've got for you today.'

And Florence glanced down at six large brown eggs, butter Gladys had churned, and a few rashers of bacon from their own pigs.

'I really can't accept all this. You only recently brought us all those vegetables.'

'Poof. Jackie's like one of the family,' said Gladys, her dark eyes twinkling, 'and a war hero. I'll not see him starve.'

'You're very kind.'

'Leastways, come the spring you'll have your own veg. But you can count on us for the rest.'

'You must let us pay.'

'We'll see.'

Since she'd been back, Florence had wasted no time in digging up a small section of the garden where she'd now sown mainly leafy crops, including cabbages and spinach, plus onions, radishes, turnips, and broad beans. It would provide for them in the early spring. She didn't dwell on whether she'd still be living there by then, or even when winter came, or whether she would, in fact, have to go back to Claudette before that.

As Gladys chattered on about the weather and the need for Jack to buy some laying hens, Florence began to sweep the floor. Being at the cottage, with a garden and a kitchen, and Jack to cook for, reminded her of home and helped to make this new life less strange.

'I've written to my sisters again,' she told Gladys.

'Heard from them, have you?'

Florence shook her head. 'Not yet.'

She didn't mention that although she'd told Hélène and Élise she was staying in Jack's house temporarily, she had implied that Jack was rarely there. Well, it was more or less true, and yet she'd felt the acidic taste of guilt on her tongue again. She knew Hélène would be looking for mentions of Jack. Just then, Florence heard the front door open and both she and Gladys looked up.

'Must be Jack home a day early,' Florence said with a grin, wiping her hands on her floury apron and straightening her hair a little.

She'd been lonely without Jack these last two weeks. She'd always had her sisters close by, had never spent much time totally on her own, so had never thought about feeling afraid to be alone. Not just about the things that went bump in the night, but the inexplicable fear that somehow hid beneath your surface armour. She'd been careful not to make a fuss when Jack left, certain that he wouldn't appreciate a woman who made a scene about every little inconvenience, but she *had* missed him terribly and had been secretly counting down the days until his return.

She opened the door to the hall, ready to greet him. But it wasn't Jack. Florence blinked in surprise to see a tall, well-groomed, blonde woman standing there, wearing an immaculate pale blue suit. It was similar in style to the simple utility clothing most women sported, with padded shoulders, nipped-in waist, and a hem that fell just below the knee, yet this woman looked so much more stylish. The fabric seemed expensive and, somehow, she was better presented than anyone else Florence had seen in a long time. And she was standing there, nonchalantly swinging a bunch of keys, with a suitcase at her feet.

The world hung still and then suddenly, before Florence could understand what was happening, it moved too quickly.

'Oh,' the woman said, her thinly pencilled brows raised. 'I didn't know Johnny had hired a housekeeper. Or are you the cleaner?'

'Johnny?' Florence repeated.

'Jonathan Jackson. He owns the house. Who are you?'

'I'm Florence. I'm staying here. I thought this was Jack's house.'

The woman laughed. 'Well, I just told you that. Some people call him Jackie. I never have.'

'And you are?' Florence asked, aware of a layer of discomfort already threatening to darken her day.

'Belinda Jackson, of course, his wife.'

They were both motionless as Florence stared in disbelief, unable to find any words for this. Of course Jack wasn't married, he'd have said. Wouldn't he? Could this woman, with her finely chiselled cheekbones, be telling the truth? Mystified, Florence became aware first of shock and then a deeply unsettling feeling of betrayal. She glared at the woman, this Belinda. Why should she believe her?

Belinda was still standing in the hall with an increasingly impatient look on her face. 'God, I need a drink,' she said.

Florence blinked rapidly. 'Um. I can make you a cup of tea if you like. It's already brewed.'

Belinda laughed. 'Darling. I need something a lot stronger than tea. Don't worry, I can help myself. I know where the booze is kept.'

At that moment, Gladys popped her head round the door. 'Wasn't expecting to see you here again,' she said, her face grim. 'Jackie know you were coming, did he?'

Belinda looked down her nose at the woman. 'Hardly any of your business is it, dear?' she said, with sarcastic emphasis on the word 'dear'.

Gladys bristled but didn't reply.

'Well, I'll just pop my case up to the guest room,' Belinda added.

'But I'm in there,' Florence said, aghast.

Belinda looked surprised. 'Oh, not sharing his bed then? When you said you weren't the cleaner, I thought you must be Johnny's latest floozy. So, he's not got round to that yet. Funny. He was always rather a fast worker.'

'Actually, Jack brought me across the Pyrenees to escape the Nazis.'

'Of course he did,' Belinda said, her voice still dripping with sarcasm. 'Well run along and move your stuff into the box room, there's a dear, and I'll put my case in the guest room. I might just have a little snooze. Clean sheets in the usual place, Gladys?'

Gladys didn't reply, so Belinda just picked up her case and, head held high, marched up the stairs.

Florence listened to the ancient wooden treads creaking beneath the woman's clicking high heels while Gladys stood with her hands on her hips, puffed out her cheeks and let the breath out in a rush. 'Bloody little madam,' she said under her breath. 'Jackie will have something to say about that.'

The two women went back to the kitchen, with Florence in something of a daze. The gap between how things were and how she wanted them to be was rapidly widening.

'Oh, my dear girl, you do look pale,' Gladys said, concern in her voice. 'Why don't you sit down and I'll pour you a good strong cuppa.'

Florence didn't need much persuading and silently pulled out a chair. Sometimes she had the feeling of not being quite real. As if she'd walked into the world from somewhere else and was doing her best to copy real people. Be like real people. But she hadn't quite managed it. Except when she was with Jack. Then she felt real. Solid. Properly of the world. This 'wife' of his turning up out of the blue had shaken that. How could Jack have married such an odious, self-absorbed woman?

Gladys looked at her sympathetically. 'Take it Jackie never mentioned Belinda?'

Feeling more desolate than she ought, Florence shook her head.

'With good reason,' Gladys added and nodded knowingly.

'You don't like her?'

'Not after what she did.'

Florence frowned. 'What did she do?'

'I think Jackie should be the one to tell you that.'

CHAPTER 10

After an awkward night with Belinda in the house, Florence was up early, trying to keep herself busy and distracted at the same time. She swept and mopped floors, wiped surfaces, polished anything she could find, beat the rugs, plumped the cushions. She couldn't rid herself of the need to look after people, even though she was beginning to think Jack might not deserve it.

The kettle whistling in the kitchen interrupted her thoughts and she hurried there to reach into the cupboard closest to the Aga for the tea caddy.

'Busy little bee, aren't you?'

Florence stiffened at Belinda's cool tone of voice. Was the woman's arrival planned to coincide with Jack's return or had it been coincidental?

'Good morning,' she said, turning and pasting a smile on her face.

'Planning to step into my shoes, are you, darling?' She

waved a hand around the kitchen. 'You'll be darning his socks next. But mark my words, he won't notice what you've done. Is that tea you've got going there? I'm absolutely gasping.'

'It's not brewed yet,' said Florence, turning to finish her task.

'So, what's cooking? Pancakes, porridge, kippers or good old bacon and eggs?'

'I was just going to have toast with some of Gladys's crab apple jelly. She didn't have enough sugar so it's a bit runny, but it tastes nice. Would you like some?'

'Thank you. I do believe I would. Must be the country air. I never eat breakfast in London.'

Florence sliced the bread and toasted it on the Aga and then poured out the tea.

They ate in silence, Florence jigging her foot nervously and wanting nothing more than to escape and dress herself in something more stylish, aware of how childish she looked next to Belinda. She had in mind a pale celadon dress, the colour neither green nor grey but falling between the two and perfect with her grey-blue eyes and blonde hair. She'd cut the dress down from a larger, old-fashioned one Gladys had given her, in a delicate paisley fabric with hints of lilac and pink. The bodice now fitted perfectly, and the skirt, made from a full circle, flared out when she twirled around. She'd added side pockets, white buttons down the front, a buckle belt and felt pleased with her handiwork. She loved making things and had lots more plans for the house, starting with painting the living room. Had, *had*, lots more plans that is. What was going to happen now was anyone's guess. Her mother's overheated cottage beckoned, and she sighed.

Belinda drew out a Kensitas filter tip and lit it with an expensive-looking engraved lighter.

'Is that gold? Florence asked.

'It is. A present from Jack' She passed it across to Florence. 'Oh, I should have offered you one.'

Florence regarded the cream and red cigarette pack still lying on the table and then at the engraving on the lighter. *To my darling Belinda,* it said. 'I don't smoke,' she eventually replied and coughed as if to prove it.

'Of course you don't.' Belinda narrowed her eyes. 'Tell me. What is a little girl like you doing setting her cap at the great John Jackson?'

Florence swallowed and passed her another slice of toast. She tried to deny it but knew she had failed the moment she felt her cheeks reddening. Damn it. It seemed that Belinda, this paragon of elegance, could see right through her.

'Oh, he's glamorous, I'll give you that, with all his tales of derring-do. But it's what's beneath the surface that counts. Wouldn't you agree?'

Florence chewed the inside of her cheek.

'Anyway, can't sit here chatting all day. Must get on. I assume you don't mind me using the antiquated washing facilities first. Honestly, this place.'

As the woman left, Florence banged her teacup down with a clunk. Was there anything going on under Belinda's smart, superficial surface? Or was she all bitch?

Florence went through to the living room and looked out towards the road, not knowing if she wanted to see Jack or dreaded seeing him. She leant against the deep window frame. These walls tell stories, Florence thought, and she loved a good story, devouring novels whenever she could. Jack's grandmother had accumulated so many and she picked out one now. *Cold Comfort Farm*, a comic novel by an English author called Stella Gibbons. Florence needed something to laugh about.

After having had breakfast with Belinda, she'd felt like chucking the cake in the bin but couldn't bring herself to waste food, and maybe Jack had a reasonable explanation. But what? Her mind kept snagging at that, but she arranged the cake on the kitchen table along with a cake knife and some pretty plates, in case Jack arrived back while she was out. Then she pulled on her wellingtons and went outside, glancing up at banks of thick clouds. Dark in the middle, their top edges were lined with silver and in between slices of palest blue. Would the clouds bring rain, or would the blue sky win the day? She hoped the threat of bad weather would recede and even though she was wearing her best dress, she decided to get as far away from the house as she could.

Instead of walking across the flat water meadow and then the hill beyond, she opened the gate nearest to the house and climbed the steep hill behind it, where sheep were grazing. At the top she stopped to catch her breath and looked down at Jack's house cradled between the hills and the woods, now turning red and gold. The sky grew a little darker, the clouds so low she felt she could almost reach out and touch them, but Belinda's presence was too unsettling for her to go back so soon. Hopefully, the rain would hold off long enough to still get in a decent walk.

From where she now stood, she could see across the rounded rolling hills and valleys of Devonshire, the winding lanes, the thick hedgerows, the oak thickets, and the stretches of mixed woodland. She chose a direction and carried on over the crest of the hill before descending the other side and then following a track lined with blackberry bushes. It stretched as far as the eye could see, deep into the woods beyond. All she could hear was the wind, intense now as it whistled through the flickering leaves.

She walked for a long time, deep in thought, before turning to head back just as the first drops of rain began to fall. A fine drizzle, that's all, she told herself. Of course, she'd known the warm September weather couldn't last and here they were in early October and it was as if a curtain had fallen, leaving the sunshine behind it.

'It's autumn now,' she said out loud and could feel the trees whooshing in agreement. Within half an hour the rain was coming down in sheets so thick that she could barely see the path. And after such a long spell of dry weather, the ground quickly turned slippery. Florence could smell the rich dark scent of soil, as rain quenched the earth's thirst and soaked into the parched undergrowth. Normally she enjoyed the peace of walking in wet weather, the feeling of inner calm and being in tune with nature. She used to believe in rain fairies and water sprites. She didn't any more, of course, but she missed the innocent girl she'd once been and mourned the loss of her peaceful childhood world that had been so brutally destroyed.

She wasn't dressed for a deluge like this and before long, her hair was soaked, hanging in strings down her back and her carefully chosen dress was sodden and clinging to her legs. She scolded herself for dashing out without a mackintosh or umbrella, although now the gusting wind would have blown it inside out within seconds.

At the top of the hill, she glanced down, hoping to spot the cottage again, but the rain had obscured it so completely she wondered for a moment if she was even in the right place. She made her way down as carefully as she could, but the grass was so slippery she lost her footing, only just managing to save herself in time. She carried on cautiously, but the lumps and bumps on the hill were terribly uneven and she caught her foot in a hole she hadn't spotted, this time falling forward onto her front. Winded, she lay there for a second, feeling tears coming, but after a moment struggled to her feet. She glanced down at herself; her beautiful dress streaked with mud and patches of grass stain. She wiped the wet hair from her brow. Everything had gone wrong since Belinda arrived. Everything. She'd been so happy baking a cake for Jack and looking forward to seeing him, but now all she could hope was that she'd have enough time to clean up before he arrived.

As she reached the house, she saw it wasn't to be. Jack's father, Lionel, was opening his car door and about to get in, his coat pulled over his head, when he glanced up and saw her bedraggled state.

'My dear girl. What happened to you?'

She shrugged. 'I took a tumble.'

'But why were you out without a coat?'

'Didn't think the rain would come on so fast or so hard.'

He nodded. 'It can do.'

'So, I take it Jack's back?'

'Dropped him off ten minutes ago.'

'You know his wife is here?'

'Unfortunately, yes. Listen, try not to worry about Belinda. I don't think . . . well, I hope she isn't dangerous. She hasn't been . . . Well it should be Jack who tells you really.'

'That's what Gladys said too.'

'She was right. Nice to see you again, Florence.'

Unable to delay going inside any longer, Florence drew in her breath and let it out in a puff. She walked around to the back door. In the porch, with one hand on the wall to balance herself, she pulled off one wellington then the other, leaving them where they fell, and then she pushed open the door. Jack was in the kitchen, his back against the Aga and looking strained, while Belinda sipped a sherry and blew smoke rings that floated up towards the ceiling. The atmosphere felt fraught.

'Hello,' Florence said, distinctly at a disadvantage with her bedraggled hair and wet dress. 'Welcome home.'

Jack gave her a tight smile. 'Thank you.'

Florence felt an ocean of distance between them. It was far from the warm reunion she had hoped for.

'So,' Belinda interrupted, her voice slurring slightly, and Florence wondered how much sherry the woman had already drunk. The evening before she had watched Belinda polish off nearly a third of a bottle of Jack's favourite Laphroaig whisky.

Jack didn't speak and Florence edged towards the door to the hall. She didn't want to reveal how upset she was. 'I just need to change. I'll leave—'

'What are you going to do about it?' Belinda interrupted again.

Jack sighed. 'I already told you.'

'You laid down the law, yes, but my lawyer says I have a right.'

'Oh, for Christ's sake, Belinda. You have the London flat. You always hated it here.'

'I'll leave you to it,' Florence managed to say and then she fled the room. But as she climbed the stairs, she heard what must have been the crash of a plate as it hit the wall, followed by Jack's shout of anger.

'Bloody hell,' she muttered. 'If that was my cake going for a burton, I think I might just murder her.'

CHAPTER 11

Florence was sitting on the uncomfortable put-you-up bed in the box room, glowering through the rain-streaked window at the hill behind the house. The horrible little bed was so close to the sill that her knees jammed uncomfortably against it. Seething with frustration, she itched to hit out, but all she did was clench her fists, pick up her pillow and pummel it. It just wasn't fair; Jack really should have told her about his wife, and she felt hurt that he'd kept such a bloody great secret from her – and from her sister too. Hélène hadn't known anything about this.

She heard a gentle tap at her door but didn't respond. A few moments later the door swung open and Jack came in. There was no space on Florence's side of the bed, so he was forced to stand behind her. She kept her eyes steady but no longer seeing the view; she was only aware of the rapid beating of her heart.

'I'm so sorry,' he said gruffly.

'What for?'

'This godawful mess.'

'The cake, you mean?' she said, her voice as haughty as she could make it.

She could hear him almost chuckle at that and then having to restrain himself. 'Well yes the cake, but—'

'Just tell me,' she said.

'About Belinda?'

She twisted around and couldn't disguise the anger in her voice, and nor did she want to. 'Of course, bloody Belinda. What did you think I was asking about? The price of sausages?'

'Well, we aren't actually buying sausages. Gladys brings them.'

Florence rose to her feet in an instant, her anger boiling over. 'This isn't funny, Jack.'

'Sorry.'

'You should be.'

They both fell quiet. She took fierce breaths as the voices clamoured in her head. Jack's, Belinda's, Hélène's, and even her own.

'Look,' he said, 'we can't talk in this tiny room. Let's go for a walk and I promise I'll tell you everything.'

Florence narrowed her eyes. 'It's still raining.'

'Only drizzling now. Do you mind?'

'All right. Give me a chance to change out of these wet things and dry my hair a little.'

Before this, when she'd been sleeping in the guest room, the silence had wrapped around her like a soft blanket through which nothing could intrude. Knowing he was just along the landing and that with a few brave steps she'd be by his side had been comforting. Now everything felt very different.

Instead of heading through the long grass leading to the gated water meadow, she and Jack had been traipsing up the acorn-strewn track for several minutes. Neither of them had spoken, the silence uneasy. So long as I don't look at him, I'll be safe, she told herself, deciding to leave the thrust of the conversation to him. After all, it really wasn't her business if he had one wife or five of them hidden about the place. They were just friends and he owed her nothing – although her heart was aching at the unspeakable wreckage Belinda had wrought on their peaceful life.

'Belinda and I married young,' Jack eventually said. 'A whirlwind romance, you know, and we barely knew each other. Every marriage has its faults, of course, and ours began to show up early on.'

He fell silent and she listened to the wind blowing the trees about. It seemed a terribly sad kind of sound. Lonely and desolate, which was rather the way she was feeling too.

'Go on,' she said.

'I suppose I allowed myself to be swallowed up by work and spent more and more time down here or in other parts of the country, then later, when the war began, in France too. We dealt with the growing rift between us in different ways. She stayed on in London, living the party lifestyle with her glamorous acquaintances and her lover, Hector.'

'She was unfaithful?'

'Yes.'

'She seems very bitter.'

'She is. She's damaged too. We both are.'

'By the marriage failing?'

He didn't answer, just shook his head as if uncertain and kept on walking.

The silence continued as they trudged down the hill and then took their time along one of the muddy tracks that ran through the woods.

'You didn't seem damaged in France,' Florence offered in a quiet voice.

'Much easier there. Had a job to do, and I could be a different person.'

'I understand that, but what about when we came to Meadowbrook? Why didn't you just tell me you were married then?'

'I don't know. I should have.'

'And now?'

'A divorce, but suddenly she's insisting on a share of my cottage. We agreed it would remain as mine alone, and she would keep the London flat for herself. It's in Chelsea and worth far more than my cottage, which has been mine since my grandmother died. I have no interest in the London flat.'

'So why has she changed her mind?'

He shrugged. 'I'm not sure. If I know Belinda, she's just here to make trouble.'

'Maybe she's not ready to let go.'

'Of what?'

'You, I suppose.'

'Maybe. Now she's seen you here, it's certainly made her more obstinate. I'm sure she doesn't really want *me* back, but she doesn't want anyone . . . Well, you get my drift. And she still has Hector, as far as I know. But unless I give her half of Meadowbrook, she's refusing to go ahead with the divorce.'

Florence had been gazing down at the ground, but now glanced up at Jack, who was watching her with sad eyes.

'Look, I'm intruding,' she said. 'This is between you and Belinda. I'll go back to my mother's, just until the war ends and then I'll go home to France, or perhaps travel to Malta to see if I can find Rosalie.'

He shook his head. 'That's not a good idea. You know your aunt may not even be alive. The siege of Malta meant the country was bombed relentlessly for almost two and a half years.'

'Why for so long? I hadn't realised.'

'It's a strategically important island for the British, so Fascist Italy and Nazi Germany fought the Royal Air Force and the Royal Navy to try to wrench control from them. The place will be in ruins. You can't go there alone.'

'We'll see,' was all she said.

'I mean it, Florence. Malta is a bad idea. The Axis resolved to bomb or starve the country into submission. It will be dangerous. And it's fine for you to stay here. I'm getting used to you being around. It's just . . .' He paused and sighed. 'Don't go. I'll insist Belinda leaves. She has no place here.'

But Florence felt *she* was the one in the wrong place.

In France she had looked after the house, the food, the garden, the animals and, of course, her two sisters, and she'd been good at it. It had been her way of doing her bit while Hélène had worked hard as a nurse for their much-loved village doctor and Élise had been helping the Resistance to fight the German occupiers. Nurturing her family had also been Florence's own salvation when the . . . when the worst of things happened to her. She still found it hard to say the actual word out loud.

Here, in England, she didn't know where she belonged. Despite spending much of her childhood near London, it was the Dordogne where she really felt at home.

Jack smiled at her, but it was a weak smile and she could not return it.

As they walked back in silence, she focused instead on Claudette's request. Rosalie. She tried to picture the aunt she didn't know, the aunt who had run away and she felt a rush of overwhelming pity. To be so dreadfully alone like that. How had she managed? Her own loneliness derailed her at times, but her situation was only temporary. And at least she knew where her family were. Rosalie had been out of touch for twenty years. Surely she must have made another home for herself? Another family even? What had she been doing for all these years, what kind of life had she led and, if she really was alive, where was she now? Although glad it wasn't possible to travel anywhere for now and nervous of more secrets coming to light, Florence couldn't help speculating about what might have happened to Rosalie.

CHAPTER 12

Rosalie

Malta, 1925

'It's the Mediterranean fleet,' Rosalie's excitable new English friend, Charlotte Salter, said, squeezing her arm. 'British Navy. Based at Fort St Angelo.'

Enchanted by her first sight of the dancing lights in the harbour, Rosalie soaked it in. Here was a world she could never have imagined.

'Can it be real?' she whispered, as she stood on the deck looking at the island ahead of her.

'Exciting, isn't it?'

'More than that. It's breathtaking. And look . . .' Rosalie pointed at the bastions and turrets of the fort. 'They're glowing in the moonlight.'

'Wait till you see the sun rising over the battlements of

Fort St Elmo. From the water you'll see them turn red, scarlet even, so much so you'd think they were on fire, and the sky! Honestly. Shocking pink. We can go out on a *dghaisa* if you like, and I'll show you.'

'A *dghaisa*?'

'One of the brightly coloured little boats. A man stands at the prow and rows. It's great.'

Rosalie smiled at her new friend and all at once her remaining doubts faded, and she had the answer to the question she'd been asking herself. This *was* the right thing to do and she couldn't wait a moment longer to begin her new life. She had not foreseen a place as enchanting as this, and here she no longer had to endure her parents' stifling conventionality and rules.

It was late by the time the ship finally dropped anchor, which meant they had to sleep on board overnight. First thing the next morning, fizzing with excitement and newly acquired freedom, Rosalie climbed down after Charlotte and got into one of the high-ended *dghaisa* vessels bobbing in the water. It was a colourful gondola-like thing, with painted eyes on either side. A water taxi, she realised as they joined the six other passengers already stowed inside it along with their luggage. Jammed up against a large British woman complaining about the smell of fish, Rosalie turned to face Valletta, and the marvellous sight of massive walls, ramparts and bastions, rising like golden cliffs from the ocean. The standing oarsman set off and had soon propelled them across to the dock where they disembarked right next to what he said were the Custom House steps.

The place was buzzing with the clanging and clattering

of frantic activity. Animals everywhere, dogs barking, horses stamping their hooves and snorting, and donkeys standing stock-still but for their ears flicking insects away. Rosalie could smell fish, coal, oranges, and cats – dozens of cats lining up where the fishing catches were being brought in. Dazzled by the heat, the noise and the colour, Rosalie hardly knew where to look. Mooring men were tying ropes to bollards, stevedores were unloading cargo, and porters were rushing to carry their luggage. She heard growly voiced fishermen, customs guards issuing orders, and thin, eagle-eyed, barefoot children begging and trying to scavenge food. She wished she had something to give them, but she had nothing and had to turn away.

'Phew,' she said. 'I thought it would be quiet.'

Charlotte laughed. 'Fat chance. Where are you staying?'

Rosalie evaded the question. The fact that she hadn't secured a job yet, nor anywhere to stay, would probably make her sound reckless; all she had was a newspaper cutting tucked safely in her handbag, and she knew the words off by heart.

EXPERIENCED FOREIGN ACTS WANTED
CABARET DANCERS, SINGERS, AND
ACROBATS.
IN THE FLOURISHING HEART
OF VALLETTA, MALTA.
CONTACT: GIANNI CURMI AT THE EVENING
STAR, STRAIT STREET, MALTA.
EXCELLENT REMUNERATION

She'd spotted the advertisement in a paper one of the customers had left behind at Johnny's Bar and had cut it out for future reference. The written words had quickly settled in her mind and even before she knew she was going to come to Malta the name of the place had called to her. Valletta sounded exotic, and she felt that fate had planned for the newspaper to be carelessly abandoned for her to find. Of course, that had been before everything went terribly wrong at home. She could still see her parents' shocked faces in her mind as clearly as if she were there again. The broken expression in her father's eyes, her mother's bitter, accusing fury.

A wave of homesickness hit her as she remembered tiptoeing into her father's study in the dead of night to retrieve her identity card, steal some francs and pick up travel documents from his unlocked desk. She'd used some of the money to pay for a false identity card so that in Malta she'd be able to use a different name and that had taken an extra day. She'd contacted her sister Claudette to ask for help, but her sister had refused, said she should stay and resolve things with their parents. But she couldn't do that. So she had been forced to relieve her mother of more valuable jewellery, '*that she never wore anyway,*' she whispered. Then she'd sold some of it to buy a ticket at the beautiful Gare de Lyon.

In her hurry to escape before the true extent of the brewing scandal was likely to be unleashed, Rosalie had had neither time to write to Gianni Curmi in Valletta, nor to wait for his reply. Instead, she'd done what she needed to do and with fear in her heart, she'd boarded the train before she was banished or worse. Now she was here, she had to find a way to make it work.

'I have the address in my bag,' she said to Charlotte. 'I'll get a taxi.'

'If you're sure. When Archie's chauffeur arrives, I'm sure he'd be happy to take you wherever you need to go.'

Archie Lambden was Charlotte's fine, upstanding fiancé and there was no way Rosalie was going to admit her situation to anybody, least of all to someone like him. 'Thank you, but I'll be fine,' she said. 'I'll probably see you around then?'

She smiled at Charlotte. Her new friend was pale with red hair rather like her own and an almost transparent complexion. Rosalie wondered how she would fare in the relentless heat of Malta, although this wasn't Charlotte's first visit so she must have found a way.

'Absolutely,' Charlotte was saying. 'I'll be having a beach party or maybe a dinner soon. You must come. You have my address so drop by and I'll tell you when it's going to be?'

Rosalie nodded. 'Look, there's a man with a horse-driven cab just over there.' She gave Charlotte a peck on the cheek then picked up her case and made a dash for it.

Having left the Grand Harbour, the driver, who spoke heavily accented English, told her they would be heading downtown. She nodded; glad she had spent a little time brushing up her reasonably good schoolgirl English with Johnny's English waiter in return for a little petting.

When the driver pulled up, he said, 'Here you are then. This is *The Gut*.'

She frowned. 'But . . .?'

'Strait Street. We call it *The Gut.*'

When she climbed down and saw a long sunless, cobbled alley, she felt the ache of disappointment. In contrast to the harbour, the buildings were eerily silent, with no sign of life and all shutters firmly closed.

'Umm. Do you know where The Evening Star club is?' she asked him.

'About halfway down. Won't be open now.'

Her heart sank and she felt a sudden flash of homesickness for sizzling Paris.

'There's a good café around the corner in Old Bakery Street.'

'You know a lot about Valletta, do you?'

'Everything. Any time you want a guided tour just knock on the door and leave a message with my wife.'

He dug in his pocket and passed her a card.

'So, I'll take you there, shall I? Old Bakery Street? You can get a bite to eat and hop along to The Evening Star later.'

She got back in the cab and a few moments later he had halted. She paid him and her mouth watered at the aroma of hot sugary pastry as she pushed open the glass door of the café. It was warm and cosy. The owner – a short, fat, middle-aged man sporting a wide curling moustache and ferocious eyebrows with spiky silver hairs flying off in different directions – gave her a broad smile.

'Welcome. Welcome,' he said and twirled his moustache.

She thanked him, her spirits lifting.

'So, an espresso or a *kafe fit-tazza*?' he asked, wiping his hands on his large striped apron. 'Coffee in a glass, best with a sweet ricotta-filled *kannol* or a hot *pastizz.*'

She ordered the coffee and a *pastizz*, though she had no idea what it was, and he told her to take a seat and he'd bring it over to her.

She sat at a window table and glanced out at the people passing by the tall houses on the other side of the street, wondering what her next move ought to be.

A few moments later, the man came across with a tray. 'Here's your *pastizz* and your coffee,' he said as he laid the tray down.

She glanced down at the little half-moon-shaped puff pastry pie on her plate. 'What does it taste of?'

'Kind of cheesy, but you can have it filled with curried peas if you like. Very popular around here.'

'It smells delicious.'

'Not English, are you?'

'No. French. In fact, I wonder if you might know where to find a room to stay. I'm hoping to become a performer here.'

He grinned. 'You saw one of my son-in-law's adverts? Married to my daughter Karmena he is.'

'I certainly saw an advert.'

'Always on the lookout for foreign artistes he is. Tell him you met me. Karmena has a lodgin' 'ouse in St Joseph Street. The British called it that when they arrived, but we always call it the street of the French. She'll rent you a bed.' He frowned. 'A bit rough for a lady though.'

'Why is it the street of the French?'

'On account of being near the French Curtain on the waterfront. A fort.'

'Well, thank you for your help.'

'Any time. My name is Nikola, but everyone calls me Kola.'

He told her the price and she felt in her bag for her purse, paid, finished her delicious *pastizz*, drank her coffee, and got up to leave. The British pound was the currency used on the island and thank goodness she had changed some of her francs while still in Paris.

'Oh,' she called to him. 'How do I find St Joseph Street?'

'Easy. Go to the bottom of Old Bakery Street, turn right, then second left. Strada San Giuseppe is at the very end of Strait Street. It's only 400 metres long and runs parallel between Fountain Street and Republic Street. See you around,' he said, and gave her a wave.

She followed his directions but when she arrived in the street of the French her heart sank. She had expected something akin to the perhaps shabby but nevertheless elegant streets she was accustomed to seeing in Paris. This dingy row of tenement buildings, six floors high, with washing hanging from wooden balconies, half-dressed barefoot children running wild, and a repulsive smell of stale cooking mixed with the stink of lavatories was the last thing she'd hoped for. She heard a shout and leapt out of the way of a man whose mule was pulling a cart at speed, piled high with cans of paraffin just in time.

She wondered if this was the sort of place Irène had lived in back in Paris. If it was, Irène deserved a medal for being as well turned-out as she was. Rosalie sighed deeply. She missed her friend. But there was no point thinking of Paris. Not now, not ever. And yet this place! She glanced up at the tenements again and, filled with nostalgia, pressed a hand to her heart. It was so different from her home. What had she been thinking? As usual she'd made an impulsive snap decision without giving any thought to the consequences, and it was now too late for regrets.

CHAPTER 13

Inside the lodging house it didn't get any better. A small scraggy woman was descending the stairs carrying an overflowing bucket and the hallway smelt of something Rosalie couldn't at first identify.

'I'm looking for Karmena,' she said in English.

The woman nodded and pointed to a door that was slightly ajar. Rosalie pushed it open. 'Karmena?' she asked.

The woman, who was almost as round as she was high, nodded. 'Who wants to know?'

'Kola sent me. I need a room. Do you have one available?'

The woman frowned. 'You could say I have. But best if I show you.'

Rosalie trailed her up the stairs and through a warren of corridors, past dormitories, family rooms and up even more stairs. She asked where the bathrooms were but was told there were no toilets, no bathrooms, and no kitchens as such.

'So how do people cook then?'

'On a *kučiniera*,' the woman said, and instantly Rosalie could smell the paraffin that fired such stoves mixed with the pong of a strong disinfectant. Of course, that had been what she'd smelt.

'A paraffin cart comes round most days.'

'I saw it. The mule nearly ran me over.'

Karmena laughed. 'That would be Spiru's mule. Can be a bit spirited.'

Rosalie glanced around. 'Where do people wash clothes?'

'Boil 'em in a bucket on a primus stove.'

Rosalie was shocked by the lack of basic facilities. 'No single rooms?'

The woman shook her head.

'Anywhere on this street?'

The woman shrugged. 'Most lodgin' 'ouses just for sailors, seven or eight beds each room. They get drunk, need somewhere to sleep.'

'So where should I go?'

'You got work?'

'I'm a dancer.'

'But you got a job yet? Yes or no?'

Rosalie shook her head.

'The Evening Star gives performers places to stay. Start there.'

'It's closed.'

'At one o'clock. My husband Gianni is there to do accounts. He runs the place for bigwigs. Hires too. Tell him Karmena sent you.'

Rosalie glanced at her wristwatch. It was still only eleven in the morning. 'What should I do until then?'

'Leave your case here. Go for a walk. Valletta, beautiful city.'

Rosalie hesitated and the woman chuckled. 'I take care. Now you go.'

Rosalie left her case with Karmena and headed off through the cobbled Valletta alleys where thin dogs slunk along the walls and fat cats eyed them haughtily. Plenty of mice, she thought, maybe rats too. Yes. Definitely rats. She listened to the hum and rumble of the city and soon understood all the streets were straight, some very narrow indeed, and very steep, whereas the main city streets were much wider. Turning down one of them, she passed peeling doorways the colour of port, and roads that rose and fell with giddying flights of steps everywhere. She loved the rows of wooden balconies on the sandstone townhouses – she later learnt they were called *gallariji* – reaching out over the street and painted in dozens of different colours.

A dark-eyed child ran up to her from one of the narrow alleys. 'I take you somewhere, lady.'

Rosalie shook her head.

'English?'

'No, French.'

'Better,' the boy nodded.

'You don't like the English?'

'My mother works for English. My father, he does not like.'

'What does your mother do?'

The little boy shrugged. 'Take you somewhere,' he said again. 'Gardens. Nice view.'

As they walked, he chattered while she was gradually getting her bearings, which was not as hard as she'd thought it might be because all the streets were part of the same grid layout.

'Upper Barrakka Gardens,' the boy proudly said as they arrived.

After she gave him a coin he grinned then darted off.

The boy had been right. The view of the Grand Harbour was stunning. The air was drenched with the scent of geraniums, roses and jasmine and a breeze carried the salty spray rising from the glittering jewel-like Mediterranean Sea below – lovely after the heady mix of urine, sweating horses, street vendors, and exhaust fumes in the city.

Rosalie felt the tension leave her body for the first time since she left Paris.

The train had taken her through Switzerland and then on to Italy. All the way to Genoa she felt terrified she might be hauled off and arrested for stealing her mother's jewels. The trains had been great until Rome but not nearly so advanced after that. With some trepidation she'd joined a train heading south swarming with people, chickens, and even goats. Children wailed, dogs barked and the women gossiped endlessly in rapid Italian. She tried to ignore them as rural Italy spread out before her – the gnarled wiry farmers bending over their work in the fields and the women clustered together, wearing black. The train rattled on, its closed windows trapping smoky, greasy air inside the carriage. Hence her relief when she eventually found her way onto a ferry to Sicily and then to Malta. It was the furthest she'd ever been from home – but she was free.

Now, in the gardens overlooking the harbour, the sun was scorching and she really needed a hat. In the early morning, the sun had cast a gentle golden light on the baroque buildings of the town but at this point in the day everything seemed bleached of colour.

She felt the sweat dampening her dress. Her back. Her underarms. Even her eyelids. She spotted a bench in the shade of an umbrella pine tree and moved towards it but at the same time a young man wearing a straw hat and a bright blue shirt approached. He paused, and with a slight bow allowed her to proceed towards it ahead of him, though as soon as she sat down, he joined her.

'Tourist?' he asked, turning his face towards her.

She scrutinised this blonde, blue-eyed, well-groomed man then said, rather archly, 'No. A dancer.'

Despite her tone, he smiled. 'I see. And where do you dance?'

Not this again, she thought. 'The Evening Star,' she lied.

'You're not English.'

'No.'

'You sound, I don't know, maybe French?'

'You speak French?' she asked.

'A little, but I am English. We're terrifically bad at languages.'

She snorted. 'Because you are all too superior to learn.'

'Oi,' he said in mock dismay. 'That's not entirely fair.'

'So what are *you* doing here?'

'Visiting my uncle.'

'So, *you* are the tourist.'

He tilted his head and smiled. He really had a lovely smile, she thought, and extremely white teeth.

'Not really,' he said. 'I spent most of my summers here as a child. It's a home from home.'

'Where is home?'

'Good old London.'

'Ah. Well, I'm from Paris.'

'Wonderful city.'

'You've been there?'

He smiled again and his eyes lit up. 'Oh yes. I love Paris. You must miss it.'

She shrugged, and knowing she could never ever go back home, felt again that pang of homesickness.

'I could show you around here,' he was saying. 'I say, are you all right?'

'I'm perfectly fine,' she said, pulling herself together.

'I was suggesting, if you like, I could show you around Malta, in your spare time of course. Mdina is a magical place with wonderful hidden palaces. Very ancient. Its walls are intact and there's only one way in or out. You'll like it.'

She didn't know if she would, but she did like *him*. Like many of the British, he was full of arrogant confidence, but in his case it was rather attractive.

'Robert Beresford,' he said and smiled.

Something told her this man was going to play a significant part in her life, so she smiled back and tried out her new name again. So far, she had only used it once when she'd met Charlotte on the boat.

'Riva,' she said, turning to him and extending a hand. 'Riva Janvier.'

Goodbye, Rosalie, she thought.

CHAPTER 14

Florence

Devonshire, 1944

While Florence was preparing supper, Belinda came into the kitchen then began pacing the room and muttering.

Florence looked up, her eyes stinging from slicing onions. 'What is it?' You're making me nervous.'

Belinda bit her lip.

Florence sighed. 'Look, I'm cooking, and I need to concentrate or I'll cut my finger or burn myself. If you've got something to say, just say it. If not, could you please sit down.'

'You think you know everything about Jack, don't you?' Belinda eventually said.

Florence frowned. 'Of course not. Why would you say that?'

Belinda tilted her head to one side with a curious look on her face. 'He told you everything did he, on that cosy little walk you had?'

Florence shrugged, not wanting to get into this.

'So, he's told you about Charlie then?'

'Who's Charlie?'

'Just as I thought,' Belinda said, her voice scornful, and then she left the room.

Puzzled, Florence threw her hands up in the air. What was that all about? Did it even mean anything? Through the window she spotted the pheasants running for the hills for no apparent reason and felt a stirring of unease. Their capers were usually funny but not tonight. She turned back to slide the onions into the frying pan and couldn't help wondering who Charlie was. Somebody significant? If not, why had Belinda mentioned him? Maybe Charlie was a girl. A girlfriend of Jack's perhaps? But then, Jack would have said something, wouldn't he? Then again, maybe not. After all he hadn't mentioned having a wife, so what else might he be concealing?

Later she sat looking out of the sitting room window as the setting sun turned the sky red and gold. She felt awkward being alone with Jack as he lit the fire and couldn't settle to her book. Belinda was now striding around upstairs, and she knew they were both listening to her footsteps. She recalled the closeness she and Jack had shared during those weeks crossing the mountains and sighed deeply. Nobody here really understood – or wanted to know – what they'd been through. The war was dragging painfully on, and it seemed everyone had a story to tell.

'That sounded heartfelt,' he said. 'You okay?'

She nodded, but as a distraction counted the panes on each of the three triple casement windows. Each one had pretty arches at the top. The one at the back had twelve panes, another facing the front had eighteen panes and the little one at the side had just nine. She stood up to close the heavily lined floral curtains against the oncoming night. Weighted with lead pellets at the hems, they kept out the worst of the cold.

Just as she was closing the final curtain, Belinda waltzed in wearing a low-cut, clingy crepe dress, with ridiculously high heels. The dress was black and she wore it with panache, accessorised only by a single string of pearls. But her eyes were red from crying, or too much alcohol – Florence couldn't tell which – and she held a full glass of whisky in her shaking hand. She was too thin but still incredibly beautiful.

'Oh for God's sake, Belinda, give me the glass and sit down. You're spilling it,' Jack said as he got to his feet.

Belinda settled into a wooden Windsor chair by the back window and pulled back the curtains to peer out. 'I like it better with the curtains open. All that darkness approaching, you know. I like to see it. In London I never close them, do I darling?'

Jack snorted. 'Don't be ridiculous, Belinda. You have blackout curtains in London.'

Belinda's words hadn't been slurred, so maybe she *had* been crying, not drinking, Florence thought. As she picked up the book she'd been trying to read, the woman spoke again. 'Well, you two are very chummy, but Florence, I wonder if you could give us some privacy. I rather need to talk to Jack.'

Jack started to object but Florence was already on her feet. 'It's fine,' she said, raising her shoulders in a shrug of feigned indifference. 'I've things to get on with in the kitchen.'

'Just like the proper little housewife that you are,' Belinda said in a sickeningly syrupy voice. 'Didn't think that was your cup of tea, Jack.'

Florence left the room, closing the door behind her. Part of her felt sorry for Belinda, but the other part of her quivered with irritation. Belinda hadn't said, 'Run along, dear,' but to Florence it had felt as if she had.

But could she really blame her?

She'd thought of Belinda only as someone who stood in the way of her own life with Jack, although her loyalty to Hélène did that too, and Belinda had a right to be there, a right to try and patch things up with him. Florence was the intruder, and she should leave them to it. She resolved to pack her case and leave the next day, though her heart sank at the thought.

With no job or alternative accommodation, she'd have to go back to her mother's, at least until she could find work. She didn't want to leave, and she didn't want to go back without learning anything about Rosalie but she couldn't go to Malta until after the war ended. She longed to talk to Hélène or Élise, ask for their advice or better still go home to France and see them. It had always helped to chew things over with her sisters and she wished she could do that now.

The next morning, when Florence woke to the rosy blush of dawn, she stretched luxuriously for a moment before it all came crashing back. She had to leave. She felt an ache in her chest as she dragged her suitcase from under the bed and began to pack. When it was done, she stared out of the window at the cirrus clouds streaming across the sky. She would miss this place.

Even before breakfast she was ready, she left her case by the front door and her coat draped over the chair in the hall. In the kitchen she filled the kettle and set it on the Aga to boil. Then she cut two slices of bread to toast.

Jack came into the room in his striped pyjamas, his hair messy, and frowned. 'I saw the case. You're not really leaving, are you?'

She turned her back on him and hunched over the Aga, feeling the heat on her face.

'Florence, you don't have to go.'

She swung round. 'How can I stay? She's your wife. And I'm . . . nobody.'

'Don't say that. Not after everything we've been through.'

He looked appalled, but she just shook her head.

'I've spoken to her. We *are* getting a divorce. It's already underway and she isn't staying. She's going back to London.'

'When?'

'In a few days.'

'But you're going away again tomorrow, aren't you?'

He nodded.

'Well then.' The kettle was boiling so she turned away

again to warm the teapot and then spoon in some leaves, fill it with water, and stir.

'Look,' he said, 'if you stick around when I'm not here, I'm sure Belinda will go. If you leave, I think she might well dig in.'

'I can't be in the middle of this,' she said and steadied the teapot on the table. There was silence as she poured out the tea and added the milk and a little sugar.

She heard him heave a heavy sigh before he spoke again.

'Florence. Come for a drive. Let's talk about this properly.'

'I don't know what more there is to say.'

'Let's find out. Maybe take a drive to Dartmoor. I have a bit of spare petrol. You haven't been there yet, have you?'

She shook her head.

'I love it. All that space helps clear your mind. Say yes. Please. Just put your case in my room.'

'Your room?' She thought of his large cast-iron bed.

'Yes. Make your presence felt. I'll sleep in the box room.'

'Ah,' she said and attempted to smile. For just one moment she had thought . . . well, it didn't matter what she had thought. In the house Jack and Belinda's marriage still haunted the place, as if the ghosts of their previous selves still lived there. Maybe on Dartmoor it would feel different.

Before Belinda had even stirred, they were on their way.

It was a crisp autumn day, the berried hedgerows shivering just a little in the breeze. They headed for Dartmoor, driving along one winding lane after another and soon she spotted a tiny sign for Princetown, the only one she'd seen so far. After they'd passed the farms and forests and reached the wilder, emptier slopes, he pulled up at the side of the road. She got out and looked around her, walking a little way from him and feeling an unexpected lightness in her step. The bracken had already turned orange and brown but the contrast of that with the wide and incredibly bright blue sky made the air shimmer. The vibrant colours and the feeling of space so joyous she felt her whole body relax. She reached out her arms to the sky and stretched.

'See what I mean,' he said, watching her. 'I always come here when I don't know which way to turn.'

'About B—'

But she didn't finish because he grabbed her hand. 'Come on, we need to walk.'

And they walked, crushing the bracken underfoot.

'There are so many secrets here,' he said, raising his arm and sweeping it across the expanse of land and sky. 'Stone circles, standing stones, the remains of medieval settlements. Wonderful, isn't it?'

She nodded and pointed at what looked like a granite cross.

'Lots of those. I like to think of the people who lived, died, or passed through this landscape. And to know that nothing much has changed since prehistoric times.'

He sighed in the pause that followed.

'What?'

'Nothing. Just . . . well I hope we never lose our wild places. I mean in nature, of course.'

Florence narrowed her eyes in thought. 'But I sometimes want to feel wild inside too,' she said. 'Don't you?'

Jack nodded. 'Yes, although it can be dangerous.'

'Out here? Or inside?'

'Probably both.' He gave her a wry look then smiled. 'Here, it's the mists. They come down so fast that people have died.'

'How?'

'They get lost. You need a map and compass, even if you're familiar with the landscape.'

She could smell sheep dung, wet peat, and the sweet traces of woodsmoke, but more than that she could smell and feel the wilderness coursing through her veins in an almost elemental way. Thrilled by it, she turned abruptly, ready to touch him, but he had already moved on and was standing looking the other way.

She glanced again at the moor and at the luminous quality of the air. She really didn't want to leave Devon.

'In the summer,' he said, interrupting her thoughts, 'it's all about the heather, and earlier in the year the amazing scent of gorse, a bit like coconut and marzipan mixed together especially when it's warm.'

'I read somewhere that people believed witches hid in gorse bushes.'

He laughed. 'Only witches could survive the spikes. I used to come looking for witches when I was a boy.

'Ever find one?'

He grinned. 'What do you think?'

There was a momentary silence. Then he glanced at

his watch. 'How about a spot of lunch before we head back? I know a pretty decent hotel.'

She nodded as they walked back to where he'd parked.

'So,' he said, as they stood before the car. Then he jammed his hands into his pockets, looked down, and stubbed his heel into the ground. 'Did you hear from your mother while I was away?'

She shook her head and there was a short pause before she spoke.

'Jack, you never speak about your mother.'

He looked away and then back at her. 'I had a twin brother. He died at birth, and it made Mum anxious. But, like you, she was a great baker. I remember that.'

'How did she die?'

'Peritonitis.'

He glanced up at the sky and changed the subject. 'The clouds are rolling in.'

'I'm sorry about your mother, and your twin,' she said.

'All in the past.' He came closer. 'Gladys says the kittens are ready to leave the mother cat. She has a sweet little ginger one marked out for you. Promise me you'll stay.'

She glanced away and then back at him.

'Jack,' she said, recalling what Belinda had said. 'Who is Charlie?'

He lifted his hand and brushed the hair from her eyes, the movement so tender and caring it caught at her heart.

'It really does feels wild here, doesn't it?' he said, ignoring her question.

But she thought it was more than wild. It felt savage and would be dreadfully harsh under a leaden wintery sky.

'I come here for the emptiness of the moor,' he said. 'And the feeling that there's more to life than we allow ourselves to acknowledge.'

She nodded and there was a long silence. She watched a bird, a thrush maybe, hopping just a foot away from Jack, then taking flight and heading for a hawthorn bush. She stood very still, expecting him to answer her question, when a huge flock of speckled gold-and-black birds flew into sight and settled further away on the moor. He spoke quietly, almost to himself. 'Golden plovers,' he said. 'They'll be moving to the lowlands any day now.'

Then he turned to her, and as the moments slid past slowly, she noticed the faint lines around his eyes deepen.

'Charlie was my son, Florence,' he finally said. 'My little boy.'

The indescribably sad look on his face took her breath away. A painting of a Madonna and child came into her head as she stifled her shock. They never painted the fathers, did they? And yet looking at Jack the grief he had kept hidden was now plain to see.

'Once we knew she was pregnant, Belinda and I tried to patch things up as best we could.' He stopped to look up at the sky then back at her. 'Florence, I'd have died for that little boy. But . . . well it wasn't me who died.'

She took a long silent breath, dreading hearing what terrible thing had happened to his son.

He didn't speak at first but turned away and continued walking, but more slowly now. Then, speaking in a detached voice, he said, 'I was away, and Belinda was in London, already smoking and drinking too much. One night, during what she thought was a lull in the bombing in September 1940, she ran out of cigarettes. Charlie was asleep so she left him and ran to Hector's house just around the corner, during the blackout. He and Belinda had been seeing each other again. She swears she wasn't gone for long, and Hector says it's true, but while she was out more bombs fell.'

Florence clasped a hand over her mouth.

'When one of them hit the apartment building, Charlie was killed outright. He would have known nothing about it.'

Florence couldn't even swallow for the tension in her throat.

'He was four years old,' Jack said, now with a tremor in his voice. 'Four.'

'I—'

'You don't have to say anything. The thing is, when the war began, I pleaded with Belinda to come down to Devon with him. It was so much safer here, but she refused point blank.'

'I don't think anyone could make Belinda do something she didn't want to do.'

He sighed. 'Maybe, but I will never forgive myself.'

'Or her?'

'Quite.'

'I'm so sorry about your little boy. You must . . . well, I can't even imagine how awful it must have been.'

He nodded slowly but didn't meet her eyes.

'Still is really,' he said. 'At times. But life goes on. And I don't even know if that's good or bad.'

She almost didn't dare to speak. After an appalling loss like this, well . . . it was no wonder he hadn't wanted to tell her or anyone else either.

'What happened to Charlie is why you kept things close to your chest in France.'

'It was easier in France. And don't forget I was there as part of the SOE.'

They walked on in silence for a little while, Florence staring at the ground, her head and heart bursting with anguish for Jack. She wanted to reach out and help him. Somehow. But maybe this was not the time.

'After Charlie died this is where I used to come,' he said. 'It helped.'

'I'm glad.'

He smiled and held out his hand. And just for a second there was that wonderfully deep moment of connection between them again. 'The plovers have gone,' he said, looking up at the sky again.

And then he pulled his hand away.

CHAPTER 15

Jack was away and although he had said Belinda would be leaving too, she still had not and now Gladys was due to pick Florence up in the truck. She was certain they had a map of Malta or maybe Italy knocking about somewhere at the farm, and she'd suggested Florence might like to see the kittens while they were there. This despite Florence reiterating that she didn't know how long she'd be at Meadowbrook, although at Jack's insistence she had agreed to stay for a while longer at least.

Just as she was putting on her coat, she heard the postman's familiar knock at the door – three sharp raps followed by a pause and then three more.

'One for you m'dear,' he said and handed her an envelope.

A thick white Basildon Bond envelope. She recognised her mother's unmistakable handwriting, as perfect as it always had been, and in her mind's eye she saw the squat bottle of Quink, blue ink, and her mother dipping her fountain pen to fill it. She thanked the man and took the letter inside. With some trepidation she slit open the envelope, and she saw at once that it was little more than a note. From her mother's very first words, Florence realised it was an apology. This was something new. Claudette never usually apologised.

Chérie,

I hope you will forgive your mother for her breach of hospitality when we last met, and forgive me for my rather bad humour.

Hmmm, Florence thought, 'bad humour' barely touched the reality of her mother's violent rage, but still this was a step forward.

You were honest with me, and my response was not well-mannered. Moreover, I pray that you might understand these matters from long ago are difficult for me. In future I will attempt to amend my response. I had hoped to secure the door on the past, but if you could contemplate visiting again at some point, I will try to be more obliging and maybe talk about what happened to my sister, Rosalie, too. I loved her as you love your sisters, and the thought of not knowing what happened to her haunts me. I hope you will reconsider helping me find her.

You remain welcome here.

Maman

Florence wasn't sure what to think. She loved Meadowbrook and didn't want to leave but it wasn't really her home. And yet her mother's cottage wasn't either. She wasn't in any hurry to return there, but at least when she did it looked as if her mother might be more forthcoming. She felt intrigued by the thought of what might have happened to Rosalie – after all a family mystery was exciting. Who wouldn't want to know more? But until the war was over there wasn't much she could do. The next time she visited she would encourage her mother to open up about her sister as well as her affair with her German lover – Florence's real father, Friedrich. She craved more details about him and about what had happened between them all those years ago.

A little later, as Gladys drove her battered truck to the farm, Florence was still thinking about her mother *and* about Belinda. Both of them mothers, and both suffering in different ways.

'You seem quiet, love,' Gladys said with a sideways glance at Florence.

'I was thinking about Belinda. I feel sorry for her.'

'Well of course. It's terrible to lose a child. I should know. The maps we have in the house, you see, they were all my boy's. Mad keen on seeing the world he was.'

For a moment Florence froze. Then she found her voice. 'Oh Gladys, I'm so sorry. I didn't know.'

'Early on in the war. Edward. We had him late in life, but all the more special for that. His ship went down. *Lost at sea* we were told.'

'Your only child?'

Gladys nodded and Florence reached over to pat her hand. They were silent for the rest of the short distance to the farm. This time, when Gladys pushed open the peeling blue farmhouse door and they walked in, Florence was prepared for the chaos. The cats were there, of course, but on this occasion the wallpaper struck her too. How had she not noticed before? Pictures of carrots, oranges, apples, jugs and jars, in shades of orange and yellow replicated over and over on a spotted beige background, so busy it made her eyes spin. But also, a rather good-looking young man in civvies was sitting at the table and reading a newspaper, his spectacles pushed back on to the top of his head.

'Bruce,' Gladys said, sounding pleased as punch. 'Didn't know you'd be here. Not on duty?'

He stood up, smiling broadly. 'Two whole days off. I just dropped by to let you know Mum can't make it to the WI this evening, so no need to pick her up.'

Gladys turned to Florence. 'This is my friend Grace's boy. Bruce, this is my neighbour, Florence.'

He stepped round the table to shake her hand. Florence studied him. Tall and slender with dark curly hair, cut short, he had warm hazel eyes. She liked the look of him *and* the way he was so comfortable with Gladys.

'Well,' he said. 'Message delivered. Better be making tracks.'

'On that old boneshaker of yours?'

'Of course.' He smiled and pecked her on the cheek. 'Be seeing you. Cheerio, Florence.'

Gladys had a sparkle in her eyes and, as soon as he had

gone, said, 'Only twenty-eight and a registrar, you know, at the Royal Devon and Exeter Hospital. Known him since he was a nipper.'

'I'm sure you must be proud. He seems lovely.'

'You might wonder why he hasn't been snapped up.'

'Not really, but I'm sure you're going to tell me.'

Gladys gave her a studied look. 'I wouldn't want to see him hurt, mind, but you could do worse than our Bruce. He was engaged to an Exeter girl, but when he went away to work, she went off with one of them Americans.'

'Oh dear.'

Gladys pulled a face. 'Flibbertigibbet she was.'

Florence hid her smile. 'Sounds like he's well out of it, Gladys.'

'Did you know when the bombs rained down on Devonshire towns during the Blitz, expectant mothers in the maternity ward of Exeter hospital were given enamel bowls and blankets to wear on their heads as protection.'

Florence laughed. 'Goodness. Not sure that would have helped much.'

'Well as it turns out the hospital wasn't hit, so we'll never know. Bruce will tell you all about it if you ask him. Now, would you like to see yours now or later,' Gladys said, in an innocent voice.

'Mine?'

'The little marmalade kitten I've saved for you. I've called him Bart and he's adorable.'

Florence smiled. 'I know what you're trying to do.'

'There is one added benefit,' Gladys added conspiratorially.

'Oh?'

'Belinda is allergic to cat hair.'

Florence burst out laughing. 'You devious so-and-so, but you know I can't adopt a cat when I don't even know where I'll be living.'

As Florence lay on the bed in Jack's room resting on one elbow and staring at the map of Malta she'd borrowed from Gladys, she felt completely in limbo. Now that Belinda was still here it had changed everything; her own future was unsettled, and she really didn't know what to do. There was nothing satisfying about this kind of uncertainty. With nowhere to really call home, if she could go to Malta right this minute, she believed she jolly well might. At least it would give her something useful to do with herself. It would make her mother happy too, and Florence liked making other people happy. She'd already written back to Claudette thanking her and saying she would visit again.

Florence loved Jack's room. It had a window to the front and another to the back. Not as masculine as she expected but, with pleasing honey-coloured beams, striped blue and white curtains, polished floorboards, and a couple of Persian rugs, it had a cheery air. A wooden filing cabinet took up one corner and shelves stuffed with box files and books lined part of one wall. She couldn't stop herself peeking in his wardrobe but forced herself not to examine everything on, or in, his large desk beneath the window at the back. She curled up on his bed and read for a while, but by late afternoon was hungry so made her way down to the kitchen. No sign of Belinda, thank goodness, but she still felt a bit wary.

She went to the larder and saw that the last bottle of sherry was gone and what had been a small block of treasured cheese was lying under its net cover hacked to pieces. Florence frowned. No prizes for guessing what had happened there.

Hearing odd noises coming from the drawing room, she paused. It sounded like Belinda muttering, maybe arguing with somebody, but when Florence listened carefully, she could hear the woman was arguing with herself. With an anxious fluttering in her tummy now, Florence wasn't hungry any more. She went into the hall.

'Ah, there you are. Come in,' Belinda drawled, her eyes glittering. 'Drink?'

'I don't much like sherry.'

'There's whisky.' She held up the bottle. 'Oh, not much left. Sorry, darling.'

Florence sighed. 'Thanks, but I really only drink wine.'

'Ahhhhh.' She pointed her finger at Florence. 'That's because you're French. Tell me exactly what you are doing here in England?'

Florence remembered Claudette telling her you had to look your enemies in the eye. Was Belinda her enemy? She drew back her shoulders. She'd had enough of being meek.

'Look Belinda, I need to tell you I'm not leaving, but that I think that you should go back to London.'

'Oh, is that so?' The woman's voice was thick and she suddenly hiccupped. 'Scuse me.'

'What good is staying here doing you, or Jack?'

'Christ! You ask me that? This is about you. It's you you're thinking of.'

'I'm Jack's friend.'

'And I'm his goddam wife.' And then to Florence's horror, Belinda began to cry.

Florence froze. Should she attempt to comfort her?

Before long Belinda was sobbing and moaning as if her heart was truly breaking, her hands in tight fists thumping herself in the chest. Florence stepped forward and tentatively put a hand on Belinda's thin shoulder. Eventually the woman noticed she was there, and Florence handed her a handkerchief.

'It's clean,' she said.

Belinda took it but her face was blotchy and creased, her eyes puffy and rimmed with red, her make-up smudged. She wiped them and then her cheeks too and she tried to run a hand over her hair, but she was still gasping for breath. She doubled over with a fresh wave of sobs, tears running down between her fingers and dripping onto her lap. The depth of her grief brought tears to Florence's eyes too.

When Belinda managed to stop again, she wrapped her arms around her body and began to rock, keening in a high-pitched tone.

'It's my fault,' she eventually whispered. 'He blames me, and he's right.'

'How can I help?' Florence asked, but knew there was nothing she could really do.

Belinda didn't seem to hear. 'There's a hole inside me. Never stops hurting, so I drink. It numbs me. Jack doesn't understand.'

There was a slight pause.

'I want oblivion. Do you see? I let my little boy die. My own little boy. I let him die. And, you know . . . I hate myself. I hate myself far more than Jack hates me.' She'd spoken the last few words softly, haltingly, as if she could hardly bear to say them.

'I'm sure he doesn't hate you.'

She laughed bitterly. 'Are you? Well, he certainly doesn't love me. Our marriage is over and all I want to do is end it all. There . . . I've said it.'

For a moment Florence wasn't sure of the other woman's meaning. Was she talking about her marriage or her life?'

'Look, if you want to stay here, I can be with you. Maybe I can help.'

'How? How can you help? How can anyone help? Don't you understand? I can't bear to go on living with my little boy dead and knowing he died because of me. . . .'

That night they sat together for hours, Florence keeping hold of Belinda as she lost herself to grief.

The next day Belinda stood on the doorstep, doing her utmost to blink the tears away, her mask of make-up once more firmly in place. She gave Florence a weak smile and a restrained pat on the back. Then she got into the taxi. As Florence watched it make its way up the drive and away from the house, her heart was hammering in her throat. Belinda was beside herself with the most terrible grief imaginable, the enormity of which surpassed anything Florence had ever known. She took a breath and let it out slowly, hoping Belinda would find her way through whatever lay ahead.

She thought about Jack, too. His own grief must be why he held his emotions so tightly inside him. If Jack allowed himself to love, he would also have to allow himself to feel his pain. You couldn't choose. She'd learnt that from her own experience after the rape. She hoped to have children one day, but along with such all-encompassing love came the risk of an equally all-encompassing loss. She imagined that when a child died, the guilt must be dreadful, an impossible weight to bear. A parent's job was to protect their child, and if you failed at that, what did it make you?

CHAPTER 16

A week later Florence took a short stroll up the track, gravel crunching underfoot, before heading for the village to look for work. Now that Belinda had gone back to London, she had decided to stay put and she absolutely had to find a job as soon as possible. She loved the peaceful mornings here, but as she walked a burst of movement ahead drew her attention. She froze, narrowing her eyes to see more clearly. A long, rust-coloured tail appeared, and then an entire fox heading towards her through the long wet grass. The animal stopped moving and stared as if weighing her up, its eyes a stunning bright amber, but then with the swiftest of movement it spun around and was gone. She knew how quickly foxes could navigate the woodland, how easily they squeezed through narrow gates, jumped over ditches, or ran along the estate walls. She'd seen them in the daytime before, but it was rare for one to stop and stare. It was a wonderful start to the day. Maybe her luck would be in.

Back at the cottage Florence wheeled out Gladys' old bike to cycle to the village. It was early November now and the cold was beginning to bite. The landscape had altered so much since her arrival in the height of summer. Now it was windy, much of the autumnal colour gone and the skeletal trees stood black against a wintery sky.

Barnsford was surprisingly quiet.

First Florence went to the newsagent's to scan the job advertisement cards in the window. But though she'd hoped to maybe spot someone needing a gardener some-where she might be able to reach on her bicycle, she found only requests for odd-job men, or plumbers, or other jobs requiring skilled labour. When she spoke to the old man behind the counter, he suggested the local paper, so she bought one and headed for the WI coffee morning Gladys had told her took place in the village hall near the Royal Oak pub.

She bought a cup of chicory coffee and a rock bun. After she sat down and took a bite, she realised how well-named it was. Then she opened the paper and found what they called the small ads page, running a finger down the columns, but with no luck.

A heavily built middle-aged woman, sighing deeply, deposited herself at the same table, almost tipping up her coffee as it wobbled on the saucer. As she caught her breath, she also caught Florence's eye.

'Don't mind me, dear. Just a bit out of puff,' she said. 'Not seen you here before, have I?'

'No, my first time. I'm surprised how quiet it is.'

'You should have been here before D-Day. You wouldn't believe it, but we were bursting at the seams. My name's Mrs Wicks by the way.'

'Pleased to meet you. I'm Florence. Do tell me more about what it was like it was like before D-Day.'

The woman sighed and took a sip of her coffee. 'Oh, busy. Our lads coming in from the camps and military training up on Dartmoor. And then in 1943 the Americans started arriving too. Some of their officers were billeted at the manor house up the road, the Hambury place.'

'Oh, I live near there.'

'Nice part of the world, that. We had dances for the soldiers here in the village hall. You could have come if you'd been here.'

'Sounds like fun.'

'Not for the likes of me, but my daughter, Jennifer, she went. Stepped out with an American called Shane for a while. Imagine that for a name. Not that I can blame her. A handsome bunch, if I say so myself, those Americans. Good teeth you know.'

Florence laughed. 'I've heard.'

'They had money too, though we hadn't a clue what they were doing here. Come D-Day we knew and overnight the village . . . poof, just like a ghost town.'

'You must miss the excitement.'

Mrs Wicks wrinkled her nose. 'I do, and I don't. The land girls still come to the pub on a Saturday evening. And when Plymouth was bombed again at the beginning of May this year, a young family came to stay with relatives here. Their house, you see, gone up in smoke. Destitute. Next door to me now. Noisy bunch.'

Soon after that the woman started to do up her coat, so Florence rose to her feet and held out her hand. 'It's been lovely meeting you, Mrs Wicks.'

The older woman got up too and shook her hand. 'Call me Freda, dear. I live just behind the pub. Number eleven. Pop in any time. I'll tell you all about Slapton Sands.'

'What happened there?'

'Only rumours mind and it was very hush-hush at the time. We only found out in early August.'

'Found out what?'

The woman drew closer and spoke more quietly. 'Mass graves, my dear. That's what. Anyway, I have to be getting back to hang out the washing.'

'I need to be getting back too.'

'Off to work, are you?'

Florence sighed. 'I wish. I'm staying with a friend, and I've been trying to find a job.'

'Why didn't you say. Any good at cooking?'

'I love to cook.'

'Well, there you are. Get yourself up to the manor. My next-door neighbour, Deirdre, she's cook there, but going part-time on account of her old man being sick. Could be something going.'

Florence beamed at her. 'Thank you!'

'You're very welcome my dear. See you again, I hope.'

Before Florence left the village, feeling excited about the chance of work at the manor, she nipped into the library, signed herself up and borrowed a book about

Malta. Just as she was wheeling the bike to the edge of the village, she noticed a man climbing down from a motorbike with a sidecar attached to it. When he took off his helmet, she recognised him at once. As he looked up, she took a few steps towards him.

'Hello again. Florence, isn't it?' he said, and smoothed a palm over his hair. His very curly hair.

'Yes.'

He smiled and his hazel eyes crinkled up. 'We met at the farm,' he said. 'I'm Bruce.'

'Of course. Is that your boneshaker?'

'A Douglas 1936 Aero. Do you know about motorbikes?'

She laughed. 'Not at all.'

'My pride and joy. I'd offer you a lift back home but——' He raised his hands and shrugged. 'I only have fifteen minutes to nip into the village hall and collect my mother before I have to head to Exeter and start my shift.'

She laughed. 'It doesn't matter, and in any case, I have my bicycle.'

'Another time maybe.'

'I'd like that.' She smiled and began to move away.

'Hang on a minute, Florence. If you're serious and really would like a ride in the boneshaker . . .' He dug out the nub of a pencil and a little notebook from his coat pocket and wrote in it. Then he peeled the top sheet off and handed it to her. 'I share the house with three other doctors; no obligation, but you can leave a message, just let me know when it suits. My Mum sees Gladys so I can get back to you that way. I assume you haven't got a telephone.'

'Sadly not, but thank you.'

'No problem. Be seeing you.'

While he went off, she twisted to watch him stride away, long-legged, and rangy. Then she cycled home full of hope and smiling to herself. She'd known it was going to be a good day.

As soon as she opened the front door, she spotted a letter on the doormat and picked it up, her heart jumping when she recognised the handwriting. It was from Hélène and she itched to open it immediately, but first made herself a quick cup of tea and only then sat at the table, tearing open the envelope and reading.

Dear Florence,

I hope you are still well. Please do write again and let us know.

As you already are aware, Allied troops with the help of the French Resistance and led by General Charles de Gaulle, liberated Paris on August 25th.

The thing is that finally, after four years of German occupation, it has taken a little while for it to really sink in. Gradually we are becoming used to being able to breathe without looking over our shoulders or fearing the knock on the door. With the Nazis gone our daily lives are improving, shops are open again, and we can go out for a meal. But I'm afraid some dreadful things have been happening during the liberation and the country is in terrible chaos.

But dear Florence, I have some truly terrible news. There have been reprisals, vendettas, just as we expected. You remember Henri, the owner of the chateau? Well, his wife Suzanne was killed. During the war she had frequently been seen in the village accompanied by Nazi officers with whom she appeared to be friendly. She'd had no option. They were living in her home, the chateau, and she had to make the Nazis believe she could be trusted. But all the time she was feeding Violette and Élise news of German activities and movements. Élise spoke up for Suzanne when she heard of her capture, insisted she'd been working undercover for the Resistance all the time. But because Suzanne had been so good at maintaining her cover, the hotheads, not even real Resistance, didn't believe Élise and took their revenge. As you can imagine, we are all broken-hearted.

I'm so sorry to be sending such awful news. Good news to follow very soon, I hope. We don't think it will be too long before Élise gives birth. Her dates are a bit unclear, but she is already enormous. I will send you a telegram the moment the baby arrives.

Please look after yourself, Florence.

With love from me and from Élise.

Hélène

P.S. I know you said he was away a lot but do you see much of Jack?

Florence glanced up, but everything was blurred. Tears slid down her cheeks and she let them fall. She wanted to be back there in France. She wanted to be able to hug her sisters at such a dreadful time. She missed them, missed her life in France, missed her village and the villagers.

Poor old Madame Deschamps, whose daughter Amelie had been killed, ninety-year-old Clément, a stooped old fellow who still carried his chair and accordion out to the pavement and played the classic street music of Paris. And she even missed brassy blonde Angela who owned the sweet shop and was rather a busybody. Here, despite growing up in England until she was fifteen, Florence felt like a stranger. Even with the possibility of a job in the offing, her mood had plummeted. Poor Suzanne. Poor Henri. She glanced at the book about Malta lying on the table beside Hélène's letter. Had Claudette missed her sister Rosalie in the same gut-wrenching way as she was missing Hélène and Élise?

CHAPTER 17

Rosalie

Malta, 1925

Rosalie looked up at a shabby eighteenth-century Maltese town house in the village of Kalkara. With rooms inside that were let only to foreign performers, it was to be her new home. She went inside and was shown a large bedroom on the second floor, with a balcony wide enough to sit out on. She caught her breath when she saw the spectacular views of the Grand Harbour and Valletta itself. From the Kalkara peninsula the city stood just across the water, shining and golden, and above it fluffy pink clouds floated by lazily. The liquid shine of gold from the city seemed to spill out onto the water, but of course it was just the reflection. After her experience at the lodgin' 'ouse Rosalie hadn't expected anything as beautiful or convenient as this, only about seven miles from Valletta by road.

'Quicker to get a ferry or a *dghaisa*,' Gianni said.

Thank you,' she replied as he prepared to leave. 'For this and for the job. I won't let you down.'

He grasped her hand and shook it. 'Be sure you don't.'

Gianni was a tall muscular man with astonishing dark eyes, a hooked nose, and a powerful presence due, she felt, not merely to his physique. Two gold teeth had gleamed when he smiled at the mention of his wife Karmena and he had whistled with pleasure when Rosalie auditioned for him. And yet when he'd shaken her hand with his own gnarled ones, she had felt gripped by the strongest feeling you wouldn't want to cross a man like that.

Soon after he'd gone, she hung a few of her clothes on a rail behind a gaudy gauze curtain and then wandered down to explore the village of Kalkara itself where she found a square, a church, a café, and a small shop. She bought fresh fruit and tomatoes from a grocery cart, plus bread, olive oil and cheese from the shop, and decided she would eat on her balcony as the sun went down. She wasn't due to start work until the evening after next. Until then? She wasn't sure. She seemed to have landed on her feet, but this was a new and different world and she had yet to learn the rules. On her way up the stairs, she heard the clatter of crockery in the kitchen she was to share with several other girls, so she pushed open the door and entered shyly.

'Ah,' a curvaceous blonde said, the moment she spotted

Rosalie. The girl had eyes the colour of a stormy sky and spoke in strongly accented English. 'You are the new girl.'

'I am.'

'English?'

'French. Riva Janvier.' Her new name felt strange on her tongue.

'Welcome. My name is Erika. I am from Hungary. You working tonight?'

'Day after tomorrow.'

'Come with me tonight and you'll see what it's like.'

'Thanks. I'd love to.'

Erika laughed. 'Don't say that until you've seen it.'

Later Rosalie was sitting on a leather stool at the highly polished mahogany bar of The Evening Star, a mirrored room painted in colours of crimson and gold and lit only by gaslight. It was deeply atmospheric and already heady with smoke, but she liked it. On their way Erika had pointed out the Cairo Club, the Egyptian Queen music hall, the Four Sisters bar, and so many others Rosalie could not recall.

'Everything is here,' Erika said. 'Restaurants, dance halls, jazz bars.'

'I love jazz,' Rosalie said. 'In Paris . . .' but then she stopped herself. Best not say too much about Paris.

It was still early and nothing much was happening yet at The Evening Star. She was talking with an English-speaking barman, a Maltese man named Ernest, who was filling her in on what lay ahead.

'Some of the bars are seedy.' He shrugged. 'So the street

gets called The Gut. Military come here for a good time one way or another.'

'And they get what they want?' she asked.

He raised his brow and gave her a knowing look.

'So, who works here?'

'In the street?'

She nodded.

'Maltese in the clubs and bars as waitresses and barmen like me.'

'And those?' She pointed to a glamorous but extremely young woman in an evening dress.

'She's one of the hostesses.'

'What nationality are the clientele?'

'Americans, British, Italians. You name it.'

'I'm sharing with a Hungarian girl.'

'Yes, Erika. Good girl. You're either one or the other.'

As the club began to fill up Riva – as Rosalie really had to think of herself now – saw that dozens of sailors were beginning to pack the bar. They jostled and laughed and flirted with her, but mostly they bought drinks and moved away to watch the show.

First up was Erika, with two other girls she'd seen earlier but had not been introduced to. All three looked fabulous in turquoise costumes embellished with feathers and silver sequins. The dancing was quite tame, Riva thought, though maybe it would hot up as the night went on. After that, a cross-dressing artist named Tommy-O took the stage. Dressed in silk and satin with a fabulous red wig that curled onto his shoulders, he was wonderful, making the audience gasp and laugh at the same time.

But when he sang and played the piano, he had them eating out of his hands and you could have heard a pin drop. The moment he finished the applause, foot stomping, and whistles were deafening. He was tall and wore dangerously high heels, making him even taller, and when he'd taken his final bow, he came swaying across to the bar, his gait languorous.

From then on, the noise from the raucous crowd was deafening. And whenever someone opened the main door for air, the sound of men carousing outside was even worse. Riva went out to look and a mob of sailors staggered past waving beer bottles, arms around each other, singing and weaving down the street. Barely even singing, she thought. More of a drunken racket. The air was thick with the smell of smoke and cheap perfume, and something else. You couldn't smell menace, but you could feel it.

Riva stepped back in retreat from the catcalls and whistles from three men who were heading directly for her. One caught her by the elbow and while she was grappling with him, she bumped into a small group of heavily made-up women, smoking and leaning against the wall.

'Watch out,' one called and pushed her away.

She stumbled, managed to right herself, edged behind the women and made it to the door of the club. It was the interval and inside the crowd had thinned, maybe some had moved on elsewhere. The sound of jazz was now coming from a club lower down the street.

Tommy-O spotted her and beckoned her over. He wore a slinky black dress over which a scarlet satin robe reached the ground. His lips were painted to match and his eyelids were iridescent green. She noticed tiny bubbles of sweat seeping through his heavily powdered face.

'So, darling, who are you?' he said, offering her a cigarette.

She shook her head and told him her new name. Stick thin and outrageously handsome, he was courteous and held out his hand. She took to him immediately.

'Sooo, what brings you here? Escape?'

She blinked but managed to hide her surprise. 'How did you know?'

He nodded sagely. 'Pretty much everyone who comes here is escaping something. Politics, families, prison.'

He smiled at her, showing perfect white teeth and an unexpected dimple in the cheeks of his angular face.

'Guessing yours is a family matter. Doesn't matter. We're all equal here. Even the ghosts.'

But Riva was soon to find out that wasn't true when the next evening, under a clear starry sky, she called on Charlotte.

The address Charlotte had given her turned out to be a tall buttery stone building with the ubiquitous enclosed wooden balconies. She spotted an enormous iron door knocker in the shape of a shell which she thumped on the studded central door.

Moments later the door flew open in answer and Charlotte appeared wearing an immaculate white silk dress dotted with little sprigs of lavender. Riva felt a little underdressed, but Charlotte didn't seem to notice and ushered her in.

'Darling, I'm so happy you came. Tea?'

'Please.'

'We're upstairs. Come on.'

Riva followed Charlotte across the front hall and then a second enormous hall with a large round table in the centre and finally up a grand stone staircase, the decorative upright railings painted gold. She ran her hands over the smooth ebony handrail. 'Do you own this place, Charlotte?' she asked.

'God no. Archie and Bobby, a friend of his, have rented it. Rather gaudy I think, but that is real gold on the railings.'

'Bloody hell.'

'I know and please call me Lottie. Charlotte makes me feel like my mother. Anyway, this place is sixteenth century and belongs to a Maltese nobleman, a marquis of some sort, but he and his family live in Mdina now.'

'So . . . you're living with Archie already?'

Lottie grinned at her. 'Not officially. I have my own apartment here.'

She pushed open another door and Riva followed her into a bright salon with tall windows, the panelled ceiling painted white with all the mouldings picked out in gold. She glanced towards the end of the room where a wide flight of four or five steps led up to a large archway and a bedroom, as if up to a stage.

'Wow!' she said. 'It's stunning.'

'Isn't it just. Lucky old me. Now, write down *your* address in my book, or I'll never know how to get hold of you. What have you been doing with yourself?' Lottie planted a cigarette into a silver holder.

Riva hesitated but decided to be honest. 'I'm a dancer, I've got a job in Strait Street.'

Lottie stepped backwards and would have paled if her complexion were not already so light. Her eyes widened as she faltered over her next words.

'Um . . . oh . . . well . . . I was about to invite you to a dinner party at The Malta Union Club next Sunday evening. It's a gentlemen's club except for these dinners they do, then we girls are invited.'

'I'd love to,' Riva interjected. 'I don't have to work on Sundays. What should I wear?'

'Ah. The thing is . . . it's a bit awkward . . .'

Riva understood instantly. 'Because I dance for a living?'

Lottie pulled a face. 'Exactly. Certainly at the Union Club. I don't mind, of course.'

Riva bristled. 'I wouldn't want to embarrass you in front of your friends. I won't come.' She headed for the door.

'Wait,' Lottie said, holding out her hand. 'You won't be able to tell anyone what you do, but maybe we can come up with a story. I hope we can still be friends. Do come with me. Please.'

'And my dress?'

'Glamorous but not too low-cut. Some of the members are rather stuffy. No Maltese of course.'

'Oh. Why's that?'

'Well, it's an old-fashioned British club, isn't it? Founded in 1826 for British officers but now civilians too, and a few dishier types will be there. It's in the Auberge de Provence, in the Strada Reale. Archie is sending a car for me, so I'll ask the driver to pick you up in Kalkara first.'

* * *

Riva's first week at work went well, although the over-powering scent of cheap cologne mixed with cigarette smoke and beer became increasingly nauseating. At least in Paris the perfume had been expensive. But this was Malta. Sometimes marvellous. Sometimes terrifying. And yet she was here now and here she must stay, at least until the way ahead became clearer and the wind called her from another direction.

In general, she liked the island. On the surface it seemed so British and yet really it was not, and the island's thrilling history fascinated her. The tales of the Knights of St John, the Catholic warriors who vanquished fero-cious Ottoman troops in 1565 and built the cliff-sized fortifications that she could see today. The folklore too. The ghost stories. The strange mix of exotic cultures, Mediterranean culture as well, plus the British of course. And as she peeled back the layers of history, she discovered when the French had invaded as well.

She had started off dancing with the other three girls, but then graduated on Saturday night to a slot of her own, just after Tommy-O's performance. She was to dance to the music of a new black American jazz player and on her first night she danced her heart out to rapturous applause. When Erika spotted her after she finished, she came running up and gave her a hug. 'I *should* tear your eyes out,' she said, 'but you were amazing. Hats off! *Bravo! Ez már derék!*'

Riva grinned. 'Er, thank you . . . I think.'

'Not sure about those two,' Erika added, glancing at the other two girls who were glowering at Riva. 'Pay no attention. They will come round. But *how* did you learn to dance like that?'

'I trained as a ballet dancer but grew too tall.'

Tommy-O joined them, languid and droll. 'You're a dark horse,' he said and clapped his hands slowly. 'Tonight, my friends, a star was born.'

The next evening Riva dressed carefully in the one evening dress – as opposed to show dress – she had brought with her. Short, sleeveless, and made of black silk, it was designed to be loose – just skimming her body – and was decorated with silver beads in clusters at the neck, hip, and at the hem which fell just below the knee. Before she'd dyed her hair so dark and cut it short, the black of the dress had been a startling contrast with her lustrous red curls, and now she wondered if the overall effect might be a bit gloomy. She decided on a little glittering headband to add some extra sparkle with earrings to match. Both were just costume jewellery, whereas Lottie would undoubtably be sporting the real thing – but needs must.

When the chauffeured vehicle arrived at the Auberge de Provence, Riva got out of the car and stared at the front edifice of what could only be called a palace. If she'd imagined Lottie's place was grand – she thought of the whole building now as Lottie's place – this was doubly so, with an imposing baroque doorway flanked by stone pillars. The front edifice was dotted with countless windows, glittering with light from the chandeliers she could see inside.

'Come on,' Lottie said.

As Lottie slipped off her coat, leaving it in the car, Riva glanced enviously at her friend's silver dress, beaded all over. It must have cost a fortune – the more beads, the more expensive the dress.

They passed a footman in evening clothes who welcomed Lottie warmly and then they climbed the stairs. At the top they were ushered into an anteroom where people were gossiping in clusters while sipping cocktails and smoking.

A rigidly upright man, possibly in his forties, with short salt-and-pepper hair, ice-blue eyes and an ebony silver-tipped walking cane came over. He smiled at Lottie, but there was no genuine warmth there.

'And who is this delightful specimen?' he asked, and something off about him made Riva shiver.

'My new friend Riva, over from France. Riva, this is Mr Stanley Lucas.'

He held out his hand, scrutinising her. 'How do you do?'

She shook his hand and replied, although she hadn't liked being called a specimen, and his hand was cold.

'And may I ask—'

'Ah, there's Archie,' Lottie interjected excitedly, pointing out a solidly built, cheerful-looking, red-faced man with sandy hair talking to another man who had his back to her.

Mr Stanley Lucas bowed and took his leave.

Archie had a broad smile for Lottie the moment he spotted her, but he was not the least bit glamorous; more what Riva's mother would have called suitable husband material. He marched over and shook Riva's hand warmly.

'How jolly to meet you,' he said.

She was about to reply but her attention had been caught by the man he had been talking to and who had just turned round – and at whom she was now staring.

'Oh, that's Bobby,' Lottie said.

Riva had all but let her mouth fall open, because striding across was the man she had met on her first day here, now wearing an exquisitely tailored suit.

'Robert Beresford,' he said, and winked as he reached her.

'Sir Robert Beresford, Baronet,' Archie corrected with a chuckle.

'I—' Riva stammered.

'What the lady is trying to say,' Bobby interrupted, clearly finding her surprise amusing, 'if she won't mind me telling, is that we've already met. I do believe I offered to show her around Malta.'

'Yes,' Riva said, collecting herself and inclining her head. 'You did.'

Lottie gave her a wide-eyed sideways glance and Riva shrugged.

'Let's see where you're seated,' Bobby said. 'Talk amongst yourselves.' And he sauntered around the long table nonchalantly picking up and putting down name cards as if he owned the world.

He probably does, Riva thought as she watched him discreetly switching one or two. When he came back, he whispered to her behind cupped hands. 'Feign surprised delight when you find seated yourself next to me.'

She grinned at him, loving his confidence but then, horror of horrors, her heart started to race as she recalled what she'd told him on the day they'd first met. She had said she was a dancer with a job at The Evening Star. Not only was she a financially struggling cabaret dancer on Strait Street while he was a blooming English baronet – but he could very easily expose her to the whole party. Oh God. What was she going to do? She glanced at the door wondering if she might be able to make a break for it. He touched her on the elbow and whispered again. 'No running away. Your secret is safe with me.'

CHAPTER 18

Riva slipped on a yellow cotton dress that made the most of her curvaceous figure and grabbed her high heels and straw hat before climbing down into a *dghaisa* and setting off for Valletta. At the dinner, Bobby had wheedled her address out of Lottie and had written to invite her to meet him in the gardens as before. She was in an especially good mood. Her week at work had gone well, although she'd wondered about the age of some of the girls working in the club. Some looked barely sixteen and many of them spoke hardly any English.

She had already spent several afternoons sitting peacefully in the shade of the Lower Barrakka Gardens, either reading or watching the shimmering Mediterranean and the vessels entering and leaving the port. She loved the little sailing boats painted blue, green and red, and when she asked, she was told they were from Gozo. Today, however, she headed for the cranky old lift that would take her up to the upper gardens and Bobby.

As she stepped out of the lift, she saw him before he spotted her, and she stood for a moment to stare. He wore no hat and his blonde hair looked almost white in the scaring sunshine. He turned, as if feeling her eyes on his back, and waved. She walked across and stood before him, suddenly shy, yet feeling – again – that this man was going to have a huge impact on her life. Somehow.

'Hello,' she said.

He kissed her on the cheek.

Riva had always sensed things before they happened, although she didn't necessarily believe her own imaginings. And today everything was exactly as it should be. He was here, she was here. What more could there be?

'I thought we'd have lunch with my uncle,' he said as he took her hand. 'In Mdina.'

'All right,' she said, but hadn't expected that. She would have preferred a day alone with Bobby.

'How about a drive to the Dingli cliffs before lunch?'

'Perfect.' She smiled at him. 'Where's your car?'

'Just around the corner.'

He had clearly parked it for maximum impact, and she stared goggle-eyed as he pointed out the gleaming vehicle.

'Alfa Romeo RLSS,' he said. 'Italian. Easy to import to Malta. My uncle has lent it to me.'

She was gazing at the most elegant automobile she had ever seen.

'It's not painted. It's polished metal,' he said, and he walked round to open the passenger door for her.

She could tell he was pleased with her reaction, and she stepped up into the car and sank into a luxurious maroon leather seat.

'What if it rains?' she asked.

He glanced up at the seamless blue sky and laughed. 'It won't, but if it does, I lift the top.'

He sat in the driver's seat and glanced at her. 'Ready?'

She nodded.

'Hold on to your hat.'

And she did.

They sped through the green and fertile landscape ripe with orchards and agricultural terraces, the dusty white road dipping and curving in front of them. She gazed at little fields and stony ground with low walls separating them, a breeze carrying the scent of wild herbs. And windmills on the outskirts of villages. She loved the windmills.

'It's a wonderful sight when the orange pickers are out in December,' he said, 'and the citrus scent in the air is amazing. I hope you'll be here for it.'

They passed barefoot rural women wearing long skirts and blouses with pretty headscarves tied under their chins and carrying chickens in large baskets balanced on the heads. And now and again a cart pulled by a donkey. In one village a man in a hat with a brightly coloured scarf draped around his neck sat on a step playing a guitar.

'We're less than seventeen miles by ten you know,' he said. 'The ocean is never more than twenty minutes or so away.'

When they arrived at the western cliffs of Dingli, he parked the car close by and came round to open the door for her. She was utterly charmed by the way he looked at her, as if there was nobody else in the world he wanted to be with.

They walked towards the edge along the flat rocky top and marvelled at the sheer drop, the sapphire blue of the sea and the milky white foam as it rolled against the base of the cliffs.

'Over eight hundred feet high,' he said. 'Dizzying, isn't it?'

Delighted by it all, she listened to the gulls calling.

'And that's the Mediterranean.'

The view of the sea was spectacular. She was a city girl and although she had spent her summers in the Périgord in France, she was not accustomed to being beside the sea. The smell of the salt was strong and would remain in her hair later, she thought. He reached out to take off her hat, his hand softly grazing her cheeks.

'It'll blow off,' he said and handed it to her.

He was right. She'd had to hold on to it during most of the car journey.

'I like your hair,' he said and smiled at her. 'Very modern.'

They walked for a while just enjoying the day.

'Look at all the yellow wildflowers,' she said.

'It's always like this in spring. In the summer it's the yellow of wild fennel and the sweet fragrant flowers of caper bushes. And when you walk it's the aromatic scent of thyme you can smell drifting up around you. Look,' he said, changing the subject and pointing at a tiny island. 'That's Filfla. Completely uninhabited.'

A fierce longing overcame her – the irresistible urge to stand right at the edge as if on the very line between life and certain death. She walked close, then even closer, daring to put herself to the test, and maybe Bobby too, by inching her toes just a tiny bit over the top of the cliff.

He quickly came up behind her and with an arm around her waist pulled her back. 'Don't be an idiot,' he said. 'The cliff can crumble.'

She rotated her body so she could look at him. She remembered how she'd longed for a more exciting world. Well, now she'd found it. And Bobby was going to be at the heart of it. He bent towards her and very gently kissed her on the mouth. He pulled back from her, but feeling sultry with heat and desire, she threaded her fingers into his hair and drew his head towards her again. Moments later, he was kissing her more deeply and she was digging her nails into his back urging him on. She pressed her hips against his, feeling the strength of what was unfolding between them.

'Oh God,' he whispered in her ear. 'What are you doing to me?'

He stroked the back of her neck and nuzzled her hair.

'What about your uncle?' she reminded him breathlessly.

'Oh damnation. I'd forgotten.'

'There's always next time.'

'Would you like there to be?'

She laughed. 'What do you think?'

She patted his hair down where she'd messed it up. It felt strangely more intimate than the kiss and then he took her hand and walked her back to the car.

When they approached the fortified city of Mdina – rising above the fields and perched on a large hilltop above centuries-old bastions and a solid bed of rock – the high golden walls looked majestic but also a little unnerving. A medieval city, with its domes and towers and cupolas – utterly unspoilt, and completely unassailable. When she asked Bobby about it, he told her it had existed in some form since Roman times and that it had been Malta's first capital city.

'It's mainly Maltese nobility who live here.'

'Is your uncle Maltese?'

'No.'

'So how come he's living here?'

'He married Filomena, a Maltese woman. She died, I'm afraid, so now the place his. It's a seventeenth-century building. Quite beautiful. Of course, there are a few British here too.'

He drove through the massive stone gateway and parked, then they walked around the shady curving streets for a little while. Riva stared open-mouthed at what he called *palazzi*. These imposing houses lined the narrow cobbled streets in every direction, their shutters closed, their magnificent doorways bolted. Everything she saw said 'keep out'.

'The Silent City, they call it.' He lifted his hand and pointed at the stunning baroque architecture all around them.

She stopped walking to listen. All she could hear was the wind.

'I'd get lost here on my own.'

'Yes. It's labyrinthine. After the Knights of the Order of St John arrived it stopped being the capital. They needed to be closer to their ships. And now the British administration is focused mainly in Valletta too.'

He stopped walking and removed an iron key from his pocket.

'This is it?' She gazed up at the immense double door and the two heavy brass lion's head door knockers.

He nodded.

'Gosh. It looks like a fortress.'

He slid the key into the lock, turned it and then pushed open one side of the huge creaking door. It was dark inside, and it took a while for her eyes to become accustomed to the gloom. He crossed the large hall and into another one, this one vaulted, full of shadows and odd shafts of sunlight.

'We need to cross the courtyard.'

They passed along a corridor and an arched gallery and then went outside to an internal courtyard surrounded by honey-coloured stone walls. She stopped to look around and breathe in the scent of early jasmine.

Climbing plants crept up the walls and others cascaded from a gallery lined with decorative iron railings running around three sides of the next floor up.

'What a gorgeous garden,' she said, looking at the stone tubs full of lilies.

'Fig tree over there,' he said, nodding towards a tree in the corner. 'The best figs you'll find anywhere in the world. And there, two orange trees.'

She heard the trickle of water and saw a fountain,

not in the centre as you might expect, but falling from three decorative spouts into a stone trough up against a wall.

'Water sprites,' he said, seeing her looking. 'The spouts.'

She took a long breath and let it out slowly. 'So,' she said.

'So,' he replied. 'Ready to meet the old boy?'

They crossed the courtyard and then went through another archway into an anteroom which led to a stone staircase. The stairs eventually opened onto a grand vaulted corridor perfumed with beeswax and the smell of lemons and lined with floor to ceiling windows on one side and portraits on the other.

'This is a hidden palace,' she whispered. 'And absolutely glorious, not a fortress at all.'

He laughed. 'You're right but I think it may have once been both.'

Tapestry chairs and tall brass lamps polished to a shine stood at intervals and half a dozen oriental rugs that must have cost a fortune lay along its length. She glanced out of one of the windows and looked across at another sumptuous building with statues perched along its stone balconies.

'Goodness!' she said.

'Wait till you see the view from the other side.'

They went through a hall and then he knocked on a door. It was opened by what she assumed must be a butler dressed in black. 'Sir, miss,' the man said with a little bow. 'Follow me.'

'Does your uncle have an apartment here?' she whispered.

'The entire palace is his, but he prefers to live in just one apartment.'

'Who lives in the other apartments?' she asked.

He was about to reply but she stepped away catching her breath as they were led to an uncovered upstairs terrace with a view right across the island.

'Great, isn't it?' he said with a grin. 'Ah, there's my Uncle Addison.'

The man who had been sitting in a cane armchair gazing over the balustraded terrace at the view, sprung to his feet. 'I never tire of it,' he said and bounded over to hold out his hand. 'Pleased to meet you my dear. I'm Addison Darnell. Do call me Addison.'

She stopped herself from curtseying just in time and managed to say, 'Riva Janvier.'

The man before her was tall, over six foot, broad-shouldered and with the same cornflower blue eyes as his nephew. He wore a velvet waistcoat in navy over a crisp white shirt. His face was tanned and covered in a network of fine lines, but what she found extraordinary was the vitality that seemed to spring from him. That and his long white hair tied back at the nape of his neck.

'Come and join me, Riva,' he said and turned towards the view. 'Not too hot for you?'

'Not at all. There's a lovely breeze up here.'

He smiled back at her. 'Isn't there? And so much sky. That's why I love it.'

'Only when we can drag him away from his work,' Bobby said, and when he saw Riva's look of surprise he added, 'My uncle is a rather well-known painter.'

'I dabble,' the older man said.

'Hardly.'

'Those portraits in the corridor?' she asked.

'Yes. Afraid so.'

'But they're beautiful.'

'You can come again,' he said and grinned at her. 'Maybe you might sit for me one day.'

She smiled but beneath the banter Riva detected something in his eyes she couldn't name. He must miss his wife, she thought, as the butler arrived bearing drinks. Or maybe she was just imagining things.

'Do you have other relatives who live here?' she asked Bobby as she sipped her drink.

He shook his head. 'Mother visits occasionally.'

Addison pulled a face. 'My little sister Agatha does not enjoy the dust.'

'Nor does she approve,' Bobby said, exchanging a look with his uncle and then bursting into laughter.

'My nephew is correct. My sister doesn't approve that I work. Especially after she married Bobby's father and became part of the British landed gentry.'

Bobby lowered his eyes. 'My father was never a snob.'

'Indeed, he was not. You must miss him terribly. I know I do.'

'Yes,' Bobby said. 'But the snobbery, it was always mother. Still is.'

'That's my sister, I'm afraid. But come, we are boring our young visitor.'

Riva had been glancing around at the pots of plants and felt herself blushing. 'No, not at all,' she said.

'Tell me all about you,' Addison continued.

She glanced nervously at Bobby, who laughed. 'You can be honest. I've already shared your dark secret.'

She blushed again, feeling the warmth rising up her neck and into her cheeks. But she told Addison about her job in Paris, though not about the manner of her leaving, about seeing the advert and how, itching to broaden her horizons, she'd set out for Malta.

'I admire your courage my dear. And have you made many friends?'

'Well, there's Bobby and Lottie, of course, and one of the girls I work with.'

'You must come here more often. Malta is not just full of stuffed shirt Britishers.'

'My uncle throws fabulous parties. People come from all over Malta and Gozo, and from all over the world too. Artists, writers, actresses and so on. You'll love it.'

His uncle raised one eyebrow. 'I used to. Not so much these days. Ah, there's the bell. Lunch is served, milady.'

Riva laughed and followed the butler to the loveliest dining room, also in fresh air with views over the countryside but this time with pillars supporting a glass roof. A cut-glass bowl filled with large yellow daisies sat in the centre of a table laid with a brilliant white tablecloth. Bobby pulled out a chair for her, so she settled herself and took in the sandy terraces, trees and bushes that surrounded Mdina.

'As you can see,' Addison explained. 'This palazzo is partly built into the fortifications.'

'I've never been anywhere more lovely.'

'I hope you'll approve of the food too. We'll have no figs until later in the year, but you must try them then, even if Bobby isn't over here at the time. He'll be training to be a pilot soon.'

She hadn't thought about Bobby leaving and her spirits dipped momentarily. She felt a sudden premonition of something she was unable to identify, and she shivered despite the heat. What nonsense, she scolded. Everything was going to be fine. Everything *was* fine.

They ate a zucchini risotto to start with, followed by lamb and then a delicious Grand Marnier and orange soufflé. The time passed quickly with Addison and Bobby teasing each other, always including her if she didn't understand, and before she knew it, they were getting up to leave. Addison kissed her on the cheeks, and she told him she'd had a wonderful time.

'Come again soon,' he said and handed her a gold embossed card, his blue eyes so intense she felt he could see right into her. 'Should you ever need a break, do just drop by. I have plenty of guest rooms in this old place. Or let me know if there's anything I can do for you.'

Then, at the door, he whispered in her ear. 'He's never brought a girl to meet me before. But I'm so pleased he did today.'

CHAPTER 19

The sun-filled images still transfixed Riva as they reeled through her mind in the days after her outing, but a week had passed during which she hadn't heard from Bobby at all. And now she was beginning to doubt herself and doubt what had happened between them.

'This won't do,' she muttered as she took down a cup from the cupboard above the sink and examined it for dirty rings. A coffee out on her little balcony with a slice of buttered toast had become part of her morning ritual, but with all these thoughts of Bobby and his uncle's hidden palace she was feeling a bit forlorn.

'To hell with him,' she said, then glanced out of a window that overlooked the back of the building opposite, its windows already shuttered against the heat.

A scuffle of feet behind her interrupted her thoughts and she came away from the window to see Paloma and

Brigitte, the two other girls she shared with, strolling into the kitchen.

'Hello,' she said with a bright smile, determined to win them round. 'How are you both?'

Paloma glowered, darting her a venomous look, but didn't speak. She was tall and slender, but with a full bosom, and curving hips. Brigitte was smaller, more energetic, quick to speak and even quicker to anger. She narrowed her dark eyes and then nodded as if reaching a conclusion. She came across and poked Riva in the shoulder.

'You . . . think . . . you are better than us, don't you?'

Riva stepped back.

'Because you're French. Oooh la la.' And she performed a strange little wiggle that didn't quite come off.

'Of course not,' Riva said, astonished more by the wiggle than by what the girl had said or by the poking. Although she actually *was* a better dancer. 'Look, I'm ballet-trained, that's all. I was forced to go.'

And she went up on her toes and just about managed a pirouette. It didn't help. The girls just rolled their eyes and sniggered.

Riva tried again. 'I've no more experience of cabaret dancing than you. Probably less. You've been here longer. I have all sorts of bad habits that I need to get rid of. Ballet habits that don't work in cabaret. Even Gianni said as much.'

Brigitte narrowed her eyes. 'He did?'

Riva nodded. It wasn't quite true, but Brigitte seemed

mollified and gave her a patronising smile. All the girls had minimal job security and any one of them could be axed the moment someone younger or prettier came along. Brigitte and Paloma probably needed to believe they were superior to feel secure.

'Friends then,' Riva said and held out her hand. Brigitte shook it.

'So, who's your rich boyfriend?' Paloma asked, still looking dubious.

Riva frowned.

'We saw you getting into his car.'

Riva snorted. 'It's not his car. He borrowed it.'

Paloma looked happier hearing that and Riva realised she would have to be more discreet if she weren't to cause jealousy among the girls.

'There's a new girl coming,' Brigitte said.

'Dancer?'

'Hostess. I saw her with a man coming out of our spare room.'

'With Gianni?'

The other two exchanged looks. 'No.'

'Then who?'

She winked. 'The one they are all scared of.'

'Who's he?'

Paloma gave Brigitte a look and the other girl clammed up. 'See you later,' she said and grabbed her friend by the elbow and pulled her from the room.

Well, Riva thought, what was that about?

Her thoughts travelled back to Bobby again. Had she imagined how it had felt? Certainly, some of the shine had rubbed off from what she'd thought had been a perfect day. A day of seamless blue skies and sapphire seas to hold in her heart forever. She remembered Addison's kindness and the way his paintings expressed something deeper than just the surface of a person. Hope and love, but also suffering.

And she remembered Bobby's kiss; felt his proximity even though he wasn't there now, and the feeling of it still rippled through her.

Later, at the club, Riva was sitting at a table and surveying the scene with Tommy-O during a break. Tonight, his wig was black, long, straight and dramatic. He wore an almost transparent dress of gold sequins sewn onto net, big, hooped gold earrings and a fur stole. Bangles of gold set with glittering rubies circled his wrists.

'Are those real?' she asked.

'The rubies? Nah. I'm not made of money.'

His eyes were made-up with thick black kohl and he looked stunning.

'Mixing it up with the Egyptian princess look tonight darling,' he said, shouting to be heard over the clatter of plates, clinking glasses, and chattering men and women. The bar was packed with sailors yelling for service and sultry girls clinging to their prey.

'You're wasted here,' she replied equally loudly. 'You should be in Hollywood.'

'Don't I know it, doll! Follow me.'

They picked up their glasses and found a quieter niche away from the bar and the noise faded a little.

'So, is that real?' She reached across to touch the stole.

'This one? Sure is, honey,' he said, and winked. 'Genuine mink. Gift from a rich admirer. Wanna try it on?'

He handed it over and she wrapped it around her bare shoulders then pouted wildly as if she were a film star, making him roar with his great barking laugh and then splutter on his cocktail.

'You got your badge yet?' he asked her.

'Gianni will have it for me tonight. Will it be the same as the hostesses wear?'

He nodded. 'Pretty much. Theirs are stamped with the initials of the Malta Police and a licence number. Officially they have to be over twenty-one.'

'Some look younger.'

He pulled a face. 'Hmmm. They have to scarper when the police come checking.'

'Are they paid well?'

'They earn a *landa* – a kind of token – each time they persuade a punter to buy a drink. They do well enough.'

'Do they, you know . . .' she tilted her head, 'go with the men?'

He grinned. 'Not here, darling.'

'There are brothels?'

He wrinkled his nose and kind of winced. 'Officially they're banned. Some bars have cubicles upstairs though. For a while the girls were examined for venereal disease, supposedly four times a month.'

'Not any more?'

'No, chérie. The Naval Shore Patrol and the Military Police come around most nights, but they deal with brawls and fights, not so much the girls.'

'Who looks after them? The hostesses and bar girls, I mean.'

'Murky area. Here at the club, Gianni. But he's small fry.'

At that moment Riva saw Gianni ushering in a slight young girl with pale blonde hair, elfin features, and tiny pointed chin. She didn't even look sixteen. 'Look at her,' she said.

With them was a man with salt-and-pepper hair and a cane. Even though he was turned sideways to her she felt sure she'd seen him before.

'That girl might be the one staying at your place,' Tommy-O said.

'I heard there was someone . . . Do you know who the man is?'

'Yes, and I wish I didn't.' He took her face between his hands and kissed her nose. 'Sorry, darling girl, but I'm up next. Much as I love discussing the rights and wrongs of prostitution with you, I need a quick frock change before the natives grow restless. And by natives, I am not referring to the Maltese.'

She laughed and watched him sashaying across the room on his high heels until he was swallowed up by the dancing crowds. Just being with Tommy-O made her feel more optimistic and her earlier low mood had dissipated. It would be fine. Bobby would be around soon.

The long narrow room was filling up; although lined with mirrors it always seemed as if there were three times the clientele. The band had begun playing something bright and bouncy and the men were shouting, crazy for it – mostly intoxicated sailors with their arms around heavily painted girls with whom they'd be leaving a little later. At least at Johnny's Bar in Paris there were no upstairs cubicles. She recalled how she'd had to rub off the scarlet lipstick and rouge before her enraged father collected her from the police station. It felt like a lifetime ago. She drew in her breath and exhaled slowly. Her father. What was happening to him now? Had the scandal broken? Or had they managed to hush it all up? She supposed she might never know. She thought about writing to Claudette to let her know she was all right – she didn't have to leave an address. If she could talk to her that would be better still, but she knew she could not. She felt a pang in her chest, thinking of her sister. She longed so much for news of her and of her three daughters too – Hélène, Élise, and little Florence.

CHAPTER 20

Florence

Devonshire, Winter

Florence was chewing her pen and gazing out of the window. Hélène's last letter was still circling through her mind. She could not believe Suzanne had been killed after all her bravery over the past few years. Thinking of Suzanne, of Henri, of her sisters and the uncertainty they were still living in, Florence's mind was returning more frequently to her memories of the war in France. And of that dark day she wished she could forget.

Now she picked up her pen and began scribbling in the notebook she'd started back then, after what had been the worst day of her life. Jack had been there. Helped her. Carried her away from the dead bodies of the two men who had held her down and whom Élise had shot.

Jack had witnessed Florence lying bruised and trauma-tised, half-naked and bent double over the kitchen table. He had seen, and she felt a wave of shame. He had carried her away from what had happened there. Could seeing her like that, so vulnerable and exposed, have affected how he viewed her now? She recoiled at the awful memories of that day. Dirty, sullied, she hadn't been able to speak, wanting only to wipe the violation from her mind. The journal became her only outlet. The only way she could face the shame, the guilt, the rage. Logically she knew the rape had not been her fault and yet the feeling of blame lingered.

It comes back to me, she wrote. *The danger that lurks behind the door. The closed door. The door that I, in my innocence, freely opened. The door I opened myself, through which the violence came into my house – into my body – into my soul. Even as I fought and struggled, I knew I had been the one who'd let it in. And now the danger behind the door never quite leaves me.*

Her eyes blurred and she put down her pen. Since coming to England, she'd forced it to the back of her mind, especially while so much of her life had been in limbo. But now that things had settled a bit, and she'd started her job at the manor – preparing the evening meals and lunch and dinner at the weekends – the memories kept coming back. Back, back, back. And she couldn't stop them.

With her notebook before her on the kitchen table, she forced herself to face them and eventually, one page at a time, found some solace. Where once she'd baked and made jam, now she wrote down her darkest feelings.

Jack was away all the time – usually in London she thought, though he would never quite say – and despite her work at the manor, Florence felt very alone. She just needed someone to talk to and thought about tramping up to the phone box at the crossroads and calling the number Bruce had given her, but something kept stopping her.

She turned on the wireless. It was battery-operated, and she knew she'd need to get it to the garage to charge it up or it would soon die on her. The news was still all about the V2s the Germans had been using since early September. They'd got the nickname 'flying gas pipes' because the government had hidden the truth and blamed the damage and deaths in London on gas mains explosions. Now everybody knew they were 'bloody Hitler's' rockets.

She turned the wireless off; it was too depressing. Instead she read for a while. The book about Malta she'd borrowed from the library was full of words, but not enough pictures. Most of all she wanted to *see* it, so she imagined a sunny place with a sparkling blue sea and soft breezes.

She glanced at the freezing day beyond the kitchen windows. No soft breezes out there. Winter now held the countryside in its grip. Every morning icicles hung from the outer frames of the windows and inside the house Jack Frost had been at work, decking the glass with elaborate frozen ferns, although not in the kitchen. The Aga saw to that.

She fetched her woollen tweed coat, wrapped a thick

scarf around her neck, pulled on her hat and mittens, and left the house to tramp along the flat water meadow in front of it. The hoar frost she had woken to was still very much in evidence and already the cold was creeping into her bones. She'd thought the stream might have frozen over and walked over the rough grass to look. There was ice but the water was still flowing. She spotted a strange little bird that appeared to be swimming underwater. She took a closer look and was enchanted when it bobbed up, shook itself and curtseyed before balancing on a stone to sing, and when it began a sweet melodic song, she decided to look it up in Jack's bird book at home. Such a jolly, fat little bird, dark above, with a huge white bib in front and a short tail, it shouldn't be hard to find.

She turned back for home.

Long before she reached the house, she saw the ravens. Four of them – big, black and bossy. She didn't like them one bit and since their arrival a week or so before she'd felt uneasy.

That night she fed the kitten, glad that she'd finally agreed to take him, and he curled up next to her on the bed. But the wind howled around the house, the windows rattled as the rain beat against the glass and the walls seemed to be closing in on her. She switched on her bedside lamp but then there was a loud crack, and the lamp went out. In the dark she fished for matches and candles in the drawer of her bedside table. Jack had told her the electrical supply was fragile during the winter and insisted she must always be prepared. She eventually found what she needed and stuffed the candle into a holder before putting a match to its wick. The little flame flickered, and elongated shadows loomed in the corners of the room.

The storm went on and on, battering the cottage until Florence felt the assault might never end. She pictured the boiling, turbulent sky, the angry gods, her own body spinning off into the clouds and she pulled the blankets over her head. It didn't help. The world had stopped feeling real and in the middle of the night she dreamt she was losing Hélène just as Claudette had lost Rosalie. In the tangles of her dream everything was wrong. At the edge of the world, it was black. So awfully black. Hélène appeared out of the shadows like a spectre in the mist and Florence called to her, shouted until her throat was raw. 'Stop! Stop!' In the end Hélène turned, looked straight through her as if she didn't even see her and then she laughed, a bitter strangled laugh, before walking away and disappearing over the edge into the blackness. The abyss. Hélène had fallen off the edge of the world, but no, she hadn't fallen after all. Florence had pushed her. Pushed her own sister over the edge into the blackness. She woke screaming and gasping in horror, her heart pounding and her cheeks wet with tears.

Although feverish now, she managed to sleep a little more as the wind howled and phantom ravens flew around her room. When she woke and tried to get up her legs gave way. She shivered and climbed back into bed where she lay all day, veering between icy cold and unbearable heat. She sweated until the bedclothes grew damp but felt too sick to change them. She moved to the other side of the bed where the sheets were dry. When that side grew damp too and she realised the kitten was gone, she curled up into a ball to comfort herself.

Florence woke to an icy room, with a pounding headache and so cold she felt as if her bones had frozen. Was it the next day, or the one after that? She pulled the bedclothes over her head again but when she thought she heard someone moving around downstairs she attempted to get out of bed. She could tell she wasn't as ill as she had been, but her legs still felt weak and she soon gave up. Back in bed again, she listened anxiously. Could it be Belinda? Then she heard her name being called. Jack. Thank goodness. She called out in a feeble croaking voice, 'In here. I'm in here.'

She heard him climbing the stairs and then the door opened wide, and he was there.

'Dear God, what the devil . . .?' He marched over to open the curtains as she struggled to sit up. He came over to her, concern in his eyes. 'You're unwell.'

She nodded.

He stroked the damp hair from her face. 'Jesus, you're freezing.'

'I've been hot, I've been cold, and I can't stand up.'

'Aga's gone out. That's why it's so cold up here.'

'I'm sorry. You said to never let it go out.'

'You were too sick.'

'What's wrong with me?'

'Bad case of the flu, I reckon. It's going round. Now

I'm going to fetch you a glass of water, then I'll stoke the Aga and light all the fires, including the one in here.'

'I don't usually get so ill.'

'I know. Lie back down for now. Once the house is warm, we'll see what's to be done. This room needs airing.'

'I can't get down the stairs.'

He smiled. 'I'll think of something.'

'There were ravens. I knew something bad was going to happen when I saw them.'

He brought her a glass of water and she held it in a shaking hand. Then he went to warm up the house.

A little later he was back, and she struggled to sit up again as he perched on the bed beside her.

'The fire is going great guns, so I'm going to carry you down to the sitting room. I need to change your sheets and open the windows. I'll light a fire in here a little later.'

She nodded.

'The Aga takes longer to heat up so I can't make you a hot drink yet. Now I'm going to put an arm around your shoulders and then your legs. Ready?'

He lifted her out of the bed.

'Goodness. You weigh nothing at all. Have you been eating while I've been away?'

When Florence woke the next morning, she knew she was on the mend. She'd slept soundly, with no ravens flying around her room and no new dreams that she could recall. 'I must have been a bit delirious the other night,' she thought, shivering at the recollection of the nightmare about Hélène. Gingerly she slid round to sit on the edge of the bed and then tested her legs. So far so good. But something was different. Apart from the spluttering sound she could hear coming from the Aga below, the outside world seemed to have completely silenced. She managed to creep across to the window and opened the curtain. 'Oh,' she gasped.

The whole world had turned white. The hill behind the cottage, the naked trees, the bushes. She found her dressing gown and opened her bedroom door. Jack must have heard her from downstairs as he was instantly there, coming to help.

'I'm so pleased you're up.'

'The snow.'

'I know.'

'We've got no food.'

'We've plenty. While you were dozing by the fire yesterday, I got some bits and pieces from Ronnie. Plus I'd already brought back a few leftovers from London. Come on, you need to eat.'

He supported her with an arm around her waist and slowly they went down to the kitchen, which was now warm and cosy. He pulled out a chair for her where she could look out across the frozen water meadow.

'It's beautiful,' she said, smiling at him. 'Bracing. Maybe we could go for a walk in the snow.'

'Not today. There are huge drifts at both the back and front doors. I'd have to dig us out.'

'Tomorrow?'

'Let's just wait until you're well. In any case, the cold snap is set to last a few days. Porridge do you?'

'I should say so.' Relieved to be feeling better, she laughed for the first time in ages, and it felt so good. While he stirred the pan, she sat transfixed by the view from the window. 'It's snowing again. Look. Isn't it magical?'

'You are just like a child,' he said, pointing the spatula at her.

For three days they remained indoors and watched the snow as it kept on falling and swirling beyond their windows. Aside from the beauty of it, Florence felt as if the outside world beyond the snow had stopped existing and there were only the two of them. She had never been happier. Jack read to her and told her funny stories and she shared a little about writing in her journal. Much of the time she slept, curled up in the big armchair beside the fire in the sitting room while Jack cooked for her and made sure she was comfortable.

On the morning of the fourth day, he said, 'By the way, a chap I know has a place in Sicily and wants an architect to check if it's still sound, and he's asked me. He's absolutely loaded and it's a marvellous place apparently, but quite possibly damaged. Just a stone's throw from Malta, you see.'

She studied him, uncertain what he was suggesting.

'You could come too . . . if you like,' he said casually. 'Obviously not until the war ends, and even then I'm not sure how we'd get there. Would you like to?'

As he glanced at her she rose to her feet, went to the

sofa and threw her arms around him where he sat. She felt his warm breath on her neck, and they held each other for a beat longer than was strictly necessary.

Then she pulled back. 'Have you heard from Belinda at all?'

He nodded. 'Yes. We met. She's still not willing for the divorce to go ahead unless I relent over the share of the cottage.'

'You'll just have to stick it out. Wait for her to change her mind.'

'I almost feel like giving in. I just don't want Belinda to be my responsibility any more. But mark my words, she'll be engaged to Hector the moment we do eventually divorce. Anyway, I'm off up to the farm now.'

'Can I come?'

'I've cleared the path but I think the walk in the snow may still be too much for you.'

'I so want to get out in it.'

'All right. Why not have a little wander with me and then I'll go to the farm afterwards.'

She grinned, pulled on her boots, arranged her hat, coat, and scarf and was ready by the front door before he'd even managed to get his wellingtons on.

'Come on slowcoach,' she said and laughed.

'I think you may be a little stir crazy, madam.'

'A little?'

He grinned and opened the door to a blast of freezing air. The snow was still pristine and, spellbound, Florence breathed in the cold then headed for the water meadow. It was so peaceful that her mind felt empty, calm.

'Not that way,' he said, reaching for her. 'It's too risky. We won't know what's solid ground and what isn't.'

'I went that way before I got sick and saw a sweet little bird swimming for food under the water.'

'Ah, that'll be a dipper.'

'It more than dipped.'

'What did it look like?'

'A fat little thing with a white bib.'

'Definitely a dipper. Sometimes called a water ousel. Let's walk up the track. It's safer. Here, hold on to me,' and he held out his elbow for her to link with him. 'You can look in the bird book while I'm up at the farm.'

The branches of the trees hung low with the weight of the snow and the track was still completely white with a deep drift on one side. The sky was a seamless blue and the sun shining on the snow dazzled them, while the air felt as if it were made of crystals, fresh and cold.

Their breath puffed out in front of them as they trudged slowly uphill. A flurry of powdery snow lifted and blew away in the wind, and then halfway to the top they turned back. Florence carried on a little ahead of Jack and while he was gazing at the view across the valley, she bent to the ground then yelled, 'Snowball fight.'

She threw one at him, missing by inches.

Laughing, he made a snowball of his own and threw it in response.

Invigorated, she made another, as did he. They threw at the same time. His missed but hers hit him in the chest and then she ran away, stumbling over the snow. He caught up with her quickly, grabbed her and they toppled over into a deep drift, laughing and spluttering. His cheeks were pink, so was his nose and his green eyes were glittering. She felt his warm breath on her face and her heart thrumming as everything stilled. She listened to the silence brought by the snow, waiting breathlessly. There was a moment of uncertainty . . . and then Jack swiftly pushed himself up and rose to his feet, ending it.

CHAPTER 21

The next day, when Jack answered a knock at the door, a messenger boy stood there. Jack took the telegram from him and called Florence.

'For you,' he said as she came running down the stairs having seen the boy from her window.

With her heart pulsing in her throat, she ripped it open. Good news or bad, you never knew.

Then Florence gasped in delight. 'Oh my gosh. It's brilliant news. Élise has had her baby.'

'When?'

'Two days ago. A girl,' she squeaked. She gulped and then exploded into exuberant laughter. 'We have a niece. Hélène and me. We have a niece.'

Jack beamed at her.

'I can't believe it. I must write straight away. I'll send Élise my congratulations and tell her about the snow.'

'Did you tell her you have a job?'

'Yes, in my last letter.'

She didn't tell him how surprised Hélène had been to hear she was staying on in Devon. But Florence had written back emphasising how peaceful it was, and reiterating that Jack was rarely there – which had been true, at the time. She'd already written about Claudette asking her to search for her long-lost sister, Rosalie. She had mentioned the row too, but reassured Hélène that things with their mother seemed to be on a better footing now.

Once she finished the letter of congratulation to Élise, she danced around the kitchen unable to fully absorb the news. It felt like such a miracle.

'I'm an auntie,' she said, whooping. 'I'm an auntie.'

And then she began to cry.

'Whoa,' Jack said, drawing her towards him. 'It's all right.'

As he held her to study her face, she looked back at his eyes so full of compassion and felt something deep inside her. She began laughing and crying at the same time, not even knowing what it was, like a child giddy with joy who then can't then help bursting into tears. 'I wish I were there so much, Jack. It hurts not to be with them.'

He wrapped his arms around her. 'I know. A new baby, a new life in a family is so significant and not to be there must be awful.'

'Yes.'

He let her go and stepped away. 'Well, I think a celebratory glass of port is in order.'

'You have port?'

'I've been saving it. Oh, and Ronnie gave me this.' He

handed her a tin. 'It's Christmas cake. And he let me have a small chicken, six eggs, four slices of bacon, a tiny chunk of cheese, bread, potatoes, apples, and some root vegetables.'

This time Jack had insisted on using his ration coupons. Florence was thrilled because the vegetables she was growing were now hidden somewhere beneath the snow and wouldn't be ready yet anyway. While Jack was away, she had been living on oats, winter cabbage from Gladys, and the odd fried egg, so this was bounty.

'I'm going to make us a sumptuous celebration meal for supper tonight,' she said.

He narrowed his eyes. 'Let's just wait and see how you're feeling later.'

She nodded but wasn't really listening. She felt full of beans, as if she could climb the highest mountain. Well, perhaps not that. She'd had enough of mountain climbing to last a lifetime.

A little later, though, and Florence was surprised by how weary she had become, as if the plug had been pulled suddenly. So, telling Jack she would take a short nap, she left him lighting the sitting room fire.

She undressed, put on her nightdress, and fell asleep instantly. When she woke, she couldn't believe it was already dark outside. She fumbled for the switch on her bedside lamp, turned it on, and as low light flooded her room, she yawned. How long had she been asleep? She located her slippers, grabbed her thick candlewick dressing gown, then headed for the stairs but, pausing at the top, she sniffed. Roasting chicken. Jack was roasting the chicken.

'Hello, sleepyhead,' he said when she entered the kitchen.

'Sorry.'

He smiled at her. 'Not at all.'

'Thought you said you couldn't even cook eggs.'

'I said I couldn't cook them apart from frying them.'

So, you remembered too, she thought, but said, 'Well, it smells wonderful.'

'Take a pew, mademoiselle. Here, catch,' and he threw a box of matches and pointed at the table where four fresh candles stood in their holders.

She lit the wicks while he busied himself with the food.

'Do we have wine?' she asked.

'Coming up. Red, already uncorked and breathing. I know it's traditionally white with chicken but I'm a red wine man.'

'I love red wine too and I don't give a fig for tradition.'

'That's my girl.'

'Hardly a girl any more.'

He faced the room to look at her, narrowed his eyes just a fraction and something passed between them she desperately needed to understand. Then she had it. Recognition. The way his lips parted – as if he were a little surprised – told her he was properly seeing her for the first time. 'No,' he said very softly and more to himself than to her. 'You're not.'

'What?'

'A girl.'

He has noticed, she thought as her heart thumped. He has noticed.

Then he dished up the roast potatoes and vegetables and brought the chicken to the table. He carved some for her and then handed her a plate piled high with food.

'Crikey, I can't eat all that.'

They clinked glasses once he'd poured the wine, the candles flickered, and Florence was content. He seemed to be too, and she didn't want to ruin it, but after the way he had just looked at her . . . she knew she needed to ask him about Hélène. Couldn't avoid facing it any longer.

As they finished the meal, she stifled her nerves and said, 'There's something I need to discuss with you.'

'I thought there might be.' There was a flat tone to his voice and a moment's silence as he looked at her with a serious, unwavering expression. 'Fire away.'

She felt herself blushing, the heat rising in her cheeks. 'I have to ask how you feel about Hélène.'

He nodded.

'Well?'

There was a long uncomfortable silence. All Florence could hear was the wind outside.

'I've seen the question in your eyes,' he said. 'But I have been too cowardly, or . . . I don't know . . . In any case I've been resisting it.'

'Resisting?'

'You know my relationship history is complicated.'

'Belinda?'

It took a moment before he spoke again. 'I was very . . . I suppose, fond of Hélène. She's a terrific person and I admired her strength of character, but I wasn't ready. And I wasn't in love with her, not then and not now.'

Florence nodded, feeling relieved but knowing there was more. 'You slept with her though?' she said softly, trying not to sound accusing.

'Once.' He paused for a moment and shook his head. 'It shouldn't have happened. It was wrong, and I blame myself, but she was so upset . . . Anyway, on my last night in France I stayed away.'

'I remember.'

'Almost as soon as we got back to England, I wrote to her, via Geneva of course, to clarify things between us.'

'You didn't say.'

'No. It was a difficult letter to write. Besides, it was between me and Hélène. I thanked her, told her how much her friendship had meant to me, and I wished her well for the future. I knew how she felt when I was in France, although she never said, but I wanted her to understand there was no chance of anything more developing. I said I hoped we'd always be friends.'

Florence felt a pang and hung her head. 'Poor Hélène,' she whispered, thinking how hurt her sister must have been.

'Does that answer your question?' he asked.

She didn't reply at first, then raised her head and met his gaze. 'I think you know it doesn't.'

He lifted the bottle of wine aloft. 'Empty.'

She nodded.

He shook his head as if remembering. 'Coming across the mountains with you was extraordinary. I saw how terrified you were every single day, but it never stopped you. You were brave, Florence. Very brave.'

'Jack, I feel . . .' Desperate to touch him, she reached out, heart pounding, but he didn't respond, and feeling rejected, she withdrew her hand. She took a long slow breath to steady herself.

'I can't give you what you need, Florence. I'm an old, grief-stricken divorcé and if we hadn't been thrown together that would have been the end of it. Do you see? I'm not the man you need. I'm just the man you're temporarily stuck with.'

She nodded her head slowly, but the muscles in her throat constricted and she couldn't speak. Yes, she saw. It was humiliating, but she saw.

She rose to her feet. 'I'm feeling tired,' she managed to say in as normal a voice as she could. 'I think I'll go to bed now.'

And she climbed the stairs, crawled into bed, and with her pillow over her head, she cried silently.

CHAPTER 22

One morning in the gap between that last conversation with Jack and Christmas, Florence faced up to the truth. It was time to be pragmatic. Jack didn't love her and although she pretended it was no big deal, she felt heartbroken because she *did* love him. But Jack had built walls around his heart and there was absolutely nothing she could do about it. That he had not been in love with Hélène either didn't really make much difference to anything – her sister would still be devastated if she knew that Florence harboured such deep feelings for him.

A letter had arrived from Claudette, in which she described her sister Rosalie as fun-loving and affectionate. Her mother explained that their parents never understood Rosalie, that she'd always been the odd one out, and that they tried to stifle her spirit because it had frightened them. Rosalie must have felt so unloved, Florence realised, and felt such a surge of sympathy for the young girl. No wonder she ran away. So now, having considered everything, Florence made the decision to go to Malta just as soon as the war ended, and she would go alone.

In the meantime, she would contact Bruce. He might turn out to be a good friend for her and she already liked him. She'd hesitated about calling, but knew she needed to spread her wings, get out more, and stop brooding about Jack. So, standing in the phone box, she dialled the number in a rush before she could change her mind. She hadn't expected him to answer in person and was a bit taken aback to hear his voice.

'Florence! It's so good to hear from you,' he said. Reassured by the warmth she could hear in his voice, it reminded her of how decent he had seemed.

'Sorry it's taken so long. I've been awfully busy. I'd love to go for a jaunt in your sidecar just as soon as the snow melts.'

'Goodness. You're game. The forecast is that it will hang around for a couple of days. So . . . how about Thursday? I know you're not far from the farm, but where exactly do you live? I'll pick you up at ten in the morning.'

'I have to work in the evening.'

He laughed. 'We'll be back long before that. It's freezing on the bike this time of year. Remember to wrap up.'

On Thursday she heard the motorbike from her bedroom window and ran downstairs in haste, hoping to grab her things before Jack had the chance to open the door. She slipped into her coat and pulled down her woolly hat but couldn't find her mittens. While she was looking for them, she heard Jack open the door and then the sound of voices. She found her mittens and hurried out.

'Sorry, Bruce, I couldn't find—'

He smiled at her. 'No problem, I've just been having a chat with Jack here.'

'You know each other?' She was surprised, hadn't expected or prepared herself for that.

'A little,' Jack said rather gruffly and then stepped back into the house, closing the door behind him.

The ride didn't last long. It really was too cold, but she enjoyed feeling the wind burning her cheeks and she had fun being with Bruce too. He pulled up and parked on the edge of a forest and they walked for a while, kicking at the leaves on the frozen ground while talking effortlessly about the war, and about his job and hers. She told him about her sisters and how much she missed them. He listened carefully and said there was only him and his mother. He'd wanted to join up, but as a doctor he was exempt from conscription, which had been a relief for his mother. So instead, he'd worked in a military hospital in Plymouth for two years before returning to Exeter where he was now specialising in cardiology.

'Have you always wanted to be a doctor?' she asked.

'I was born wanting to be a doctor. When I was young our cats and dogs used to hide when they saw me running towards them wielding strips of newspaper and glue which I claimed was ointment to make them better.'

She laughed. 'It must be hard though at times, being a hospital doctor.'

'Not as hard as it is for the soldiers who come back

from the war. It's not just broken bones or missing limbs.'

'Yes, I know. My sister Hélène is a nurse in France.'

'I'd like to meet her one day. Compare notes.'

Bruce was different from Jack, more direct, with fewer complications and contradictions. He knew what he was doing, had a clear purpose in life. She liked that. On their way back to the car she slipped on the icy ground, so he linked arms with her. She liked that too.

When he dropped her back home, he grasped her mittened hand and squeezed it. 'I'd love to see you again,' he said. 'And maybe when the weather improves we might try another trip on the bike? Perhaps to the coast. Though any beach suitable for amphibious landing is likely to be mined so we'd need to choose carefully.'

At the cottage Florence did her best to behave as normally as possible. Jack didn't say much about her outing with Bruce but seemed more taciturn than usual and refused to meet her eyes. But then, on Christmas Eve, he cut down a pine tree and dragged it into the house. It was a surprise and she felt as if he'd done it as a kind of peace offering.

'There are some tree decorations in the attic, I think. My grandmother was always so fond of her tree. I'll look later.' And then he went outside and brought back holly, ivy, and a cardboard box. 'There are pinecones in there,' he said.

She clapped her hands, pleased. 'I'll do the decorating while you look for the tree baubles.'

'There may be carols on the wireless,' he said. 'Would that help?'

'Nothing like carols to get us in the festive spirit.'

'Talking of spirits,' he added. 'I've discovered an old bottle of Armagnac at the back of what remains of the booze store. Should still be good. Thought it would remind you of home.'

She nodded but kept her face turned away.

'You all right, Florence?' he asked.

She nodded again but still didn't look at him, missing home so much but steeling herself not to cry in front of him.

As she sang along to all her favourite carols, she felt better, and draped the ivy over the mantelpiece adding pinecones and holly. It was a great year for the cheery red berries and before long she had the whole room looking festive. She noticed he hadn't brought in any mistletoe.

Sometime later he came downstairs carrying a wooden box. 'I think this is it,' he said.

He placed it on the coffee table, then lifted the lid. She carefully rummaged in the box and saw there were individual packages wrapped in silk. Once he'd sorted out the tree and it was firmly held in place with broken bricks and a layer of pebbles on top, she lifted out one of the packages. She unwrapped it to find a little white woodpecker with green wings and a hole in the top concealed by a metal cap with a little wire loop.

'These blown ornaments of hers were all handmade and hand-painted,' he said.

'It's so delicate. I'm scared I'll break it.'

'You won't.'

He took out a package from the box, this time revealing a tiny glass gingerbread house, gold and covered in hearts. He held it up for her.

'I'll get some thread and scissors. These need to be safely tied onto the tree right away.'

Once she'd returned, they carried on opening the packages and hanging glass ornaments in the shape of hearts, more birds, stars and angels. All high enough up so the kitten couldn't reach them.

'There's an invoice or something here,' she said. 'Handwritten from . . .' and she peered at it. 'Ah yes. Lauscha, Germany.'

'Then some of those baubles probably date from well before the Great War.'

She unwrapped two heavy glass bunches of red grapes.

'Heavens above,' he said. 'I remember those. Haven't seen them for years. Those are original German kugels . . . I must have been only five or six years old when my grandmother let me hold one. She had bunches of grapes, but also apples, pears, pinecones, berries. Let's see if there are more.'

They unwrapped more packages, finding several more kugel ornaments in cobalt blue, green, gold, and amethyst.

'Lined with real silver,' he said. She showed me when I broke one and she said they'd be valuable one day. I wonder how she got them.'

Florence shrugged. The German baubles had given her a funny feeling in her stomach. So much information was missing from her life. What might her German father,

Friedrich, have passed on to her that she had no idea about? There must be millions of little things, not just the love of gardening she and her half-brother Anton already knew they shared, but other unknown things. What was Friedrich's favourite colour? Did he like fish? Anton had said *he* enjoyed fishing. Did Friedrich too? And what about swimming? Florence loved to swim. And there would be bigger things, too, that at present she couldn't begin to fathom. Since finding out about her father, she'd felt as if her psyche had altered. She could still feel the music of her French life beating in her heart, but something about the rhythm was no longer the same.

She and Jack spent the rest of Christmas Eve peacefully enough, demolishing Gladys's delicious Christmas cake, heavily doused with home-made cherry brandy, drinking Armagnac, which did remind Florence of home, and listening to the BBC Home Service on the wireless in front of the fire. After the news they enjoyed an adaptation of *Alice Through the Looking Glass*, and later, at half past nine, there was Christmas Eve music from the BBC Symphony Orchestra. They didn't refer to their conversation about Hélène, or to her outing with Bruce, and went to bed at half past ten. But Florence still felt a trace of tension hanging between them.

CHAPTER 23

It was quiet when Florence woke on Christmas morning except for the purr of little Bart, who had somehow managed to fall asleep right beside her face, making her sneeze. She thought of Christmas in France with her sisters before the war and how noisy it used to be, and she wondered how it would be with a new baby in the house. They would have already had the long feast they called *Le Réveillon* – the French Christmas Eve midnight meal, though she wasn't sure who would have cooked it or what they'd have had to eat. Supplies must be getting awfully low without her to manage them.

She pictured them before the war. Hélène madly polishing everything until it shone before everyone arrived – she'd have polished Florence and Élise if they'd let her; Hélène always did run a tight ship. And Élise would be dragging in greenery at the very last minute and pinning it everywhere. There used to be mulled wine in the bars.

Mulled wine. And the thought of that brought tears to her eyes. But she wiped them away and remembered how she would have been in the kitchen roasting the goose. She could almost smell her old kitchen and longed again for that feeling of home.

Then, in the old days, Marie and Doctor Hugo would arrive bearing a huge *bûche de Noël*, a decorated yule log made of chocolate and chestnuts. And Marie would also carry in a box full of fruits, dried figs, hazelnuts, walnuts, almonds, nougat, and dried grapes. To bring good luck for the coming year, after the meal was over you had to taste thirteen different sweet things representing Jesus and the twelve apostles.

But then the war had come, and Christmas had never been the same, although they'd done their best. And now it was changing again. How unsettled it made you feel – you thought your world would remain unchanged and go on just as it always had but then suddenly, without you doing anything, anything at all, it completely turned on its head. She wondered if Friedrich and Anton would be eating *stollen*, dusted with a thick coat of powdered sugar and baked with aromatic spices. And would they be thinking of her?

She got out of bed and glanced in the mirror. Her eyes were pink and teary. This wouldn't do. You were supposed to be happy on Christmas Day, so she tried a cheerful face, checking her success in the mirror. Hmmm. Not brilliant. But they were going to see Gladys soon, and no matter what, Gladys always cheered her up.

She washed, dressed and went downstairs.

'Happy Christmas,' Jack said, and looking self-conscious, handed her a small box.

'Oh, I wasn't expecting—'

'Last-minute thought,' Jack said, interrupting her.

She opened it, and nestled in red velvet was the prettiest bracelet she'd ever seen. Two silver chains with small pearls and blue stones threaded through it.

'It was my grandmother's,' he said.

'It's beautiful.'

'The pearls are real and the little blue stones are sapphires. I think my grandfather brought it back from India.'

'It must be terribly valuable. A family heirloom. Are you sure you want to give it to me?'

He smiled. 'Who else? In any case my grandmother would be delighted to see it worn.'

After a light breakfast, and when they were finally ready, she and Jack went outside to check the weather. As they did it began to snow again. He glanced at the heavily laden sky. 'A steady fall, I think. Wouldn't want to take the car.'

'That's fine. We'll walk,' she said.

He went back inside and she stamped up and down on the ground to keep herself warm while she waited. He came out carrying a box.

'What have you got there?'

'Wine, brandy and dried fruit. Brought it back from London.'

'My God! How did you get it?' she asked, frowning. 'Not with ration cards?'

'It's not black market, if that's what you're thinking. A

contact of mine gave it to me for smuggling him out of France safely. I told him he owed me nothing, but he insisted.'

'The whole boxful?'

He nodded. 'His family are fabulously wealthy so he raided their Gloucestershire home and gave me some of the spoils.'

When they knocked on the farmhouse door, Ronnie answered and ushered them into the kitchen. 'We're all in the sitting room,' he said, pushing them in front of him along a corridor.

Florence, who arrived in the room first, gasped at what she saw. A huge Christmas tree reaching all the way to the ceiling glittering with dozens of flickering candles. Tiny real candles in exquisite little holders. Tears sprang to her eyes and Gladys, who had been standing by the open fire beside a sleeping collie, smiled.

'I know you can't be with your family, my dear, so I wanted it to be extra special for you.'

The lump in Florence's throat stopped her voice for a moment but she went straight over to Gladys and the two women hugged. 'Thank you,' Florence whispered. 'Thank you so much.'

'Now let me introduce you to my friend Grace from Exeter. I've told her all about you.'

'Hello,' said a woman with chestnut hair and skin the colour of clotted cream who stood and shook Florence's hand.

'And of course, Gladys continued. 'You already know Grace's son, Bruce.'

'How lovely to see you,' she said. 'I didn't know you were going to be here.'

He smiled warmly and rose to give her a kiss on the cheek. 'I wasn't supposed to be,' he said in a loud whisper, 'but I knew you'd be here, and after a lot of cajoling, and a last-minute shift swap, here I am.'

Florence felt herself blushing.

'Come on, Florence,' Gladys said, 'You sit down on the sofa beside Bruce.'

Florence glanced across at Jack, who was still standing staring at his feet. 'Jack,' she said. 'Why don't you give Gladys the box?'

When he looked up, Florence saw something new in his eyes. They were not accusing. Not that. But they had a look she couldn't fathom, like an ache maybe, deep in his eyes. Although the moment seemed to stretch out for ages, it had not really been long at all, and it seemed nobody else had noticed. Jack passed the box to Gladys, and she opened it, showing them all the contents. Ronnie said, 'Well I'm blessed, and here we've been on the home brew.'

After a few seconds, Florence saw Jack struggle to rally and brush it – whatever it was – off, and her heart twisted. She weighed the moment and found it dreadfully heavy. Jack did feel something for her, she knew it, even if he would never admit it. But he had recovered now and was laughing.

'I was given it all, so best place for it was here.'

'Got any sweet sherry?' Gladys dug in the box. 'Blimey, what the dickens is this? Dramb . . . how do you say it?'

'Drambuie,' said Jack. 'Scottish whisky, honey, herbs and spices. Courtesy of my friend's father's cellars.'

'How the other half live, eh? Let's try it then.'

'It's usually for after the meal,' Jack said.

'Oh, who gives a fig. Give it here.' And Ronnie went to the kitchen, returning with a tray of glasses. He poured and they drank. He poured again and they drank again.

Florence followed Gladys into the kitchen to help with the lunch and as they were working, Gladys whispered, 'Like Bruce, do you?'

'Yes, he's very nice.'

'He's got a crush on you, my girl. You could do a lot worse. But like I said, mind you don't hurt his feelings. He's a good lad.'

Florence laughed. 'Honest to God, Gladys, what are you like?'

When the food was ready and they'd all been served, you could have heard a pin drop as they tucked in. Delicious, everyone agreed, while Ronnie secretly slipped titbits to the ravenous collie. Then Gladys placed a flaming Christmas pudding in the centre of the table to multiple 'ooohs' and 'aahs'.

'Not brandy, just home-made stuff,' Gladys said. 'But it lights up well enough.'

Florence glanced around at everyone. Happy faces, red cheeks, sparkling eyes, especially Bruce's. The war forgotten.

'Any more for any more?' Gladys said, slurring her words a little now.

Florence shook her head, and in her mind, she sent a

Christmas blessing to Claudette, Hélène, Élise and baby Victoria, and to all their old friends in France.

They turned on the wireless to listen to King George broadcast his Christmas speech to the Empire.

When it was time to leave, Florence noticed a huge bunch of mistletoe had miraculously appeared above the front door. She could have sworn it hadn't been there when they'd arrived, and she spotted Gladys winking at Ronnie. Bruce stood up and came across to give her a hug.

'See you soon I hope,' he said, and Florence nodded mutely. Then he kissed her on the cheek, and she knew she was blushing but hoped everyone would think it was the wine.

She and Jack donned their coats, scarves and hats and they walked towards the door.

'You gotta kiss her, man,' Ronnie called out.

Jack stood awkwardly beneath the mistletoe, his hands in his pockets. He bent and gave her a peck on the cheek.

'Nah! That won't do at all,' Ronnie added. 'Go on, son. Give it some welly.'

Ignoring him, Jack just pushed open the door and strode out. Had Florence seen longing in his eyes, just for a moment? Or was that only her wishful thinking?

The sky was clear and the moon was full as they walked home without speaking.

CHAPTER 24

Early April, 1945

Florence had postponed her second visit to her mother, but now that the weather was so much nicer, she asked for a few days off and took the train just as she had before, this time arriving as the blossom was at its prettiest. The war wasn't over yet, but the cheerful flowers blithely declared that it soon would be. She remembered Claudette's pinched white face the last time she'd seen her, but this time her mother met her at the door and immediately took both her hands in her own. Florence had worried Claudette might still be buried somewhere in her lost chances and broken dreams, but instead she was smiling. If there had been soul-searching since Florence's last visit it wasn't showing.

'Chérie, it has been too long. I was hoping you might come sooner.'

'I've been working, saving money to go to Malta. I did explain. And I'm trying to figure out how I might get there. Even when the war ends, I don't think it's going to be easy.'

'You said your job was part-time.'

'It is, evenings and weekends, but *every* evening and weekend except over Christmas.'

'I can help you with money to get to Malta,' Claudette offered. 'Anyway, I'm glad you're here now. Come on in and I'll make some tea. I'm afraid it's only mint tisane: just can't get hold of decent black tea. They sweep it off the floor along with the dust, I'm certain.'

'The shortages *are* getting worse. But it will be over soon won't it, the war?'

Her mother nodded. 'Just a few days ago I heard on the wireless that American troops had taken Okinawa, the last island held by the Japanese.'

At first, Florence thought her mother had forgotten her promise to be more open, as they spent much of the afternoon peacefully working together in the garden and listening to the wireless in the evening. The door to the past remained firmly closed, but her patience was rewarded on the evening of the second day when Claudette spoke up, almost out of the blue.

'I did love the man you believed was your father,' Claudette said. 'You asked me about that when you were here before.'

Florence wondered if her mother was about to rewrite history, wondered if she might hear some anodyne version of the truth and she held her breath for a moment, aware of the open door to the hall and the ticking of the grandfather clock.

Exhaling slowly, she tried to hold in her own emotions. 'Yes, and honestly I'm so relieved to hear it.'

'He was a good man, but Friedrich . . . well, he was different.'

'I liked him,' Florence said simply. 'And his son Anton, my half-brother. I don't know how long after the war it will be until I can see them again.'

Her mother narrowed her eyes. 'You definitely want to see them?'

'I think so, but I'm not sure I could go to Germany. . . . You said Friedrich was different from Father. Do you mind telling me in what way?'

Florence felt the atmosphere in the room change and a distant look came into her mother's eyes. 'Oh chérie . . . he was my soul, my life.'

Florence reached out a hand and her mother squeezed it.

'When you were here before I was too shocked to speak. I had concealed everything for so long, buried it, tried to stamp it out. I thought I'd succeeded but when you said you'd met him and my secret was out, I wanted the ground to open up and swallow me.'

'Maman,' Florence murmured, feeling a little guilty to have caused such distress.

Claudette sighed and her eyes glazed over.

'You don't have to tell me, Maman, it's all right.'

Claudette held up a hand to silence her and it seemed as if she were suddenly there, lost in the time when all this had happened. 'I could not bear to go to him and

208

leave you girls behind. Friedrich would have been happy to have you all, but how could I take you away from your father in England? It would have broken his heart.'

Florence spoke softly almost in a whisper. 'So you stayed with him because of us?'

Claudette glanced at Florence with a puzzled expression but then nodded slowly. 'Yes. I suppose that is what I did.'

'And you were unhappy.'

'I don't see what else I could have done.' Her eyes had grown wide and bleak. 'But I could not even breathe without Friedrich . . . there was this eviscerating pain in my body. Every day I lived after that, I felt I might die from it. I *wanted* to die from it. It sounds ludicrous now, but I wasn't on solid ground. I held on to the furniture when you girls were at school or with the nanny. I needed to be tethered or I would fall apart. That's how it felt. They were dark, dark days, chérie.'

Florence was shocked, her heart twisting for her mother, her eyes brimming with tears. This was raw and almost too upsetting to hear.

She watched Claudette sitting with a trembling hand covering her mouth.

The pain her mother had never shared or expressed was plain to see. It had hardened her over the years until the person she had once been became trapped behind a brittle shell.

Claudette was speaking again. 'Looking back, maybe there might have been another way, but I couldn't see it. I did what I thought was best for all of you.'

'You sacrificed your own happiness.'

'It was not mine to have. I was married . . .'

Florence felt her tears beginning to spill now.

'But you're right, I wasn't happy. One day something collapsed inside me, and I took an overdose. Your father found me and forced saltwater down my throat until I was sick.'

Florence stared, her tears still falling, her breathing shallow. This was so much worse than she'd imagined, and she hadn't known any of it. Had Hélène or Élise known?

'It . . .' Claudette paused. 'It hurts so much to admit it, but I wasn't a good mother.'

Florence's heart twisted again. 'Please don't say that,' she begged.

'It is the truth. I am so sorry, Florence. You were my precious girls, and I didn't know it. I see my failure in Hélène's eyes, I see it when Élise glowers at me and I see it in you too, my darling girl. Too wrapped up in my own unhappiness, I wasn't there when you needed me. I was never there. That's why I sent you to France. Better that than rely on a mother who was present in body but not in heart or mind. In France you would learn to rely on each other instead.'

Florence didn't speak, couldn't speak. But, taking a breath, she rose from her seat and went to her mother, wrapping her arms tightly around her. Claudette was thin, much too thin, and Florence could feel her trembling and then her poor mother began to sob. Florence closed her eyes and continued to hold her. It had cost her mother a great deal to speak about the life she had hidden for so long.

They went to bed soon after that and the next day Claudette told her why Rosalie had run away. The family in Paris had been on the verge of a scandal for which they blamed Rosalie. In fact, it hadn't been her fault at all. She'd merely been the messenger but was so unhappy she'd felt there was no choice but to go. And, of course, Rosalie had never got on with her strict strait-laced parents who wanted her to marry a suitable man and settle down. She didn't want that, she wanted to be a dancer.

'Here,' Claudette said, just before the taxi arrived to take Florence to the station. 'This is for you.'

She dropped a glittering silver charm bracelet into Florence's palm. 'Wear it all the time. Rosalie has the same one, with duplicate charms. She wore it every day, said it brought her luck. If you find the identical bracelet, you'll find Rosalie.'

'Is there anything more you can tell me about her?'

Claudette looked pale, as if her revelations the day before had worn her out, but her eyes were strangely bright.

'Just that she was a cabaret dancer in Paris. Our parents didn't know but she confided it to me.'

'All right, but Maman, you don't look too well,' Florence said. 'I could stay, help you here.'

'Don't be ridiculous,' Claudette snapped. 'I'm absolutely fine.'

And the look of irritation in Claudette's eyes made Florence smile, glad – well, almost glad – to see her mother hadn't lost the irascible self that had been her protection for so long.

'I love you, Maman,' Florence said, gave her a hug and then the taxi arrived. For most of the journey her eyes were blurred with tears and when Jack picked her up from Exeter station, she still could not speak. Back at Meadowbrook he asked if she was all right and could he turn on the wireless and she nodded. It was 12 April, and they heard the news that after twelve years as President of the United States of America, Franklin Delano Roosevelt had died from a massive stroke.

Florence listened in shock. This was the man who had led his country through the worst of times to the impending defeat of Nazi Germany, with the Japanese in full retreat.

'Oh,' she said, her voice choked. 'It's terribly sad that he didn't get to see the very end.'

Jack held out his arms to her and she went to him. She cried then for the American President, and she cried for her mother, for herself and Jack, for her two sisters and all they'd been through, and she cried for a world in which war and so many senseless pointless deaths were possible.

As they waited for an end to the war, Florence swung between a growing sense of relief and anxiety that something might still go wrong. Jack assured her it wouldn't, and he seemed not to have to go away so much, except for occasional days to somewhere in Dorset when he took only a penknife, a change of clothes, a toothbrush, and a compass. He'd said the SOE wouldn't be wound up until the end of the year or maybe the beginning of the next, but most of his work would be tying up loose ends. It was the most he'd ever said about what he was doing.

The good news was that Belinda had finally accepted the divorce must happen and had given up insisting on a share of Meadowbrook. Jack seemed happier after that, although he hadn't known what had changed her mind. Florence suspected that with the end of the war in sight Belinda, like everyone else, wanted to make a fresh start.

Jack was talking about Sicily again and long before any date was set, or even a definite decision about going, Florence began to read about the island, to talk about it, and even to dream about it. Although she had decided to go to Malta alone, it would be so much better if Jack came too. When she thought of Sicily, she saw herself soaring free like some mythical winged creature flying over sunlit buildings and shimmering blue seas. In her dreams she walked barefoot on empty beaches, feeling the warm sand as she wriggled her toes, the water lapping at her feet.

She looked at the island in Jack's world atlas, followed its contours with her fingertip. Strangely Sicily called to her in a way that, so far, Malta had not. Might Rosalie have felt the same way, stayed on in Sicily, swum in its surging seas and decided to stay put?

'What do you think of this one?' she asked Jack and in her mind's eye pictured the characters from the Sicilian legend she was reading about in her library book.

He murmured something indistinct.

'The legend of the Fountain of Arethusa in Syracuse, Jack. I'd love to go there. Do you think we might?'

'Well, *if* we go, and remember nothing is settled yet – this wretched war needs to end—'

'Yes. Yes, I know,' she interrupted irritably.

He laughed at her, not unkindly. 'The ferryboat to Malta sails from Syracuse so I suppose it's possible.'

Florence glanced down at the book again. 'The water flows out from a fissure in the natural rock and forms a pool. They say the goddess Artemis changed a Grecian nymph called Arethusa into a spring that flowed underground and emerged at Ortygia to help her escape pursuit.'

'She had direct access to the goddess then?' Jack said.

Florence smiled. 'Doesn't every beautiful nymph? Apparently the fountain is enchanted, a place where people in love touch the waters and pray for fertility and happiness.'

'And well they might. I just think the legend of Etna and the giant Enceladus, or the story of Cyclops, is more my cup of tea. I was forced to study classics at school and had to read some of Ovid's *Metamorphoses*.'

'Ugh. One-eyed giants. No thanks.'

He covered one eye and pulled a ghastly face.

She grimaced and threatened him with her cushion. 'You like non-fiction don't you? War stories, battles and so on.'

He narrowed his eyes. 'Not entirely true. I like Graham Greene's novels and Joseph Conrad's *Heart of Darkness* is one of my favourite books.'

'What else?'

'*Madame Bovary*. You'd like that, I'm sure.'

'Who wrote it?'

'Flaubert, first published in 1856. It's about this woman,

Emma Rouault, who marries thinking she'll have a life of luxury and passion. But her husband is dreadfully dull, and she has an affair. But then her lover betrays her, and she spirals into deceit and despair.'

'Sounds grim.'

'What makes it wonderful is the way the author reveals a world of flawed individuals with narrow lives and narrow minds. Nobody comes out smelling of roses.'

Florence thought about what he'd said. The mention of betrayal made her itch with guilt. Wasn't that exactly what she was doing by falling in love with Jack even though Hélène loved him? By not leaving and staying here in Devon, despite the fact he had more or less said he didn't love her, and she had made her own decision to move on? Yet still had not.

CHAPTER 25

Florence swung open the library door, nodded at the librarian and headed straight for the reference section. They were fortunate that Barnsford library was well-stocked, also serving several nearby villages. It was still early and the place was quiet, so Florence quickly found the dictionary she needed and settled herself at a small table in the corner. It was close to a side window over-looking the bakery, in a spot where she was unlikely to be disturbed. She dumped her shoulder bag on the table and delved into it for the ancient, dog-eared recipe book. Her boss, Lord Hambury, the old boy at the manor, had handed it to her saying, 'You'll find it in there, along with an English translation stapled to it.'

Before she began, she looked up from the books and thought about Bruce. She'd seen him at a New Year's Eve party, and then once more when they'd been hoping to reach the coast on his motorcycle, but again it was too cold and the trip had been aborted. They'd spent the afternoon in a cosy teashop instead, talking for hours and it had felt like being with a friend she'd known for years. Today was his first day off since then and, a little later, Florence would be meeting him outside the picture house in Exeter. She hoped the cinema would be showing *Casablanca,* for Gloria had seen it and with stars in her eyes had waxed lyrical about Humphrey Bogart.

Florence opened the recipe book and glanced at the dedication inside it – a gothic German script she couldn't decipher, although when the book fell open at the page she wanted, the name of the cake was just about intelligible.

Berliner Pfannkuchen

'Berliner Pfann . . . kuchen,' she whispered, trying out the strange words.

It turned out that Lord Hambury had been a junior diplomat in Berlin before the First World War and the embassy there had employed a top-notch German chef. At least that was what Florence thought he'd said. Most of the time he seemed to be drifting in and out of the past and Nurse Carol, who came in twice a day, had told her he was heading towards senility. Anyway, the old boy's wife had learnt his favourite recipe for German doughnuts, and this was it. With tears in his eyes, he'd begged Florence to make them and, feeling such pity for him, she'd agreed. Now she fished out the piece of yellowing paper, no longer pinned to the page, and read through what remained of the English translation.

4 cups flour
1½ oz yeast
¼ cup sugar
¾ cup milk plus 2 tbsp . . .
5 . . .

That was all she could make out, plus a few words.

. . . fried doughnuts . . . drain on . . . jam using.

She sighed. At least half of it had been water-damaged. There was nothing for it but the dictionary. She'd only fished out the German-English dictionary from the shelves out of curiosity and hadn't expected to really need it much. For a few moments she studied the recipe in its original German. She couldn't understand the words, of course, but also the script was terribly old-fashioned and impossible to read. She glanced at the title page and saw it had been published in 1905.

She checked her watch. This was going to take a while and she had to leave for Exeter on the eleven fifteen bus. Slowly, achingly slowly, she concentrated on making out the words and then looking them up in the dictionary, jotting down what she hoped was the correct translation in her notebook.

A little later she was started by a rustle behind her and turned to see a heavily built, middle-aged woman standing there staring at the books.

'Hello, Mrs Wicks,' Florence said, pushing back her chair and rising to her feet. Mrs Wicks was the woman she'd shared a table with at the WI, the one who told her about the possible vacancy for a cook at the manor. 'I'm so glad to see you. I must thank—'

'German,' the woman hissed, interrupting and pointing a finger at Florence. 'You're one of *them*.'

'What?' Florence replied aghast, not only shaken by the look of distaste on the woman's face but also how close she'd come to the truth.

The woman's eyes narrowed. 'I've heard about people like you.'

'What do you mean?' Florence's voice had come out high and squeaky. She took a deep breath to steady herself.

'Spies, living amongst us. Why are you reading in German if you're not one of them? Speak it too, do you?'

Florence tried to stay calm although her heart was racing. 'Not at all. Lord Hambury asked me to make some doughnuts he liked when he worked at the British embassy in Berlin. That's all. This is the recipe.'

Mrs Wicks bristled. 'Well you would say that, wouldn't you?'

'Really, if I were a German spy, would I be looking something up in plain view in a public library?'

The woman gave her an angry glare and Florence began to stow away her things in her bag. She had to get out of there.

'I thought you sounded a bit strange. I thought about it after I met you at the WI and talked it over with my neighbour. You seemed like a nice girl, but there was something. My neighbour said I should go to the police.'

Florence swallowed her anxiety and stood tall. 'Well,

I'm not German and I feel very offended that you should say so.'

Hands on hips, the woman smiled grimly. 'Prove it then.'

'Oh, for goodness' sake!' Florence said in a fit of pique, completely forgetting to tone down her response. 'This is ridiculous. I was trying to do Lord Hambury a favour, that's all. He's old and he's lonely and I wanted to make him happy. And if you must know I lived in France for a while, so think what you bloody well like. But maybe that's why I sounded a bit *strange,* as you put it.'

Mrs Wicks smiled in satisfaction. 'There, you see. I knew it. Around here we don't have much sympathy for the Frogs either. Letting that Hitler stomp all over them.'

Florence sighed. Dammit. Why had she mentioned France? Goodness knows what lies the woman would be dishing out behind her back. Nothing spread as fast as a good scandal. Before long the whole village would assume she wasn't English and would maybe even believe she was German if Mrs Wicks repeated her worst suspicions. She felt close to tears, swinging between anger and shame – after everything she'd been through in France to be accused like this, no matter how unfair it was. She'd had to run away from France because of it. Was she going to have to run away from Devon too?

She took the bus to Exeter, listening to the clippy calling everyone 'dear' and 'love'. She couldn't help overhearing a couple of old biddies gossiping in the seats behind her and felt even more upset. She'd agreed to meet Bruce on the corner of North Street and the alley where the cinema was located. The exchange with Mrs Wicks in the library had left her seething and miserable, but as she left the bus she saw Bruce looking so pleased to see that her it lifted her spirits a little.

'How was the journey?' he asked, after giving her a brief hug.

'Fine. Sorry I'm late.'

'We're still in time but we'd better get our skates on.'

'A couple of old women were blethering on about how terrible the Germans are. And the Nazis are, of course they are, but not all Germans are terrible. I hate the way war makes everything us or them.' She didn't tell him about the scene in the library.

He smiled. 'You know you sound very English. I don't mean your accent. It's the colloquialisms.'

'Comes from spending time with Gladys.'

The Gaumont was the only cinema to reopen after the bombing of Exeter in 1942, and today there was to be a showing of a British war film. She viewed the outing as a stolen hour or so of hope in all the muddle of her life. The house lights had darkened as they took their seats and the Pathé news was already showing. The usherette shone her torch in the direction of where they were sitting, about halfway down the stalls, and they whispered their apologies as they sidled past the already seated and now grumbling people in their row.

She was disappointed the film was not *Casablanca* but an adaptation of a Graham Greene story – *Went the Day Well?* As the rousing patriotic music at the beginning began to play, Florence felt very aware of Bruce sitting beside her. His presence as close as this confused her, and she was wondering if they might spend time together afterwards at his house. Suddenly the screen flickered for a moment then turned black. People muttered and complained and there were a lot of 'bloody hell's and one or two shouts erupted from the audience. It wasn't unusual. Films were always breaking down. But then the house lights came on and a shrill-sounding woman began to speak to them over the loudspeaker.

'We apologise for the interruption, ladies and gentlemen,' she said, and they all groaned. 'The picture will be restored as soon as possible.'

As the lights went down again and the film stuttered back to life, Florence settled down and tried to enjoy it. But the subject matter didn't help her state of mind. As a group of German paratroopers disguised as British Royal Engineers took over a peaceful English village, she became more and more unsettled. Gradually it became clear there was a traitor among the villagers who was enabling what they realised was a German occupation.

At that point there was a gasp from the audience as they turned to each other muttering their disapproval.

When the entire village was held at gunpoint in the church and the vicar, who'd tried to ring the church bell as a warning, was shot in cold blood, you could have heard a pin drop. But what really disturbed Florence were the scenes which, naturally enough, showed the villagers fighting back; even the postmistress took an axe to her German guard and killed him outright. It wasn't that they shouldn't fight back, of course they should, but she couldn't help feeling vulnerable. What might happen to Florence herself if anyone found out that her father was German? Now that Mrs Wicks had inadvertently hit the nail on the head she didn't feel secure. Meadowbrook had been her sanctuary but was this going to follow her all her life?

'The area is being evacuated,' a gutsy woman in the film was saying. 'We need to release the children first.'

But a young boy had already climbed out of a window to run for help and Florence flinched when he was shot trying to escape the German soldiers.

'All right?' Bruce whispered.

She nodded but didn't speak.

At the end the audience cheered. The plucky British villagers had won the day and now people were standing up, laughing and chatting about the film.

The disembodied voice of the loudspeaker broke into the general hubbub. 'An unexploded bomb has . . .' A loud crackle broke up her words.

'What was that?' Florence asked Bruce and heard other people saying the same thing.

The voice continued, '. . . so, in the light of this will you please vacate your seats in an orderly fashion and head—'

They began to move but heard an explosion from somewhere outside the building, and the house lights went out again.

The older lady who had been sitting in the seat next to Florence gripped hold of her by the elbow. 'Can I stick with you, m'dear? I dropped my spectacles and I don't see too well in the dark.'

'Of course. Hold tight. We just need to head for the exit.'

'Did she tell us where the bomb was? The lady on the loudspeaker?'

'It went off already, somewhere outside. We heard it. Don't worry,' Florence said. 'Just hang on to me. Best to get out quickly now.'

By then Bruce was a few steps away from her, heading up the aisle, although in the dark she couldn't see him. Somehow, she'd let go of his hand but she could hear him call out to her.

'I'm here,' she shouted above the general noise and confusion. 'You carry on.'

People were used to unexploded bombs, but you didn't want to be trapped inside in the dark. She felt the sting of fear. You never knew if there might be another about to go off. She clasped hold of the woman and almost dragged her along the aisle. Whether there was any danger or not, people were still pushing and shoving, and you couldn't help holding your breath until you were safely outside. But then an usherette appeared on the balcony above and shone a torch onto the stairs. The light made everything better and, relieved, Florence scrambled towards them making sure the woman was still holding tight.

A few moments later, along with a flood of excited people, they reached the top of the stairs and were swept across the foyer to the open front doors. Once outside, with unshed tears glistening in her eyes, the woman thanked Florence for her help. Florence smiled, told her it was nothing and then glanced around to look for Bruce. An acrid smell of burning filled the air and everyone was milling around asking each other what they'd seen.

Bruce waved and motioned for her to follow him, and they walked down a narrow alley to an area behind the cinema which was being cordoned off. Florence saw policemen, wardens, and parents in clusters clutching their children. She stared at smoke still drifting from scattered fires, and debris spawned by the explosion that had been propelled in every direction. But worse, a crater about fifteen feet wide with raised edges met her eyes, a dreadful wound in the earth. The children's schoolyard had been destroyed. She glanced at the school itself, its walls blown outwards, drainpipes dislodged, windows shattered and evidence of the blast in the holes that peppered its walls. In the distance, the sound of children's voices.

'Dear God,' she whispered and turned to see the back of the cinema covered in blast holes too. 'We were awfully close.'

'Bloody UXBs. Even more dramatic than the damn film,' Bruce said wryly. 'Although that postmistress with the axe – the look on her face. Terrifying. Next time let's make sure we come to see a love story.'

'Or a comedy,' she suggested. 'I don't think I can take any more shocks. A good laugh is what I need.'

After the drama had faded, Florence focused constantly on the incident that had happened in the library. The thought of what the woman might be spreading about her haunted her and her life in Devon felt fragile. She hadn't seen Bruce since that night. He had written to her, twice. Once to say how much he'd enjoyed the film with her despite the dramatic ending to their outing. And then, just before they were due to meet again, he sent her a note saying his mother was ill and between looking after her and his duties at the hospital he wouldn't be free for a little while. She felt disappointed but wrote back wishing Grace well.

Although she longed for Jack to hold her, to feel his body strong and comforting – which it would be, she knew it would be – she hadn't shared her worry about whatever gossip Mrs Wicks might be circulating. Instead, she told Gladys, who didn't know the truth about her father, and Gladys had said not to worry and promised to have a word in the village. Of course, Florence did still worry. How could she not? And the thought of Friedrich and Anton frequently played on her mind too, and she hoped they were safe.

And now, in these days of waiting, she and Jack listened to the wireless in nervous expectation, as the news came fast and furious. On 2 May, when they heard that Berlin had surrendered to the Russian Army, Jack cheered and Florence clapped, and then again two days later, when a section of the German Army surrendered.

'Jack,' she asked, 'how will things be in Germany? For Friedrich and Anton, I mean.'

'I really don't know. One thing is certain, their lives won't be easy. At least not for a while.'

On 7 May, the newsreader on the wireless announced

that the new German President, Admiral Karl Dönitz, had authorised the unconditional surrender of the armed forces of Nazi Germany. The newsreader added that the very next day would be celebrated throughout Great Britain as Victory in Europe Day.

Florence and Jack gazed at each other with tears in their eyes. So much had happened to them both during this interminable war, it was almost impossible to believe that in Europe, at least, it was over. She closed her eyes for a moment as her thoughts travelled to her sisters in France and to all the people who had suffered so terribly there. And then, unable to stop herself, she wept with Jack holding her in his arms.

CHAPTER 26

8 May 1945, VE Day

The next day Florence wore a blue and white spotted dress with puffed sleeves. She'd added red piping and red buttons to be especially patriotic and was delighted with the result. The weather was overcast but dry and now she, Jack, Gladys and Ronnie were heading to the village in the farm truck. Florence couldn't help smiling at the idea of what the 'jollifications' – as Gladys called them – would be like. After six long years it would need time for everything to fully sink in, but this really was going to be a day to remember, as long as Mrs Wicks hadn't done too much damage with her gossip-mongering.

Before they parked, Gladys pulled up so they could take a peek at the main street and the scene that met their eyes was exciting. Doorways and windows festooned with boughs of greenery interspersed with spring and early summer flowers gave the village a feel of times gone by. People wearing home-made red, white and blue paper hats were setting out trestle tables, carrying chairs on their shoulders, or delivering precariously wobbling piles of crockery. Children in fancy dress – elves, princesses, soldiers – were racing around waving streamers and squealing, while a brass band tested its instruments, and acres of Union Jacks and red, white and blue bunting fluttered overhead. Florence felt a surge of absolute jubilation. The war in Europe really was over.

'Can't imagine what they think we're all going to eat,' Gladys muttered as they swerved away from the main road and parked down a side street. 'We'll share, of course, but I haven't got enough to feed the entire village.'

'Everyone will bring something and there'll be home brew,' Jack said. 'Lots of it.'

'And cider,' Gladys added.

She and Jack unloaded a small table and four chairs from the back of the truck.

'I'm guessing a lot a people will be relieving themselves behind the hedges,' Ronnie muttered.

Oh God, really? Florence thought, but then laughed out loud. In this fantastic dizzying moment it didn't matter. To hell with it. To hell with the Nazis. To hell with everything. Nothing mattered today but letting your hair down and having fun. They'd waited long enough, hadn't they? It was a glorious day. A wonderful day. A day to rejoice.

And rejoice they did. First the brass band played 'Land of Hope and Glory'. Admittedly not terribly well, and Florence suppressed a smile behind her hand, but still she clapped and cheered with the rest of them. Then came a parade of the Home Guard, followed by police and local servicemen with old boys from the First World War proudly joining in, their polished medals shining. A dense crowd of jostling villagers and children came next, and the entire motley crew ended up at the parish church where a banner proclaiming *God Save the King* hung jauntily on the church railings. Nobody gave her funny looks so whatever Gladys had said, it must have put to bed anything mean Mrs Wicks might have been spreading and Florence felt relieved.

Once inside the church it was time for prayers of thanks and hymns.

But there were bittersweet moments, too. Florence heard sobs coming from a woman at the back, because although this was a day of celebration, too many women had lost their fathers, husbands, sweethearts, sons, or brothers. And the fact was that some of the menfolk were still away fighting the Japanese in Malaya and Burma. She heard Churchill's words ringing in her head. 'Japan unsubdued . . . unspeakable cruelties.'

Sitting next to her in the pew, Gladys was clutching a handkerchief and dabbing her eyes and Florence's heart went out to her. Jack, too, was staring at his lap, clearly thinking of his little boy. Florence put a hand on his arm, and he glanced sideways at her, nodding his acknowledgement. She felt her eyes grow damp at the thought of her sisters in France without her, the little niece she'd never seen, and everything they'd all been through. The vicar told them that while the darkness and danger were over and it was a day to rejoice, they must never forget the fallen, nor the terrible price that had been paid.

'As a strong brotherhood of man,' he added, his voice catching, 'we must put our faith in God and build the future together.'

When the church service was over, and while the bells were ringing, Florence asked Jack if he was all right. He smiled such a sad smile it almost made her cry again. 'I'm so sorry, Jack,' she said.

'Come on,' he replied. 'We can't dwell on the past. Not today. The only thing to decide now is beer or cider?'

Florence pulled a face at the thought of beer, and soon after was happy to rapidly down a pint of home-made cider. 'To the future,' she said and smiled at him. She'd been about to say 'to us' but had caught herself just in time.

The cider went straight to her head, as even though Jack had suggested it might be a good idea to eat lunch before the party, she'd been too excited.

The children got up a rowdy tug of war to loud laughter when both sides let go at the same time and they all fell on their bottoms. Then Florence watched in amazement as the vicar's son wheeled out a piano.

'This will be good,' Jack said. 'Geoffrey's a professional.'

When he began playing, she and Jack stood side by side swaying and joined everyone else belting out the tunes they all knew, starting with 'Daisy Bell', a song they tended to call 'A Bicycle Built For Two'. They followed it with 'Pack Up Your Troubles' and ending with a raucous 'It's a Long Way to Tipperary' and then a gentler 'Goodnight Sweetheart'.

By now the drink was flowing freely and a young man with a limp had brought out a 1930s, hand-cranked, wind-up gramophone, which he set up on the table next to where Florence now stood a little distance from Jack and the others. As he wandered further off, she drifted down the street in the other direction. She smiled at everyone and grinned at the children as they wove around people's legs, tables, chairs, shrieking and laughing whenever they tripped an adult up. Florence had already drunk another pint of cider and felt light-headed.

It was then she saw Bruce standing behind his mother, who was sitting at a table looking pale but recovered. Bruce waved and she went across to say hello.

'I'm so happy to see you,' he said, smiling broadly, his hazel eyes shining. 'Sorry not to see you since our cinema trip.'

'My fault,' Grace said. 'But I'm much better now.'

'Mother insisted on coming,' Bruce added. 'Even though I offered to stay at home with her.'

'Poof!' Grace said. 'What kind of celebration would that have been?'

At that moment, the man with the gramophone began cranking up. After a few crackles they heard a dance tune begin to play.

Bruce glanced at his mother. 'Go on,' her look seemed to say, and he held out his hand to Florence. For an hour they danced wildly to 'In the Mood' by Glenn Miller and other lively tunes. Later, towards the end, they kind of rocked together to the romantic 'Wonder When My Baby's Coming Home' by Jimmy Dorsey & His Orchestra.

Florence felt rather drunk and very carefree in Bruce's arms. At the end the man with the record player put on Vera Lynn singing 'There'll Always Be an England'. The dancers stilled and Florence felt the tears that had been threatening all day flow over and run down her cheeks. Bruce handed her a handkerchief.

'It's clean,' he said, and smiled sympathetically.

She glanced about her and saw that practically everyone had tears in their eyes. The bombs, the destruction of so much of their beautiful country, the buildings that lay in ruins. The fear. The lost lives. But it wasn't just about the past. Their transitory sadness was also tinged with anxiety about what might lie ahead – how they would live with what had happened and what kind of future they faced. And so the afternoon passed by and as dusk fell there was to be a huge bonfire in a meadow beyond the village. Bruce had gone to take care of his mother and Florence, realising she hadn't seen Jack for ages, looked around for him. She couldn't see him anywhere. Surely, he hadn't already gone home? He must be helping with the bonfire.

Soon after that Bruce joined her again and put an arm around her shoulder. 'Are you cold?'

She shook her head. 'Not at all.'

'Mum's having a rest in a friend's house.' He glanced to the right. 'There's tea over there. Would you like some?'

'Oh God, yes. I'm dreadfully thirsty.'

They shared a mug of tepid and very weak tea then he linked arms with her as they set off to walk through the meadow. 'Are you hoping to go to France to visit your sisters soon?' he asked.

Florence sighed. 'I wrote to them yesterday. I don't know how things are over there. It was chaos after the liberation and still seems to be.'

She didn't tell him she was also thinking of Rosalie and how likely travel to Malta might be. Claudette had written again of Rosalie in her last letter, and Florence hadn't been able to put it out of her head since. *I must know what happened to her, Florence, before it is too late,* she had written.

As they reached the bonfire, she watched the golden flames flickering on the drunk, happy faces of the people opposite. She felt light as air. Probably the cider – but still, it was wonderful to feel so free from care for once. Bruce gently turned her around. 'I've missed you,' he said. Then he kissed her on the lips, and she leant into him and forgot about everything else.

CHAPTER 27

Riva

Malta, 1925

With a towel wrapped turban-style on her head and another knotted loosely around her body, Riva heard someone knocking on the front door. It was her day off and she'd just washed her hair, but she could hardly go down to the street like that. She heard one of the girls on the landing and then from downstairs some murmuring. A few minutes later Bobby walked into her room armed with chocolates and flowers and beaming at her.

'Well, you look—'

'Undressed,' she said, more forcefully than she meant, feeling that she had somehow been negligent to let him see her like this. 'Déshabillée?'

'Gorgeous, actually. Pink-cheeked and fresh. Come over to Lottie's with me?'

'Why?' She was feeling annoyed and a little hurt that he was just springing this on her without so much as an apology for not being in touch for at least three weeks.

'She and her beau are over on Gozo until tomorrow. We'll have the place to ourselves.'

'Why not the apartment you share?'

'Not as nice. Messy. Male. Smells of booze. The maid will be there.'

'Lovely,' she said and raised a brow, deciding not to give in too easily. This was a new world for her and outside of the club it felt very English, so she wasn't entirely sure what the rules of behaviour were. She wished again that she could speak to Claudette, maybe pick her brains about Englishmen.

'I'm rather busy actually,' she said.

His face fell. 'Oh. I'm so sorry, I know I should have let you know beforehand. Thing is . . . it's been a bit tricky. My mother has been over.'

'From England?'

'No. She has a place in Italy.'

'Not staying in your . . . now what was it . . . messy, boozy, smelly apartment? Have I got that right?'

He laughed. 'At the best hotel in Valletta, actually.'

'And you preferred not to call me while she was here?'

He pulled a face. 'There wasn't time.'

'Well,' she said, knowing he was making excuses. 'I'm only teasing you. It really doesn't matter about your mother.'

'So you'll come to Lottie's? I have champagne.'

She laughed and, meeting his unwavering gaze, she saw hope in his eyes. 'As I said, I am rather busy.' She lifted a hand to push back a stray lock of hair and her towel slipped.

In a heartbeat he was beside her, kissing her on the forehead, on the cheeks and finally when he put his mouth on hers, she let him. With one hand on her buttocks, he pulled her tight against him. It was one of those long melting kisses, and for those few moments time swelled and then stilled, and she was lost.

'You have a beautiful bottom,' he murmured in her ear.

She was ready to give in, let him have what he wanted, right this minute, here and now, because more than anything she wanted it too, but still she pulled back.

'I've missed you so much,' he said. 'I'm so sorry about my mother. Please come.'

Her heart was pounding, and she could feel sweat blooming under her arms, but she tried to sound matter of fact. Even though her breath was coming too fast, and he knew it, she managed to turn away and with her back to him coolly said, 'All right. Maybe. But you can wait in the street while I get dressed and you can take me for breakfast before anything else.'

'I could watch you dress.'

'Get out of here,' she said and, now laughing, she bundled him through the door.

She took her time brushing her hair. As she glanced in the mirror, she heard her mother's admonishing voice. *'No one likes a cheap girl.'* Was she really planning to spend the day and night with Bobby? She wanted to get drunk on champagne and allow him to undress her. Wanted to kiss him everywhere, all the way down to his navel and beyond. She wanted, no she longed, to feel everything. She had never made love, just fooled around, nothing like the explosive images she imagined now.

She pulled herself up short. It was ridiculous. She barely knew him. They'd been out together only once, and he hadn't called her afterwards, just turned up out of the blue today with no warning – just assuming she'd comply. Well blow that! He clearly thought he was the bee's knees, and she was someone to be dallied with, a dancer, not much better than a call girl. And yet he *had* taken her to meet his uncle. She made a snap decision to not simply do what *he* wanted and slipped into her glad rags. Today a navy blue cotton dress with a gently fitted bodice and a skirt accented with crisp white zigzagging lines, and at the hips a white bow. She had recently bought a new white sunhat which she twirled in her hands. A dab of make-up and she would do very nicely.

During what turned out to be a fabulous breakfast – croissants, fruit and especially good coffee – he raised his cup and said, 'Cheers. Here's to us' just as if it had been a fine wine. She dabbed her mouth with her napkin and gazing right into his eyes, she haughtily told him it really was for the best if they weren't seen together in public.

He looked surprised but also curious. 'Why not? I want to show you off.'

She glanced up as three inky black birds flew past and then she saw a man standing on the other side of the street, shading his eyes with one hand, the other resting on his cane.

'Do you know that man?' she asked. 'I've seen him before, and he appears to be watching us.'

Bobby glanced across and raised his hand in a greeting of sorts. The man tipped his hat and moved on. 'I rather think it was you he had his eye on. He has quite a reputation.'

'With women, you mean? But he's old. Must be over forty.'

Bobby laughed. 'The worst sort.'

'So who is he?'

'Stanley Lucas. You probably saw him at that godawful dinner Lottie dragged you along to. Local businessman and well-connected fixer. But you haven't answered my question. Why shouldn't we be seen out together?'

She could give him any reason she liked but she decided on the truth. 'The girls get jealous. Valletta isn't a great place for us to be out and about together.'

He frowned. 'Let them be jealous.'

She sighed as if to a child. 'I have to live with them.'

'Ah.'

'And they can be mean.'

'All right. We'll be secret lovers!'

She narrowed her eyes. 'Aren't you rather assuming something?'

'I thought—'

'You thought?'

'I thought . . . I thought we were going to Lottie's.'

She shook her head. 'I said *maybe*.'

He had the grace to redden. 'Oh . . . Of course . . . I'm so sorry. If you don't want to. I wouldn't want you to think . . . well we can do something else. Of course we can.'

She smiled, enjoying seeing him squirm.

'Do you have something particular in mind?'

'How about you show me more of the island, just as you promised when I first met you.'

'Absolutely. We'll take a picnic.'

'I'd love a paddle in the sea.'

She waited in the car while he bought the ingredients for their picnic and then he drove them northwest from the city. As they neared a small village he said, 'We can drive down to Riviera Bay from just beyond here.'

'Riviera?'

'Don't get your hopes up, it's nothing like the French Riviera. Just small and rural, but very lovely. The locals call it Għajn Tuffieħa. It's Maltese for 'Apple's Eye' and it's my favourite beach.'

'I'm sure it will be lovely.'

'I've heard they are closing the road soon and then there will only be steps down to the beach,' he said.

Once he'd driven the dangerous slippery road towards the beach she got out of the car and stood gazing at the panoramic view of the deeply curving bay and the turquoise sea. Completely alone, they were surrounded by clay slopes and high cliffs on either side of the bay.

He unwrapped some of the food he'd bought and on a small rug he placed *ġbejniet* which he said was sheep's cheese, *zalzett* a coriander-infused sausage, plus rustic bread, olive oil, anchovies, and a bottle of wine.

'Race you to the water,' he said when they had eaten, and he began to run.

She kicked off her shoes and followed him, running unevenly across the fine reddish sand, then paddling in the clear water, loving the bright colours of the shells and pebbles. After a few minutes she looked up to see him watching her.

'Like it?'

She looked around at the stunning beauty. 'I love it.'

'Are you a strong swimmer?'

'Of course,' she said, not wanting to admit she wasn't.

'There are currents, so we do need to be careful. Better in high summer really but it should be fine now. And we haven't had too much to drink.'

She hung her head, digging her toes into the sand. 'I'll just sunbathe.'

'Of course. Addison always has towels and mats in the boot.'

He went to fetch them and once he had returned, he laid two straw mats on the sand, smoothing them out until they were completely flat. Then he handed her a towel.

'What?' he said, clearly sensing her unease.

'I don't have a costume.'

'You were the one who suggested the beach.'

'I know. It doesn't matter.'

He glanced up at the bright blue sky. 'It'll get hot soon.'

He was right and there was no shade. Then, aware he was watching her, she carefully undid her buttons and wriggled out of her dress. She felt self-conscious standing only in her pink drawers, a chemise and a petticoat, all of them in a new material they called rayon. But it was sweaty, and she wished it were silk. She didn't usually bother with a corset here in Malta, although her mother would have been incensed at the very idea. Her mother. Her shoulders sagged at the thought.

'What?' he said again.

'Nothing. Just thinking of my mother.'

'You must miss her.'

'Oh, my good Lord. Not at all.'

He laughed. 'I know the feeling.'

'But your mother was just over here to see you. I bet she thinks you're the best.'

'Hardly. Anyway, it wasn't just to see me.'

'What then?'

'A bit of a kerfuffle at the bank. Something very boring. She's a rum old bird. Likes to sort everything out herself.'

'Well at least she came.'

He shook his head but didn't say anything more and simply concentrated on removing his cream cotton trousers, and his blue shirt, under which she saw he was wearing a short-legged, short-sleeved, union suit. He walked to the water's edge and with his back to her he removed his underwear. She watched spellbound. This was the first time she'd seen a man completely naked, even if only from behind. He was fair-skinned with clearly defined muscles in his thighs, buttocks and back. He glanced back at her, and she felt herself blushing to have been caught staring like that which, of course, she realised, had been his intention.

He plunged into the sea, and she walked to the edge where the water lapped around her toes as she tested the temperature, then she waded a little further to watch as he swam. After a while he stopped and waved.

'Come right in. The water's gorgeous.'

'It feels cold,' she shouted back at him from the shallows, shifting her weight from foot to foot as she studied the haze on the horizon.

'Not a bit of it,' he said, then carried on swimming, this time out of sight.

She plucked up her courage, walked out of the foaming water back to the sand, slipped off her petticoat, leaving only her chemise and drawers, then stepped into the water again up to her waist, shrieking as icy waves broke against her tummy.

'It's freezing,' she yelled as he came back into sight.

He laughed and swam to her.

'I've never swum in the ocean before,' she said and felt the weight of his eyes on her semi-naked body.

'Where then?'

'The River Dordogne in France.'

'Well, it's perfect here. You'll warm up once you get moving. Just don't go out too far.'

'Not like you?'

He inclined his head and kept pace with her as she began to swim a slightly hesitant breaststroke. Then he pulled away, his professional-looking crawl enabling him to slice through the water at speed.

'Don't go any further out,' he called back to her.

She was enjoying her own leisurely pace, lost in the

beauty of the sea and the expanse of periwinkle blue sky. There was barely any wind and once she'd warmed up she closed her eyes and floated, feeling peaceful without any sense of how far out she might be. But suddenly, with no warning, the sea surged and her legs were swept under her as she was forced further out. She shouted for him, her arms flailing as she thrashed at the water, trying to resist the force of a current that was now dragging her along. In her panic she went under, then managed to come up for air, but with water in her mouth and nostrils she coughed and spluttered. She tried to swim sideways to free herself from the current, but it held her in its grip and she was moving along much faster now. Oh God, why hadn't she listened to him? Every time she surfaced she was dragged back under. She felt herself sinking again and again but each time was able to rise and stay afloat for a few more moments, keeping her face just above the surface, long enough to gasp for air. She panted as images began flashing through her mind. She could not let this happen and yet it was. The pulling sensation became even more powerful and now, as it took her under, she had nothing left with which to struggle. As the overwhelming power of the current held her down, she knew she couldn't fight back and was going to sink . . .

With one final burst of energy, she fought and rose again, screaming. Terrified she was drowning, she screamed once more before swallowing water. Suddenly Bobby's arms were around her, hauling them both out of the current and back towards the beach.

Once on the sand she fell to her knees coughing and crying at the same time. When she could finally manage to speak, she staggered to her feet and faced him.

'You absolute bastard! I could have died out there. Why the hell weren't you keeping an eye on me?'

He stiffened. 'You said you were a strong swimmer.'

'I told you I had never swum in the sea before.'

She tried to maintain her dignity as she stalked up the shifting sand to where she'd dropped her clothes then, with difficulty, tugged them on over her soaking wet things, not caring how it looked. He followed and tried to hand her a towel which she ignored.

'Now take me home,' she hissed. 'And after this I never want to see you again for as long as I live.'

CHAPTER 28

That night Riva dreamt of sinking, felt the sea dragging her away from life and that awful sensation of going under again, the stinging salty water in her nostrils, in her throat, and in her eyes. When she woke she struggled for breath, gasping, choking, crying. She hated Bobby for caring so little about her and yet a small voice in her head was whispering that she was to blame. He was right. She had lied about being a strong swimmer and he had warned her about the currents. She had been stupid, wanting to impress, but still she couldn't let go of her anger.

She got out of bed and as she threw open her shutters, she blinked at the harsh light of another bright day. Missing her misty Parisian mornings and her early morning chocolate in a favourite cup brought in by the maid, she sat on her bed and glanced at her clock. Still early. What was she going to do with herself until she could go to work? Maybe she could go and see Lottie. She didn't want to be alone today feeling so blue and out of sorts. Her mind was in turmoil as she roamed over the events at the beach, and she wished she hadn't sounded so accusing. The image of Bobby's naked body, his back towards her, kept repeating over and over and she only partly succeeded in shaking it off.

She grabbed her robe and went out onto the landing where she heard subdued sobbing. She listened at Paloma and Brigitte's doors but there was only silence there. The sobs seemed to be coming from the floor below, and as she tiptoed down in her bare feet she realised something was going on in the new girl's room. Riva froze. Should she intervene? She didn't want to intrude on her private distress, but what if this was the girl she had spotted at the club? Pale, young and yes, now she thought about it, frightened.

Riva tapped gently on the door. Nothing. She opened it just a crack. 'Can I do anything to help?'

The girl just moaned and shook her head.

Riva pushed the door open a little further. 'Won't you let me get you some water?'

This time the girl nodded and lifted her face up, her eyes so puffy and rimmed with red that she looked as if she'd been crying most of the night.

'Oh sweetheart,' Riva said. 'I haven't got a hankie. Look I'm going to get you some water and a face flannel.'

The girl didn't speak but sniffed and wiped her eyes and face with her hands.

A few moments later Riva was back, relieved that the door was still ajar. She padded in and placed a glass on the girl's bedside table and handed her a damp flannel.

'There. It's clean. You'll feel much better once you've wiped your face and drunk some water.'

The girl was compliant and did exactly as Riva suggested.

Riva looked around the room and spotted one small case and a couple of dresses hanging on a rail. When the girl had finished Riva asked her where she had come from.

'Russia,' the girl said and let out a wail.

Worried she was about to start weeping all over again Riva patted her hand. 'I'm Riva,' she said. 'Will you tell me your name?'

'I am An . . . ya,' the girl stammered.

Her English was halting, lacking in confidence. Riva put an arm around her shuddering shoulders, which were so thin she looked as if a gust of wind would blow her away.

'Those are pretty,' Riva said, pointing at a row of wooden dolls on the windowsill.

The girl's eyes lit up. '*Matryoshka* dolls. Mother has child inside and child has child inside. Many. All fit together. It is life.'

'Inside each other?'

'Yes.'

'How many?'

'Eight.'

Riva went across to the window and picked up the largest doll, a woman holding a black rooster beneath her arm. Clearly handmade and hand-painted, the yellow and pink looked a little faded in places but beautiful all the same.

Anya smiled. 'She is mother. My grandmother gave me. Is very old and valuable. I take everywhere.'

'But there are only seven.'

'I hide last one.'

'Why?'

The girl shrugged and looked sad. 'I do . . . not want to come here. I do not know where my family is. They made me come.'

'Your family made you come?'

'Maybe. I don't know. I am think . . . ing my father and brother are dead.'

'And now you are a hostess.'

Anya glanced sideways at her from under her lashes as if she were trying to work out how much was safe to say. 'That is what they say. I do not like.'

'How old are you?'

'I cannot say.'

'Who told you not to say?'

'Please . . . no more questions.'

'Will you come for tea with me later today? I know a nice café. It's perfectly safe.'

'I am sacred, no, I am *scared* . . . the men will come. Take me away again.'

'Don't worry. I'll be with you. Just rest today and I'll come back later this afternoon. You know the bathroom is the next door along from you?'

Anya nodded.

'Mind if I just nip in first? I'll be quick. I'll tap on your door to let you know when I'm done, but you take as long as you need.'

Riva ran up to her room for her towel and then back to the bathroom before someone else got in. When she'd finished, she let Anya know it was free and then went back to her own room to dress. She had managed to order a few cotton dresses run up cheaply by a local seamstress and chose one in green then brushed her hair. No matter how hard she brushed, the curls always bounced back. She had also managed to dye her hair dark again, but the colour faded too quickly and she wasn't sure how long she could keep it up.

On her way to Lottie's she told herself it wasn't with the hope of seeing Bobby and in a way it was true. She'd be terribly embarrassed about how she'd reacted at the beach if she saw him. Besides, although it was all over with him now, that shouldn't stop her from seeing Lottie who, after all, was her only real friend here.

'Oh, I'm so pleased to see you,' Lottie said, standing in the doorway. 'Come on up.'

They climbed the stairs and when Lottie threw open the door to her apartment Riva looked about in surprise. Clothes were strewn everywhere. Over the backs of chairs, in piles on the floor, and there were three large semi-filled cases lying open on the bed.

Riva frowned. 'You're leaving?'

'Back home for a bit. Daddy's not too well and I've been summoned.'

'Oh dear. I hope he's all right.'

'Probably a storm in a teacup, but I have to go. And I could do with getting away for a bit.'

'What about your beau?'

Lottie shrugged and Riva saw something in her friend's eyes she didn't understand. 'You are happy to be marrying Archie, aren't you?'

Lottie bit her lip but then recovered and smiled brightly. 'Of course. And now Mummy sounds as if she's lost the plot . . . Have you seen much of Bobby?'

Riva pulled a face.

'I saw him last night with a hangdog expression on his face, couldn't get a smile out of him at all.'

'We fell out.'

'Ah, the course of true love. I've never seen him like this with anybody else. Want to talk about it?'

Riva shook her head. 'Want help with the packing?'

'Would you? I'm useless.'

And for the next couple of hours the two girls went through every item of clothing, only choosing things that Lottie would wear in England.

At one point she looked at Riva and said, 'Actually, this is crazy. I've got loads of clothes at home. Maybe I'll just take one case.'

'Good idea, Lottie. Only take what you need for the journey.'

When they had finished Lottie went to her bedside table, fished out a set of keys and handed them to Riva.

'What's all this?'

'Keys for this apartment. Stay here as often as you like.'

'You're sure?' She had felt envious of Lottie's life and now, in the face of this generosity, she felt ashamed.

'If things . . . well if you and Bobby make up, you'll need somewhere to go. I'll let Archie know.'

'He won't mind?'

'Not at all. But don't bring anyone else here. Apart from Bobby, or Archie of course. Is that too mean?'

'Course not. It's awfully kind of you but I don't think I'll be needing it.'

'You never know.'

Later, when Riva eventually returned home having left Lottie happy with her one case neatly packed, she went straight to Anya's room and knocked. No reply. She knocked again. Still nothing. If Anya was sleeping, she didn't want to wake her. It wasn't time to go to work yet, so it was probably best to leave the girl to get some rest. She was about to turn away, but something nagged at her, so very quietly she opened the door just a tiny bit and peered in. Anya was not there. Riva went into the room and closing the door behind her, she took in the bed now stripped of sheets and blankets. Anya's absence felt weirdly unsettling and Riva had a bad feeling so she checked the cupboard, the wardrobe and the small bedside table. Anya's clothes, her dolls and her small case were gone. There was nothing left of the girl at all.

CHAPTER 29

Time passed and nobody seemed to know anything about it and if they did, they weren't saying. For a while Riva questioned anyone who would listen about the Russian girl, Anya, who had vanished from their shared house so suddenly. She felt wretched knowing that somebody could disappear like that without leaving a trace, and nobody even cared, so she decided to spend her night off in Lottie's apartment. She needed to cheer herself up and a little bit of luxury might be just the ticket, she reasoned, but as she was climbing the stairs, she met Bobby coming down.

They stopped short, gazed at each other and then both spoke at the same time.

'I have wanted to—' said Bobby.

'I need to—' said Riva, and she knew that more than anything she wanted them to be friends again.

They both wavered, but then he held out his arms. Relief washed over her as she fell into them and any remaining shred of resentment about his lack of care at the beach evaporated.

'You on your way to Lottie's?' he asked once he'd let go.

She glanced towards the door. 'Yes, she said I could use the apartment.'

'Super. I've had a bottle of champagne chilling in Lottie's refrigerator ever since she left.'

'Really?'

'Yes. It's a Frigidaire from America. We don't have one in our apartment.'

She laughed. 'I meant the champagne not the refrigerator.'

He raised his brows. 'Ah, yes. Well, I can't tell you how many times I've walked up and down these stairs, or how many times I've sat on the top step waiting for you to turn up. Oh Riva, I'm so sorry. You were right and I was a stupid thoughtless fool—'

He was talking rapidly as if he couldn't wait to get it all out and she was forced to interrupt. 'No. I lied. It was my fault. I told you I was a strong swimmer.'

'I've missed you,' he said.

'I've missed you too.'

'So, champagne?'

They didn't make love that evening, nor on her next night off the following week, nor on the one after – each time he had returned to the apartment he shared with Archie in the wee small hours. But on the fourth night together she sat looking at him as he sprawled on the sofa smoking and listening to the wireless. She was evaluating her own readiness when, 'Why don't you stay?' she said. The words had just slipped out but then, more definitely, she said it again. 'Stay with me tonight.'

She curled up next to him on the sofa and kissed him. There'd been plenty of kissing and talking, and now she felt as if she'd known him all her life. But not like an old friend. This was very different.

They went up the wide steps to the bedroom where she encouraged him to undress her slowly, item by item, until she was standing naked before him, not feeling at all bashful. One thing Riva was secure about was her body. She was healthy, strong, curvaceous, and she knew men found her attractive.

'Shall we?' he said, but then he stopped as if words had entirely failed him.

She sat on the bed moving deliberately slowly as she then lay back with her legs just slightly apart. In that moment, as he kept his eyes on her, the energy coursing between them was thrilling.

'God, Riva,' he said and tore off his own clothes. Still standing he leant over her and trailed his fingers from her throat down to her navel. A charge swept through her, and she instinctively raised her hips

He grinned. 'Oh no, not yet.'

She laughed and held out her arms to him. 'Come here, you clown.'

He shook his head.

'I haven't, you know, before,' she said.

'I guessed.'

He placed a palm on her stomach and then slid his fingers down to her thighs, parting her legs further, stroking her until she could no longer bear it. She pulled him down on top of her and ran her hands all the way down his back and then, grasping his buttocks, she tried guiding him into her. With little experience she was counting on instinct.

But then he whispered, 'Not so fast,' and searching his face, she wondered if she might have done something wrong.

But he didn't look bothered and reaching down for his trousers he drew something out.

'What?' she said.

'"Gentlemen's rubber goods" they call them. You must have heard of them. Ghastly things,' he said laughing, 'though I'm reliably informed the Americans will come up with something much better soon.'

After he had rolled the *ghastly thing* on – she'd watched through fluttering lashes and semi-closed eyes – he went slowly, taking his time, and when he finally entered her she cried out, partly in pain and, for a moment or two, partly in frustration. Frustration because an unwelcome voice in her head was commenting, remarking, making notes. But then, without noticing how it had happened, she realised something had changed and instead of feeling weird and somehow under observation, she and Bobby were suddenly in tune. She stopped thinking altogether and seemed to know exactly what to do. Why had nobody told her it would be like this? There she was, lying in Lottie's bed with nothing in her head at all. She closed her eyes. It was fast. It was furious. And it was over.

Afterwards they both panted from the exertion and until they could breathe normally neither spoke.

'Well,' she said eventually. 'Can we do that again?'

'What, now?'

She nodded.

He laughed and his blue eyes crinkled up. 'Give me a minute to recover.'

But a little later he guided her, and she learnt how to help him recover and that would happen another time that same night.

In the morning she woke to see him gazing at her. 'Hello,' he said.

She breathed him in, the smell of him. Bay leaves and cloves. Something old-fashioned anyway. Nice. Spicy.

'Look, I meant to say this last night, but other things seemed to be happening and I got distracted.'

'What?' she asked.

'My mother.'

'Your mother? That's a funny topic after what we've just spent the night doing.'

He guffawed. 'You're right. But she'll be here for a couple of weeks. I won't be able to spend the night here.'

'Oh.' She got out of bed and stretched, and he sat on the edge of the bed watching her.

'Thing is, she's not going to a hotel this time. She'll be staying here.'

'In this apartment?' she said, taken aback.

He laughed. 'No. In mine and Archie's.'

'Really? Why not the best hotel like before?'

'She's suddenly got a bee in her bonnet about money. I've got someone coming to clean the place.'

She grinned. 'You could always nip down here for a quick fix.'

He laughed. 'Something tells me nothing I do with you will ever be quick.'

'Oh, I don't know, it could be rather fun,' and she swayed her hips provocatively in front of him, bending down so that he had no option but to take one of her nipples in his mouth. And they had their first attempt at fast unprotected sex, with Bobby withdrawing only just in time.

'Are you regular?' he said.

'Why?'

'Because there's also the rhythm method. It's not foolproof but at least we'd know which days to be more careful.'

'I've heard of it. I'll draw up a plan. A sex plan,' and she roared with laughter at the thought of what her mother would say if she knew. She had no idea how her parents had managed to produce two daughters.

He smiled and kissed her on the nose. 'I've got to go.'

'Oh no, really?'

'She's arriving later today and I need to tidy up the apartment before the cleaner gets here . . . You know I may be away soon don't you. I'm doing my pilot's training here in Malta,' he said, 'but sooner or later will be completing it in England.'

'Will you be gone for long?' she asked.

'Don't know yet, but let's not worry about it now.'

'All right. Off you trot then. Back to Mummy.'

He grinned at her.

'By the way,' she said. 'I meant to say earlier, I don't know how I could have forgotten, but a girl from my house disappeared. Three or four weeks ago. I've been asking around, but no one seems to know anything about it. She was young. Underage I think, and Russian. I heard her crying. She said she was afraid.'

'Do you know what she was afraid of?'

Riva shook her head. 'No. Of something or someone, that's all she said, and then she just vanished.'

'I'll ask around.'

'Discreetly.'

'Of course.'

Then he dressed and came to kiss her where she now sat on the edge of the bed. She pulled him towards her and undid his trouser buttons and his underpants.

'Oh God,' he groaned. 'You have very quickly become such a wicked woman.'

CHAPTER 30

After Bobby's mother had departed, and on a day when Riva had the night off, they were driving to Mdina to see Bobby's uncle for the second time. She felt delighted to be seeing Addison and his beautiful hidden palace again and was looking forward to a night with Bobby too. She began to happily sing something she'd recently heard on the wireless.

Bobby reached across and brushed a stray curl from her cheek. She turned to smile at him, took his hand, and kissed it.

'Careful,' he said. 'I'm driving.'

It was a beautiful day although a bit windy and she leant back to enjoy the feeling of sun on her face.

'By the way, I have information,' Bobby said, 'about your Russian girl. At least I think I do.' His eyes were focused straight ahead.

'Good news?' she said and looked at him hopefully.

But as he shook his head, she drew in her breath.

'What then?'

'I'm so sorry. It's pretty awful, but the remains of a young girl turned up on one of the beaches.' He turned briefly to her, his eyes grave.

Riva gasped. 'Oh no!'

'I have a friend at the *Times of Malta*. I happened to mention what you'd said about a missing girl, and he told me about it. The authorities tend to hush these things up.'

'When was she found?'

'About two weeks ago. She'd been in the sea for a little while.'

'Oh God. That's awful. But why do you think it was her?'

'Someone from Strait Street identified her as a Russian girl who'd only been here a couple of days before she didn't turn up for work. They didn't worry because people come and go so frequently.'

'It could have been another Russian girl.'

'They called her Anya.'

Tears welled up in Riva's eyes. She dashed them away but felt terribly sad for the girl. If only she could have done something to help her while she'd had the chance. She shook her head feeling awful, knowing she'd chosen not to stay with Anya that day and now it was too late and there wasn't anything she could do for her.

He sighed. 'Look, darling, there have been rumblings about goings on in Strait Street. It's likely the police may toughen up. I wish you would leave.'

'Toughen up in what way?'

'I don't know exactly but my friend at the paper wants to talk to you.'

'Me? Why me?'

'He's a journalist with a nose for ferreting out trouble. But he's a good guy, one to have on your side. He suggested you might like to meet him for tea.'

'And you think that's a good idea?'

'Maybe. You needn't say anything about what happened in France or tell him your real name. I just think, well . . . I just think he'd be a friend if you ever needed one.'

She stared at him, wondering if it had been a mistake to tell Bobby the truth about herself. 'You're my friend.'

'More than a friend, I hope. But if I'm not here . . .'

He glanced over, gave her a peculiar look that she didn't understand, then turned back to keep his eyes fixed on the road. 'You must know you mean the world to me.'

'As you do to me,' she replied, and leant across to kiss him on the cheek.

She felt joy, of course, at what Bobby had just said. It should have been a special moment, and it was, but she felt uneasy too, her happiness marred by the thought of what had happened to poor Anya. How awful it must have been. How frightened and alone she must have felt. Instead of spending the day with the lonely girl she had swanned off to Lottie's, but if she'd stayed with Anya the girl might still be alive. And yet she'd had no way of knowing what was going to happen. Nor did she know what *had* happened. How had Anya ended up in the sea? Surely someone did know. The young girl continued to haunt her thoughts until they arrived in Mdina.

Bobby's Uncle Addison was as magnanimous as he had been before and they ate a delicious lunch of *lampuki* pie, a fish dish like nothing she'd ever tasted, and for pudding *kannoli* — sweet tubes of crispy fried pastry filled with ricotta. This big man with his equally big-hearted kindness cheered Riva up and as the wine flowed they laughed and ate, and laughed and ate some more. After coffee Addison wiped his mouth and said, 'I have something to show you both.'

He rose to his feet, went indoors, and collected something from the top drawer of a desk. 'Come on. Follow me,' he said then.

They followed him out of his main door and down the stairs. There he stopped at another door, unlocked it, and ushered them into a pale hall. This opened onto a beautiful high-ceilinged sitting room, full of sunlight slanting through floor-to-ceiling windows with a narrow open-air terrace beyond.

'Oh,' Riva said, glancing around at the soft paintwork and feminine furniture. 'It's so pretty.'

'Yes, it was my wife's favourite place. So, here are the keys. Might as well use the place, Bobby.'

'Are you sure?'

'I don't like renting it out, although I do let the ground floor from time to time. In any case, the whole place will eventually come to you.'

'Well, thank you,' Bobby said, blinking in surprise. 'It's generous of you. But I hope you'll be around for a lot longer yet.'

'Indeed.' He turned to Riva. 'My wife Filomena and I never had children and as you can see, Bobby is like a son to me.'

'I thought you might leave this place to my mother,' Bobby said.

'Good God, no. She hates it here, she'd only sell it. No, this old place means so much to me I'd rather keep it in the family. I've given you two keys, although I do have another, in case of emergencies.'

For a moment Riva couldn't help comparing her own critical parents with this wonderfully generous man and she sighed.

'You don't like it?' Addison asked.

'No, I love it. Sorry, I was just thinking of something else.'

Riva smiled at him and after Addison had gone upstairs again, they explored the apartment. It was bigger than Riva first realised. She opened the tall glass doors and went out to the terrace where she stretched her arms out wide and whirled around feeling as if the whole world was spinning. Back inside they found a dining room, and beyond that a kitchen. In the other direction were two bedrooms with a bathroom shared between them and another washroom just off the hall.

'I can't believe we can stay here,' she said.

He threw her a key. 'If I'm not around jump on a bus and come here any time. Think of it as a haven.'

'I will,' she said, with no idea how much of a haven it would one day become.

'Would you like to stay the night?' he asked.

'Are we allowed?'

He furrowed his brows and twisted his mouth as if deep in thought. 'Err . . . yes.'

She laughed. 'In that case I'm going to have a bath.'

He grabbed hold of her arm. 'Before or after we christen the bed?'

'Before,' she said.

'Nooo.'

'Yes. I want to be pink and glowing and smelling of those gorgeous toiletries I spied in the bathroom.'

She searched for, and found, some fluffy white towels and a lavender-coloured silk robe.

'There's food,' Bobby called out, 'and wine.'

Addison had clearly not only ensured the place had been spring-cleaned but had also provided everything they might need. She took a long breath and let it out slowly. How had she managed to land in paradise?

She ran a bath and sat on a stool, watching as the water filled up.

The bath was gorgeous, with gold clawed feet and gold taps. Real gold, she thought. She opened the glass cupboard, took out bottles of scented oils, rose, neroli, eucalyptus, and poured them liberally into the bath. As the fragrant steam began to rise, so did her hopes for the future. Bobby had pretty much said he loved her. She dared not look ahead too far because life could be contrary, but still couldn't help picturing herself with him and even saw a brood of children. Marriage wasn't something she had longed for, had never been what she'd aspired to; she was going to be somebody in her own right, after all. But maybe, just maybe, she might make an exception for Sir Robert Beresford, Baronet, and then she called herself an idiot and slid under the water.

After a while she climbed out, dried herself and towelled her hair. Putting on the silk robe, she went to find Bobby and saw him, apparently asleep, on the sofa with his head resting on the back of it. She allowed her robe to fall open and then she straddled him. His eyes remained closed as she moved back and forth, feeling him grow harder beneath her. The slightest hint of a smile told her he was feigning sleep. She undid his shirt and kissed his chest then raised herself up so she could undo the buttons and pull down his trousers. He wore nothing underneath and she stared at him, not expecting that. Still he did not open his eyes. With a bit of effort, she eventually managed to lower herself onto him and moved slowly at first, enjoying the feeling of power, and then faster and faster while he continued to fake sleep. She finished quickly, heart racing, her breath short. She'd never experienced anything like that before. It had thrilled and shaken her and she felt invincible to have taken *him*, but then his eyes flew open.

'And now, in punishment,' he said, and still inside her he rolled them both onto the floor and then he finished too.

Swimming in the afterglow of it, she laughed and laughed until she was nearly crying.

'I knew you were awake,' she said.

'Yes, but I wanted to surrender.'

'Robert Beresford. Who would have thought it?'

'What?'

'That you'd let a mere girl be the boss.'

'Nothing mere about you, my darling. And I rather like you being the boss.'

'I love you, Bobby,' she said.

The next day, Anya playing on her mind again, she met Bobby's friend at the British Hotel on the Grand Harbour for high tea. He rose to his feet as she approached and took her hand. He was older than Bobby, maybe thirty-five, taller too and darker-skinned with curly brown hair and kind amber-coloured eyes with flecks of gold in them.

'I'm so pleased you decided to come,' he said, shaking her hand. 'Ottavio Zampieri.'

'Riva Janvier.'

They took their seats and a waiter was instantly there with a menu. As they ordered tea and cakes, she looked Ottavio over. Well-heeled but with a slightly dishevelled look, he wasn't unattractive. Then she turned to the stunning view of the Grand Harbour, golden and glowing in the late-afternoon sun.

'Have you been here before?' he asked.

She shook her head. 'No. You have an unusual name, if you don't mind me saying, Mr Zampieri.'

'My father was Italian, and my mother is Maltese. Do please call me Otto.'

'Well, I'm happy to know you, Otto, although I'm not at all sure why you wanted to meet me.'

'Bob tells me you are a dancer.'

'Yes.'

He glanced around and, his face thoughtful, he spoke in a hushed tone. 'And you had a friend who went missing and was sadly found washed up on the beach.'

She sighed deeply and leant forward. 'Anya, yes, I was terribly upset to hear what had happened to her, but she wasn't a friend really. I only spoke to her once.'

'Would you mind telling me about that?'

'We lived in the same house, although I think she was only there for a night or two. I heard her crying and went to see what was wrong. At first, she didn't want to say but then told me she'd been forced to come here.'

'Anything else?'

'She just seemed very frightened.'

'Did she mention any names?'

Because Otto had spoken even more quietly, she lowered her voice. 'Names?'

'Of whom she may have been scared.'

Riva shook her head. 'No. And the next thing I knew she was gone.'

'That same day?' he said, frowning.

'Yes. When I came back later her room was empty, and all her things were gone.'

'And why did you look into her room again?'

'I promised her I would. I said we'd have tea together.'

'I'm wondering—'

But then the waiter arrived bearing a cake stand. He was accompanied by a second waiter who placed a silver pot of tea on the table, plus milk and sugar. He poured their tea and then left.

'This looks very British,' she said as she added milk and sugar to hers and noticed he took neither.

'Yes. And you are French of course,' he said in a conversational tone.

'I am. These cakes look delicious. Mind if I help myself?'

'Not at all.'

She chose a slice of sponge cake, an eclair, and what looked like a chocolate biscuit. 'I've just remembered something. Before I met her, I think I saw Anya with someone at the club I work in.'

'Who was that?'

'It may have been a man called Stanley Lucas. Could he be involved?'

Otto shrugged. 'I don't know. But,' he continued in a whisper as she ate the sponge cake. 'I'm wondering if you might assist me. I want to find out what is happening to these girls.'

'Girls!' she said, swallowing rapidly and almost choking. She held up a hand and coughed a couple of times before she hissed, 'You mean Anya is not the only one?'

'Several foreign artistes have disappeared, some never found, but three others have turned up dead. Anya was the latest. The other two were a French and a Hungarian girl.'

'Dear God. I didn't realise.'

'It gets hushed up. The problem is that prostitution is flourishing and it's a market which, to some extent, relies on the trade in human trafficking. Apart from how terribly wrong that is, we are also attempting to develop tourism. The two don't really fit together.'

'I see. Tourists are unlikely to want to come to a place where girls regularly turn up dead.'

'Or a place whose reputation is tainted by tales of a trade in foreign women and girls.'

'Anya was Russian and terribly young.'

'Yes, they usually are. The island is beautiful but there is an undercurrent, and it flows right through Strait Street. Because you work there, I thought you might be well placed to pass on anything you see or hear. I would pay you, of course.'

'You want me to be a spy. How thrilling.'

He laughed. 'I suppose you could say that.'

'Can I think about it?' She bit into an eclair and chewed. But she already knew. She had wanted to be changed, to be different from her bourgeois parents and now she would be. A spy! How about that? Of course she would do anything to protect other young girls from going missing.

He glanced around and spoke even more quietly. 'Many of these girls are working for dangerous men, criminals. They live on immoral earnings and mistreat the girls. You would need to be extremely careful.'

'I can take care of myself.'

'All the same. And as you said, give it some thought.'

'Can I tell Bobby?'

'I don't think he'll be happy but yes, you can tell him, nobody else though, and I'll meet you here in a week.'

'Perhaps I shouldn't be seen with you in public. Won't people put two and two together.'

'I chose this hotel because it's entirely British and the paper I work for is pro-British, so anyone who spots us here will think nothing of it. Don't worry. You're safe here. It's in Strait Street that you will have to be careful. That's where you need to keep your eyes open.'

CHAPTER 31

Malta, 1926

'You'll have to remove your mask at the entrance,' Bobby said as they drew close to the building. The ball was being given by the Civil Service and open to all, just so long as you could afford the entrance fee.

'You have to reveal your identity there, but nowhere else. You can wear it once you go inside. But it's also prohibited to wear masks in the streets after sunset.'

'Why?'

'Long story. Who knows what the government are afraid of? Probably *undesirables*, I suppose, getting away with murder behind their masks. Maltese people resent unmasking though, it's their tradition and I don't blame them. Once you're inside the hall and masked, everyone is equal, not like the ghastly balls that used to be held at the Governor's Palace. Terribly snobbish affairs.'

Riva had hired a costume and was dressed as Nefertiti, a queen of Ancient Egypt, and the wife of wife of Pharaoh Akhenaten. She had a gold dress, a tall headdress and a black mask. Bobby was dressed as Pharaoh in black and gold and they made an imposing couple. A bit too imposing, Riva realised, as she saw how many eyes turned towards them when they entered the brightly lit hall. In the months they'd been together, this was the first time they'd been out in public. A tall man approached dressed as Sherlock Holmes and she realised it was Otto. He drew her aside. 'Can you come with me?'

She glanced at Bobby, who tilted his head. 'I'll find you,' he said.

She followed Otto to an alcove away from the milling crowd and the band.

'Aren't you hot in that get-up?' she asked him.

'Yes. Crazy idea.'

'You have news?'

'I do. You remember telling me about seeing Stanley Lucas with Anya at the club.'

She nodded. 'Yes, and about ten days ago I saw him with two other young girls. I was waiting to tell you. I've not seen those girls since.'

Riva had been keeping her eyes open and meeting Otto now and then to report her findings. So far nothing had seemed especially significant. New girls had come, and new girls had gone, but none had turned up dead – as far as she knew.

'Well, Lucas has been arrested,' Otto said.

'For trafficking?'

'No. For fraud, but I'm hoping it might convince the police to ferret out more about him. So far I have no proof he's actually part of the trafficking gangs.'

'He's British, isn't he? And wealthy?'

'Yes, and that would make it unusual. Maybe others are procuring the girls for him, and he's not actually involved in the mechanics of it, so to speak.'

'Might he be passing the girls on elsewhere? Yesterday, Tommy-O told me he'd spotted Stanley Lucas with a girl who has not gone on to work in Strait Street.

'He could have passed her on for a price. But thank you. You're good at digging. Would you ever consider doing more to help the cause? You know, maybe work as my assistant? In your free time.'

She laughed. 'I don't think so. Maybe when I'm old and grey.'

He pulled a face.

'Oh sorry, I didn't mean *you* are old and grey. It's just that I love dancing and I don't have much free time.'

'Well, if you ever change your mind. . . . I'm going to start a campaign to rid us of white slavery and the traffic in women for prostitution.'

At that moment Bobby found them and pulled Riva away. Forgetting Otto, she lost herself to the joy of the ball, spending the night dancing and drinking until she could barely stand. Later, when they really couldn't dance any more, they held on to each other, feeling overheated and sticky. The smell, smoke, and sweating bodies became too much for Riva; her head fizzed with all the champagne, and jostled by the inebriated crowd she could barely move.

After a while Bobby took her hand and pushed them through the crowd to the garden beyond, where they sat in a courtyard beneath an indigo sky peppered with stars.

'I'm too drunk to drive to Mdina,' he said. 'Can we go to yours?'

They rose to their feet and staggered along the streets, forgetting to remove their masks, laughing drunkenly about nothing, and holding each other up. Riva's vision was blurred, and she was surprised when she finally focused on the bulky silhouettes of two policemen approaching them.

'Leave it to me,' Bobby muttered as he pulled off his mask.

'Well done, sir. Silly rule if you ask me,' one of the policemen said, instantly recognising him.

'Sorry, Officer.' He steered Riva away without her having to reveal her identity.

They walked to the gardens overlooking the harbour where they took their masks off and sat on a bench gazing out at the lights. 'Let's just stay here for a while,' she said dreamily.

'It's four in the morning,' he said, checking his watch.

'Where's your spirit of adventure?'

He laughed. 'In bed with you.'

And then she had an idea. 'Let's go out on a *dghaisa*. I want to see the sun rising over the battlements of Fort St Elmo. Lottie told me it's stunning and even after all this time I still haven't seen it.'

'And we can go for early morning coffee and doughnuts when we come back,' he said, warming to the challenge.

They talked for a while, and he told her the rest of his pilot's training would definitely be in England soon but that he'd be back after two months.

'I don't want you to ever feel tied to me,' she said.

'I want to be tied to you. There's no one else.'

'I wish we could go out with each other openly.'

'It was you who said the other girls would kick up a fuss.'

'Perhaps not now that they know me.'

He held her tight, and she rested her head against him, almost falling asleep. After a while he shook her gently. 'Time to look for a *dghaisa,*' he said.

They found one easily and as they were taken out on the water, she looked back at the town. And then, as the fat morning sun came up, it painted everything pink and the battlements gradually turned red, scarlet even. 'Ah,' she whispered. 'Just as if they are on fire. Isn't Malta the most wonderful place on earth?'

CHAPTER 32

Malta, 1929

Time, the years, and life moved on. Now Riva was sitting alone, decked in beads, feathers and ribbons, feeling tawdry and listening to the sounds of stomping feet coming from the dance hall and drunken men shouting the odds in the street. Worse than unwholesome, the place was turning her stomach. She hadn't been to the doctor, after all she wasn't married, but already curvaceous and even more so recently, she was certain she was pregnant.

'All right, darling?' Tommy-O said as he made himself comfortable on the stool next to her and tipped his head to one side. 'You look a bit blue.'

'I'm twenty-three and sick to death of the smell of smoke, beer, fried fish and garlic.'

'Oh dear. You've got it bad.'

'Got what?'

'The "there must be a better life than this-itis".'

He was right. She had become repulsed by the brightly coloured lights and the artificial enchantment that was not enchanting at all. It was killing her, and she had to find the courage to make a change before it became clear she was carrying a baby.

Tommy-O stood up and patted her on the shoulder. 'We all go through it sooner or later. And now, my love, I have to slip into something fabulous.'

She blew him a kiss. 'See you later.'

She and Bobby had been happy together since 1925 – four years now – but he had missed their last date almost two weeks before with no explanation and she had been worrying ever since. It wasn't that their relationship had been all plain sailing. Like any couple they squabbled, argued, irritated each other. She could be fiery, opinionated, and at those times he had been mainly conciliatory, which only made her worse, but they always made up and survived his absences in England and her difficult working hours. She had planned to tell him she was pregnant the day he hadn't turned up and really needed to tell him soon.

And now that she was growing more and more jaded with the dancing life, and had a baby on the way, she didn't know what to do. Strait Street was cheap and gaudy, but Bobby was still the one light at the end of the tunnel, although she still enjoyed the bits and pieces of detective work she did for Otto.

On the second day off after Bobby hadn't turned up, she was determined to track him down. In all the years they'd been together he'd always been as good as his word, always letting her know if he was held up, always telling her if he was going to be away. So, what had happened? She had no idea how he'd feel about a baby. She had no idea how *she* felt about a baby. Part of her was thrilled, but they had never discussed marriage and the thought of having a child out of wedlock terrified her.

They'd often talked about life and how best to live it. 'Grasp hold of every chance,' was his mantra. 'Make every single day count.'

They talked about commitment and he always confirmed how much he loved her, buying her presents, taking her wherever she wanted to go and these days in public too. Nobody gave them a second glance. She accompanied him to cocktail parties at Addison's in Mdina, spent time in the apartment there, and met all sorts of interesting people, elegant men, glamorous women, the rich, the not-so-rich but entertaining. But Bobby never mentioned marriage and neither did she. It hadn't seemed to matter. They were young with their whole lives before them. He knew her real name and that she'd run away from Paris. She told him she wanted to be more than just the wife and mother her own mother had insisted she was born to be.

'I'm not going to fall into the trap my sister Claudette has,' she'd said defiantly. 'It will never be enough for me.' Now she wondered if that had been a mistake. Should she have sounded so adamant? She wished she'd said more about her parents and her childhood, explained more about what she meant.

And now where was he and why hadn't he let her know?

She tried not to worry but failed. Apart from feeling nauseous there was a pain in her chest that didn't quite go away. A breath she couldn't quite draw. A feeling of life being on pause. She wandered disconsolately through Valletta's main thoroughfares squinting into the bright light as if by doing so she might conjure him tucked away somewhere and waiting for her. As luck would have it, she found Lottie sitting in the window of one of the nicer cafés. Her friend smiled, beckoned her in.

Inside, Riva pulled up a chair. 'I just called at your apartment,' she said.

'Someone else lives there now. Archie still has his 'bachelor' pad, as you obviously know because Bobby stays there, but we have a house on Gozo now.'

'That's what I thought Bobby said, but I hadn't seen you around for ages, so I called at the apartment on the off-chance.'

'You were looking for me?'

'In a manner of speaking. I'm actually looking for Bobby.'

Lottie coloured slightly and fidgeted in her seat.

'What?' said Riva.

Lottie pulled a face. 'It's tricky.'

'Come on. If you know something, tell me. We are still friends, aren't we?'

'All right. The thing is, Bobby's gone.'

Riva frowned. 'Gone? What does that even mean?'

'He went back to England.'

'For work?'

Lottie shook her head. 'No. Because of the Wall Street Crash. His mother sent a telegram demanding his return.'

Riva was stunned. 'But why didn't he let me know?'

'Maybe he didn't have time. It was very sudden and urgent. He packed a bag and left. Hardly said a word. Just looked stricken and left.'

'You saw him go?'

'Yes. The telegram came to the apartment while I was there.'

'So, you don't know how long he's gone for?'

'No. All I know is the crash has affected them badly. I got the impression . . .' she hesitated, biting the skin around her thumb.

'What?'

'I got the impression it might be a while.'

'Well, that's all right. I just wish he'd let me know.'

Lottie nodded then stared at her hands.

'Is there something you're not telling me?'

Lottie didn't look up.

'Well, thank you anyway.'

It was very odd and Riva sighed, feeling more distressed than she was ready to admit. But then she realised Lottie wasn't looking at all well herself. 'How's married life suiting you?' she asked.

Lottie looked up now. 'It's fine.'

'Fine? Is that all? Aren't you gloriously happy?'

'He goes out a lot. I get lonely on Gozo. Nothing happens there.'

'Go out with him.'

Lottie shook her head.

Then when Lottie's sleeve rolled up a little, Riva noticed a bruise circling her wrist. Riva reached out a hand and her friend almost winced. 'How did you get that?'

'It's nothing. Forget it.'

'Surely Archie didn't do that?'

Tears filled Lottie's eyes.

Riva sighed. This was awful. 'Does he hurt you often?'

Lottie lowered her eyes and did not speak.

Riva wasn't sure what to say or do. 'Is there someone you can talk to?'

'God no!' Lottie exclaimed, looking mortified.

'Well, let's at least keep meeting for coffee like this, shall we?'

Lottie shook her head.

'What?'

'Archie wouldn't like it.'

'Well blow, that. Do you have to tell him? Does he tell you everything he does?'

Lottie laughed a bitter little laugh. 'He doesn't need to. He leaves plenty of clues.'

'Not other women?'

'Maybe.'

'Oh Lottie, I'm sorry.'

Two months passed by and Riva heard nothing from Bobby. She didn't have his address in England, just his old flat in London, which wasn't even his any more, and no other way to contact him. It didn't make sense, but surely Bobby would be back sooner or later? Or he'd write? Maybe he had already written but the letter had gone astray. She was sure he wouldn't just leave her like this. There had to be a good reason, although the longer it went on the harder it was to keep believing that. She threw herself into her work as a distraction. She still wasn't showing much, thank goodness, but worried constantly about what she was going to do. Thank heavens she had the work with Otto to occupy her when she wasn't dancing, and she was learning more and more as time went on.

She now knew that journalists, politicians, and various organisations had been campaigning against the traffic in women and children for some time. In 1927 the League of Nations had published a report detailing the way women were lured into the sex trade tempted, unbeknown by them, by false theatrical contracts to work as music hall artists. Riva logged every case she thought she saw of girls being brought in illegally and presented it to the chief of police who, she found out later, had immediately filed it in the bin. For all the noise the campaign had generated in England, nothing had changed in Malta.

One evening she was in the ladies' lavatory when the door flew open, and a man walked in.

'Wrong place,' she said, thinking he was a drunk. 'Yours is next door.'

He gave her a cold smile and took a step towards her. 'You listen to me,' he said. 'My boss wants you to stop interfering in his affairs.'

She tilted her head. 'Your boss? Who is your boss?'

Then, before she had a chance to scream, he was on

her. He covered her mouth with his hand and pinned her against a wall.

'My boss—' he began again, but she bit him. He removed his hand and rubbed it and then with his other hand he formed a fist and struck the side of her head. She stumbled and fell back against the wall.

'Take that as a warning,' he said as she straightened up.

She rubbed the side of her head.

'Got it?'

She nodded, feeling sick to her core. And in that moment, she decided to quit Strait Street altogether.

Two days later she met Otto at the British Hotel. He sat in the same quiet corner where they usually met but when she drew closer, she saw there was something wrong. He looked tired, but it was more than that.

'Are you all right, Otto?' she asked. 'You look a bit peaky.'

'I'm a bit under the weather. No big deal, I promise you.'

She narrowed her eyes. 'You're sure?'

He nodded. 'More to the point, how are you?'

She rubbed her head. 'A bit sore. Seen anything of Stanley Lucas?'

After they'd found out that Stanley Lucas had been released without further charge – despite the evidence of fraud and even more rumours of him living off immoral earnings – the man had seemed to disappear.

'Why do you ask?'

'I'm just wondering if he could be behind the man who threatened me,' she said.

'Maybe. Did you let the police know?'

She shook her head. 'No, but I'm leaving Strait Street. The thing is I haven't heard from Bobby and I'm thinking of going to England. I've had enough of dancing. I need a new start.'

'Look,' he said, seeming hesitant and dismayed at the same time. 'I've been wondering what to do about this.' He delved into his jacket pocket and drew out a newspaper cutting. 'I didn't know if you'd already seen it. Or what you might know. But from what you've said . . . well. You'd better read it.'

He unfolded it and then passed it to her.

She read the small item cut from an English newspaper and her heart almost stopped.

Sir Robert Beresford, Baronet, to marry blonde Texan oil heiress Joanna Walton in May 1930.

The waiter arrived with their customary high tea, but Otto waved him away. Riva's eyes stung, blurring with unshed tears. She rose to her feet and crashed her way out of the Hotel's tea rooms and into the street. It couldn't be true. She was carrying his child. He couldn't be doing this, not after their four years together. His eyes full of sincerity, he had told her he would always love her. She had believed him. He was her life. Had become her life. She became aware of Otto steering her by the elbow.

'Let's get away from here – is there anywhere you'd like to go?'

She nodded. 'Mdina. Can you take me there?'

He ushered her away from the crowds to where his car was parked. Numbly she got into the vehicle.

'Shall we stop to get your things?'

She shook her head. She just wanted to get away from Valletta, from Kalkara too, as quickly as she could before anyone could see her breaking down. After that he drove in silence. When they arrived at Mdina a little later, she said, 'Could you tell Gianni I won't be coming back to the club. He knows I'm planning on leaving anyway. Tell him I'm sorry.'

Otto opened the car door for her and she stumbled out.

'Can I do anything?'

'No,' she said. 'Thank you.'

He got back in and as she unlocked the huge front door, she knew she was going to be sick. She raced up the stairs to their apartment. *His* apartment. Then reached the bathroom just in time.

After she had splashed her face, she glanced in the mirror expecting the desolation to show. It didn't. She wandered into the bedroom and there on the bedside table was an envelope. She ripped it open and read four words. *I am so sorry.* That was all, followed by his name. She shredded the paper into tiny pieces and went out onto the terrace where she let them float away in the breeze.

So, he'd had time to come here and leave that pointless note. What a fool she'd been. He could never have married someone like her, a cabaret dancer for God's sake. But it hurt so much to know she would never be good enough. She'd given herself to him, trusted him, and he hadn't even had the grace to tell her himself.

She remembered all the nights they'd spent in this apartment and now she wouldn't be able to come here again. He would come here with his wife. *His wife.* It was unbearable. Worse than unbearable. Had she been wrong about what he'd felt? It had seemed so real, so true, the love they'd had. The ways they understood each other. All the little things. The newspaper must be mistaken, because if it were true, how could he not have told her himself?

As the sitting room became saturated with evening sunshine, she opened a bottle of wine and drank it all. Then she opened another and howled and howled while her heart broke over and over.

She wanted to hide in the apartment, in their bed, but eventually fell asleep on the sofa. That night she felt the first wrenching pains in her tummy. She ran to the bathroom and felt warm liquid trickle down between her thighs. In the brightly lit bathroom she saw the blood, touched it with her fingertips, and tried to wipe it away. But she couldn't. Too fast, it kept on coming. She wrapped her arms around her belly, panicking now, her heart galloping. No. Please no. The baby, *their* baby, was all that she had left of Bobby. She hadn't even known if she wanted it, but now? Yes. Yes. Now she wanted it with all her heart. Lying on the bathroom floor with a towel under her head, she drew her knees up to her chest as the cramps grew worse. It went on and on. Then later, as well as blood, she saw the first thick clots and she knew it was far too late. Everything was coming out of her, and she could do nothing to stop it. She wept, shocked, terrified, and feeling more alone than she had ever been before.

In the morning she felt hollowed out. She cleared up the blood, filled a bath, made a cup of tea, and then wrapped herself up in bed where she slept all day and most of the next night, where the shock, grief and loss could not reach her. Except that in her dreams they did. She didn't dream of the broken child who had so briefly been inside her and who hadn't even had a chance of life. Instead, she saw a little boy playing with a ball and a golden retriever puppy in the garden of a house. In England, she thought. A little boy who called her Maman. A little boy with blonde hair who looked just like Bobby.

With tears drying on her cheeks, she woke to the sound of the apartment door opening and went through. He was back.

'Bobby,' she called out and tried to stand but then fell onto the sofa as Addison entered the sitting room.

'I have coffee,' Addison said and scrutinised her. 'Heavens you are looking pale.'

'I . . .'

'No need to speak. Try to drink some coffee. I have aspirin too.'

'My head,' she muttered feebly. She couldn't tell him about the miscarriage, nor the pain in her belly, nor the awful mix of emotions that coursed through her in its aftermath. She felt numb, angry, sad, confused, all of those and all at once.

'No need to speak,' he said.

She sipped the coffee and Addison opened the terrace doors to let in some fresh air. She turned away from the bright light.

'You knew?' she eventually managed to say.

'No, but I saw the announcement in the newspaper. I was going to come and find you today. I wasn't sure if you knew.'

She shook her head.

'He didn't tell you?'

'Not a word.'

'It's a bad business. My nephew is a good man, and I've always loved him, but I'm afraid he can be something of a moral coward. Mark my words, this will be his damn mother's doing.'

'How so?'

'Already overspending, she then lost heavily in the Wall Street Crash. Needs Bobby to marry well to restore the family fortunes.'

'And he always does what she wants?' she muttered bitterly.

He shrugged.

'Are you affected by the crash too?'

He shook his head. 'Not me.'

She leant her head against the back of the sofa and felt as if she were falling into a deep hole. Despite the daylight her mind was thick with dark thoughts.

'Sit up,' he said. 'I don't want you to pass out.'

'I've left my job and my house. I don't know where to go.'

'You can stay here as long as you want.'

'What about Bobby and this woman? What if they come?'

'I've already written and told Bobby that he's to stay

away. Anyway, I have another idea that might interest you. We can talk about it when you're feeling a bit stronger. Do you think a spot of lunch later might help?'

She pulled a face.

'Well let's see. Just knock on my door if you need anything.'

'Thank you.'

He nodded slowly. 'You're a good girl, Riva. As I said, this is a bad business. You deserve better.'

Settling into a chair after he'd gone, she felt too numb to cry any more. She wanted their baby. She wanted Bobby. She wanted anything but being alone like this, she needed him to hold her and yet, if he tried right now, she'd probably kill him. Her thoughts roamed endlessly, snagged, roamed again, as she tried to figure out if she'd made a mistake without knowing it. How had it ended like this? Without her even realising it was coming. Should she have tried to control her temper? Had she missed the clues? Not guessed how much the crash would have affected him or his mother. He'd spoken of his mother's growing money worries, but it had never sounded serious, and she hadn't probed. Hadn't wanted to know. Perhaps if she'd asked him about it. And yet, although she tried to find ways to blame herself, it came to nothing. Bobby was marrying a rich girl because his mother needed him to. Perhaps this is what would have happened all along. Crash or no crash. He had never introduced her to his mother. Not once. That should have told her all she needed to know.

And in this place of endless silence another doubt took

hold, making her feel hot and panicky. What if Bobby actually loved this American girl? What if he'd never seriously been in love with Riva? She cried again, keening with a depth of sorrow she had never experienced before.

Consumed by memories of him she mourned the loss of their time together and the loss of their child. The days passed. Somehow. And then the weeks. Three of them. The longest and loneliest three weeks of her life. She thought about her parents, even worried about them, wondering what had happened after she left Paris. She felt sad about it all now, the way she'd left. But the truth was she felt sad about everything now. The narrative of her life had seemed so certain after she'd met Bobby. It had felt significant with a shape to it she understood. Now there was only turbulence and uncertainty.

Gradually anger took over from sorrow. She stormed around the apartment, thumped cushions, glared at her own reflection. How dare he dismiss her like this, set her aside, like an old unwanted pair of shoes? Well, she'd show him. She'd show them all. But inside the anger, a little voice was whispering. What on earth are you going to do now?

I don't know. I just don't know.

CHAPTER 33

Florence

Palermo, Sicily, September 1946

Florence finally stepped foot on Sicilian soil just over a year after the end of the war in the East. She had hoped to leave for Malta far sooner but the chaos following the German unconditional surrender in May 1945 and then the Japanese surrender in August, meant travel had been highly restricted. Florence had wanted to visit her sisters in France and with Jack's help had contacted the Foreign Office in London to ask about how to get there. She had been sternly warned against attempting it, as only diplomatic and military persons were currently advised to go. Visiting family was not considered vital given the dreadful conditions there.

Hélène had written about those conditions, too.

Florence had wept when she first read the letter but had brought it with her on the trip to Sicily, for on the back of it was a tiny line drawing Hélène had made of Élise nursing her baby. Florence took the letter out now to look at the drawing and then read it yet again.

My dear Florence,

It was lovely to hear from you but I have to tell you it would be most unwise to visit us. France is on its knees. People are sick and hungry, two thirds of our children have rickets, and it's heartbreaking to see many not even surviving childbirth. Everything is completely disrupted and it's impossible to get around except by bicycle as there are shortages of just about everything, including fuel for cars. We will have to rebuild everything and start from scratch. Despite the end of war, I find it hard not to feel bitter about how France has suffered.

Hundreds of thousands of buildings have been destroyed and we hear that industrial and agricultural production is running at less than half of what it was before the war. The appalling state of ports, railway tracks, roads, and bridges, means even our medical supplies are not reaching us. Doctor Hugo is beside himself with worry, and his wife Marie has still not been repatriated from London. In parts of the countryside the farmers barely know where it is safe to work because of the landmines.

For all these reasons I think it will be some time before you can safely visit us, or us you. Oh, my dear sister, we both miss you terribly as always, and send our

love. I hope you like the little drawing I made for you.
How is Jack? I was surprised to hear that he may be
going to Malta with you, and that you stayed on in
Devon so long, but Maman writes that by doing so
you've been able to save enough money for your travels.
I wish you luck in your search for Rosalie.
　　Hélène

Florence folded the letter and put it away, shaking her head, and brushing the tears away. Even though she'd read it several times hoping for something different, of course the words remained the same and she couldn't help feeling sad and worried for her sisters and for France.

Jack had managed to secure berths on a Royal Navy vessel delivering medicines and other supplies to Rome, Naples and Sicily, though not Malta. For Malta they would need a ferry from Syracuse.

She'd been thrilled to be going at last, but the journey had been slow and uncomfortable. The many metal staircases were narrow and slippery, and the deck always wet from sea spray, which meant it wasn't easy to get around the winches, coiled ropes and lifeboats lined up ready for use. There had been a smell of metal and tar, as well as the odd whiff you get from thick orange tarpaulin. The sea had seemed vast, and she'd been very seasick until she eventually found her sea legs. But she managed to enjoy the final few days, running her fingers over the salt on the ship's railings and feeling the wind in her hair. And at last she was making a start with her mother's request to find Rosalie.

As for Bruce, after he'd kissed her on the evening of VE Day she had realised that, much as she liked him – and she really did like him – she had not fallen in love with him, and knew she never would. She still loved Jack. So, she'd met Bruce to tell him they could only ever be friends and over the past year that's what they had been. He'd been the first among the people she knew to predict the Labour landslide in July 1945 and Churchill's failure to retain power.

And now Jack was going to have work in a place called Lipari, which turned out not to be on the Sicilian mainland at all but more remotely on one of Sicily's tiny Aeolian islands. Although she had longed to see Sicily, Florence had started to fret over how long it would be before she could go to Malta.

After arriving in Sicily and a few moments of gazing back at the sea, they heaved up their bulky canvas bags, walked away from the docks and into the hot, still air of the blazing town itself. Palermo sat in the plain of *Conca d'Oro* – the golden shell – surrounded by a semi-circle of purple mountains, although nothing much looked golden in the afternoon. Florence stared in shock, taking in the rubble piled up in the narrower streets of Palermo, the collapsed walls, the bullet-pocked plaster, the bombed remains of aristocratic houses the colour of soft pinkish cream.

Deeper into its dark passages the houses were either faded or crumbling and decayed, doors hanging at angles, red-tiled roofs absent. She hadn't seen London since the Blitz, although Jack had told her about it, but they'd sailed from Portsmouth and the bomb damage there had been enough. And, of course, she'd seen first-hand the damage an unexploded bomb could cause. Here in the ruined stony streets she coughed as the wind lifted the ochre dust to swirl in the air.

They reached a garden, where cypress and Judas trees gave way to the green of an orange grove. A few columns and arches stood undamaged, plus a building with the glass blown out from its windows but with intricate old ironwork still intact. From there the tall spires of the cathedral were visible too.

'It's awful to see this, Jack. It must have been so frightening.'

'I know. This was one of the loveliest cities in the world.'

'Until the war.'

He nodded. 'The carpet bombing of Palermo was designed to destroy the port, airfields, military bases, railway stations and so on but there's always civilian damage. And naturally that discouraged resistance when Allied troops finally invaded.'

Florence found herself almost speechless, imagining Malta must be in the same dreadful state. She had seen the horrors of the Nazis close up in France, but somehow seeing the terrible destruction brought home the scale of the world war.

'Come on,' Jack said. 'Give me your bag.'

'I can carry it.'

'Fine. But we need to get a move on before it gets dark. I don't think we'll get to Lipari tonight. What we need is a hotel, if such a thing still exists.'

They wandered on and he asked a few locals for directions. It seemed that along with his native English, Jack not only spoke French and German, but also had a smattering of Italian too.

'The trouble is,' he said as he shook his head, not always understanding the replies. 'The Sicilians don't exactly speak Italian. They virtually have their own language.'

Many of the people looked destitute, thin children ran about with no shoes and gaping holes in their ragged clothes and old ladies dressed in black sat with covered heads on stools outside what must have once been their homes. Donkeys roamed freely as did the dogs, all as thin as each other. A pitiful sight. Florence knew Sicily had a weighty history, heavy with the blood, sweat and tears of its people, she just hadn't expected to see quite so much of it now.

After questioning more locals, Jack found a pension that had once been a private villa.

The owner now was a widow called Margarita and when Jack asked if she had rooms, she laughed bitterly and swept an arm around her. 'See for yourself. Does it look like I have rooms?'

Jack did look. So did Florence.

'It's all right, Jack,' she said, 'let's just find somewhere else.'

A few locals were wandering in and out of the pension and, apparently not ready to give up, Jack frowned. 'Madam, if you do have any space, we can pay you well.'

Margarita narrowed her eyes and then she shrugged. 'Most of the wiring and plumbing has gone. My beautiful rooms . . . well you see for yourself.'

Jack and the woman agreed a price and she took them out into a garden with a large terrace. The scent of roses tumbling from a pergola took Florence by surprise. How, amid all this destruction, had it survived? Dazzling geraniums cascaded from pots as well and two broken stone benches sat either side of the terrace beneath a couple of palms. Margarita led them through a pint-sized orchard of gnarled olive trees to the end of the garden and a small barn that had no door. Florence felt hot, dirty and hungry but all she wanted was a bed.

'There is a well.' The woman pointed to one side. 'It is good water. So, there is your room.' She nodded at the barn. 'After the Germans, the Allies. Now only the homeless or destitute.'

She sighed heavily and left them to it.

Jack entered the barn first and turned to Florence. 'You okay to bivvy up here?'

'Sure. I don't mind straw for beds,' she replied, keeping up the appearance of being fine with them sharing the space but aware there was still a trace of awkwardness between them. 'Sheer luxury.'

'Are you sure? We can go elsewhere. There's bound to be something better.'

'I'm too tired, Jack. I just want to sleep.'

'I'll check out the well.'

She lay down on the straw relieved to be on dry land at last, but instead of falling instantly asleep there was too much going on in her mind and she lay awake wishing she could write it all down in her journal. Over the last year, she had begun to write a novel too, inspired by her life in the Dordogne, and she was itching to return to it. She sighed. It would have to wait and with that last thought she fell deeply asleep.

When she woke in the morning, she had to shade her eyes from the brilliance of the day. She glanced around the barn for Jack then went outside and saw he'd filled a pail of water and was chewing on what looked like a bun. 'Here,' he said and handed one to her. 'They're still warm.'

'Thank you. What is it – some kind of brioche?'

'Sicilian style, with almond paste inside.'

She took a mouthful and chewed. 'Delicious,' she said, savouring it.

'I have milk too. Goat's milk.'

He handed her a tin mug full of it.

She drank it rapidly.

'I can make myself scarce while you wash and change.' He pointed at the bucket of water. 'Did you sleep all right?'

'Like a baby.'

He wandered off and after a cursory wash she dug out a clean dress from her bag and dragged a brush through her tangled curls. When he came back, she began packing and said they'd better plan the day.

'We need to get a bus to Milazzo,' he said. 'There we'll find someone to take us across to a small port on Lipari. There are ferries, but none today.'

She straightened up. 'Can you never tell me anything about what you were doing while I was in Devon and you were away? Now that the war is over.'

'Still classified,' he said and pulled a face. 'But I *can* tell you I was working in association with the SIS and the Free French. And I was offered a job with MI6.'

'You turned it down?'

'I'm an architect, remember?'

She laughed. 'So you say. And I am still going to Malta to find Rosalie. You too, the minute you've finished here?'

'Absolutely but for now, let's just focus on the job in hand. I know so little about where we're headed. My friend Edward's place is on the north coast of Lipari but it's a tiny island so shouldn't be hard to find.'

'What does he want you to do?'

'Initially just to inspect the place for bomb damage. See if the place is still sound.'

'And then?'

'Well, I gather he has great plans for it although I don't yet know what, or if he'll hire me to be the architect.'

'Surely he wouldn't ask you if he wasn't going to use you?'

'Maybe. He's rich. Has property all over the world and before the war was developing a network of exclusive hotels.'

'The place must be big then?'

'It may just be his own place. He's being cagey. Wants me to get in touch when I know what's what.'

'Best figure out if the ferries have a timetable, then. For when we come back.'

The little fishing boat bobbed about on a dazzling azure sea and before long it was discharging them onto a narrow jetty. Florence clutched her canvas bag and smelt the salty seaweed air while Jack arranged for a cart to take them to their destination.

The island was dusty and mountainous. Dear God, she thought, as they set off, where has he brought me? Malta seemed further away than ever. The driver sat astride the donkey pulling the cart along a stony path – you couldn't call it a road – past the occasional bleak farmhouse. Then it rattled and jolted along narrower dirt trails that ran up and over the parched hills. All she could see were endless ochre crags rising higher and higher as they left the sea behind. The wind was alive, blowing dust into her eyes and she rubbed them, only making the stinging worse.

Jack noticed. 'You okay?'

She nodded but her spirits were sinking.

'Bad time of year,' he said over the noise of the wheels rolling and bumping over the stones. 'Dry. Looks greener in the north east.'

She turned away and kept her eyes closed. Would any time of year here be better?

They reached the peak of the mountain they'd been climbing and then began the descent through the sun-bleached landscape. She opened her eyes wide. 'Oh,' she said and drew in her breath at the sight of the sea. It seemed endless and such a deep violet blue.

He grinned to see her surprise.

They jolted down the hill and she saw volcanic cliffs plunging into the sea where brightly coloured fishing boats bobbed about.

'Should be plenty of fish,' Jack said.

'Man cannot live on fish alone,' she said and smiled at him.

They arrived at a long tree-lined track, road, she wasn't sure what, leading back towards the mountains again but flat here. She spotted a tanned workman in a long leather apron who waved at their driver. Could you call a man on a donkey a driver? The drive, she decided it was a drive, was now lined with sculptures on squat columns, some of them damaged, and then she saw it.

She whistled in amazement.

A mansion, for that is what it appeared to be, was coming into view.

The driver spoke in guttural Sicilian and Jack said. 'I think he's telling us it used to be a palace and, but for a housekeeper, it has been unoccupied for decades.'

The two-storey terracotta and cream building spread out before them in a long, high rectangle. She counted the first-floor windows, all with delicate wrought-iron railings. Ten? No. Twelve. At least twelve. All of them with their canvas blinds down but held away from the windows on rods at the bottom to allow air into the rooms.

The man steered the cart round to the side of the house which turned out to be the front.

Jack helped Florence climb down.

She felt suddenly exuberant, a feeling that had been absent for some time. Something important was waiting for her here, she knew it.

Florence looked up at the main doorway of the grand house. It was on the first floor with two large windows either side and surrounded by ornate stonework with a

balcony in front. From the balcony a staircase descended
on both sides curving to the front. Beneath the main door,
tall gates enclosed a huge archway. The stone of the
building shone like gold in the bright sunshine, purple
bougainvillaea crept up the walls and a strong scent of
lemons wafted in the aromatic air. Herbs too she thought,
certainly thyme, mint, rosemary. She inhaled deeply and
pinched her arm. Could this place be real? Behind the
house the volcanic mountain rose, magnificent, pink, hazy,
and when she turned the other way, she saw the smudge
of silvery sea glinting not far away.

Jack looked almost as surprised as she was.

'He didn't tell you?' she asked.

'He did not. This place is enormous.'

A woman in a faded black dress with a tiny white collar
and small bib apron came through the archway. She didn't
smile or speak but indicated they should follow her up
the stairs. She was tall and stick thin, with a grey plait
wound into a bun at the back of her neck and eyes as
black as midnight.

As she climbed the wide white steps Florence couldn't
wait to see inside but had to curb her impatience as the
woman moved so slowly it seemed as if her every joint
needed oiling. At the top she unlocked the bronze door
– oxidised by time or weather, or probably both, it had a
delicate patina of greenish blue. They entered a long room
with a dozen open windows along one side where cream-
coloured Italian lace curtains billowed in the breeze this
side of the blinds she'd seen on the outside. Florence saw
Jack's eyebrows rise, as awed by it as she, for it felt as if

they had been ushered into a world that had long gone. The room was pure nineteenth century, a place where the passing years had touched nothing. No electric lights – and she doubted there'd be running water – yet everything looked exquisite. Dark carved furniture and chairs upholstered in a striped gold fabric. Candelabra on the side tables and the most stunning tiled floor she had ever seen in intricate Arabic patterns of blue, ochre, white and terracotta.

'Incredible,' Jack muttered. 'Completely intact.'

He glanced up, whistled and she followed his gaze to a frescoed ceiling where cherubs danced among the clouds.

The past was all around her, and the spirits of the past too. She heard whispering and the ringing of a ghostly bell. She pictured the people who'd lived there, and they didn't seem gone. Not gone at all. Had they just slipped out for a minute? Maybe headed off to the beach with a picnic, returning at any moment to wonder what these travellers from another age were doing in their home? She could hear the whoosh of the distant sea and felt an uncomfortable shiver. There was something menacing in the air, and she felt the spirits here were not the happy kind.

The housekeeper smiled grimly and spoke to Jack.

'What?' Florence asked.

'She says her name is Claudia and we are to follow her to our rooms.'

They passed a few rooms where open doors revealed furniture covered in dust sheets and at the end Claudia showed them two rooms, one on either side of the corridor. He glanced in both then tilted his head at her.

'Choice is yours, Florence.'

The rooms were identical save for the fact that one looked out at the mountain, which seemed incredibly close, and the other faced the sea. She dithered, drawn by the mountain and yet it was . . . intimidating? Ominous even? Still, despite that, she pointed to the mountain side.

'You're sure? You wouldn't rather have the sea? It's lighter.'

She looked and shook her head. 'I'm sure.'

Claudia spoke to him again and he translated for Florence. 'She says she will take care of all the meals, and she has a letter for me.'

'Really? How come?'

He shrugged. 'Search me. She's gone to fetch it now.'

The woman had left the room while Jack was talking and returned now with a white envelope with his name scrawled on it. He put down their bags, tore it open and read.

'Who is it from?' Florence asked, curious.

'Edward, the one who owns this place. He's already in Sicily.'

'Coming here?'

'No, I'm to go to him at his place in Donnafugata apparently, take my report with me.'

'Has he asked you to take charge of restoration?'

'No. He only wants an honest view of its condition before he goes any further.'

'How long before we can go to Malta?'

'It'll take a while to survey this place properly and then to see him about it.'

Florence fingered the silver charm bracelet she wore round her wrist and remembered her mother's strangely bright eyes as she'd given it to her. She had seen how thin Claudette had been then, had felt it when she'd hugged her, but when she'd asked, her mother had grown impatient. 'I'm absolutely fine,' she'd said.

She had hoped Claudette would visit her in Devon before they left for Sicily, and in fact a visit had been planned, but when the time came, her mother had written to say she had a touch of flu, nothing serious, and couldn't make the trip. She thought of Rosalie and of her mother. How must it feel not to have seen each other for twenty years? It was unimaginable not to see your sister for so long and she wished she could tell Claudette how close she was to Malta now.

CHAPTER 34

While Jack worked, measuring, checking, examining, Florence wandered the estate but didn't dare go too far afield. Something about the unyielding little island disturbed her and she felt she needed to stay in the vicinity of the house. So she reached for her notebook and began to write notes for her novel. She often watched the mountain changing colour, purple, blue, green, grey, even ochre, depending on the light, but there were times when her skin crawled, and she felt its malevolence. People had died on that mountain and in this house; she was sure of it and their deaths had been violent.

She had not seen even a glimmer of another person but for the same driver of the donkey and cart, and he'd only come by to make a delivery. She listened to the plaintive sound of the sea and wind and felt again that something was waiting for her here, although what it was seemed no clearer than it had been before. She picked flowers, heavenly scented roses, and pungent bunches of herbs which she dotted about the place. It should have been paradise but there was no birdsong and there was something awfully forbidding about that. The mountain was too imposing and the house too still, as if all the life had been stolen from it. Discordant notes rang in her head. Bells, whistles, and a shrill high-pitched ringing. She didn't feel safe and tiptoed around the house dreading that someone might be about to leap out of the shadows and carry her off. She felt that phantom people were calling out for rescue, their voices drifting in with the sea breezes. As she looked around, she could almost feel their sadness, their pain, their trauma, and it scared her. Yes, it was beautiful here in a way, but also chilling and she felt as trapped as the people who had once lived here must have been. And when Jack had asked the housekeeper about what had happened to them, the woman wouldn't say.

When Florence told Jack she felt disturbed by the menacing atmosphere in and around the house, he said, 'We'll be gone soon. I agree it's atmospheric, but there's nothing to worry about. It's just your imagination.'

She knew it was not.

The days slid into each other and at the end of the first week he declared a day off.

'I have a surprise,' he said. 'I've organised us a boat. Well, it's a dinghy, really, but Claudia has made us some lunch to take.'

'She likes you.'

He laughed. 'She knows you won't understand a word she says, so she speaks to me.'

'She speaks to you because you are the man.'

He pulled a face. 'And terribly important,' he said in a mock-pompous voice.

She shook her head. 'Idiot.'

'Well, this idiot would like to invite mademoiselle on a little boat trip, and it needs to be today while the weather holds.'

She was happy to leave the house, although she usually loved old things, forgotten things that left a trace of what had gone before. In France she'd searched the local book-shops for out-of-print cookery books and gardening manuals. As a child it had been fairy tales. In Devon she had become a hoarder of ribbons, string, safety pins, buckles, pencils, hair clips and so on. But this old palace was different. There were bullet holes in the walls at the back of the house, and whatever had happened she felt it still there.

After crossing the island and once settled in the dinghy with its Johnson outboard motor, they chugged south-wards from Marina Corta. The flat areas they passed soon gave way to jagged hilltops.

After a while she spotted a beach. 'We could swim there,' she called above the sound of the waves and the motor.

'Let's see what else there is first. We can always come back.'

They continued past immense cliffs falling sheer into the glittering sea, then a promontory where the lava had formed an arch. More low cliffs, and then higher cliffs, and after that then a shingle beach, totally deserted.

Further on a stunning stretch of coastline with tiny islands, caves, coves, and copper-coloured cliffs with the purple mountain rising above.

'This is the best yet,' she said.

And then they found it. A tiny sheltered beach behind a cliff where he moored the boat and they clambered out.

Despite the sea breezes Florence was hot and sticky but the air was filled with the scent of pine and euca-lyptus from just a couple of trees. Mixed with the salt of the ocean and the baking sand, it felt good, and with a rush of pleasure, she stripped down to her underwear and hurled herself into the sea. It was not cold, so she splashed and shrieked and then swam for what felt like miles and miles.

Jack had already come out of the water and was exam-ining their lunch. The day had grown brighter, the sky lemony and the sea was tinged with depths of purple.

'Come on,' he called when he saw her swimming back. 'Lunch.'

'Sky's a funny colour,' she said, looking up. 'Is it all right?'

'I should think so.'

Invigorated, she shook herself and sat down on a rock to dry herself in the sun.

He took out a few packages wrapped in waxed paper. 'Cheese, I think,' he said and unwrapped it. 'Here. Pecorino flavoured with peppercorns.'

She picked out a larger packet. 'This one is bread.' She broke a piece off and handed it to him.

'Have you had enough cheese?'

'Yes. It's a bit salty.'

'Aha!' he said. 'I spy salami. Already sliced.'

He passed her a couple of slices and she sniffed it. 'A mix, I think, of pork and lean beef. She took a bite. 'Gorgeous. Really chewy.'

'There are some tomatoes too, and wine.'

'It'll send me to sleep if I drink wine.'

When they'd finished their lunch, and the wine, Jack lay back with his hands behind his head and his breathing instantly slowed.

Florence went in search of some shade, getting a little wet as she clambered over the still water in the weather-worn rock pools, picking her way carefully over the rocks but grazing her knee a little. She found a craggy inlet with a small cave that seemed ideal. If she nodded off in the midday sun she'd get a headache, but this shade was perfect, and it would be lovely to fall asleep to the gentle rhythm of the sea.

Later, when she woke, she heard Jack calling her name through the rising sounds of a storm. She rose to her feet and realised that the sea had swollen while she had been sleeping, and waves were now smashing against the rocks. She couldn't work out how to reach the beach where Jack had been without clambering right into the swirling water which she feared might sweep her away. She couldn't even see Jack as she stared at the sea, nor the little boat either. Huge waves were battering the cliffs, foaming as they leapt into the air and the ominous violet sky was shifting to black. She stood on a section of rock pushing her back hard against the cliff face to stop herself slipping. She shouted his name, but the wind whipped her voice away. Her heart thumped. This did not look good.

Maybe the water wouldn't fill the cave and she could just wait it out. The sand felt quite dry at the back of it. But really, she had no idea. She shouted for Jack again. Nothing.

She glanced up to see if there might be another way to get out and saw him standing on a rock many feet above and to the side of her staring grimly at the water. She flapped her arms to attract his attention. He spotted her and she could see the relief flooding his face.

'Wait there,' he said. 'I'm coming down.'

Her heart lurched as he began to descend, slipping and sliding on crumbling rocks that gave way beneath his feet. Even if he does reach me, she thought, how are we ever going to crawl back up there again battered by this torrent?

The wind shrieked and the water began spinning at the cave's entrance. She'd never be able to get past this. Beyond her the sea was growing even wilder. She heard the pounding waves and the crack of thunder, the noise so loud she could hardly think. And then she saw Jack had reached her, was leaning over the cave's entrance from above and holding out his hand.

'Come on,' she managed to hear him shout. 'Come on. Now. We don't have long.'

She would have to take a leap of faith. Jump to reach his hand. But if she missed, she'd be in the water and dragged away in moments. Even Jack couldn't save her from that.

Scared to move, but also scared not to move, she took

a breath as he yelled at her to hurry. Her heart almost stopped as she stretched out and leapt and then, oh God, she felt his hands grasping hers. He began to haul her up. She scraped her flesh against the rocks and could barely breathe for fear of Jack losing his grip. But he did not and when he finally dragged her over the top, they lay together panting, exhausted from the effort. The storm seemed to pause too.

After a while he rose to his feet and helped her up, but then the wind redoubled with the force of a cyclone.

'Keep low. It will be all right if we zigzag our way. Try to feel for footholds.'

She nodded and saw what he meant. But she couldn't feel any part of her body, let alone her feet.

When they finally reached a slightly flatter patch they rested again for a moment, and he pointed a little further up. 'There's a hut. We'll head for it and sit out the storm.'

They staggered on through driving wind and rain while concentrating on not missing their footing on the shifting stones and feeling that it would never end. But then, at last, they reached the hut. He pushed open the door of the little weather-beaten place and they both fell into it, shivering but amazed that they'd made it.

'Jesus, Florence,' he managed to say, gasping for breath. And she saw that Jack, a man not given to shock, was shaken.

'I'm . . . so . . . sorry,' she tried to say, all her strength spent.

He wrapped his arms around her. 'You gave me a fright.'

'I gave myself a fright.'

She heard the rolling sea, the waves thundering against the cliffs and the rain beating on the tin roof and stumbled into a corner where her legs gave way. Like a rag doll, she collapsed onto some blankets that smelt as if they had been there for years.

He sat next to her, knees drawn up. Neither spoke and Florence fell into a kind of stupor.

Sometime later she roused herself to find the noise of the storm receding – just the hum and thump of the water now – and Jack had lit a candle.

'Lucky the first match wasn't damp,' he said.

'Lucky?'

He gave a grim little laugh. 'I found it in here along with the candle. Only one in the box. The gods were on our side.'

'A miracle then.'

Another grim laugh, but she heard something else in the laugh. Fear maybe?

After that the conversation fizzled out and there was a long silence. He held her close, and she could feel his heart beating. While out in the storm she had felt the wind behind her back driving her. Propelling her. She had felt terrified that she was about to die. But now all that was making her think, making her feel, forcing her to speak her mind.

'You shut yourself off from me, Jack, from life,' she suddenly burst out. 'Why?'

'What?'

He sounded irritated. Nevertheless, she continued. 'After what we both just went through, I must ask. We are connected. Be honest. You know we are and yet you keep denying it.'

'I haven't said a word.'

'Does it need words?'

'I don't understand you.'

'Oh, but you do. You keep me at arm's length. What are you so frightened of?'

'That was a confrontation with death today,' he said, sounding exasperated. 'That's what I was frightened of.'

'No, that isn't true, you aren't scared of dying. It isn't that. What you're scared of is living.'

He drew away from her in silence, the atmosphere tense. He didn't reply immediately, then he said, 'Can we just drop it, Florence?'

'What are you avoiding, Jack?'

He snorted. 'You have no idea.'

'Then tell me,' she said, raising her voice.

She heard his sharp intake of breath. 'Very well. You're right. I wasn't scared of dying. I was scared of *you* dying.'

'Me?'

'You are my responsibility,' he said, his voice catching.

That's it, she thought. That's it. 'You're still holding so much pain inside you,' she said almost to herself.

He didn't speak for a moment. When he did his voice was ragged and deep. 'I didn't keep my little boy safe. And I didn't keep you safe from the BNA men who raped you.'

She heard the anguish and longed to make him feel better, but sensing he was on the verge of telling her everything, she kept quiet.

'The loss of a child is indescribable.' He paused for a

moment and when he spoke again there was a tremor in his voice. 'It was my job . . . but I couldn't protect him.'

Her heart twisted and she ached to reach out to him but he carried on speaking so she simply listened.

'I can't allow myself to love, Florence, do you see? I did not deserve the child I lost. When Charlie died, I reached the end of the line. I could never endure grief like that again.'

'Oh Jack.'

She heard him sob and then suddenly he was weeping and taking great gulping breaths. She did not try to stop him and felt her own eyes grow damp. Had he ever cried about the loss like this? She doubted it. Men like Jack rarely cried.

She stroked his back and after a while, still shuddering, he ran a hand over his wet cheeks. 'Sorry.'

She didn't speak but reached for his hand.

'Hélène once asked me if I wanted a family,' he said.

'What did you tell her?'

'I wanted to tell her the truth but being in France was my only escape. If I spoke of what had happened while I was there . . . well, it was impossible. I just told her I couldn't think of it.'

'It was the truth.'

'Yes. But I did feel I'd short-changed her.'

She hugged him close. 'You can move beyond this.'

He shook his head and spoke very quietly. 'Florence, I just don't know how.'

'It wasn't the same thing, of course, but after the rape I discovered that unbearable pain can pass through you without destroying you. Little by little you let it in, feel it, and it passes.'

'Does it?'

'Yes, and that's how you learn to live again. In the middle of something that seems so impossible there can be peace. Moments only, but peace all the same and they grow longer. But if you spend your life suppressing the pain it really will destroy you.'

'You know I love you, Florence.'

'Yes . . . I do. And I know you've been trying not to.'

'Will you help me?'

She blinked hard, wanting to cry herself. 'Of course. Of course I will. Only you can do it, but you don't have to do it alone. I'll be there, Jack. I'll always be there.'

He nodded.

'And you know, everything passes, everything, no matter how loved or how precious. We all live with that knowledge. It's life. And yet we still have the courage to love knowing that one day that same love will break our hearts.'

And then he kissed her. Properly. Longingly. Passionately.

CHAPTER 35

Riva

Malta, 1930

It was Addison who saved her, Addison who got her back on her feet after she recovered from losing the baby and it became clear Bobby was never coming back . . . Addison who, several weeks after she tore up Bobby's note, came to her door and asked her to accompany him although he didn't specify where to.

She had been listening to the radio where the news was still all about the Wall Street Crash the year before and the ongoing global economic depression. Millions were unemployed, hungry, and desperate and in Germany people were turning to the Nazi party for a cure. While it was clear that peace was fragile, it seemed far enough away not to be a problem for Riva, and she'd rather be listening to the news from afar than having to face the real world outside her front door.

Rather unwillingly she followed Addison out of the apartment, along the corridor and then down the main stairs.

'Where are we going?' she asked.

He half turned back to look at her, his eyes sparkling. 'You'll see.'

'You know I don't really want to leave the house yet.'

He laughed. 'You won't have to. I promise.'

When they reached the ground floor and the grand hallway, he crossed it and unlocked a small door opposite the stairs. She had no idea how much he was opening a door to a different future, had just assumed it was a cupboard of some sort, but he asked her to follow him along a narrow dark corridor.

'Good grief, Addison, are you going to hide me away in a dungeon until I grow old and grey?'

He laughed again and at the end of the corridor, opened another door. She shaded her eyes at the blinding sunlight that flooded in.

'Come on,' he said, and stepped outside.

She glanced out and then, as her eyes adjusted, walked into the prettiest courtyard garden she had ever seen. She heard the gentle trickle of a fountain set right in the middle, surrounded by flowers that grew out of blue enamel pots and roses that climbed the surrounding walls. An Arabic-looking archway on the opposite side led to what looked like a covered alcove.

'My Moroccan garden,' he said. 'My wife and I went

to Marrakech on our honeymoon, and I promised her I would build her one.'

'Did she love it?'

He shook his head. 'Filomena died before I got round to doing it. So many things I should have done and then it was too late.'

She glanced at the pretty jewel-like colours of the tiled floor – blue, white, ochre and turquoise. They surrounded the cup-shaped fountain and also rose halfway up the walls while patterned terracotta tiles paved the edges of the courtyard where two rectangular sections had been planted with orange trees. The sight of it lifted her heart. Over by the archway two giant palms in terracotta pots stood sentinel like exotic birds, their wings stretched out either side as if ready to take flight. She detected a scent that seemed to waft all around her.

'What?' she asked, sniffing the air.

He smiled and pointed at some white blooms that grew around the fountain. 'Angel's trumpets.'

'The scent is heavenly.'

'It's good to see you looking happier,' he said.

'How could I not? This is paradise.'

'And that's plumbago,' he said, glancing over at the archway. 'I trained it to shade the alcove beyond. It's an evergreen.'

'You did the work here?'

'Some of it . . . until my arthritis got the better of me.'

'Oh, I'm sorry, I didn't realise.'

He grinned. 'Well, it may surprise you to know that I am in my late seventies. I don't usually admit it. Either way, the arthritis is creeping, hips, spine and so on, but the worst thing is that it's happening in my fingers and wrists.'

'Can I do anything to help?'

He seemed to study her face before saying, 'Maybe.'

Absorbed by her thoughts, she hung back as he headed for the archway where a white sofa with pretty patterned cushions sat in the shady alcove. She glanced back at the garden and inhaled the scent again, but Addison turned right and opened another door.

'This place is a rabbit warren,' she said.

'More than you realise.'

They entered a small and rather gloomy hall which opened onto a bedroom and a bathroom, both painted a pinkish terracotta but with high windows from which you could only see the sky. He flicked a switch and a lamp burst into light, making the walls glow as if lit from within, and she saw an embroidered Moroccan wall hanging behind the bed.

'Oh,' she said. 'How lovely.'

'I bought that in Marrakech. As you know the electricity on the island is limited so a part of this little place is lit only by oil lamps. We'll go up now,' he said.

Back in the hall she saw a spiral staircase in the corner. 'I didn't spot that before.'

'I hadn't turned the light on. You go first.'

She climbed the stairs which led straight into a large bright kitchen with a dining table at one end. She felt puzzled by this charming, but odd, little upside-down house.

'There's a refrigerator,' he boasted. 'American of course, made by General Electric. Carry on up.'

She did and when she reached the top she gazed around in surprise. A spacious, high-ceilinged sitting room decorated in the palest blues and greens overlooked the landscape of Malta. Delicate silk scarves hung over two large lamps. Strings of silvery beads hung from a mirror and embroidered cushions were stacked up on a navy blue sofa. There was no large terrace beyond, just double glass doors that opened onto a balcony just big enough for one small cast iron table and two chairs with a tiny pergola above them for shade.

'Do you like it?'

She smiled. 'I adore it. But it's so odd. I've never seen a house with just one room on each floor.'

'I've arranged for coffee and pastries if you'd like to follow me.'

On one side of the sitting room there was a wall with just one door in it and no windows. He unlocked it and she followed. There was a small gap and then another door.

'There's more?'

'No. This is my apartment, and we,' he pushed the door open, 'are in my study. Come on through.'

'I never expected that.'

They made their way on to his balustraded terrace where a table was already laid with a coffee pot, two cups and saucers and a plate of delicious-looking pastries.

'Help yourself,' he said.

She poured the coffee, selected two pastries and tucked

in. It was the first time she hadn't had to force herself to eat for weeks.

When she'd finished, he asked if she'd like to hear the story of the little apartment, he'd just shown her.

She nodded but thought of it more as a little house.

'This palace is a labyrinth, like many of the others here, but it was some time before I discovered all its secrets. The door we just came through into my study had been bricked up, and for a long while I hadn't the slightest idea.'

'Why was it bricked up?'

'Well, it could have once been a priest hole. But I think smugglers more likely. Contraband.'

'How did you discover the doorway?'

'A bird had got in. I heard the awful flapping noises. As you know the palace is built into the exterior walls of Mdina and of course, from the distance, I could see the little balcony, but assumed it was part of the building next door but when I asked, he said there was no sign of a trapped bird in his place.'

'How thrilling. Like one of those dreams when your house has entire wings you never knew about and you wake up excited and it's so disappointing when you realise it's not true.'

'I'd say those dreams are hinting at something.'

'What?'

'Perhaps that there's more to you than you currently understand and whole possibilities you've never even imagined.'

She smiled. 'Hope you're right . . . Please go on.'

'Well, I quickly hired an architect who worked out that

there was most probably a connection via my study. You should have seen the place when the builder broke through. Yeasty. Mouldy.'

'So when did you restore the apartment?'

'Oh, not for ages. But then I had the strangest feeling that it would be needed.'

'Really? By whom?' she asked and noticed he was staring intently at her.

'Well as it turns out, you, my dear. You.'

She blinked rapidly, not understanding.

'I can see that staying in Bobby's apartment isn't ideal for you. The hidden little upside-down house in the palace walls is empty. If you like it.'

'I love it,' she said, astonished. 'But I can't stay here. I need to work, earn a living.'

He held up one finger. 'Ah well, I have thought of that too. Throughout my life I've written journals and, believe it or not, poetry. And now a British publisher is going to publish my memoirs.'

'So, not only an artist.'

'Writing was my first love, but I failed to make any money. Besides, painting came more easily, although once I married money was no longer an issue.'

'And you carried on painting.'

'Not right away. But you can't make another person your purpose in life. I found that out when Filomena died.'

She gave him a sympathetic look.

'So yes, after she died, I carried on painting, and I did do rather well. But now my fingers are stiff with arthritis and my publisher is coming over in a couple of months to see how far I've got.' He raised his hands hopelessly. 'I urgently need someone to help me choose and collate. Someone I like.'

She could feel her mouth falling open in surprise. 'Me? I . . .'

'Don't decide straight away. Mull it over. I would pay you, of course, and I think it might take six months or so. Something like that. You can use my automobile if you need to get about.'

'I don't drive.'

'Easily sorted.'

'My typing isn't brilliant either. My mother forced me to take classes, but a trained secretary might suit you better.'

He shook his head. 'I need someone I trust, someone with the right heart for the job and I think it might help you too.'

'I'm touched you think so. But . . . well . . . the thing is, I don't know how to tell you this but I'm not who you think I am.'

He smiled indulgently and patted her hand. 'My dear girl. I know who you are. You are Rosalie Delacroix, from Paris.'

Hearing her real name, tears stung Riva's eyes, but she managed to stop them falling.

'Don't blame Bobby for telling me. Not for that anyway. I wheedled it out of him. And I have news about your family, too.'

Her hand flew to her mouth.

He told her there had been a high-profile police

investigation, but it transpired the entire thing had been a swindle. There had been no fraud, although her father's hidden addiction to gambling had been exposed. He lost his job because of it, and because of that and his debts, they had been forced to sell the Paris apartment and her mother's jewellery. They then moved to a small town in the countryside where they lived a much-reduced quiet life. Riva was relieved her father hadn't gone to prison but felt desperately sad to think of his humiliation. And now, thinking of the life and people she'd left behind, the tears did fall.

CHAPTER 36

Malta, several months later

Riva hadn't needed time to think about Addison's offer and accepted it the day after he brought it up. She had put her work for Otto on pause but expected to resume at a later stage. Now the lovely little apartment had become her solace and the work she was doing with Addison her respite. All the time she'd been staying in Bobby's apartment she had dreaded he might turn up with his American girl, despite his uncle's warning to keep away. She had buried the grief over her lost baby; it hurt too much. And now she was living in her little upside-down house, doing her best not to dwell on Bobby's betrayal. She still missed him though, still felt the crushing grief, the inconsolable loss, the memories, the anger. Never again would she wake up next to him and yet he was not dead, only lost to her.

She dressed carefully in a navy cotton dress and slipped into white high heels, wanting to make a good impression on Addison's publisher, Gerard Macmillan. She wasn't sure what to do about her hair. The dye was fading rapidly, and she had decided to go back to her natural bright red, but you could still see a dividing line. She found a blue and red scarf among her things and tied it turban-style round her head, grimaced as she looked in the mirror, added some red lipstick, then rubbed it off again. She wanted to look serious, not like a cabaret dancer from Strait Street.

Later, as she walked into Addison's study after knocking on the door that divided his apartment from hers, he looked up at once and smiled.

'Will I do?' she asked, still feeling dubious.

'Darling girl, you always look beautiful. Coffee?'

She nodded.

He rose and went to call the butler who brought them both coffee a few minutes later.

'We don't have long, because I need you to pick Gerard up.'

'Oh God. Really?'

'Think you can do it?'

She tipped her head and grinned at him.

A little later she set off in Addison's beautiful car, petrified she might crash it, but determined to prove she could be trusted. Every day he'd taken her out for lessons along the quiet lanes in the countryside around Mdina and she had regularly driven to the nearby town of Rabat to buy groceries. This was the first time she had driven to Valletta harbour.

As she neared the city, she grew more uneasy. The harbour was as hectic as ever, but she spotted Mr Macmillan immediately. A tall, pale, lean man of about thirty-five, he was dressed in a cream linen suit with a white shirt and blue tie. He wore a light panama hat, plus round, thin-framed black spectacles and was shading his eyes from the glare and blinking in what Riva thought must be surprise. She recalled how she had felt about the bustle and noise when she'd first arrived and hurried forward to greet him.

After she introduced herself, trying to look more in control than she felt, he shook her hand vigorously and they walked to the car where he hauled in his tan-coloured leather case.

'N . . . nice motor,' he said, and she noted the very slight stammer in his voice.

'Addison's.'

'And have you been driving long?'

'Not long,' she said breezily, hoping not to reveal how tense she was feeling, not so much because of the driving now, but because this man had come to evaluate Addison's work, her work too, and would be with them for a fortnight.

Together with Addison she had spent hours going through the endless brass-handled drawers of three floor-to-ceiling mahogany chests in which he kept his writing.

'I had them made especially,' he'd said. 'The chests.'

She'd sorted through his journals and poetry, line drawings too, and had been overwhelmed by how moving his words often were, especially when they concerned his late wife. She'd frequently felt tears forming and was protective about the work, hoping this Macmillan man wasn't going to pull it all apart. The trouble was there was far too much material for one memoir, and they needed the publisher's help.

On the journey back along the bumpy country roads they exchanged a few words about London and the economic situation. She recited a list of the invaders and settlers Malta had endured, Phoenician, Arabic, Italian, French and British, soon arriving at the point where the umbrella pines on either side over the road pointed the way to Mdina. 'Here we are, Mr Macmillan,' she said a few minutes later as they drove through the massive entrance gate into the ancient city.

'Oh, please c . . . call me Gerard. Gerry actually, if you don't mind.'

She parked and after they got out, Gerard looked around him. 'Well, I'm stunned. I had no idea it would be so beautiful. I knew it would be impressive but this . . .'

Gerry, as he kept on insisting she call him, turned out to be a mild-mannered man with an unexpected grin which lit up his light blue eyes. He was polite and diplomatic and as the hours went by, he gently steered Addison in the direction in which he wanted the book to go.

'The thing is,' he said, 'we need to settle on the story.'

'Story,' Addison stiffly replied. 'This is my life, not a novel.'

'All the same, your readers will want a story. We want

a story too and I suppose it's which story you choose to tell that's the tricky question.'

Addison huffed and puffed. 'Not sure I'm with you, old man.'

'Well, for example, is it a love story?'

Addison muttered something Riva didn't quite hear but felt sure he must have been cursing.

'Or is it a story about finding one's feet as an artist. Or is it more about the shows you've mounted all over the world?'

Addison looked uncertain and after Gerry had gone for a walk to give them time alone to talk, Addison asked her what she thought.

'Truth?'

'Truth.'

'I think the most affecting story is the love story. People will want to know how you found the love of your life, how you lost her, and how you survived to become the most generous, kind-hearted man I have ever known.'

'Oh my dear,' he said, and she could see he had tears in his eyes.

And thus it was decided, although Addison didn't give in for another two days, during which time he persuaded Riva to show Gerry the island of Malta.

But before going further afield she led him around the city of Mdina.

'Its medieval name was *Notabile*: the noble city,' she said as he contemplated the silent streets. 'Mdina's noble families who live in these palaces are descendants of the Norman, Sicilian and Spanish overlords who built it.'

'It's extraordinary,' he said. 'Timeless.'

'It's not all beauty. There are dungeons beneath at least one of the palaces.'

'Sounds intriguing.'

'Addison has books about them. What they were used for and so on. Torture chambers mainly, from what I've read. During the Roman era, Malta was a slave colony, but the tortures went on throughout time, even during the French Occupation.'

While Gerry marvelled, the streets reminded Riva of Bobby. She felt as if she might turn around and see him smiling at her, her heart lifting and then lurching when she understood it would not happen. Could not happen. If she ever saw him here, he would not be smiling, and neither would she.

'Shall we get out of the city now?' she suggested. 'I can show you St Paul's Cathedral another time. You can't miss its red-and-white striped dome.'

She took Gerry to Ħaġar Qim, the prehistoric temple complex situated on a ridge on the southern edge of the island, where they walked around for half an hour. After that they drove to the village of Qrendi, where they found a coffee shop and then went further south to the caves.

'You can see something of them from high up on the cliff,' she said. 'We just need to walk a little. Though the best way is to take a boat out.'

She didn't mention that Bobby had hired a boat and shown her caves and the amazing blue sea, and she fell silent.

'Anything wrong?' Gerry asked, after a while.

She swallowed and shook her head.

They walked on and looked down from the cliffs, Gerry blinking behind his glasses.

'Maybe tomorrow we can go to the Dingli cliffs,' she said. 'They're my favourite.'

'I'm hoping that tomorrow we can get back to work.'

'Of course.'

'I didn't mean to sound brusque.' He paused. 'Look, I can see something is wrong. Is there anything I can do? I'm a good listener.'

In fact, that evening turned out to be the time Riva did talk. After a late supper, Addison rose to his feet and yawned. 'I'm going to call it a night, but feel free to take a bottle of wine and this charming young man to your apartment, Riva. I will see you both in the morning.'

'You don't have to come with me,' Riva said, once Addison had gone. 'But I'd better go. It's just Addison's way of saying he wants some peace and the apartment to himself. Sifting through his memories of his wife must be emotionally exhausting.'

'I'd like to come with you,' Gerry said, glancing at his leather-strapped wristwatch. 'If you don't mind. It's only ten.'

After that she could hardly say no, so nodded but found Addison had locked the study door to her apartment. He always kept the key with him, so they would have to go down the stairs and into her apartment from the hall and the little Moroccan garden.

She led Gerry there, but when she unlocked her door,

she immediately saw she'd left the bedroom door open and the lamp on. Apart from the waste of electricity, it plainly looked like an invitation. He took hold of her hand very carefully and studied her eyes, as if working out what she expected of him. When he smiled, she knew immediately and nodded.

He bent to kiss her gently and afterwards she tried to speak. He put a finger to her lips then removed the scarf from her hair. She'd worn a different one every day.

'I've been wondering about your hair. Why do you hide these gorgeous curls?' he said, running his fingers through them.

'I'm growing the black colour out.'

'It's almost gone. Your red hair is glorious.' After a moment he added, 'Riva, Addison put me in the picture about his nephew, Robert.'

She suddenly felt vulnerable, more unsure than she had been.

'Only if you want to,' he said, glancing at the bed. 'No strings.'

Instantly she knew this had been Addison's doing. He wanted her to get over Bobby and thought this kind, gentle man might help her. Addison had known all along he was going to go with the love story.

She began to laugh. At Addison's boldness, at his audacity, at his wisdom.

Gerry smiled. 'What?'

'Did Addison ask you to make love to me?'

He shook his head. 'No. For Christ's sake. No. He only said you might need a bit of cheering up.'

'Oh my God. He's such a wily old man.'

'So?'

She laughed again. 'What can I say but welcome to my boudoir.'

The sex was not the same as it had been with Bobby. It was sensitive, caring, and more careful. There was none of the wild animalistic passion and it was not driven by a deep-rooted desire to possess or the ravenous longing to become one being. But it was nice. Really nice. He clearly knew what he was doing and left her in no danger of becoming pregnant.

'Tell me about you,' she said, intrigued.

'Well, Yvonne, my wife, she's French. Taught me every-thing I know.'

'You're married?'

'In name only. She didn't like England, headed back to the sunlit lands of Provence after the war, taking our son with her. Her family are perfumiers and own lavender fields near Greoux-les-Bains in Provence, but my work . . . it's in London.'

'You must miss them.'

'I miss my son.'

There was a short silence.

'Look,' she said. 'I just need to say I don't want any commitment. I don't want a new man in my life. But I'm glad this happened. I didn't know how much I missed being held.'

'We all need to be held sometimes,' he said rather sadly.

She swallowed hard, deliberating before she spoke again. 'I've never told anyone this, not even Addison, but

I was pregnant with Bobby's child when he left. I was so upset and shocked by his disappearance I drank too much, and I lost the baby.'

He stroked her hand. 'You poor girl.'

She blinked rapidly to hold back the tears spiking her eyelids. 'It still hurts. I think it may have been my fault, you see. The miscarriage. I can't stop blaming myself.'

He shook his head. 'I'm sure it wasn't your fault. Yvonne had one too and we read that a miscarriage tends to happen when there's something not quite right with the foetus.'

'If you're right, that does make me feel a bit better.'

'And it should. Don't carry the weight of all that guilt. These things happen sometimes.'

She didn't say but had noticed that his slight stammer had completely disappeared.

'Look, if you ever feel like a change, I might be able to get you work in publishing. In London, of course, as a trainee. It can be enormous fun.'

He was so easy to be with, great to talk to and the way he gave her his complete attention meant she really felt heard. He wanted nothing from her except her presence and she felt the same way about him. And she began to see herself through his eyes. There would never be a romance but what if she were to take him up on his offer of finding her some work in London?

CHAPTER 37

Malta, December 1932

Over the ensuing two years Riva had carried on working for Addison, despite calls from Otto asking her to come back to Valletta to help him out and Gerry's entreaties to decamp to London. But in 1932 Addison finished his second volume, swearing there would be no more, and Gerry returned to London for the final time. And Riva had reached a point where she could no longer ignore the rising danger for young women in Malta.

Both the *News of the World* and the *Daily Herald* printed stories describing the 'shameless' music halls of Malta. *'English women lured to work in dens of iniquity'* the headlines proclaimed, then went on to assert that with promises of inflated remuneration these innocent young girls were enticed abroad and away from the safety of English shores. They found themselves forced to live in filthy lodgings on scant wages and with not enough to eat. These 'poor' English girls were expected to entertain the sailors privately in so-called 'homes' which were nothing of the kind. *'Brothels'* the headlines screamed. *'Nothing but brothels'*. They also claimed that 'prudish' Maltese locals loathed the girls and threw rotten food at them in the street. With no money the girls found themselves imprisoned in a music hall industry that was really a cover for white slavery.

White slavery.

The words echoed around the world.

After the stories were repeated in the *Daily Malta Chronicle* Otto telephoned Riva and asked to meet.

He was still working for the pro-British newspaper, the *Times of Malta,* and nodded at acquaintances as they were led to their table in the window of the British Hotel.

'It's causing uproar here,' he said after they had greeted each other. 'Look at this.' He pushed a copy of the *Daily Malta Chronicle* towards her.

'Crikey,' she said as she read. 'The locals are furious.'

'Spitting nails, and quite right too. I don't believe any of the girls have had rotten food thrown at them.'

'Well, I never had. It's ridiculous.'

He told her he'd already published an article calling for the resignation of the minister responsible for the police. 'He hasn't done so of course,' he added. 'But now the *Chronicle* is demanding an enquiry and the word on the street is the minister has agreed.'

'That's a good thing, isn't it?'

He twisted his mouth to one side as if he wasn't sure.

'Could be. Rather depends on whether the enquiry ends up being a whitewash.'

She sighed. 'You think it might?'

He nodded. 'Everyone is worried. People believe the repercussions of the cabaret scandal, as they call it, will destroy Malta's good name, deter the visitors we need. The enquiry will probably be a cover-up.'

'I wish I could help.'

'You can. With your background in Strait Street, together we might be able to keep up a stream of articles to keep the police on their toes about what's really happening there. What do you say to working with me on a more regular basis?'

'In what capacity?'

He grinned, looking pleased with himself. 'It wouldn't be anything fancy, just a freelance role, as my assistant.'

She grinned. 'Sounds like a plan.'

But time had passed since she'd worked in Strait Street and she didn't know if any of her old contacts would still be there, however she decided to have a quick word with her old friend Tommy-O.

As she walked across the almost empty Evening Star, Tommy turned to look and patted the leather stool next to him. She kissed him on his heavily powdered cheek then perched on the stool next to his, concerned about how old and tired he looked. The venue hadn't changed, still mirrored and painted in crimson and gold, lit only by gaslight, and smelling of cheap scent and stale beer.

'I didn't know if you'd still be here.'

'Well as you can see, here I am. But I didn't expect to see you. Thought you were working for our island's most famous artist.'

She shrugged. 'I was.'

'You've seen the newspaper articles?'

'Who hasn't? That's why I'm here.' She lowered her voice. 'Otto at the *Times* wants me to help him. You know everyone on the island. Is there any way you could you get me an interview with the chief of police, on the quiet I mean?'

He puffed out his cheeks and let the air out. 'I can try. But it's a big ask.' He shook his head. 'The police and the Church *are* looking into the scandal, but they're looking in the wrong direction.'

'How do you mean?'

'The girls at risk are not English. Even in the 1920s they were mainly from Italy and France, as you yourself were. Now they're nearly all Hungarian. Not British. Ask in any of the bars, *tabarins* or music halls. Same story all over.'

'Even if the girls aren't British there's still the issue of prostitution and exploitation.'

He nodded. 'Yes, but they don't care about that. The articles claim that it's English girls who have been used in this way. The enquiry will have no difficulty proving that isn't true.'

Gianni came in and nodded at Riva. He still hadn't forgiven her for upping and leaving without notice.

'Be careful, Riva,' Tommy said and touched her hand.

A few days later Riva was sitting on a bench in the gardens overlooking the ocean waiting for someone. She wasn't quite sure who. She'd received a message from Tommy telling her to be there at ten but to keep her wits about her. It was now half past ten and she was about to get up and leave when a bespectacled man walked across to her. She studied the measured way he was walking and then his face. His rust-coloured hair was thinning and with a spiky face and sharp chin, he looked like a predator of small creatures. A gimlet-eyed weasel; she almost expected him to bare his teeth.

He gave a slight bow. 'Miss Janvier?'

She nodded.

'There is somebody who wishes to speak with you. Would you be happy to accompany me?'

'You're from the police?'

He nodded. 'No names, if you don't mind. We don't want any trouble. Understand?'

'I do,' she said, aiming for nonchalance, although she wasn't sure. Trouble from her? From him?

'You may be aware that withdrawal of the Constitution is on the cards. If that happens the island will revert to being a British Crown Colony. Everyone would prefer to avoid that.'

She followed him into the centre of the town and then along a side road. 'Is this a back way to the police head-quarters?' she asked, feeling increasingly apprehensive.

He laughed. 'Sensitive matters are rarely dealt with at police headquarters. Ah, here we are.'

He unlocked a heavy wooden door and ushered her in and then up a wide stone staircase to a room at the back of the building. He knocked, walked straight in, and held the door open for Riva. She glanced around at floorboards polished to a high shine and paintings of wild animals hanging on cream-coloured walls.

'Sir,' he said.

A thin man with his back to them was staring out of the window. As he turned round another man who had been standing just inside the door coughed. Riva spun on her heels to see who was there.

'Miss Janvier,' he said, and with a sinking feeling she instantly recognised the man with salt-and-pepper hair and a walking stick. Stanley Lucas. 'We meet again,' he said and gave her a smile. 'How delightful.'

She stood hands on hips. 'I thought you'd moved away from the island.'

He waved the other two men off and they left the room.

'For a while. As you may know the police cleared me of those scurrilous accusations of fraud.'

'Corrupt police in your pay?'

He laughed. 'I like your sense of humour. But there it is. If you have evidence to the contrary, be my guest.'

She inhaled deeply before she spoke, feeling uncertain, but despite that came out with it anyway. 'I saw you.'

His eyes darted momentarily as if he hadn't been expecting that. 'Saw me?'

'With young girls. The Russian girl, Anya, for example.' She studied his face, then tilted her head to ask the question. 'Did the police clear you of murder too?'

He bristled, puffed out this cheeks, and darted her a look of loathing. 'I rather think you may be something of a fantasist. In the past women were put away for less.'

'Your wife maybe?'

His face went red and then purple. 'Ariadne died.'

There was a long silence while he turned his back, lit a cigarette. She wasn't sure what to do. Leave now? Stay?

'Anyway,' he said, clearly having collected himself and coming back to face her. 'Like you, I have made my home here. I am a collector.'

'A collector?'

'Of *objets d'art*.'

And people, she thought.

He waved his hand vaguely at the glass-fronted shelves behind his desk where a host of ornaments were displayed.

She looked and her heart lurched. A row of wooden dolls sat on his shelf behind the glass, among all the other ornaments. Anya's old, rare Russian dolls.

She heard the girl's voice in her head. '*Matryoshka dolls. Mother has child inside and child has child inside. Many. All fit together. It is life.*'

Riva stared at the largest doll – the woman holding a black rooster beneath her arm, the yellow and pink looking a little faded – and she felt sick.

'I understand you are interested in the enquiry into these shocking allegations of human trafficking in the newspapers,' Lucas was saying, but all Riva could think was that she needed to get out of there and fast. She took a sharp breath and struggled to reply.

'Of course,' she said, hearing the tremor in her own voice. 'They're absolutely dreadful if they're true.'

'And naturally you'd like to find that out. However, it is of the utmost importance to all of us here in Malta and to the British Government in England that this matter is dealt with as swiftly and fairly as possible.'

'Of course.' Her heart was racing as she spoke.

'Under the circumstances it would be wise for you to step back and not attempt to delay things.'

'Wise?' she managed to say.

'Well, you're a pretty girl. And you know . . .'

In the stuffy smoky room, her skin began to crawl, but still she stood her ground. 'I don't respond to threats, Mr Lucas.'

'Not a threat. Think of me as a well-wisher. There are shady characters mixed up in this. I wouldn't want to see you hurt. Leave it to the police. They'll do a good job. I understand the enquiry is due to report in February. Not long now.'

'What's your role in this?' she asked, finding enough strength to stand up to him. Despite her fear, she knew this might be her only chance.

He frowned, raised his hands and shrugged in an open gesture of surprise. 'I have no role, but I do have an enterprise. We are building a chain of hotels. Top notch, you see. Restaurants, casinos, tennis courts, swimming pools. You get my drift. Tourism will be our future once the military leave. We all want to wipe out this current blot on Malta's reputation.'

He was dangerous but still she couldn't hide her disdain. 'And you're the man to do it.'

'If you had known poverty, real poverty, you would understand. I will not permit you to destroy what I have built up.'

'Poverty? What are you talking about?'

Clearly rattled, he shook his head. 'I am originally Hungarian. My parents were poor and died from the Spanish flu . . . I became a homeless orphan.'

For a moment she almost felt sorry for him. 'You sound British.'

He gave her a cold smile. 'You do what you have to do.'

Riva narrowed her eyes. 'But your name?'

'Was Lukáč. Zoltán Lukáč.'

'So, you're not Stanley Lucas. Why are you telling me now?'

'Your friend at the *Times* already knows. But I am not the only person using an assumed name, am I? Take good care, Miss Janvier.'

'I'm free to leave?'

He smiled. 'Naturally. I wish you well.'

As she walked away Riva's heart was racing.

Back in Mdina, she roughed out an article for Otto in which she refuted the English newspaper claims that English girls were being abused but said the problem for foreign girls still existed. And at least the police were now interviewing all the girls working in Strait Street and beyond. Her next stop would be the Church authorities whom she knew were anxious to stamp out immorality on the island. She was not going to let the likes of Stanley Lucas win. He could threaten her all he liked; she wasn't backing down.

CHAPTER 38

Riva sat with Addison on his balcony. Thick cloud blocked the moon and stars and she complained bitterly about the Church authorities. When she'd spoken to them, they refused to countenance any issues of exploitation and took the stance that the problem was the immoral character of the women. In their view women needed to be subjugated, kept docile and deferential, or the social fabric would fall apart. At least that was the attitude of one religious leader she spoke to.

'He didn't actually say if you keep them ignorant then the evil within them will not rear up, but he might as well have done,' she said.

Addison sighed. 'Awful. In this day and age.'

'Such damn prejudice,' she continued. 'Everyone knows what's going on. Everyone. Yet nobody is prepared to deal with it. Nobody is prepared to help.'

'Mark my words, the enquiry will also blame it on the

women,' Addison said, 'rather than examining how British colonial rule and the presence of the military in such huge numbers has encouraged the exploitation.'

'I don't know what to do. They ignore Otto's articles and I've talked to everyone I can think of. I'm wondering about holding a meeting.'

'What kind of meeting?'

'An open one, to point out the hypocrisy and start a petition to call for immediate action to ensure the safety of the girls.'

'Be careful, Riva. I don't want them to find you dead in an alleyway.'

At the beginning of 1933, despite Addison's warning, Riva did go ahead with her meeting in a hall not far from Strait Street. She paced the room feeling exposed, while at the same time she worried nobody would turn up. In the end, a few church members trickled in with placards calling for an end to prostitution. This wasn't the angle or focus Riva had been hoping for but she eventually managed to persuade them to take a seat, saying everything would be addressed in due course.

She was pleased when a few girls came in and sat at the back, hair covered, and eyes fixed on the side door. Riva's own hair was fully red again now, the waves tumbling to her shoulders. She'd long given up the pretence of having dark hair to protect her true identity. When no one else appeared to be coming, Riva stepped forward and began to speak, passionately arguing for human rights and against the violation of those rights, and for an end to the exploitation of young women brought in from other countries. She talked about her own experiences as a dancer, and without naming names, told them about Anya.

'It's time the authorities took this seriously,' she said as she neared the end of her speech. 'How much longer must we wait for action that actually makes a difference to these girls? Please sign the petition you see on that table over there and tell your friends I will hold another meeting at the same time next week. If we can achieve enough signatures, I'll deliver it to the chief of police and the ministry will have to take notice of our demands for more safety controls.'

She glanced at the main door and spotted a stream of men coming in. They stood at the back of the hall, feet wide apart, arms folded. Her heart raced as the atmosphere became heavy with unspoken threat. At first nothing happened, and she continued to speak. That was her mistake.

The heckling started as a whisper and carried on as a kind of low-key chanting with words she couldn't quite make out but that had an ugly undertone. She couldn't believe it when she realised it was coming from the women, the look on their faces completely blank. The women!

Didn't they realise she was trying to help them?

Soon after that the girls hid their faces and sidled out of a side entrance, their job done. Riva was gripped by an immediate fear but carried on. 'I don't want to argue with you,' she told the men, who laughed and blew raspberries.

'Go back to where you came from, Frenchie,' one of them shouted.

She stood her ground and went on trying to be heard above the growing noise of catcalls and whistles. They'll calm down, she told herself. But they weren't there to calm down and the heckling continued until the voices became more aggressive, the stream of invective uglier. *Whore. Bitch.* She saw their faces screwed up in anger as they chanted. *Whore. Bitch. Whore. Bitch.* Although shaking inside she was determined not to let the vitriol stop her and raised a hand to plead for silence. She noted a policeman standing with his arms crossed a little away from the other men. Would he step in?

He did not.

She glanced around her as the voices continued. *Bitch. Whore. Slut. Bitch. Bitch. Bitch. Bitch.*

'Frigid cow, I know what I'd do to her, boys,' someone sneered, and they all laughed approvingly.

And now she glanced at the side door, realising she would have to cut and run before it became physically violent. She should have got out of there before all this.

Someone threw something at her. It missed but the church people at the front who had been sitting in shocked silence began shrieking and ducking their heads as pebbles began to whizz through the air.

'Take it as a warning,' someone shouted and laughed when one hit Riva on the cheek.

'Next time, missy, it'll be bullets.'

The men clapped each other on the back and finally left the room.

Shaken, Riva felt blood tricking from her cheek and abruptly ended the meeting. No one had listened. Not the religious women, not the girls, not the men. What had she expected?

Night came down thick and black as a taxi dropped her and she walked towards Addison's place that evening. Hearing something behind her, Otto's words came back to her. *The island is beautiful but there is an undercurrent, and it flows through Strait Street.* But this was Mdina, not Valletta, and yet her skin still prickled uncomfortably. She stopped dead, felt the fear in her bones. Silence. Was there someone loitering in the shadows? Lying in wait? The feeling of foreboding deepened as she glanced around. Nothing. Whoever had been there was not visible. She walked on and then she heard the rumble of an engine. Just someone leaving Mdina then. Probably one of the locals. Nothing sinister. She'd been imagining things.

At Addison's she sat alone on his terrace while he went inside to fetch a second bottle of wine. Her mind kept clicking back to the meeting with Lucas. Subdued and disheartened, she felt the pull of the past. Not her life with Bobby. Not that. But Paris where she was born. And where, nearly eight years ago, and with barely a backward glance she'd packed her bag and run away from home. She thought of her sister Claudette, and how much she missed her, and she thought of her parents too; even though she had never fitted in or felt she belonged, she couldn't completely erase the pull of home.

'Do you have a never-ending supply?' she said as Addison came back out with a bottle.

He laughed. 'Something like that.'

She smiled.

'I've been thinking,' he said. 'Why not take up Gerry's idea of working in London—'

She began to interrupt him but he held up his hand. 'Your apartment will still be here for holidays or if you change your mind about London and want to come back. I'd miss you, of course, but you've done all you can.'

'Have I?'

He shrugged. 'I don't know, but think about what I've said. At least do that. I'm worried for your safety.'

She nodded. 'Thank you for caring.'

'Of course I care.'

'I think I'll turn in now if that's all right. I'm dead on my feet.'

As she started to turn away, she glanced out into the darkness as a pair of headlights caught her eye. The vehicle seemed to be approaching carefully, then it disappeared. She went down to her apartment and forgot about it. She didn't even undress, just climbed into bed, flicked the switch and the room plunged into darkness. She fell asleep instantly but awoke very soon after to the sound of thunderous knocking on her door.

She grabbed her robe and found Addison standing at her open door with a police officer.

'What?' she gasped.

'It's Otto. He's been hurt.'

'An accident?'

'No. He was attacked. He's asking for you.'

Otto remained in hospital for a week with broken ribs and concussion, unable to remember much of what had happened. When he was allowed home, she visited him and spent time in the apartment. 'Safety in numbers,' she laughingly said to explain her presence to him, but she had already arranged for stronger locks to be installed on his apartment door.

'You didn't see who did this?' she asked, hoping something might have come back.

'No. It was too dark. More than one, I think.'

'They say anything?'

'Threatened me with worse. You too. That's all I remember.'

'You think Stanley Lucas was behind it?'

Otto shrugged.

A week later the enquiry was published. As Addison had predicted, its findings focused on the immorality of female foreigners and unfortunately that had fostered the growing feeling of xenophobia on the island. It was not only clever but easy to prey on people's semi-dormant fears. Just beneath the surface lay so much hate; God help them if it ever found a way to erupt.

Women To Blame, screeched the headlines.

The enquiry's solution was to denounce the corrupt girls and make them shoulder the blame, rather than confront the impact of British rule on Maltese society. And the British military authorities focused on the threat of sexually transmitted diseases to their labour force, rather than exploring their own accountability.

No British girls exploited, screamed more headlines while non-British girls were ignored.

Any mention of white slavery was completely denied. It did not exist. All the girls interviewed, barmaids and cabaret performers alike – and most of them foreign workers – had arrived in Malta willingly and none were involved in prostitution. Anyone who read the report, or the newspapers, would reach the conclusion that there was no prostitution in Malta and no exploitation of women at all.

Riva sought an interview with a minister from the Treasury to complain. Declined. She wrote to the minister who dealt with National Security and Law Enforcement. Also declined. Not a single soul in charge of the Government of Malta either in Valletta or London was prepared to discuss the issue. With Otto out of action, she wrote an article condemning the enquiry's findings. No one would print it.

When she met Tommy-O for coffee, he shrugged his shoulders, bemoaned what was happening politically and warned Riva from going any further on the human trafficking issue.

'It's getting more dangerous, my girl. All that fuss, and prostitution has just become even more clandestine. The girls are kept in debt by the criminals who control them and dare not speak. Nothing changes.'

Riva sighed. 'They'll never give evidence?'

'Threats from the traffickers make sure of that. And the agents with their offers of extortionate rooms, and the *matrones* who "loan" the girls jewellery and clothing. It keeps them trapped.'

'So if the girls can't speak out, what's the solution?'

'Legalise the industry. License the prostitutes and the brothels and move them out of Valletta.'

Riva thought he might have a point.

'I really think you need to back off now,' he added. 'For your own safety.'

The enquiry was soon forgotten in the furore surrounding Malta reverting to full Crown Colony status, with power resting in the hands of the governor just as it had been way back in 1813. There had been a grant of self-government in 1921 and during the decade following *that* British concession, Maltese politics had become more diverse and complicated. Maltese nationalism had blossomed with many of its people working towards true independence sometime in the future. Now this would put everything back by years and there was a great deal of anger.

On the day it was announced she passed Stanley Lucas in the street, and he smiled smugly. *See. Girlie. There's nothing you can do.*

She knew there was nothing she could do about him, at least not at the moment. And she accepted she needed to step back and get on with her life. She might never find out what had happened to Anya and the others who had died or gone missing, but she would do what she could to help Otto improve conditions for the girls who were still there.

But then the enquiry, the Crown Colony status, and everything else slipped into the background because at the end of the decade, a different kind of trouble was brewing. The kind of trouble that nobody could believe was really going to happen again.

CHAPTER 39

Florence

Sicily, 1946

Back over on the main island of Sicily, Florence and Jack got out of the taxi into the hot white sunshine accompanied by the sound of church bells. They stood outside an ochre-walled farmhouse surrounded by open fields and wild scrubland. Florence was thrilled to have left Lipari behind. Since Jack's admission about his feelings for her, and the kiss they had shared, an unspoken anticipation had been growing and building between them.

She pushed open the wooden door which gave onto a courtyard, the floor tiled in beautiful sand-coloured stone which the late-afternoon sun had painted with stripes of gold.

'Limestone,' came a voice.

Florence whirled round to see a small wiry man smiling as he came towards them arms outstretched. 'Extracted from the area of the Iblei mountains here in Sicily. Jack, welcome.'

Jack and the man shook hands and then he turned to her. 'This is Florence.'

Edward smiled and kissed her on both cheeks. While she glanced around the courtyard at succulents and feathery bamboos growing in giant terracotta pots and the flowering plants cascading from the windows above, Edward explained that two communal 'salons' or sitting rooms opened into the courtyard.

'Just use whichever one you like. Make it your own. There's only myself and Gloria here. And there's a pool through there. Well, a pond really, but you can dip your toes into it. The fish don't bite.'

Florence sighed with pleasure as he then led them inside and through a hall into one of the bedrooms. It turned out to have a vaulted ceiling, a chandelier, and was painted pale blue, with cream linen curtains framing two faded blue doors and diaphanous gauze pulled to the side of both the windows. She glanced at the view of golden hills, delighted to be away from the palace on Lipari with its forbidding atmosphere.

'Gloria is the interior designer,' Edward said. 'And my niece. Come and meet her.'

A few minutes later, a tall, elegant woman wearing a pink and orange silk kaftan flowing around her as she walked, called hello. Her blonde hair fell in a sheet to her waist and her eyes were electric blue.

'We are aiming for sustainable living,' she said. 'Everything happens at a slower pace here. It's so nice to meet you.'

'You have a kitchen garden?' asked Florence.

'We do. Aubergines, peppers, courgettes, melons, onions and strawberries.'

'I used to grow all those in France.'

'Well this is our first year. You know, the war . . .'

'Did you suffer much damage?'

'Some.'

'You live here all year round?'

The woman sighed and, holding Florence's elbow, steered her towards another faded blue door with glass panels that revealed a small patio shaded by palm trees. The air vibrated with the sound of bees, birdsong too. It was so different from France and England, and Florence wondered if there might be something Moorish about it. Bougainvillaea climbed the stone walls, three small ferns grew in earthenware tubs and there were two rattan armchairs, a small table, a comfy chaise longue, and a lemon tree.

'This is yours. See that door? It opens directly to your room.' Florence glanced at Jack, wondering if he would say they needed two rooms. He remained silent.

They had a light supper washed down by local red wine and went to bed early, claiming tiredness. In their private bathroom, lit only by candlelight, Florence washed first and then Jack. He extinguished the oil lamp in the bedroom, and they lay down on crisp white sheets beneath a fan listening to the sound of the fountain as the scent of thyme drifted in from the open window. It was the end of summer but still warm.

She had never felt anything like this before and reached over to touch his skin with her fingertips. She felt his shiver in her own body and heard his sudden sharp intake of breath. She turned her head to the side to look at him lying beside her, something she'd longed for, but could only see the silhouette of his face in profile. She forced herself to wait, secure now that he wanted her. And she was sure of herself too, despite her earlier worries of not being able to be intimate with a man after the rape. Now she was balancing on the delicious moment before anything more happened, but in the absolute assurance that it would. She traced the muscular curves of his arms and then rolled completely onto her side, facing him in the darkness.

He kissed her gently and then more forcefully.

'You're sure you want to?' he asked.

'You need to ask?' She laughed and he stroked her neck, her breasts, her thighs, with the lightest touch and so, so tenderly. 'I won't break, you know,' she said and could feel his smile.

'I've recovered from what happened to me,' she added. 'Truly.'

After waiting so long she had expected the sex to be over swiftly, but it wasn't. There were interludes of almost unimaginable elation as they took their time, other moments when she felt tears on her cheeks and the heat coming off his body in waves. She kissed his wrists, felt his pulse, and awed by the sensation of his heart on her lips she allowed him to engulf her. She'd long wondered about how Jack would be and now she knew. Immersed in him, her heart pounded so fast she thought it might break through her ribcage. And it was thrilling. Beyond thrilling and Jack was everything she wanted him to be.

At breakfast they held hands under the table as the white tablecloth lifted gently in the breeze. An orange butterfly had become trapped in a fold of the gauze curtains behind them. As if caught in a dream she watched spellbound as Jack got up, cradled the butterfly in his hands and released it into the garden. Gloria brought out a pot of coffee and home-made pastries as well as bread and local cheese.

'I've forgotten the orange juice,' she said.

Jack rose to his feet, but she waved him down.

Later they went for a walk across rocky scrubland above a deep valley, from where they could see caves built into the cliffs.

'I think I'll avoid caves for the time being.'

He laughed and drew her to him.

Further on they saw rolling woodlands and jagged hills.

'We could go to Noto itself, if you like. Edward says the town is a maze of honey-coloured buildings. I thought it might be your sort of place.'

'Are you meeting with Edward today? I mean for work.'

'After lunch.'

'Is this place his, or Gloria's? I asked if she lived here all the time, but I don't think she replied.'

'She lives in New York, I believe, but spends part of the

year here. She's making quite a name for herself in the world of design, or she was before the war. This place is her latest project.'

While Jack met with Edward, Florence took a nap, or a riposo as she liked to call it now. She spent an enchanted hour half awake, half asleep, hearing sounds but not engaging with them, just daydreaming happily as the world drifted by. But then Hélène slipped into her mind as image after image of their lives in the Dordogne arose. Compelled to re-examine every moment, she saw herself with her sisters climbing the hills before the early morning mist dissipated. Saw herself staking out her beloved goats. Saw herself swimming with Hélène, who'd always been like a mother to her. Florence liked to think she was a good person but, oh God! She loved Jack, truly loved him, and he loved her, but she loved her sister too and she worried about how Hélène would react when she knew. The upsetting thoughts continued and the deeper she went into her own sense of failure, her own wrongdoing, the worse the violation of her relationship with her sister seemed.

By the late afternoon when Jack rejoined her, his beautiful green eyes looking so much more relaxed than they had been, she felt better for seeing him. She knew she was shifting and growing and that meant confronting difficult things. It would turn out all right with Hélène, she told herself. In the end it would have to. This new changed relationship with Jack was still so fragile, and they were only just discovering each other – she didn't want anything to spoil that.

'Are you all right?' he asked. 'After last night.'

She smiled. 'I'm very all right after last night, Jack, although I can't help thinking about Hélène.'

'She'll be fine, Florence, I'm sure of it. She's a good person.'

Florence nodded and hoped he was right.

'Edward has decided to delay work on the palace in Lipari but has given me a contact in Malta who might, I don't know, maybe need a hand with some of the restoration work there. They took a terrible battering during the Great Siege.'

'Who's the contact?'

'Someone in a governmental department involved in the rebuilding. Apparently, the destruction there is worse than in Palermo.'

'Hard to imagine, isn't it?'

'Makes me wonder, if Rosalie is even still there, how badly she may have been affected.' Jack shook his head. 'I mentioned before Malta's strategic importance as a British Crown Colony.'

'Yes, and how it suffered during the bombardment by air.'

He squeezed her hand. 'What I'm trying to say is there's a chance Rosalie may not even be alive.'

There was a moment's silence as Florence considered this. 'You might be right,' she eventually said.

'I really hope I'm not . . . By the way, changing the subject, Edward told me something about the house in Lipari. You were right about the atmosphere. Apparently three generations of the family were slaughtered there. A

Mafia vendetta, he thinks. Few of the locals will go anywhere near the place. They believe it's cursed.'

Florence could believe that. Given how she'd felt there, it made sense.

They sat quietly for a few moments and then the air in the room seemed to grow lighter.

'There's something else I've been waiting to say,' he continued and took hold of her hand but then didn't speak.

She smiled at the way he looked so uncertain and yet so earnest. 'You can say anything you want to me, Jack. Anything.'

He avoided her eyes by glancing down. 'The thing is . . .'

She tilted her head, waiting.

'I'm not much good at this sort of thing, Florence, but I want to love without fear . . . and your absence from my life . . . Well, I couldn't even contemplate it before, and when you were seeing Bruce, I . . . well . . . I wasn't comfortable.'

She couldn't help smiling at the way he described his feelings.

He looked up and searched her eyes. 'All right, the truth is I was dying inside . . . I need you to understand, I mean really understand, that I am not trifling with you, Florence. That I will never trifle with you, and I don't want to take advantage in any way—'

He gently stroked the hair from her brow. Then, as she began to speak, he put a finger to her lips before he kissed them.

CHAPTER 40

The next day their host Edward knocked and then called out as he opened the door and entered the sitting room.

'Out here,' Florence replied.

He walked out to the little patio she shared with Jack. 'I found these,' he said and handed her some newspapers. 'They're mostly old Maltese papers. Thought you might find them interesting.'

Florence pored over the papers in case there might be any references to Rosalie but, although she looked carefully, she spotted nothing. She was surprised when she read in a newspaper from 1944 that women in Malta still hadn't been given the vote, and something called The Women of Malta Association had been formed to campaign for female suffrage. From what Florence had heard Rosalie was the type to stand up for what she believed in, so could she have been part of that?

She scanned the names of eighty women who had been involved but found no sign of her.

She read that although the Constitutional and Nationalist parties were undecided about the role of women, the Church was strongly opposed to female delegates being allowed to be included in the National Assembly. *And* strongly opposed to women having any political presence that would affect their traditional role as mothers and homemakers.

'And they still haven't,' she said, throwing down a second more recent newspaper in disgust as Jack came into the room. 'Even now. Two years later.'

'What's two years later?'

She picked up the newspaper again and held it out to him. 'Read it. Women still don't have to right to vote in Malta. Can you believe it? They finally have it in France now, but not Malta.'

'Perhaps before we go haring off on what might well be a wild goose chase, we should think about what your mother told you about her.'

'How do you mean?'

'Claudette said she was independent and wilful, didn't she? Maybe Malta is so old-fashioned it really wouldn't be the type of place she'd want to live. At least not for long.'

'Let's go to Noto and have a think about it.'

A little later, as the bus crawled along winding roads passing olive groves, small vineyards and orchards full of ripe pears and apricots, Florence hung her head out of the window and smelt eucalyptus and something else. Wild fennel, she thought.

This bumpy old bus with its metal seats was so different from an English bus to Exeter, with the cheery female conductors, or clippies as they were called, nattering away. This was full of Sicilian voices, and she couldn't make out a single word. Eventually they arrived in Noto, where the maze of old stone buildings led off from its two main arteries, the Corso Vittorio Emanuele, and the Via Camillo Benso Conte di Cavour.

'Some of the Allied troops landed nearby in the Gulf of Noto,' Jack said. 'Tenth of July 1943 was when it began.'

Florence closed her eyes for a second, imagining what it must have been like. 'At least the bomb damage here doesn't seem as bad as it was in Palermo.'

They approached the baroque cathedral from a flight of wide steps, but the midday heat was building and Florence was sweltering, her thighs sticky with sweat.

'It's beautiful,' she said, peering up at its magnificent facade. 'But perhaps we could find somewhere cool for a drink.'

The nearby café was cool and peaceful inside and she was happy to kick off her shoes and relax as Jack made himself understood somehow and ordered a simple meal of enormously fat tomatoes, delicious sheep's cheese and crusty bread washed down by local wine.

'There must be so many stories here,' she said. 'In Sicily, I mean. The history never quite disappears does it?'

'Did you know the Sicilians rebelled against the French in the late thirteenth century?'

'I did not.'

While they lingered in the café the two of them thought about where they might start their search in Malta.

'Well,' Jack said, 'the government offices would be a start, and the police of course.'

'They'll have records of who died in the war, won't they? And there will be newspaper archives.' She paused. 'They might even have a census.'

'Guess we'll find out. It's a shame we don't know more about Rosalie.'

'All I really know is that she was the wild child of the family,' Florence said, 'gave their parents no end of trouble. Rebellious, just like Élise.'

Jack smiled. 'A force to be reckoned with.'

'And, as you said, Malta does seem very traditional.'

He nodded. 'Not the kind of place a woman like Rosalie would like. It's up to you, of course, but I wonder if we should just go home to England when I'm done here and forget about Malta.'

She didn't reply. Wasn't sure what she thought about that, although surely for her mother's sake and to satisfy her own curiosity, she had to go through with trying to find Rosalie, especially having come this far? No matter how tempting the attraction of Meadowbrook might be with its familiar routines and feeling of stability.

Later, as they sat on their little patio sipping wine, the scents of early evening drifting in the air, she felt the collision between her hopes and her fears. Hopes for herself and Jack, fear of upsetting Hélène, and also of not finding Rosalie. So much was uncertain.

While she was lost in these thoughts, she was vaguely aware of him reaching into his satchel on the floor.

'Florence?'

'Sorry, I was miles away.'

He opened his palm and her breath caught when she saw a tiny blue velvet box.

'Florence Baudin. Would you . . .' He paused and she stared at him. 'Would you . . . What I mean is, shall we get married? Would you like to?'

Tears filled her eyes.

'Oh God. I didn't mean to make you cry.'

She laughed. 'These are happy tears, you idiot. And I would.'

He smiled almost bashfully then opened the box and lifted out a sapphire engagement ring which he then slipped onto her finger. 'It was my grandmother's.'

'How did you know it would fit?'

'I had it altered. A while ago.'

'You've been deliberating about this?' Given how reluctant Jack had been to confront his feelings, she was surprised.

'I have, though not about you. I always knew you were perfect, but about me. I worried that I couldn't give you what you deserved.'

She shook her head, reflecting on all the time they'd wasted, but maybe it wasn't wasted, maybe this was how it was always meant to be. A proposal in the most beautiful place she'd ever been.

'How did you know the right size?' she asked.

'You had taken off a ring to do the washing-up. I borrowed it.'

'The ring I thought I'd lost and then found again in the soap dish.'

He grinned.

'Honestly, Jack, you really could have just asked me then. You didn't need to half drown me in a cave in Sicily to persuade me to say yes.'

He laughed and she laughed with him. Then she lifted her hand to the light streaming in through the window. 'It's a beautiful ring.'

'From Ceylon,' he said.

'How marvellous. How utterly bloody marvellous.'

'I have another ring for you. A wedding ring.'

She laughed. 'Isn't it traditional to wait until we're actually married?'

'Malta is such a conservative place. If we do go there it would need to be as man and wife, I think. Might be best if you wore it even before we actually marry.'

'I wouldn't want to tempt fate.'

'I understand. We could have separate rooms, of course.'

'Not likely. It took me long enough to get you into my bed, I'm not letting you go that easily.'

'You, Florence Baudin, are a wicked siren!'

While she changed for supper, Florence decided she must write to Hélène and soon. Of course she had to hear about the engagement from her first, but the thought of her eldest sister triggered another fleeting moment of misgiving.

She heard crockery being laid on the table outside,

laughter too and someone clapping. Along with the smell of roasted octopus with garlic, her unease melted away.

And when, as the sky turned golden and then to a flaming red, she joined everyone at the supper table, Edward and Gloria were immediately on their feet beaming while Jack uncorked a bottle of champagne.

'Congratulations,' they chorused while Jack turned beetroot.

Florence felt so ecstatic she thought she might burst. Things would go well now; she was sure of it. Their roots were strong enough. She and Jack would be married, and Hélène would accept it.

Even before Jack had proposed, Sicily was a place that had spoken to her. Now she would never forget it.

In bed that night he kissed her palm. 'I couldn't be happier, you know.'

She smiled, feeling the warmth curling inside her. 'We've not spoken about what will happen.'

'How do you mean?'

'Will we carry on living in Devon?'

'I had thought so . . . but look, if you don't want to . . .'

'I want to,' she said, nodding vigorously. 'I love Meadowbrook.'

He talked a little bit more about Devon, the places they might go together, things they might do. Hope Cove, Lannacombe Bay, Bantham. Just listening to Jack talking about the South Devon coast soothed her, even when she felt so hot and sticky.

She thought about Rosalie too. Although going straight back to Devon was very appealing, she still itched to know what her aunt might have done with her life, whether in Malta or elsewhere in the world. And she thought, perhaps naively, this might be her chance to restore a part of her family that had been broken.

'So,' she said with a grin. 'When are we going to set off for Malta?'

'You're still determined to go?'

'Of course. I haven't come this far to give up on Rosalie now.'

CHAPTER 41

Riva

Malta, 1940

Nobody could believe the war was really happening but early on the morning of 11 June, Riva woke to an ear-splitting screech and then a deafening crash. She sat bolt upright in her bed. The building rocked and she trembled in fear, certain they'd been hit and that any moment now the roof would collapse. The noise went on and on pounding in her ears, in her head, in her brain. Then the wail of air raid sirens and anti-aircraft fire from British warships in the harbour. The wait was over. They'd been preparing for this. The inevitable war against Italy which, only a hundred or so nautical miles from their shores, left them vulnerable.

She was currently staying in Otto's spare room within

walking distance of the docks. It was easier to be in Valletta for work rather than Mdina. Had the docks been hit? Had people been killed? She paused just for a second, too frightened to move, but then threw on her clothes and boots and together with Otto she tripped and stumbled down the stairs and ran out into the street.

People were begging for assistance as dust, smoke and flying debris ballooned in the air right across the entire dockyard, and ambulance bells began to ring. Riva could barely breathe. She coughed and rubbed her stinging eyes as Otto dragged her into the new casualty station, set up just before Mussolini had declared war.

As the days went by, she longed for some guiding hand to show her the way. Tell her how best she could help. She had no idea. All she knew was that once she'd ensured Addison was safe, she would not be able to just stand by in Valletta. She had to find a way to help, but then things went strangely quiet again – the calm before the storm, she later realised.

By December, a heavier and more terrifying German air offensive had begun, and in January the Luftwaffe began its attack on the aircraft carrier HMS *Illustrious*, pride of the British Navy.

Riva was reading in bed when the German flares came down, but she saw the blue flash on the walls of her bedroom. She leapt up and ran to the window as the sirens wailed. Then came a horrifying series of explosions above and beyond the Grand Harbour, the air expanding and swelling as if it might burst open and swallow the entire island. Otto's building vibrated so much she felt sure it was teetering on the verge of collapsing. She'd been a fool and hadn't left for the shelter in time and now could only watch in horror as she saw the searchlights and then one aircraft after another tearing away from the group and diving straight into the anti-aircraft flak. These were not the Italian raids they'd experienced so far. Riva had watched those bombs leaving the aircraft with a shrieking whistle only to fall into the sea with a splash. Had even laughed at their failure. These now, were the much more ferocious German bombs dropped at close range from Stukas. She saw the sky fill with bursting shells and twisting planes as the convoy including *Illustrious* was attacked and its multiple barrelled guns fought back with a tremendous barrage of fire. She heard the appalling progress of the screaming bombs and then saw buildings crash to the ground and fires erupt.

By about ten that night, HMS *Illustrious*, listing unevenly, was dragged through the Grand Harbour's entrance, its hull burning red in the darkness. It finally berthed at a wharf in French Creek. In air thick with the fumes of explosive chemicals, dockyard workers rushed aboard, bringing with them breathing and firefighting equipment to tackle the blaze.

When it was light, Riva ran, along with hundreds of other people, to the ramparts of the harbour and saw the devastation on the other side of the water, the dust billowing, the buildings turned to rubble, the houses still in flames.

She and Otto took the ferry from the Custom House Steps over to the so-called Three Cities which had taken the brunt of the attack. As she climbed out of the ferry, she saw dozens of dead goats floating in the water. The streets were impassable, piled high with sheets of concrete, broken glass and mountains of brick, and they were turned away by police. Riva later learned one hundred and twenty-six men had died on the *Illustrious* that night and ninety-one had been wounded.

HMS *Illustrious* was caught again by two bombs during another air raid on Malta. But, although damaged, like the dockyards themselves, *Illustrious* survived. Still the Germans didn't give up. Despite further bombings the dockyard men continued to work night and day to enable the ship to be seaworthy enough to escape. On 23 January, a very battered and broken HMS *Illustrious* set sail for Egypt.

But still the bombs carried on falling.

Night after night.

Day after day.

Over the next weeks, while the raids continued and the people spent their nights in cellars and basements, 'Demolition and Clearance' were out in force. When Riva crawled out of their shelter into the dust and debris, all she could do was help get the injured to safety and make herself useful wherever she could. She knew she was not destined to be a nurse but helped as thousands of Maltese people left their dockland homes, their belongings – cooking pots, bedding, bundles of clothes – piled high on flat carts, most of their animals left behind to starve while they attempted to find shelter with relatives inland.

By day, she and Otto both wrote articles about what

was happening. She focused on the stories of everyday people, their courage, their endurance, their tragedies, and she tried to find nuggets of hope in the darkness that now engulfed them. Otto wrote about the progress of the war. It was not good news. It was rarely good news.

Riva felt a pull to see Addison, to reassure herself again that he was still all right. Exhausted from another night helping in the casualty station, she headed by bus to Mdina, having long since given him back his beautiful car.

When she arrived at the top of the stairs, she saw his door had been left slightly ajar. She knew the butler did this occasionally to allow a through draught into the apartment, so she walked straight in only vaguely aware of the hum of voices and with no idea of what she was about to see.

'Hello,' she called out and entered the sitting room.

Addison turned towards her, as did another blue-eyed man in civilian dress.

She froze.

'It's been a long time,' the man said.

'Twelve years,' she said curtly and turned to Addison. 'I just came to see how you were.'

'I'm fine, Riva. Thank you for keeping an eye on me.'

'It's not a problem. You know that.' She paused, turned back to the other man and stood motionless, her heart beating furiously. 'So, how are you, Bobby?' she managed to say.

He nodded. 'Well enough.'

She glanced around. 'And your wife?'

'Died five years ago. Cancer.'

She nodded and took a deep breath, stifling a rising feeling of bitterness. 'Right. Sorry, Addison, but I have to go back to Valletta.'

'Won't you stay for a coffee?' Bobby said, and as he took a step towards her, she could see he was walking with a limp.

No longer a pilot then, she thought as she shook her head and made for the door. 'See you later, Addison.'

She paused on the landing to steady her breath and heard Bobby say, 'Doesn't she live here any longer?'

'No,' came the reply. 'She lives with Otto, you know, the journalist in Valletta.'

She didn't wait to hear any more and scurried down the stairs.

On Sunday night she heard the whine of a bomb, then a deafening crash and the sound of gunfire. There had been no warning siren. Otto's apartment shook again, and he ran into her room to see if she was hurt.

'Were we hit?' she asked, her heart thumping.

'I don't know. You okay?'

She nodded. 'We'd better get the hell out.'

He ran after her, racing down the stairs at breakneck speed while crashes and roars thundered around them. When they finally reached the junk-filled cellar, he held on to her, both panting from the effort and cowering in fear. The attack went on and on, until Riva's head was throbbing with sound of engines and explosions and anti-aircraft fire. Hell. Sheer hell. No other word for it and she didn't feel prepared.

In the morning they surveyed the broken windows, the

glass-strewn streets and the dust, so much dust, though so far most of the buildings close to theirs seemed intact. But the people tramping the streets were angry, shouting and swearing and many so distressed they barely knew what to do. Riva comforted the elderly among them and brought them blankets and hot drinks. Reassured, they picked themselves up and carried on.

Eventually the night-time horror exploding in the purple skies above them became such a regular occurrence, they became accustomed to it. When she lay awake at night listening, she allowed herself to think of Bobby. What had he been doing in Malta? Why had he been at Addison's place in Mdina? There had been an all-out evacuation of most British civilians so it was odd that he should be there. As much as she tried to forget him, he haunted her thoughts.

Months later, at the end of a terribly long day, Riva heard from Lottie that Hugh Lloyd, the RAF AOC, or commanding officer, was looking for women – on the quiet – to be trained for duties in the plotting rooms. The war rooms were overwhelmed and needed more staff, but it was top secret work and they had to be careful who they took on. Riva, excited at the thought of it, went directly to the address Lottie had given her, but was worried they might just want Englishwomen.

She was ushered to a room where a stern-looking woman officer who called herself Roberts handed her some sheets of paper. 'It's an intelligence test. You have half an hour.'

Riva sat at a small desk in the corner and bent her head, feeling nervous. It was like being back at school with only half an hour to get it right.

When the time was up, which to Riva didn't seem like half an hour at all, the woman rang a bell and beckoned her forward. 'You are French,' Roberts said, glancing down at the top sheet where Riva had written her name. Then she pressed a button on her desk and another woman came in. 'Mark this would you, Giovanna?'

The second woman, Giovanna, nodded and took the sheets of paper away.

'I am French,' Riva said. 'But I've lived here since 1925.'

'Indeed. I have heard of your efforts to rectify the problems with prostitution. Very outspoken, I understand.'

'I did what I could.'

'Your command of English is the most important thing, although you still have to pass the test and be cleared by security. As you have been here for so long and have a good track record, that shouldn't be a problem.'

Riva crossed her fingers behind her back.

Giovanna came back in and gave the officer the papers.

Roberts glanced down at a number at the top encircled by green. 'Well, you have top marks. You have the go-ahead from me. Giovanna, take her to security please.'

In security a bald man went over her application and asked her a few questions about her background and whether she visited Italy much before the war and did she have any German ancestry. When she replied in the negative, he asked about her work for Addison. The questions went on and she worried her false papers might be her undoing. But she now had medical cards and an insurance number in her new name, plus her false passport, and nothing was said. But still when he let her go she felt sure she must have failed.

However, much to her surprise, she received a letter soon after telling her she'd got the job. Two days later she was escorted down to the underground Lascaris War Rooms, which Linda, the woman in charge, laughingly called 'The Hole'. Riva could see why. Much of it was a maze of gloomy sunless tunnels and grim chambers, reminding Riva of a claustrophobic rabbit warren. The entire complex had been formed from old tunnels built by the Knights of St John but British forces brought in miners from Yorkshire and Wales to explode parts of the rock and cliff. So, beneath the Upper Barrakka Gardens overlooking the Grand Harbour the tunnels had been extended for the RAF and the navy. The miners also developed miles of tunnels beneath the city as shelters for the people, including carving out small chambers where families could find some privacy during the air raids.

Riva was shown the different rooms. The plotting room – No. 8 Sector Operations Room – where she would work, was overlooked by a gallery from which the commanders could look down to see the enormous table below where the positions of everything were marked. She was also shown a coastal defence room, an anti-aircraft operations room, and several others.

'The air is mechanically ventilated through metal piping retrieved from ships that have been sunk in the Grand

Harbour,' Linda said proudly. 'You start on Monday, but remember we are the nerve centre of Malta's defence, and you must never talk about what we do here. Understand?'

The weekend was relatively quiet, and Riva managed some unbroken sleep apart from the dreams of Bobby that had taken her by surprise.

When she started work as a plotter on that first Monday morning, she stared at the huge RAF plotting table where she saw a map of Malta and the area around it, including some of Sicily and the Aeolian islands. When she glanced up at the gallery above and the men in the gods – as the gallery was known – she stepped back in shock.

'That's the leader of D-watch,' Linda whispered, seeing her looking. 'Our senior controller, Group Captain Sir Robert Beresford, and he's aided by Flight Lieutenant Weston.'

Riva could not speak, just nodded and longed to make a run for it. Did Bobby know she would be working here? Perhaps if she kept her head down and just got on with her work, he might not even notice her.

She put on her headphones as she had been shown and the messages from the filter room began coming in. Everyone immediately looked serious, and all other thoughts left her mind as she began to assemble and then move the aircraft blocks around. She had to use a long stick to plot the locations as the aircraft travelled south and approached Malta and she was terrified of getting it wrong. There was a rush of activity among the men above her as the pilots' voices were broadcast from loudspeakers and squadrons were scrambled. When they heard 'Tally-ho' in their headphones, all that was left for the girls to do was pray that the pilots would be safe.

Most of the time Riva had neither time to think, sleep or breathe, and it was after a night like that that she came out into the thick dusty morning air to find Bobby looking exhausted, smoking a cigarette and leaning against a wall.

'Hello, Riva,' he said and offered her a cigarette.

She took one. More from nerves than because she really wanted one. She rarely smoked.

'I've been hoping we might have a chat.'

'What about?' she said. 'I mean, what about, *sir*?'

He smiled. 'Glad to see you haven't changed.'

She snorted. 'Oh, but I have.'

'I'm sorry. Truly. But let's not quarrel. We were friends, weren't we?'

So that's what we're calling it, she thought but didn't say.

'I'm heading for the RAF Officers' Mess at the Xara Palace in Mdina. Like to accompany me? Maybe pop in to see Addison? We both have a two-day break, I believe, or will your boyfriend be upset if you leave Valletta?'

'Boyfriend?'

'Otto, isn't it?'

She shook her head and laughed. 'Otto's not my boyfriend. I'm just staying in a room in his apartment,' she said and saw a flash of relief on his face, although he hid it quickly.

'So? Mdina?'

'All right,' she said despite her mind turning somersaults as it warned her to step away.

'I have a staff car and a driver. But probably best if I drive. The RAF are a bit sticky when it comes to officers cavorting with the young ladies of Lascaris.'

'One, I have no intention of cavorting and two, I'm hardly a young lady any more.'

'You look exactly the same.'

'I'll soon be thirty-five, Bobby. There's no way I'm just the same.'

'Well, I don't think they can object to two old friends having a drink together. Do you still stay in your apartment at Addison's place? He told me all about it and your work on his books. They've been hugely successful.'

'I was happy working with Addison.'

'I'm surprised you weren't spirited off to work in the publishing houses of London or New York.'

'I had offers.'

'I'm sure,' he paused. 'And you never married?'

'No.'

They remained in silence for the rest of the way.

He slowed down as they approached the ancient walls of Mdina and suggested that before they visit Addison, they stop at his apartment for a drink. She felt hesitant. Was it a good idea? Probably not and yet she heard herself agreeing, and they climbed the stairs to the place she had spent so many happy hours with him.

'Whisky?' he asked, raising the bottle.

'A small one.'

They carried their drinks out onto the little terrace

where she sipped her whisky and neither of them spoke. She heard dogs barking in the nearby town and smelt woodsmoke in the air, saw the winding white lanes and the sloping fields where the old donkeys spent their days.

He sat opposite her staring at the tiled floor. Then he swallowed visibly and said, 'I feel I should explain.'

'No need,' she said, holding herself tight, because if she were to allow the feelings inside her to release, she would be finished.

'That isn't true. I behaved—'

'Appallingly,' she interjected. 'You behaved appallingly.'

'I . . .'

She shrugged. 'Look, it doesn't matter. It was years ago. We're different people now.'

'Are we? I never stopped loving you.'

At this she rose to her feet in anger. 'Well I stopped loving you.' She spat out the words, headed inside and made straight for the door.

'Please don't go.'

She turned, watched him stand, reach out a hand and take a limping step towards her.

'No.' She shook her head, raced down the stairs and only when she had hidden herself away in one of the narrow cobbled streets, did she lean against a wall and cry, great gulping sobs, her body wracked with pain as she bent double. How dare he come here and say that? How stupid was she to have come with him? She wasn't a child, for God's sake.

Moments later she heard uneven footsteps, tried to wipe

her face with her sleeve, began to walk away. Then he was there pulling at her elbow. She fought him off then pounded his chest again and again as if she might pound out the pain that had been buried inside her for so long. The pain that she'd never given herself permission to fully feel.

'Riva.' His voice broke.

'No.'

'Please.'

'You broke my fucking heart, you bastard.'

'I . . .'

She swayed, overcome by the ferocious anger coursing through her body, making her heart pound, her blood boil . . . she gasped for air but then she went limp suddenly, crumpled against the wall like a rag doll.

'You . . . broke . . . my heart,' she repeated. 'And I lost our baby.'

'Baby?'

The silence of Mdina seemed to deepen even further as he helped her to straighten up. He wrapped his arms around her and then they both wept – she with the relief of telling him, he . . . well she didn't know for sure, but sorrow, she thought.

When the tears were over, he whispered. 'I am so sorry. I didn't know you were pregnant.'

'Would it have changed anything?'

He looked horrified. 'Of course. I would never have let you go through it alone. I know you'll never be able to forgive me, but I'll do anything to make this better, anything you want.'

She stiffened then pulled away. 'There's nothing you can do. Some things can't be fixed. I'm going now, Bobby.'

'Let me drive you.'

'No. I'd rather get the bus. Better not waste the petrol.'

CHAPTER 42

After that Riva kept her distance. She saw him in the gallery but did everything she could to avoid them meeting again. Linda noticed she was behaving a little stiffly and took her aside.

'I don't know what's happening to you, but you have to keep your mind on the job. A mistake by any of us can result in certain death for one of our pilots. You understand that, don't you?'

Riva nodded.

'Good girl,' Linda added, not unkindly. 'This war is hard on all of us. Did you lose someone? Is that it?'

'In a manner of speaking.'

Linda patted her shoulder.

After that warning Riva kept her head down and thought of nothing but work.

A couple of weeks later, after the 'Tally-ho' had been

called, one of the other plotters broke down in tears. Linda quickly ushered the girl out.

Riva turned to Tilly, a bright young woman of about twenty with bleached blonde hair. 'What was that about?' she whispered.

'She's married. Been having an affair with someone in the military. Linda's going to have to let her go.'

Bobby instantly came to Riva's mind.

'The RAF can't do anything about unmarried staff getting together when they're off duty. But they won't have this. Not the extra-marital affairs. Bad for morale. The man involved was a pilot and I heard he's already been posted elsewhere.'

While the days melted into each other, the nights became more exhausting and even more severe. There were four watches with about fourteen women in each. An unbroken watch was kept for twenty-four hours of every single day. In the intense atmosphere of the plotting room, men and women worked closely together. Lives depended on everyone getting things right and emotions were more highly charged than under normal circumstances. Off duty they let off steam together.

Riva and everyone else who worked in the war rooms had a special pass to show the military police if they were stopped at night. They had to be so careful. You couldn't light a cigarette outside, and all the streetlights were permanently shut down. The nights were black as pitch.

Dances were held in the afternoons, between three and six, but Riva rarely went. Leave it to the youngsters, she thought. She liked to walk, though, always staying aware of where the nearest air raid shelters were. They used railway tunnels, cellars, basements, and openings in the sandstone cliffs which were riddled with passages and tunnels, formed over the centuries.

It was on one of these off-duty walks in the Upper Barrakka Gardens that she bumped into Bobby again. Though 'bumped' was not quite the word. She saw him coming before he saw her, and she momentarily froze. When he did see her, he paused then began to walk towards her slowly, carefully using his stick. Her heart melted and she bit her lip to suppress tears that had suddenly appeared from nowhere.

'Hello, Riva,' he said, and he smiled, looking so forlorn she held out her hand. She hadn't meant to. It had happened involuntarily.

He took her hand.

'Shall we sit?' she said. 'I mean your leg . . .'

'Yes. I can't walk so far these days.'

'Does it hurt?'

'Now and then.'

But she saw him wince as they reached the bench and he bent his leg to sit.

'Oh Bobby,' she said.

'I wasn't expecting to see you in the war rooms. It shook me.'

'Me too.'

'Might we at least be friends again? I know you don't want to hear it, but I've missed you, Riva. I've missed you like hell.'

She sighed. 'Why did you leave without telling me? That's what hurt the most.'

'It was cowardice. Plain and simple.'

'And your mother. It was her plan for you?'

He nodded, looking glum.

'How is she?'

'Oh, you know.'

Riva nodded. 'And children? Do you have children?'

He shook his head. 'Look, I didn't do right by you, or by my wife. I couldn't love her. I cared for her, looked after when she was ill, but I couldn't love her. It's always been you, Riva. I—'

'Stop, Bobby. Stop. I really don't want to hear this.'

He gazed at her. 'I have to say it. Leaving you was the biggest mistake of my life.'

She swallowed rapidly and her voice came out more bitterly than she'd intended. 'But in leaving me, you solved your financial problems, so that's just fine, isn't it?'

'Riva, please.'

She shook her head.

'This . . . it's eating me up. I'm begging you to forgive me.'

'I . . .' She paused and then realised something.

'What?'

'It isn't *my* forgiveness you need. It's your own.'

He stared at the ground and for a while neither of them spoke.

'Life is short,' he eventually said. 'Especially now. You know that. Riva, is there any chance we could begin again?'

And suddenly all the years had come full circle. She'd

struggled to accept what had happened but now time suddenly concertinaed, and it was as if the intervening years, the anguish, the grief, the anger had simply faded.

'Maybe,' she said.

He hugged her to him so tightly she couldn't breathe.

'Let go,' she finally managed to say.

'I will never let go of you, not until my dying breath.'

They had precious little free time but over the next few weeks, they began to spend any moments they had off duty together, mainly in Mdina, away from curious eyes. It was only a few hours they had and apart from Addison, who beamed to see them so happy, they kept themselves to themselves. This now was different, a less bright, less sparkly, more muted shade of love. Love that had been marked by experience, by betrayal, and now by forgiveness. They were meant to be together because look, despite everything, here they were. Again. She'd thought she'd understood what their love had been the first time round. She had understood nothing. It had been fuelled by desire, passion, excitement, and longing. An addiction. Drunk on love, they'd been frenzied, subsumed into each other, and almost destroyed by it.

And yet there had been joy, something ineffable, never spoken of, never identified, never needing to be identified, but now gone for ever. The kind of love that could be felt only by the young. A young Riva, a young Bobby. So, this now. What was this? A deeper love, the connection between them yet again beyond words? Did that mean the love would change in another ten years' time, in twenty, in thirty? Was she too old to still carry a child? Did it matter? He had found her again. She had found him. And it was as if they knew each other intimately and at the same time not at all.

CHAPTER 43

The bombings continued relentlessly. On 15 April 1942, King George VI awarded the George Cross to Malta. The island had become an extreme focus for German and Italian air attacks in their attempts to destroy military bases and to starve the islanders into submission.

One day, when Riva went to the bakery to buy bread, there was an especially long queue. A woman with a lined face and a headscarf covering most of her grey hair, turned round with a look of desperation in her eyes.

'It's a waste of time,' she muttered.

'What is?' Riva asked.

The woman frowned. 'They've run out of bread. What's my daughter supposed to give her little boy? He's only two.'

'I'm so sorry. What are you queuing for if not for bread?'

The woman sighed and looked close to tears. 'Goat's

cheese and butter. The dairy got bombed so they're selling it here . . . You don't look scared. Aren't you scared? I'm scared. All the time.'

Riva reached out a hand to her. 'I know. Me too.'

'We're going to run out of food, aren't we? My husband, Pawlu, he says we're all going to starve to death.'

Another woman joined in the grim conversation. 'My son reckons we'll be starving by the middle of August if no convoys manage to get through. He works at the docks, you know. Says almost nothing has come in.'

Riva nodded. It was unthinkable and she wished she could believe this was the usual exaggeration and fear-mongering, although she suspected it was not.

On 16 June all her worst fears were confirmed when she switched on the wireless at Otto's place, and turned the volume up – the Governor was about to give a live broadcast on Rediffusion.

'*I am sorry to have to announce,*' he began, '*that the latest two convoys of twenty-four ships that set out to bring us supplies have failed. One convoy was so heavily attacked by the Luftwaffe that only two small ships have reached us. The other convoy was forced to turn back.*'

Riva gasped to hear this. 'Oh God, Otto. There really will be dreadful times ahead. Only two out of twenty-four ships. What on earth are we going to do?'

'*It is a fraction of what we had hoped for,*' the Governor continued.

'You can say that again,' Otto muttered under his breath. 'And the black market doesn't help. My sources tell me that Stanley Lucas has his finger in that particular pie.'

'Why does it not surprise me? Bobby mentioned that supplies to the officers' mess in Mdina have been intercepted, petrol syphoned from army vehicles too.'

Otto shook his head. 'Despicable. But there are always the good guys and the bad guys, and a time of war is no different, in fact it simply offers new opportunities for people like Lucas.'

The broadcast continued. *'There will be deprivation and we must do everything we can to avoid waste. Our stocks of oil are low. Paraffin is almost gone. Rationing will be more stringent than ever. Supplies will come. We must remember that. But in the meantime, we are introducing severe penalties as part of the campaign to halt the black market. There will be a maximum sentence of five years' imprisonment.'*

Soon after that Riva was walking around the town desperate to see if she could stock up on the food they needed. So far, she'd only managed to get hold of some goat's milk and a bar of chocolate the shopkeeper said had been found under a box in the back and was probably mouldy. Riva didn't care and bought it anyway. What she really hoped to find were eggs. People still had chickens so there had to be eggs somewhere. The devastation she saw, the smell of destruction, the thin, gaunt people she passed, all of it was so disheartening she felt like giving up. Just sitting down in the dirt and the dust of the cobbled street and giving up. Instead, she carried on and strayed away from the areas she knew well.

Suddenly a ferocious dive-bombing attack began. There had been no warning. Petrified, she began racing back to the part of town she was familiar with. Most islanders spent their days sheltering from the long and terrifying attacks and had their favourite places in the tunnels excavated by the British miners. But people had also been digging underground through the limestone rock in the countryside, in the courtyards and beneath their homes in the town. Riva now found safety in one of those dugouts near to the bombed Opera House. Inside it, she squatted and saw someone was holding a lit candle. She covered her ears as best she could, but still heard the gut-wrenching whistle of the bombs, the thud, the crash and then she struggled for breath at the sound of falling rock, and part of the shelter caving in.

In the fetid air she could not see any light. Had the candle blown out or was it now on the other side of fallen rock? Heart racing in the pitch blackness, she felt for her bag, located it, and fumbled around inside for her torch. She always carried a torch. Why wasn't it there? She scratched around on the floor, growing increasingly frantic. She heard whimpering and then she found the torch, thank God, where it had rolled a few feet way. Its light was dim but enough for her to see that the fallen rock had formed a jagged wall. She went to look for a way through, feeling with her hands. Nothing. It was solid. Fear, absolute and immediate, gripped her.

Apart from an elderly man in the corner who looked more dead than alive, Riva and a heavily pregnant woman with two small children were the only ones trapped there. Everyone else was on the other side of the rocks. When the pregnant Maltese woman began to weep, Riva tried to comfort her, held her hand, spoke to the children, who were now sobbing too.

'Don't worry,' she said, although she felt sick from something far worse than mere worry. She went over to the rocks and shouted for help. Screamed that they were trapped. Thumped on the rock with her fists, then picked up a smaller rock and banged it against the large rocks. She heard faint voices on the other side and listened. Impossible to make out anything beyond a rumble. She screamed again to let them know. *'We are here! We are here!'*

The pregnant woman was moaning softly. Was that normal? She remembered her own pains when she suffered the miscarriage. The woman let out a sudden yell and held her belly, her eyes wide and helpless in the dim torchlight. Was it just fear? Surely the woman wasn't really going to give birth here?

Although terrified she would never get out, never see the light of day, never see Bobby again, she had to focus on helping the woman. It was a filthy place to be giving birth and Riva could still hear the now strangely muted sound of the bombs dropping on the city above them, could even hear the distant rat-tat-tat of anti-aircraft fire. An image of the small but exquisite courtyard garden in Mdina slipped into her mind. Her garden. She gulped. What if they were all going to die? The woman was panting now, her children whimpering. She tightened her grip around Riva's wrist and screamed. Then she went quiet again, her pain seeming to ebb.

In the silence Riva dipped in and out of alertness,

feeling nauseous and stifled by the heat and the smell. Time passed. Endless hours. She had no idea how long. If only she could see the light. Daylight. Any light. They only had darkness, and the weakening beam from her torch.

The bombing ended.

Then came a respite.

The children slept and when they woke Riva gave them her chocolate.

Silence again.

But soon it was broken by a low growl and then a scream. Riva could only imagine the pain the woman was in and held her hand, speaking soothingly in response to desperate pleas for help. Riva had no idea how long the labour would last.

The woman began panting between slow breaths.

Sick at heart, Riva waited and prayed.

It seemed colder in the shelter, or hotter. *Which?* How long would the oxygen last? Riva's thoughts raced and raced until she felt light-headed, longing for nothing but to be able to close her eyes and go to sleep.

But then a high-pitched, furious wail arose. It was unmistakable. The baby. Riva immediately came to full consciousness and reached down between the woman's raised knees. Amazed, her heart thudding, she felt a soft, wriggling infant on the ground. She unwrapped her own scarf and carefully cocooned the baby in it, then passed the little bundle over to its mother. The woman was talking rapidly now but Riva did not understand, though then she heard the word 'afterbirth'.

Of course. She knew about that and waited, hoping it would just happen on its own.

After a while, the woman gasped again and there was the sound of liquid gushing. Blood? Was it blood? Then a wet slithering sound.

The woman made a scissoring action with her fingers and said, 'cut.'

Riva didn't have a knife or scissors, did she? Maybe nail scissors in her bag. What if she couldn't cut it? Was it dangerous? She really didn't know. *Hurry*, she told herself. *Hurry*. She put down the torch and with trembling fingers she felt for the nail scissors and almost cried in relief when the zipped inner pocket revealed them along with a lipstick. She picked up the torch again to look. The afterbirth lay like a purple slab of lumpy liver. But where should she cut the cord? The woman indicated higher up so Riva battled the tough cord with her minute, ineffective scissors, the woman making exasperated impatient sounds. When it was done the woman used her hands to indicate a knotting action and held the baby up, pulling the scarf away. Riva quickly tied a knot in the cord quite close to the baby's belly. She hadn't realised she'd been holding her breath and now she let it out in a long juddering sigh.

The two children snuggled up with their mother and Riva went back to the fallen rocks, shining the torch trying to work out which ones might be safe to move. Which might cause another rockfall? She was frightened to move any at all but decided there was nothing else for it so gingerly she removed a few of the smaller rocks, gradually gaining confidence to roll a couple of the bigger ones away. In between moving rocks, she paused and shouted for help but now she heard no voices coming from the other side. Exhausted, her throat and chest raw, she sat back on her heels. What if they never got out?

CHAPTER 44

Florence

Malta, 1946

As the sun rose, Florence stood on the deck thinking about Rosalie and smelling the tang of seaweed and the salt of the Mediterranean Sea. After all this time, was she about to find her aunt? Discover her secrets? Find out what she'd been doing all these years? Would she be able to give Claudette the news she wanted? She gripped the railings praying for something positive and determined to do everything she could. She felt hopeful but knew so little about Rosalie and wondered if she'd even know her if she passed her in the street. All she really knew was that she had bright red hair, had been a wild child, and that she owned the same charm bracelet as Claudette, which she, Florence, now wore every day. And Florence knew, or thought she did, that at some point Rosalie had probably been in Malta. But it seemed like such a long shot, and she might well have moved on somewhere else years ago.

It was still early when the ferry from Syracuse dropped anchor in the waters of Valletta harbour. As she heard the shrieking seabirds welcoming them, Florence took in the amazing sight of massive walls, ramparts and bastions, rising like cliffs from the depths of the sea.

'What a place, Jack,' she said a few minutes later, and reached for his hand as they climbed into one of the small vessels bobbing in the water. A *dghaisa*, they were told. Painted red, blue and yellow, it was a gondola-like thing, with painted eyes on either side of the bow. As the high-ended little boat – propelled by a standing man with an oar who pushed instead of pulled – reached some wide steps, they climbed out and looked around them. Florence could smell fish and saw dozens of cats lining up where the catches were being brought in. But she stared in horror at the destruction of much of the dockland.

'Oh my God,' she said. 'They have so much still to do.'

Edward had been as good as his word and Jack had been given the phone number and departmental address of a government administrator in charge of plans to restore Malta to its former glory. He had also booked them a room at the British Hotel overlooking the harbour.

As they made their way there, they saw the heartbreaking evidence of the bomb damage – rubble, Blitz-battered architecture, and even some of the ancient buildings totally destroyed. There were temporary homes everywhere, or maybe they were shelters.

'What do you think?' she asked Jack.

'These people must have lost their homes.'

The little huts were made of tin and chunks of fallen masonry. Florence could smell charcoal and frying onions and saw a group of women cooking in the street on open fires. Other women nearby were washing clothes in tin tubs, or chopping wood while children dashed around, shrieking.

'God, but they've suffered here,' Jack said. 'The RAF operated mainly from an airfield at Luqa, here in Malta,' he said. 'It became their Mediterranean Command HQ during the war.'

'How do you know?'

'Common knowledge now.'

Their hotel was comfortable, but Florence's heart sank as she thought of the impossible task of finding Rosalie in all this chaos.

'I wonder where to start,' she said while Jack looked out of the window. 'I'd like to get to know the island a bit, find my feet, and then make a plan. You can talk to people you meet too.'

Jack went back down to reception to call the number he'd been given by Edward and set up a meeting for the following day. He didn't know if there would be any chance of work while he was here but would give it a try.

'Come to bed,' she said much later that day, after they had wandered around the town for a while.

He came to her immediately, picked her up and carried her to the bed. 'Light as a feather,' he said.

'I am not. Gladys spent months feeding me up and I ate like a pig in Sicily.'

He kissed her on the nose. 'An adorable little pig.'

Early the next morning, Florence wrote to Hélène. She'd been putting it off but now she forced herself to sit down and do it.

My dear, dear Hélène,' she wrote and chewed her pen.

> *I am now finally in Malta with Jack, hoping to find Rosalie. We arrived today. It has been very badly hit – so many beautiful old buildings were destroyed during the war. Did you know there were 3,000 raids on this tiny island? Hard to believe but the damage is everywhere. The people were starving at one point too, as supplies couldn't get through. No medicines either. It breaks my heart to think of it. It really does.*

> *But on to other things. I hope you, Élise, and my gorgeous niece Victoria are well. I want to see you all so much, but before that happens there's something I must tell you.*

> *When we were in Sicily before coming here, Jack asked me to marry him, and I accepted. I do hope this news won't dismay you. I know you and he were once close. We only got together very recently while in Sicily. As you know, when I was living in Devon, he was rarely there. But during that time, I agonised about my growing feelings for him, and I now know he was doing the same about me. I'm so sorry, Hélène. I hope you can*

understand this. Better still I hope you've found someone yourself or will do so soon.

He has given me permission to tell you about a couple of things he couldn't talk about when he was in France. Firstly, he was still married then, although now the divorce is final. It's terribly sad but he and his ex-wife Belinda had a little boy who died in the war aged four. I think it explains a lot about how he was when you knew him.

He has been grieving for his son all this time but is coming through it now.

So, there it is.

I'm sending you all my love. Please hug the others for me. Oh, I nearly forgot . . . when I last saw Maman, she looked thin. If the telephone lines are up and running again, could you call her from the surgery and see if you can find out if she is all right? She's fanatical about me finding Rosalie so I shall do my best. Maybe we can all finally be together again before too long.

With my love always,

Florence xxx

Jack had already gone out, so she dressed and decided to find somewhere to post the letter. Lured by the smell of real coffee and baking, she stopped for breakfast at a small café. After she'd eaten, the café owner came over to ask if she needed anything else and, knowing she'd have to start somewhere, Florence spoke in English.

'I'm wondering how to find a missing person here.'

The woman sucked in her cheeks. 'Many missing after the bombing. Most accounted for now. When was this?'

'I don't know. She may have been here for years. A French woman. Rosalie Delacroix?'

The woman shook her head. 'Never heard the name. Sorry. Try the city archives, what's left of 'em, or the town hall records.'

There was a pause as the woman narrowed her eyes as if thinking. 'I don't know if this will help but my cousin's son, he is a professor at the university. He knows people.' She scribbled something in her notebook, tore the page out and passed it to Florence.

Back out in the street people were picking their way around heaps of rubble still waiting to be cleared. She asked an old man where she would find the city archives and he pointed in the direction of the town hall.

'It's all there,' he said. 'What's left.'

'Could you tell me where the registry office is too?'

He scratched his head. 'Not sure now. It was moved during the war.'

When Florence asked to check the records at the town hall, the clerk was unhelpful. Frowning and shaking his head, he sat behind a neat, highly polished mahogany desk, with a painting of Malta looking golden and untouched by war behind him.

She stood her ground and gave him the broadest smile. 'How beautiful it must have been,' she said, glancing at the painting.

He muttered something she couldn't hear.

'Look, I've come all the way from England to find my aunt. I need to know if she survived the bombing. If she was even here that is.'

'You have authorisation to look at the records?'

'Where do I get that?'

'The police. They issue authorisation if you fit the criteria.'

'What's the criteria?'

'Go to the police. They'll check you out.'

'Can't you help me? Just a little bit.'

He shrugged and returned to his paperwork.

'In that case could you tell me where to find the registry office? Births, deaths and marriages.'

'First door on the left.'

Well, she thought, pleased it was so near, I hadn't expected that. But her enthusiasm soon dimmed when, after a lengthy wait on an uncomfortable wooden chair, the heavily set and very slow-moving registrar returned, unable to confirm any record of a Rosalie Delacroix.

'Anything registered during the war was lost in a fire,' he said. 'The office was housed temporarily in Rabat. We weren't expecting bombs there but we got one all the same.'

'What about after the war?'

'I've checked the name you gave me. Nothing, I'm afraid.'

Florence sighed but she wasn't daunted and decided that instead of the police she would first call at the address the café owner had given her. She prayed the building would still be intact and when she arrived was relieved to see that it was. She entered the old place, a warren of corridors and rooms, stairwells and lecture halls smelling of cinnamon and beeswax. She eventually found the room she wanted on the first floor and knocked. Silence. She knocked again and now feeling a bit unsure of herself, she heard someone moving around. The door flew open, and as a dishevelled man stood glaring at her, she backed off.

'Sorry. Have I disturbed your sleep?' she asked, aiming for a light-hearted tone as she stared at the chunky, tousle-haired fellow.

He studied her face indignantly and then burst out laughing. 'Guilty as charged,' he said, dark eyes glittering. 'Who are you?'

She told him who she was and why she was there.

'I'm Fleming Camilleri. But call me Cam. Everyone does. So, looking for your aunt you say?'

'Yes. Rosalie Delacroix. French.'

'You've tried the police?'

'Not yet. I need to get authorisation to look at the records in the town hall.'

'That's easy, I can give you an authorisation slip.'

'Really? The clerk said the police issued them.'

'Yes, and so can I, and in fact any professor here. Just wait a minute and I'll find the paperwork.'

He rummaged around in the desk drawers and eventually pulled out a pad and tore off the top slip. 'Here we are. Your surname again, Florence?'

'Baudin,' she said without thinking and then wondered

if she should have said Jackson, if they were to maintain the pretence of being married.

He filled in the form, signed it, passed it to her and studied her face. 'I don't know but . . . would you like me to accompany you?'

'Would you? That would be a tremendous help. Do you have time?'

'Free this week. No students you see. Anything to get out of collating all this.' He waved a hand at his paper-strewn desk and the countless files piled up on the floor.

She laughed. 'What do you teach?'

'Wish I knew.'

'Seriously.'

'Ancient bloody history.' He laughed. 'We call it classics. Come on, let's go.'

At the town hall they found nothing about Rosalie, so he asked if she'd like a guided tour of Valletta. She nodded, grateful to have a guide. 'I'd like to place postcards in some of the shop windows asking if anybody knows of my aunt's whereabouts or has any information about her. I've already made some.'

'Do you have a photograph of her?'

'Sadly not.'

'Pity. Never mind, we'll stop at shops as we go round. Motorcycle all right? I haven't got a car. And anyway, with the rubble still piled up, bike is best.'

She smiled, relieved to have found someone willing to help her. 'Perfect. I'd love to grasp the layout of the Valletta streets and learn where everything is.' And so, riding pillion was how she very quickly got to know her way from Fort

St Elmo to the Customs House, and from there to the Upper Barrakka Gardens. He pointed out the library, the police headquarters, and the way from the bombed Opera House to the Hastings Gardens and the Phoenicia hotel and then back to the British Hotel where she and Jack were staying. And he picked out half a dozen shops where, when she asked, the owners were happy to display her postcards in their windows.

Later, when he took her to see the cliffs, the beaches, and the little inland villages, she fell in love with the island. She hoped Rosalie had too, and that she had treasured the gorgeous blue sky, the dusty white tracks, and the shimmering turquoise seas enough to have stayed. You could see the sea from almost everywhere and when Florence felt the warm breeze on her cheeks and breathed in the scent of salt and seaweed, she imagined Rosalie doing the same.

They sped past farms surrounded by fields kept safe within dry stone walls and beyond the walls, prickly pear and carob trees. Cam was a knowledgeable guide, and the history of the island fascinated her. As they went inland her mind wandered back in time to when the Order of the Knights of St John were given the island by Charles V. Everything comes and goes, she thought, and took another breath of sweet-smelling air. 'Oh, to be a fly on the wall of history,' she said.

Cam laughed and she liked him. He was one of those people who really seemed to relish being alive. And despite teaching 'ancient bloody history' he was light-hearted and fun to be with.

When Jack returned to their hotel room just after she got back herself, she was still trying to brush the dust from her hair.

'You managed to get out, then?'

She twisted round to look at him. 'I did and it was marvellous.' She went on to tell him all about Cam.

'But no hint of Rosalie?'

She glanced away. 'No.'

'Something else is bothering you. What is it?'

Florence sighed. She wanted to find Rosalie for her mother's sake, but her chest tightened a bit when she thought about maybe uncovering something dark or unsettling.

'Nothing,' she said.

'Well, if you're sure . . . I have news . . .'

'Don't keep me in suspense.'

'Bit of a lucky fluke but I have found us somewhere to stay.' He picked her up and whirled her around. 'I saw an advertisement and followed it up.'

'Put me down, you heathen. Where is it?'

'Quite near here and we can move in tomorrow.'

CHAPTER 45

The airy second-floor apartment in Valletta was an absolute gem. It belonged to an English banker who had shipped back to London when the war began and was not planning on returning just yet. Jack had been told about it when he visited the planning officer who had placed the advertisement for someone to oversee the work, and it had seemed just the ticket. Once fabulous, with high ornate ceilings and large windows, it had been partly damaged during the war but was still habitable. Some of the plasterwork needed repairing and one of its balconies was hanging dangerously. They had the place rent-free with the proviso that Jack supervised and aimed to have it finished within three months.

A couple of large bedrooms overlooked the street of baroque sandstone townhouses, each with its coloured wooden *gallarija*, while a bathroom, kitchen and living space had views of the courtyard at the back, which seemed to be where everyone hung their washing. The owner had wired cash over to the planning officer, who would release funds to the builders on receipt of invoices.

'I love it,' said Florence when she first saw it.

'It's pretty fantastic,' said Jack. 'Just don't try stepping onto the balcony in the second bedroom.'

They settled in and the next day he asked about her plans for finding Rosalie and whether she needed his help today. She felt excited to be out of the hotel and getting going on this properly, even if there had been no clues so far.

'No. I'll be fine. I've got somewhere else I want to see before I try to work out what to do and the order in which to do it. How about you?'

'I'm meeting someone at a small church. Apparently it's in Rabat, not far from a place called Mdina.'

'Mdina is where I was thinking of going today.'

'With your friend Cam?' He gave her a look of fake indignation. 'Should I be jealous?'

She laughed. 'Don't be ridiculous. I'm going to take the bus as soon as the builder has left.'

'Sorry to leave you with that.'

'It's fine. I might be able to walk to your church afterwards if it really isn't far. Give me the address. Maybe we could meet there at lunchtime.'

The builder the planning officer had recommended arrived soon after Jack had left, a muscly Maltese man, red-faced, with a moustache and sparkling eyes. She quickly recognised he spoke just a few random words of

English, though he seemed to be fluent in Italian, which was not much use to her as she was not.

However, Jack had already met the man and told him what was needed, and now he was scrutinising the building for cracks, shaking his head and pulling faces. When she gave him a glass of water, he thanked her by nodding repeatedly and smiling. Then he held up three fingers. She nodded and he seemed pleased. But she had no idea what he was really saying.

After he left, she took a bus to Mdina, which Cam had said was worth a look, and felt awed by the sight of the centuries-old bastions, high golden walls, domes, towers and cupolas. It looked utterly unspoilt, and completely unassailable. Once past the huge arched entrance she wandered the labyrinth of narrow streets where she became aware of someone watching her from a small window at the very top of one of the stone buildings. Although the ancient city was extremely beautiful, Florence shivered. There was something ghostly about its silence and she couldn't imagine Rosalie would be living in a place like this.

'Who lives here?' she asked an old man who was walking a dog.

'Maltese nobility,' he said gruffly and walked on.

Then she hitched a ride with a passing fruit truck to Rabat, where she met Jack at the church he was giving the once-over. He was covered in dust and grime but smiled when she walked in.

'Get anywhere?'

She shook his head. 'I'm still just getting my bearings,

but it's a lovely island even with the bomb damage. I'm ready to work out a plan now.'

'Well, I've got us both second-hand bicycles and had them delivered here. That might help you get around more easily. We can cycle back to Valletta together if you don't mind hanging on for half an hour.'

Later, after they cycled back to their apartment, Florence made a simple lunch of omelette and salad and then she wrote her list.

'What's first?' Jack asked.

'Well, I've got hospitals, churches and newspapers on my list for tomorrow but I'm going to the police this afternoon.'

At the police station a burly, heavily moustached man behind a desk openly laughed at her.

'You think I can find someone who went missing, let's see . . .' he looked up at the ceiling, 'you don't know when, you don't know where, and maybe she wasn't even here at all? All you can tell me is that she was French.'

'Is French,' Florence corrected, bristling. Then, sighing, she changed tack and decided to flatter the man. 'I heard the police here are especially efficient.'

He nodded. 'We do our best.'

'They told me that at the hotel.'

'You visiting?'

Florence bit her lip and tried the damsel in distress look, whereas in reality she felt annoyed and wanted to give the man a good shake. 'I'm trying to find my aunt, you see. My mother's terribly upset about her disappearance.'

'Sorry to hear that, my dear.'

She gave him a helpless wide-eyed look. 'My mother just wants me to find her sister.'

'Very sad. So many people lost during the war, even my own cousin. But there it is.'

'She might have been a dancer. Could you possibly go through your records?'

'I'm sorry but this is not our normal station. Temporary, you see. Most of our records went up in smoke. And to be fair you really are looking for a needle in a haystack.'

'But it's such a small island.'

This time *he* bristled. 'It may be small, but many people pass through, legally and illegally, I might add.'

She bowed her head and blinked again to make her eyes water, then looked up through damp eyelashes.

It worked because he immediately relented. 'Look, if she was a dancer, you should ask around in the clubs of Strait Street one evening. What's your best bet for when she was here?'

'A few years ago.'

'Ah well.' He shrugged. 'I wish you luck.'

Back in the apartment Florence made a few small posters to put in shop windows and at dusk she went with Jack to Strait Street. It looked very run-down, with peeling posters on the crumbling walls and dozens of stray cats and dogs. They climbed over rubble and Florence almost choked on the awful smell of boiled cabbage mixed with stale beer, urine, and cheap perfume. She felt tired and sweaty and needed a long bath but despite all that, they called at every club that was open. There were many that weren't, and they were just about giving up hope when in one of the clubs an old boy seemed to want to talk. 'French, you say?' he remarked.

Florence nodded.

'We had foreign dancers, French to begin with and then mainly Hungarian and, of course, the foreigners had to go when the war began. The British stayed and some of the French. But there was a big old fuss in the Thirties.'

'What kind of fuss?'

'Buy me a beer and I'll tell you.'

Jack bought him a beer and Florence settled down to listen.

'Human trafficking, they call it now. We called it the white slave trade.'

Florence gasped, feeling sick to the core. Is that what had happened to Rosalie? Is that what she meant the only time she contacted Claudette saying she needed help?

Jack put an arm around her shoulder.

'Sorry, love,' the man said. 'Didn't mean to upset you.'

'No, I'm all right. Who should I ask about her?'

'Try the newspaper archives. We had an enquiry and it was reported in the newspaper. If she was interviewed there might be something.' He shrugged. 'It's a long shot and, like everywhere else, the *Times of Malta* was bombed. And, of course, you could try the churches too. She might have got married, or buried, I suppose.'

She nodded slowly, hoping it wouldn't turn out to be the latter.

'You'll have to phone the *Times*,' he added. Make an appointment.'

The man had been right. When she finally walked through the doors for her appointment a week later, an officious-looking man with terrible teeth, a small mouth, and bad breath led her to a poky office that smelt of stale tobacco. He told her that yes, the *Times of Malta* had been bombed, along with their archive, although part of the building was considered safe to use. After she explained what she needed she was told to put her request in writing and their archivist would get back to her once he'd been able to investigate. In the intervening week before seeing this man she'd had no luck at the churches, nor the hospitals in Valletta either and now felt completely frustrated. She'd been to Strait Street again, had spoken to a few of the dancers there but no one had heard of Rosalie or the enquiry except to say it was before their time. *And* she'd been back to the police to ask if Rosalie had ever been arrested. Nothing there either.

Much later and time was rapidly passing. Florence was running out of options and still nothing had come back from the archivist at the *Times*. Now she was gazing at an airmail letter arrived from France. Jack had collected it from the poste restante, and she turned it over in her hand several times, having recognised the handwriting and feeling nervous about opening it.

She sighed then she opened the envelope carefully, her eyes misting over as she began to read.

Dear Florence,

I have spoken to our mother and you are quite right. She is unwell. I'm sorry to be blunt but Claudette has incurable cancer. I don't know how long you are planning to say in Malta, but I believe she only has a few months left. Maybe three or four, maybe less. Now that travelling is possible, I am going to England to care for her, but Élise and Victoria are staying here in France until closer to the end.

As for Jack, I'm sorry to hear about the loss of his child. Please pass on my condolences.

Élise sends her love.

Hélène

Florence read it through several times. Her mother was ill, seriously ill. Oh God, she should have stayed with her, should have looked after her when she had the chance. Only a few months left. How could that be? She could feel an ache in her chest and her tears welling. Oh Maman, why didn't you tell me? Why did you send me on this wild goose chase when I should have been with you?

She turned to Jack. 'It's awful news. Claudette is ill. Really ill. Cancer. Hélène says she only has a few months left. Look, read . . .' She almost choked on her words and passed the letter to Jack.

As he read it, Florence sat with her head in her hands. She longed to be with her mother and it hurt to be so far away from her. It felt like they were never going to find Rosalie, so going home to Claudette was the only thing to do, just as soon as she possibly could. She pictured her mother restored to health, cheeks glowing, lips painted her favourite shade of pink, her eyelids shimmering blue. Her chignon perfect. But then another image took hold and she choked back a sob. Claudette, thin, grey, dying, and she, her daughter, not with her at her bedside. She covered her mouth with her hands and screwed up her eyes. Then she thought of how Hélène's letter had sounded so formal and cold and remembered that Hélène would be at her mother's house. She began rocking, holding her face in her hands again, her sobs tearing her apart, as the thought of Claudette dying before she got home completely broke her.

CHAPTER 46

Florence and Jack talked long into the night. Shredded by exhaustion, disappointment at her progress in finding Rosalie, and fear for her mother, Florence felt wretched.

'Could you check out how long we'll have to wait for a ship home?' she asked Jack.

'They're not frequent. I know that.'

'We might be lucky.'

'You might even hear back from the archivist at the *Times* before we can go.'

More than anything she wanted to see Claudette, but her mother had been so desperate for news of Rosalie that Florence hated the thought of returning empty-handed. Claudette was counting on her, and she so wanted to give her mother some peace of mind before she died.

'I'm going to have my hair cut,' she said as Jack

came out of the bathroom naked. 'It's the last thing I really want to do but I need to do something, or I'll go crazy.'

'Wouldn't you like to come back to bed?' he said and, reaching for her hand, pulled her to him.

'You're wet,' she said and pushed him away. 'But I've made up my mind. My hair's a fright and I need time to think. The hairdresser's is a good place for that.'

'Your hair looks fine to me.'

'Then I'm going to look at the church records,' she said, ignoring him and knowing that being resolute was the one thing that would stop her from dissolving into tears whenever she thought of Claudette.

'I thought you'd been to the churches.'

'Only the big ones, and I can't speak Maltese, can I? Cam said he'd come with me this time. It might help.'

'See you a bit later then. Shall I get the shopping?'

'What about the little church in Mdina?'

'Still waiting for the go-ahead. The wheels seem to turn awfully slowly here.'

'If we're able to leave for England quickly what will happen about finishing the apartment?'

'I'll work something out.'

She left with a heavy heart, and made her way to Paris Style, the oldest salon she could find where people had been going for decades and the magazines might be from the past. You never knew – Rosalie might be mentioned somewhere.

The woman who was to wash and then cut her hair was called Ganna, a large Maltese lady with huge hands, dressed head-to-toe in black. But her chestnut hair was stunning, long, wavy and lustrous.

'You want a short cut?' the woman asked with a gleam in her eye.

Florence shook her head. 'Just a trim. Tidy it up, please.'

Ganna threw her hands up in the air. 'A trim, always a trim. I am an artiste. I like to cut, to shape, to change.'

'Sorry,' Florence muttered.

Ganna gave in with a shrug, washed Florence's hair and was remarkably deft with the scissors despite the size of her hands.

The two women sitting next to her were talking about their offspring, when Florence thought she'd overheard something rather intriguing.

She leant forward to listen.

'Lulu says she heard it from her neighbour.'

'But is it true?' the other one said in a mock whisper.

'Well, your guess is as good as mine. Lulu's neighbour is one for a bit of gossip, I know that.'

'Hmm. Maybe it was dead horse they found?'

'Nah. A body, Lulu said.'

'Where?'

'Somewhere behind the old Opera House.'

'Today?'

'This morning.'

'Blimey. Still finding bodies even now and the war's been over for more than a year. Bloke, was it?'

'She didn't say.'

As soon as Florence could politely leave, despite her hair not being fully dry, she paid and hurried to Strada

Reale where, flanked by South Street and Ordnance Street, the Royal Opera House still lay in ruins since 1942. How sad that war had destroyed so much that had been beautiful. Not far away, the remains of a house piled high with rubble was cordoned off with two bored policemen guarding it.

'What happened?' she asked the younger one, who looked like he might be a rookie.

'Body under rubble. Must have caught a stray bomb at the end of the war. We do still find them. Sad really.'

Florence nodded. 'Man or woman?' she asked.

'Woman. Pretty bashed up I believe. Except for her hair.'

'Her hair?'

'Yeah, bright red. Must have been foreign. None of us have red hair like that.' He narrowed his eyes. 'What's it to you?'

'Where have they taken her, the poor thing?' she said with a pounding heart but trying for nonchalance.

He shrugged.

'Do you know? I'm curious, that's all.'

'Hospital mortuary,' he said, relenting.

'I see. Well, have a good day. Hope you don't have to stand here for too long.'

Florence glanced at her watch. Oh God, she thought, panicking now about the body, a woman with red hair. Could it be? Could it? And now she was going to be late for Cam too. She forced herself to calm down because there was a shortcut to his office and with luck she might just make it in time.

When she knocked on his door, he already had his jacket on.

'I was beginning to think you weren't coming,' he said.

'Sorry, I just heard they found a body. I need a favour. Can you help me?'

When Jack arrived home that evening, he immediately picked up on her distress.

'Feeling bad about your mother?' he asked, with a sympathetic look, then came to her and drew her close. 'I'm afraid there isn't a ship for ten days. We only just missed one. It left yesterday.'

She screwed up her eyes. 'It's not just Maman. You haven't heard?'

'What?'

'A woman's body was discovered today. Under the rubble in the bombed remains of a building. Cam called someone he knows at the hospital.'

'I guess they will be finding bodies, even now.'

'They think she died towards the end of the war, maybe even a couple of years ago, a stray bomb. Something about the way she was held under the rubble meant she's only partially decomposed.'

'And you're worrying—'

'I don't know. I'm going to the hospital mortuary tomorrow.'

'It might be . . . well, dreadfully grizzly.'

'Jack, they told Cam she was wearing a charm bracelet and a policeman told me she had red hair. I have to go, if only to put my mind at rest.'

'There must be other similar bracelets.'

'Maybe,' she said.

'You really think she might be Rosalie?'

'I don't know what to think. If she is Rosalie, it still doesn't explain why nobody has heard of her.'

He nodded.

She stared at him as the light finally dawned. 'Oh Lord, I've been such an idiot. She must have changed her name. I should have thought of it. Obvious, though, isn't it? I should just be asking about a French woman, never mind her name.'

'Don't give yourself such a hard time. There used to be a hell of a lot of French here, so it may not have helped anyway.'

Jack accompanied Florence to the mortuary the next day. Cam had phoned ahead to tell them she'd be coming and that she believed the dead woman might be a relative.

Florence took in the entrance hall, painted a rather sickly acidic green. Then she marched across to ask at the reception desk and was pointed towards a staircase and told to go down then turn right at the bottom. After that there would be signs. With a feeling of deep unease, Florence held Jack's hand as they followed the woman's instructions and eventually reached a door where a notice told them to walk straight in and take a seat. She turned the handle and went into a room painted the same awful green as the entrance hall and all the corridors. A notice on the wall gave the address and phone number of a funeral director, along with a small photograph of a church. She rang a bell on the wall, and then waited on a hard metal chair, her heart hammering in her throat as she tried to second guess what she would see when the final door swung open. Would the body be Rosalie's?

After a few minutes, an almost bald middle-aged man came out. 'Miss Baudin?'

'Yes.'

'Please follow me.'

He took them into a small anteroom and asked them to wait again. Florence was overcome by a feeling of doom. All this interminable waiting was making it worse, and it was chilly down here in the bowels of the hospital, with nothing to look at on the walls but for a cross.

When the man returned, he was holding something wrapped in white cloth. He unwrapped it carefully and held out his hand.

Florence stared and her throat constricted. Oh God! She recognised it immediately, knew all the individual charms. The little horse, the rabbit, the Eiffel tower, the goat, and more. She nodded at the man and showed him her own bracelet, then said, 'I want to see her body. I think I must.'

'She's not in too bad a condition, if that's what you're worried about,' the man said. 'We think she was trapped in a space that must have remained sealed and dry, probably in the basement and covered by dry dust and rubble in the air pocket.'

'Did she die immediately?' Florence asked.

'Hard to tell. She might have died from her injuries, or

from suffocation. When the building collapsed, she was contained in a kind of rocky vault, if you like. I would have expected insects to have got in, but it doesn't appear so.'

Florence and Jack were then shown to a small room where a body lay on a trolley covered by a white sheet. There was a sweet, sickly smell, and Florence held a hand over her nose. The bracelet was Rosalie's. Was this Rosalie's body too? When the attendant pulled back the sheet, her heart thumped even more wildly as she glanced at the partially decomposed face of the dead woman, her eyes open, and her skin purplish. Then she stifled a groan. Although the woman's face was damaged, her dusty hair was clearly red. Poor Rosalie had bright red hair.

Florence stepped back. In that instant she lost hope, her shoulders slumping. This had to be her aunt, killed when a bomb had fallen on the building. Somewhere along the line Rosalie had changed her name or possibly married, although none of the churches had given up a clue to a marriage. She wondered if anyone had even known of her death or disappearance. This poor dead woman had to be Rosalie, it was the only thing that made any sense, but the dead don't give up their secrets easily and they certainly don't give up a name.

She left the room and numbly sat with the attendant, trying to explain she had no idea what name her aunt had been using. The staff didn't seem to care, only keen to certify an unknown woman's death as caused by a stray bomb in the vicinity of the ruined Opera House towards the end of the war.

Later, in the awful blackness of night, Florence couldn't

sleep. Images of her dead aunt plagued her, but it wasn't that alone. Something about it seemed wrong, although she couldn't figure out what. Jack grunted in his sleep and reached out an arm to enfold her, but she slid from his embrace and left the bed, tiptoeing away from him and into the other bedroom.

She sat and thought about her aunt, wondering about her life, and feeling desperately sad that she had died the way she had, and that Claudette would never set eyes on her sister again. Rosalie was dead. And Claudette would be soon. There had to be a ship heading back home sooner than Jack had said. There had to be. She needed to look after her mother, convey the sad news, and face the music with Hélène. There was no point thinking of Rosalie any more.

CHAPTER 47

Riva

Malta, 1942

Riva had no sense of how long they'd been trapped in the shelter and was losing hope. She'd given up pleading and bargaining with God. Given up hoping for a miracle and had no idea how long they could last without water. The airless shelter was hot, stuffy, and smelt of fear and the sooner death came the better. Her eyes were stinging, her head hurt and feeling sick to her stomach, all she could do was whisper prayers under her breath. As time stretched out, no longer with any meaning, she ached with longing for Bobby to hold her. Were they going to be buried in this awful thick silence until the end? Was she never going to see Bobby again?

In the blackness she picked up a faint sound of scraping,

followed by a loud crack. She gasped, certain the shelter was about to collapse and then they'd be buried alive instantly. She flung herself back against the wall, her hands covering her ears, and waiting for the inevitable, but nothing more happened. There was a brief silence then the scratching resumed. And only then, in a lightning flash of hope, she realised where it was coming from and on hands and knees, she crept to the wall of fallen rocks where she screamed. 'In here. We're in here.'

She held her breath, heard nothing, shouted again until her throat was raw. Still nothing.

But then, thank God, a muffled voice. She couldn't hear the words but whoever was on the other side, they were moving the rocks. Moving the rocks! So close. Her breath snagged as she waited, terrified more rocks might fall. The woman began to pray, her children crying, but eventually Riva saw a thin shaft of light coming through a tiny cleft.

'Don't move,' she heard the man on the other side say. 'We'll get you out. Just don't move any rocks on your side.'

She chewed the inside of her cheeks, hardly daring to hope. Unable to keep still she went to check on the elderly man. She'd been right. He *was* already dead. Poor old boy must have died of fright when the bomb fell. She went back to the fallen rocks itching to move some herself but knowing she must not.

'How many?' the rescuer was asking as the hole grew a little larger. 'How many trapped?'

She told him.

'Right. When I'm ready I'll ask you to pass the children through first. They will need to slide on their bellies.'

As Riva trained the torch on the woman and her children, the rescuers moved more rocks. The woman spoke rapidly in Maltese and tried to push the children towards the hole. The man let her know he was ready and Riva held her breath. The children clung to their mother, too scared to let go, but the man on the other side spoke Maltese too and eventually they complied and slithered towards his outstretched hands.

'Now the woman and the baby,' the man said. 'Will she manage?'

'I think so,' Riva said.

The woman groaned in pain, but on her stomach and clutching the baby in front of her, she crawled through to the other side.

'Now you,' came the voice.

'There is a dead man.'

'We can't risk this collapsing. We have to save the living.'

'Let me just see if he has identification.'

She stumbled across to the man, went through his pockets, but found nothing.

There was a rumble and a loud crack as the rocks moved. Her heart lurched, and she hurried back to the hole, then holding her breath, she scrambled through to the other side where people were helping the woman and her children. Behind her came the sound of rocks falling again. She'd only just made it in time. She could barely stand up, was nauseous and hot, but breathing slowly in blessed relief. Someone rubbed her back and helped her out of the shelter. She felt dizzy and the world around her blurred then disappeared as she blacked out.

The next thing she knew she was in the medical centre, a scratchy blanket wrapped around her, and Bobby was sitting on her bed and gazing at her with hollowed, anxious eyes. But her vision was still blurred, and she glanced around in wonder. Was she imagining this? For a moment she couldn't believe what she was seeing. Was Bobby really there? She couldn't properly recall what had happened and when she tried nothing came to her. She felt muddled, hazy, in thick unforgiving air as if still in the shelter. But then she heard birds chirping in a tree outside her window. Saw a painting of a deer on the wall opposite her bed. She must have escaped the shelter before it collapsed. But her eyes felt gritty and sore, and although her forehead seemed to be burning up, she was shivering. She shook her head, screwed up her eyes, opened them again and tried to focus.

'It's the shock,' he said. 'You'll be all right.'

She couldn't reply, just rubbed her eyelids and then she felt it. The light seemed to turn luminous, and she was filled with a flood of so much joy and gratitude that it overflowed into great gulping sobs of relief.

'I'm alive,' she whispered when she could speak again, barely registering that Bobby was blinking back tears.

'You are and thank God for it,' he said in a choked voice, and then he caressed her cheek.

She reached for his hand and kissed it.

'I don't know,' he said, looking at her in mock outrage. 'I leave you alone for five minutes.'

'I just went for a walk while you were busy with paper-work. I wanted to stock up.' Her throat felt raw and her voice was rasping. 'I thought I was going to die.'

'You gave me a terrible fright. I was hunting for you everywhere.'

He stroked her cheek again and pulled her close.

'Sorry.'

'You're something of a heroine.'

'What?'

He smiled. 'Otto is preparing the headline as we speak. *Woman War Room Worker Delivers Baby in Bomb-blasted Shelter!*'

'Is the baby all right?'

'As far as I know. Yes.' He paused, looked suddenly serious, rubbed his nose. 'Riva, you may not realise but you hit your head. You had blood all over it and you have stitches.' He touched her forehead.

'I didn't feel a thing.'

'It will be fine. But they want to keep an eye on you in case of concussion.'

She sighed. 'Bloody hell. Bloody, bloody hell.'

The nurse brought her a mint tea. 'Sorry,' she said. 'We're out of biscuits but there's a lump of sugar in the tea. Emergencies only.'

After she had sipped her tea and rested back against her pillow, Bobby said, 'I do have some good news.'

'Tell me.'

'Four merchant ships and an oil tanker have reached us unscathed. This island is not going to starve, at least not yet.'

'Oh, thank God. Thank God.'

'Can I ask you something?'

She closed her eyes. 'Of course.'

'Riva, will you marry me?'

Her eyes flew open and she laughed, although it hurt her chest and throat. She felt jubilant, her heart dancing with triumph at having escaped death and now this. What a marvellous delicious moment to be alive.

'Well?'

'Are you crazy? You're asking a concussed woman to marry you? I call that taking advantage.'

He gave her a tired smile and stroked her hand. 'I'm serious. Do you need some time to think about it?'

'You are an idiot, Beresford. I've had thirteen years to think about it.'

'So?'

She gripped his hand and squeezed it. 'Of course I'll marry you. I would be honoured.'

And now Bobby was the one with tears filling his eyes.

'You can't cry in here,' she said and grinned at him. 'What if someone sees?'

'To hell with that. The whole world can see for all I care. Can I hold you?'

'I won't break.'

And he held her as close as he dared without disturbing her stitches.

She nuzzled his cheek and smelt his skin, his hair. Bobby. Her Bobby. And this time forever.

CHAPTER 48

Riva and Bobby chose the old stone-built church of Santa Maria Ta' Doni in Rabat for their wedding. A gorgeous little sixteenth-century church, not ostentatious but with lovely frescoed walls and a beautiful vaulted ceiling. Addison would give her away, and a few of their closest friends, including Otto, Tommy-O and a couple of Bobby's RAF pals would be among the guests. They planned a simple affair, with a small reception to be held in Addison's apartment and they kept very quiet about it. Gerry sent a telegram with warmest wishes for their happiness, sad that the war prevented him from being there. Dear Gerry, Riva thought, dear, dear man.

'But what shall I wear?' she complained as she sat with Bobby on Addison's terrace.

Addison was just coming out and overheard her. 'One moment. I have a solution to that,' he said and went back inside.

Bobby reached across and kissed her. Joy bubbled up inside her and spread tingling and fizzing throughout her body. They had reached a new frontier in their relationship. There was vulnerability – how could there not be with the war still raging? – but Riva felt little fear. The days of intoxication were long gone but this quieter love was a revelation. Of course, she had found a way to forgive him, but she'd only been able to do it because she'd allowed herself, with his help, to feel how much he really had hurt her. And she had encouraged him to forgive himself too. Brick by brick she'd removed the barriers she'd spent so long erecting, and now they were both living in the present, still with an uncertain future, but everyone shared that, didn't they?

Addison came back out with a long dress in palest sea-glass green draped over his arm. 'This was my wife's. It's silk, designed, embroidered and made in Paris. We can get it to altered to fit you.'

She rose to her feet and touched it. 'Oh Addison. It's exquisite but are you sure? I don't really mind what I wear.'

'No, my dear. You must look your best on your wedding day. It's an order. And you'll be doing me a favour. The dress has spent far too long hanging in my wardrobe. It's yours now.'

She took it from him. 'Bobby shouldn't really see it though.'

'Close your eyes, nephew,' he ordered. 'Come, Riva. Let's see how it looks on you.'

They went down to Bobby's apartment and Riva tried on the dress in the bathroom. When she came out to show it to Addison, he looked as if he were lost in the past. Then he shook himself out of it and smiled.

'You look beautiful. But since I first met you, my dear, you've lost weight.'

'I know. We all have, haven't we?'

'There's a woman in Rabat who makes my shirts. I'm sure she can take it in a little here and there. Come back when you're next off duty and I'll make sure she's here.'

'No need. I've given in my notice at the war rooms.'

He looked surprised. 'Oh.'

'We haven't told them we're getting married, but if they knew, Bobby and I wouldn't be allowed to work on the same watch. And if we were on different watches, we'd rarely see each other, so it seems the right thing to do.'

'Well, you've already done your bit what with delivering babies and everything else.'

She laughed. 'I didn't do a thing.'

He laughed and wagged his finger. 'False modesty. Now have you thought about a bouquet?'

She shook her head. 'Not really.'

'Will you leave it to me? Any preference for colour? I rather think something red or orange to go with your extraordinary hair. Thank God this marvellous island is still blessed with flowers. The Germans can't take that away.'

He came over to touch her hair which, long now, tumbled to her shoulders in her natural fiery red. She smiled, delighted by Addison's involvement in all this. With her marriage they would become family, of course, but he was already more than a father to her.

★ ★ ★

On a beautiful bright day in May, a day filled only with enchantment and love, Riva and Bobby married. The ceremony was brief, over quickly, but then came the reception. As everyone trooped up to Addison's apartment, smiling and happy, you could almost have believed there was no war, there were no bombs, no deaths, no grinding fear. Life was as it had once been with light-hearted chatter, unrestrained laughter, raising of glasses and toasts, so many toasts. The scent of roses and tobacco drifted in the air and the simple country food was delicious. Addison had opened his wine cellar, the hundreds of bottles accumulated over many years, so despite the deprivations on the island the champagne flowed. Riva saw herself and Bobby together for ever and blew him a kiss across the room, imagining herself in bed with him later. His face glowed with happiness and she knew nothing could break their bond now. And as she stood on Addison's terrace all she could feel as she gazed out across the spring green fields was hope, and the kind of spaciousness she'd rarely known before. This time their love would not stall. This time she had absolute faith in him and in herself.

The summer and autumn passed.

After days of bruised purple skies, endless rain and violent storms, the sky had been washed clean and when Christmas Eve came it was sunny and bright. Bobby, Addison and Riva took a *karozzin*, or cab, along with throngs of other people to the Porta Reale. The evening air thrummed with the scent of incense and the chanting that rose up along the streets of Valletta. The churches were overflowing and as they entered the bombed

Carmelite church in Old Theatre Street they glanced up and saw stars. It seemed significant. Special. That amid the destruction the stars still shone down on them.

All the churches were packed with kneeling people who, heads bowed, were praying for deliverance and the end of war. Riva, followed by Bobby and Addison, squeezed into the back of the baroque church of Our Lady of Victory. Inside it glowed, golden and bright, from the dozens of altar candles. Riva felt tears pricking her eyes and reached for Bobby's hand. The hope in the human heart was truly incredible.

CHAPTER 49

Ten days later, while Bobby had gone into Valletta for a lunch appointment with one of his RAF colleagues, Riva heard the sound of an air raid over Valletta. She crossed her fingers and told herself it would be fine. But an hour or so later she heard a knock at their apartment door. It was January and cold, so she threw on her robe and went to open up.

She saw Addison first, standing solemnly before her eyes, then she registered the policeman in uniform who was looking at his feet.

Riva just stared at him, already knowing, her body beginning to shake.

'I'm so sorry, madam,' the policeman said, finally glancing up.

She took a step back and tried to shut the door.

Addison moved towards her, held the door open.

'Bobby,' she whispered. 'Not Bobby. Please . . . not Bobby.'

'A direct hit,' the man was saying.

She ran for her coat. 'I have to go to him.'

Addison stopped her. 'No, Riva. No.'

She couldn't stop the tears nor the low groan that emerged of its own accord. She heard Addison talking to the man and she walked away. This was not happening. It could not be happening. The policeman and Addison followed her inside.

'When?' she asked as a feeling of icy unnatural calm took over.

'About two hours ago,' the policeman said.

'His body?'

Addison's look was anguished. 'You know how it can be.'

Riva knew. During the worst of the siege, she had seen the broken bodies. The pieces of people. The pieces of families. Had seen them so indistinguishable from rubble that only a hand or a foot was left. Had seen it all and yet they'd all believed the bombing was over and done with. How could this be? Bobby. Her Bobby. She couldn't comprehend it.

Once the policeman left, she crumpled onto a rug and Addison let her lie, just sat on the sofa, his hands resting on his knees, his head bowed. When she looked closely, she saw tears rolling down his cheeks. She went to him, and they sat together, both of them trembling in disbelief.

During the following days and nights, grief tore her apart. They had not even been married for eight months. She had thought she'd felt grief the time he had left her to marry someone else. It had been nothing of the kind. Not while he still lived and breathed. Loss, yes, betrayal too, and anger. But not the grief, the utterly corrosive grief that comes with the impossible knowing that the person you love above all others no longer exists. Does not have a body. Cannot ever walk or talk or breathe, or eat, or make love again. She circled the apartment, unable to keep still, praying that one time she might glance back and he'd be sitting there and smiling. She longed for his touch. Physically. Mentally. Emotionally. Just the brush of his hand against her cheek as he passed her as she sat lost in a book. That would be enough.

'Why Bobby?' she shouted at the walls, his chair, their bed. 'Why?'

Silence. There was no rule for death. No formula for surviving the pain as time slid between day and night. No respite.

Addison let himself in one morning. 'I've arranged the funeral. I hope that's all right.'

She recoiled, hating to think of it. 'I don't think I can be there. I'm so sorry. But few people knew we were married, and I would weep, and people would gawp. Bobby wouldn't have wanted that.'

'Of course. I've informed his mother. Travel is impossible so she won't be here either. We can talk about the headstone later.'

Riva nodded and Addison left.

The headstone! She didn't want a headstone. Bobby's death wasn't real. It couldn't be real. Her memories rose and dissolved with the beating of her heart, with the pulsing of her blood, with her ragged uncertain breath.

She didn't sleep, didn't see how she could ever sleep again. She even dragged up memories of her old life in Paris. Would she ever go back there? She doubted it. This was where she belonged now. Here, where Bobby was everywhere and nowhere.

She held wordless conversations with him and in the weirdest way she felt as if she'd known that this was going to happen. Somehow. That there had been an inevitability about it she couldn't explain. His return. Their marriage. The depth of their love, the depth of her pain. She cried and fell to her knees, her world and her life in pieces.

When the time came for Simon Wilson-Browne, the solicitor, to sit in Addison's living room to read the will, Riva sat up straight on a hard-backed chair, digging her nails into her palm to prevent herself from crying.

'Sir Robert has left you almost everything, Mrs Beresford,' Wilson-Browne said after a few moments and then read the exact wording in the relevant clauses.

She heard the words, but distantly as if happening in another room and spoken to another version of herself. 'And his mother?' she eventually asked, glancing at Addison.

He nodded. 'Taken care of. The house in England is already in her name and she has her own private income. Bobby saw to that when he became a pilot.'

'I'm glad.'

'Back then he knew the lifespan of a fighter pilot could be brief,' Addison added. 'As all of our lives on this earth are.'

It seemed as if Addison had somehow known he also hadn't got long left. Because the time came just a few short weeks later when she went upstairs and found him looking as if he was pretending to have fallen asleep in his favourite armchair. But there was no breath, no pulse, no life. She sat beside him, holding his hand in the silent room, and waiting while his butler called the doctor.

'Oh Addison,' she whispered, stroking his lifeless hand. 'I'm so sorry.'

'A heart attack,' the doctor said when he came an hour later.

A broken heart, she thought.

Confronted so soon by this second unexpected loss, she could not bear it. She withdrew, physically and emotionally, and found a kind of solace in absolute silence where she faced the darkest hours of the darkest night. Alone.

And even as the war ground on, it seemed as if she were the only one left alive on the island. She would see no one, not even Otto. And when the war ended, if it ever ended, she would stay on in Mdina, forever wearing only black.

She'd had few black clothes of her own but found Addison's wife's clothes – black shawls, long skirts, and silky blouses. All out of date but she didn't care and wore them, even though they were too big and made her look like a witch. One day she unlocked his wife's jewellery box too and wore her earrings, long dangly earrings made of gold with precious gemstones set into them. Rubies, emeralds, sapphires.

Meanwhile Otto kept on calling and knocking at her door.

Some weeks later she relented and let him in, and they drank wine together.

'Well,' he said with a grin. 'You'll be pleased to know I have news about Stanley Lucas.'

'Oh?'

'He's been arrested, charged, found guilty and sentenced to prison for the maximum five years.'

'For the girls?'

'No. That would have carried a far heavier sentence. Unfortunately, he appears to have got away with that. But he couldn't wriggle out of this one. He's been skimming off army supplies – black market profiteering.'

'Just as we suspected.' She knew Lucas would probably never face justice for Anya and the other girls, but this was something at least.

'Was he still involved with the trafficking of girls?'

'No. It seems he shifted his focus. For people like Lucas, war delivers fresh opportunities.' He paused then asked her if she had thought about what she might do next.

She didn't know. Didn't have a clue.

'You could come back to the paper,' he suggested.

She shook her head.

'Will you stay here?'

'In Malta?'

'I meant Mdina.'

'Where else?'

This hidden palace, *her* palace, had tightened its grip around her, but the meeting with Otto had unleashed something and it made her realise she had to get out before she became even more isolated and forlorn. She began by taking short walks around Mdina itself, gradually recognising one or two of the people who lived there or were servants to the people who lived there. On her third outing, a grand old lady also dressed in black stopped to talk to her outside the cathedral.

'Forgive the intrusion,' she said with a little bow. 'Please accept these and allow me to offer my sincere condolences.'

'Thank you,' Riva muttered as she took the delicate white roses, and the woman passed by. Had the woman been coming to see her, she wondered, or was it just chance that she had been carrying a bunch of flowers?

A whiskery man stopped her the next day in the public square in the heart of the city. 'If there is anything I can do,' he said. 'I knew Addison well.'

Of course, most of these people must have known Addison. He'd lived in Mdina for so long and his wife Filomena had been born there.

Riva kept the outings brief while she gathered her courage to go farther afield. She had thought hearing people speak of her loss would make her feel worse. It hadn't. In Villegaignon Street, just across the square from the cathedral, she stopped outside the Palazzo Santa Sofia, her favourite building and realised what a strong affinity she felt for Mdina and its people.

A silent woman in a silent city.

They were very private those who lived there, but some began leaving offerings at her door. More flowers, books, even a basket of fruit. They left little cards wishing her well and she had been so touched it made her cry.

Despite the kindness of strangers, grief continued to constrict her until her life became so small she felt she might disappear completely. So eventually, on a brilliantly sunny day, she braced herself, left the city walls and set off for the cliffs at Dingli. She forced herself to walk there, one foot in front of the other and, once there, she gazed at the luminescent multicoloured ocean and the haze of the empty horizon. Gazed and gazed until her eyes stung. She tasted salt on her tongue, felt the wind snatching her hair free from its clips, smelt the seaweed and remembered her first sight of the island back in 1925.

The girl she had been. Where was she now?

Grief had unleashed something wild inside her that she'd almost forgotten. It had been a different kind of wild back then and she longed for those irresistible carefree days. But this was where she was now, and she didn't know what to do. The memories tipped and wobbled inside her, and she could do nothing but lift her arms in resignation and call out to the gods of the ocean. *Tell me what to do. When the war ends. Tell me.*

And the gods of the ocean did give her an answer, or so she liked to think.

By the time the war was over, she still hadn't been up to Addison's apartment. He had left the entire palace to her, but she had been too numb to care. Hadn't been up there since the day the solicitor read the will, but now she unlocked the door and went inside, her heart in her mouth. Even after all this time it still faintly smelt of him. Cigars. Wine. Even flowers, lilies perhaps, that smelt of death. Addison's butler was long gone, of course.

The apartment was dark, so she opened the shutters and threw open the windows for fresh air. Until that moment she hadn't clearly known what to do with her loss, but then she went to Addison's study, took out all his remaining work and contemplated it. The next day she returned and a few days after that; it took all her strength, but she phoned Gerry in London. Losing Bobby had felt like a grief that could have no end and that was right. It *should* have no end. It – and he – was a part of her, but that didn't mean she couldn't live her life.

'I didn't know if the phone lines would be working,' she said when Gerry picked up.

'It's wonderful to hear your voice,' he replied. 'How are you, sweetheart?'

'You know, one foot in front of the other.'

'Are you eating?'

The kindness in his voice brought tears to her eyes.

'I wish I could be there,' he said. 'Will you come to London? I can still help you find a job.'

'It turns out I don't need money. But actually, I have a different idea. Might you be interested in publishing a third and final volume of Addison's work?'

She smiled when he replied. Gerry was thrilled and she could hear the excitement as his laughter spilled down the line.

'Oh my dear girl. As soon as I can, I'll be there,' he added. 'The very moment.'

'No, I think I might come to you in London, after all. I could do with being away from here for a while. I'll bring a case full of Addison's work with me and get the rest shipped over.'

'You have a recent passport?'

CHAPTER 50

Florence

Malta, 1946

Their passage home was still nine days away. Florence wished she knew at least something about Rosalie's life that she could give her mother before she died. Before she died. The words went round and round in her head. Florence's sleep had been dreadfully troubled because of what was happening to Claudette, of course, but something else was playing at the edge of her mind just out of reach. Something about Rosalie that she just couldn't work out.

That evening she and Jack went out for a meal at the British Hotel and were seated at a table with a wonderful view of the harbour, the reflected lights from ships and boats sparkling in the water.

'Like fairyland, isn't it?' Florence said and sighed. 'But I just can't relax.'

'Try. It will do you good.' He reached for her hand and gently squeezed it. Then, as she saw his green eyes shining as he smiled at her, something lit up in her mind and then exploded.

'Oh my God!' she gasped. 'Oh my God.'

'What?'

'My mother told me Rosalie had blue eyes. How could I have forgotten? I was so shocked at seeing her, or rather seeing a dead body like that, it just didn't sink in. All I could see was the red hair and the bracelet. But the woman in the mortuary . . . Jack, her eyes were brown, not blue.'

Jack bent towards her. 'Then—'

'Yes. She wasn't . . . she isn't, Rosalie. I don't know if they're doing a post-mortem or not. But I know she wasn't Rosalie, which means Rosalie may still be alive. May even still be here in Malta!'

They walked home slowly and made love for the first time in days. Until now Florence had felt too preoccupied but afterwards, while Jack slept, she lay awake trying to think of her next steps. But she was so tired of searching with no results that eventually she curled her body next to Jack, closed her eyes, and fell asleep too.

First thing the next morning she contacted Cam to say she needed to rescind her identification. Told him that the woman wasn't Rosalie, and that they should identify the dead woman from dental records.

Back at the apartment a letter arrived from the archivist at the *Times of Malta*. He hadn't been able to find any mention of Rosalie Delacroix. She sighed, feeling her spirits plummeting after the euphoria of the evening before.

'Jack,' she said after he made her breakfast. 'I'm now absolutely sure Rosalie changed her name. It's the only explanation I can think of.'

'Or she may have been here for such a short time that nobody remembers her.'

'Maybe, but I need to ask the archivist at the *Times* if any French women were involved in the enquiry into the white slavery issue. I'll do the search myself if they'll let me.'

As she sipped her coffee, he asked her what else she wanted to do.

'I don't know. I'm wondering if there's anything I *can* do before we leave, as well as contacting the archivist again I mean.'

'You tried the churches?'

'Yes, we went through the records, but just the big ones. There are village churches, damaged churches where they're likely to only speak Maltese. Cam knows where they all are and he was going to help me, but we got side-tracked by the news of the dead woman.'

'Well, there you are. If Cam is still willing to help, that's the one last thing you can do.'

'You mean the woman was murdered?' she said a little later, staring at Cam in shock.

'Yes. Her dental records have identified her as Charlotte Lambden. She was English, married to an Archie Lambden. Because of strangulation marks on her neck and certain historic injuries, her husband has been arrested, although he's not yet been charged. They have her marriage certificate and her birth certificate so it's all above board.'

'The poor woman. I can't help wonder why she had Rosalie's bracelet?'

'Who knows? Maybe Rosalie sold it.'

'She might have if she'd needed cash.'

They set off to look at records in some of the smaller village churches. By the time Florence and Cam had already been to three, reading through records until their eyes were stinging from heat and concentration, Cam said, 'Shall we give up? Have some lunch. I've got to work this afternoon.'

'Just one more,' she pleaded.

In Rabat they arrived at a gorgeous little sixteenth-century church called Santa Maria Ta' Doni and Florence instantly loved the charm of it.

'Will there be anyone else here?' she asked, heat bearing down on the back of her neck as she marvelled at the golden stone of the edifice.

'No, but I have the key,' Cam said.

He unlocked and pushed open the creaking door.

Inside it was beautifully cool and the place looked in relatively good condition. 'So what's wrong with it? Why is it out of use?' she asked, glancing around at the frescoed walls. 'It doesn't look too bad.'

'It wasn't damaged during the war but soon afterwards a small unexploded Italian bomb went off through there.' He pointed in the direction of a vestry. 'Don't worry, it's safe to go through now.'

While Cam looked around Florence explored the damaged vestry, sifting through papers that must have been lying around since the bomb exploded. There were letters and ledgers, yellowing newspapers with announcements of births, deaths and marriages, prayer books splayed out on the floor, orders of service sheets and hymn sheets fluttering in the breeze, and piles of old handwritten sermons.

She heard Cam calling her and was just about to go through to him when something caught her eye. A torn piece of paper sticking out from beneath a prayer book with just four letters visible. *Rosa.* She almost left it but then turned back. It couldn't hurt to look.

As she pulled the whole thing out, she skimmed the words, then read them again more slowly, her hands trembling with excitement. 'Oh my Lord,' she whispered. A letter. It was a letter.

Hardly able to breathe, she called Cam. 'Look,' she said, waving it at him as he came in. 'It's her.'

She read Rosalie's name out loud. 'Surely it must be her? Rosalie Delacroix.'

The letter was from someone called Group Captain Robert Beresford, written in 1942 asking the priest to read the bans for a wedding to take place in late May between himself and Rosalie Delacroix.

He glanced at it and grinned. 'Good grief. That is a find.'

'Let's see if we can find out when the wedding took place.'

They searched the vestry, but the register of weddings

appeared to be missing. Destroyed or moved elsewhere? They didn't know.

'Did they get married?' she muttered over and over. 'Did they? Oh, I feel so tantalisingly close. To get this far and draw a blank would be so disappointing. I need to check the registry of marriages in the town hall, again. There has to be something. Doesn't there?'

'Agreed.'

'Come on then,' she said, tugging at his elbow. 'Let's go. I want to find Jack.'

Half an hour later Cam had gone back to his office, and Florence and Jack arrived at the registry but there they ran out of luck.

The officious pimply clerk shook his head and told them they only had records from 1944 onwards, as all the rest had been destroyed during the war.

'Can you just check the names please?' Florence said. 'We think the marriage would have been in May 1942, but it might have been delayed.'

He nodded reluctantly and took them through to a gloomy room where everything was recorded in date order. 'You can look for yourselves,' he said.

But even though they searched every entry, they found nothing.

'They may have gone back to England,' Florence said. 'Left Malta and married in England after the war. Or France I suppose.'

She felt deflated. To come this far but be left no closer.

'When we go back to England,' Jack suggested, 'we can check the records there.'

She thought about it and shook her head. 'First,' she said, 'I want to find out more about this Group Captain Robert Beresford. If the War Office here is still open. They'll know.'

In the morning the girl who greeted them at the reception desk of the War Rooms frowned when they enquired about Beresford.

'I'm so sorry. I'm new. Most of us working here are civilians brought in just to wind things up. The military have gone, taking their confidential records with them.'

They thanked her and were about to leave when an older woman walked in carrying some files.

'Could you update these?' she said and briskly turned to go back to wherever she had come from.

'Oh Linda, hold on a minute,' the younger woman piped up. 'These people are asking about a Group Captain Beresford. I wondered if you knew him. You were here during the war, weren't you?'

Linda nodded. 'I was a plotter and yes, I did know him.' She turned to Florence and Jack. 'Why are you asking?'

'I'm looking for someone,' Florence said. 'I think he may have been going to marry my aunt.'

'What was her name?'

'Rosalie Delacroix.'

Linda shook her head. 'No. I don't think he ever married someone of that name. Not that I heard anyway. It was all rather tragic. He *was* involved with a woman here though. Riva, a fine woman with whom I worked. But he was killed outright. An unexpected bomb you know, just when things were really going our way. So dreadfully upsetting. Now if you'll excuse me.' She took a step away.

'I'm sorry to hear that but do you happen to know where Riva is now?'

'No. I'm afraid I haven't seen or heard from her since 1943. That's when Robert Beresford died.'

'Did she marry him?'

'I'm afraid I can't say.'

Florence felt sorry for Rosalie. She must have been devastated if he had married someone else.

'Come on,' Jack said. 'We'd better be off.'

But then Florence felt a bolt of energy run through her and suddenly she knew. 'This Riva. What did she look like?'

Linda looked surprised to be asked. 'Stunning actually. Red hair and French originally, but with perfect English.'

'Do you know anything else? Her surname maybe.'

'Ah yes. Janvier, that was it. She enjoyed quite a colourful life. A dancer and then an editor. Did quite a bit for the girls who worked in Strait Street too.'

Florence bit her lip in excitement.

'Still exists,' the woman continued. 'Cabaret, music hall and girls. Not as bad as it used to be though. Her work got the place cleaned up a bit. Now I'm sorry I really must go.'

'Where did you last see her?'

'Here. But you might try the land registry. I think Beresford had a place near the RAF Officer's Mess at the Xara Palace. She used to go there with him. Good luck with your search. I'm sorry, I have a meeting now.'

Florence gripped Jack's hand and whispered. 'I'm sure

this Riva woman is Rosalie. Remember that my mother always said she was a brilliant dancer and had secretly worked in cabaret in Paris.'

At the land registry they found a helpful studious young man who allowed them to search first for Riva Janvier. 'She might have carried on living there after Beresford died,' Florence said.

But they could find nothing about a woman called Riva Janvier.

'Linda hadn't seen or heard from her in over three years. Strikes me she must have left the island,' Jack said. 'Shall we go?'

'Hang on a minute.'

She carried on searching and after a few more moments grinned with excitement. 'Oh my God! I knew it. Look.' Her heart was racing as she tapped the line she'd spotted. It was an address in Mdina that had belonged to one Rosalie Beresford since 1943.

Jack gazed at it and continued to read. 'And before that it was owned by someone called Addison Darnell and Sir Robert Beresford, Baronet. Bloody hell!'

'Rosalie,' Florence whispered. 'Oh, Rosalie, are you still there? And if you aren't, where are you now?'

CHAPTER 51

Florence wanted to go straight to Mdina after they found her aunt's name in the land registry, but it was getting late, the bikes didn't have lamps, and Jack persuaded her to wait. By the next morning she hadn't slept a wink, so eager and excited was she, but also fearful that Rosalie might have gone back to France or even England.

Cam had told her it was Maltese nobility who lived in Mdina, so how Beresford and this Addison man had a place there that Rosalie must have inherited, she had no idea.

But at least Beresford had married her.

They cycled to Mdina slowly, Florence hanging back, hardly able to bear the disappointment if, after all this, Rosalie had gone. 'Can we stop for a bit?' she called out to Jack, who had gone on ahead of her.

He waited while she caught up. 'I thought you'd be itching to get there.'

'I am. But I think I'll cry if she isn't there.'

'And I think you'll cry if she is.'

She laughed. 'You're right. And yet, I don't even know her and if I ever met her, I'd only have been a toddler.'

'What a shame you never knew her.'

'She just upped and left, at only nineteen, and nobody knew where she'd gone. My grandparents moved away from Paris sometime after that. I never knew why. My mother wouldn't discuss it.'

Jack shook his head. 'Strange business.'

'Let's just find out if Rosalie is still in Mdina. I wasn't that keen on the place when I was there before. It's beautiful but feels so sad and empty.'

When they approached the ancient city a little later, she stopped again to take in the way it rose up on the hill, the high golden walls majestic but also a little unnerving just as she had thought before. It looked completely unassailable, perhaps because it was.

They cycled through the arch and then dismounted to walk around the narrow cobbled streets as they tried to work out if the address they'd found really existed and, if it did, where it was. They searched for a little while walking past the grand *palazzi*, their shutters closed, their magnificent doorways bolted. Everything proclaimed *keep out*. It was completely daunting.

'They call it "the Silent City",' he said, lifting his hand and pointing at the stunning baroque architecture all around them. 'And it is.'

She stopped walking to listen. 'Apart from the wind. It makes me feel a bit melancholy.'

It didn't take long to find the place they wanted and soon Florence was staring at the tall building. 'It's huge. Surely this can't be it?' She studied the immense double door and the two brass lion's head door knockers.

'I think it is,' he said and whistled.

She nodded.

'Go on then.'

She lifted one of the heavy knockers and, letting it drop, jumped at the deep resounding echo it made.

They waited. Nothing. Not a whisper.

'I'll try again.' She lifted it again and let it fall.

Still nothing.

Close to tears, just as she had predicted, her heart sank.

'We'll come back later,' Jack suggested and put an arm around her shoulders. 'Rosalie may just be out somewhere. Shopping maybe.'

'Or gone.'

'Could be, but we don't know. Come on. I think you need food and wine.'

There was nowhere to eat in the old city, but they found a café in Rabat where they ate, drank, and waited and then returned to Mdina an hour or so later. Just before they reached the house, they spotted a tall man unlocking the huge front door.

'Wait!' Florence called out.

The man, surprised, turned round.

'I'm sorry,' she said.

'Don't be. How may I help?'

'You're English,' Jack said.

He held out his hand. 'Gerard Macmillan. And you are?'

461

'I'm Florence Baudin,' she said, breathless with excitement, 'and this is Jack Jackson, my fiancé.'

He looked at them, a quizzical expression on his face.

'The thing is,' Florence went on. 'I'm looking for someone. Her name is Rosalie and she's my aunt.'

'Oh . . . my . . . goodness. I don't know what to say.'

'Is she here?'

'How did you find her? Most people know her by another name and since her husband's death she lives a very solitary life. She only allows me to come because we're publishing a book together.'

'Oh,' Florence said, surprised. 'Is she a writer?'

'More of a collator. Would you mind waiting in the hall?'

He removed the key from the lock and then pushed open one side of the huge door. It was very dark inside and it took a while for Florence's eyes to become accustomed to the gloom. He turned to go.

'Please,' Florence said. 'Could you tell her that her sister Claudette sent me to find her? Claudette's my mother and seriously ill. I have a message for Rosalie from her.'

He nodded, crossed the large hall, opened a door and disappeared behind it.

They waited for what felt like an absolute age, Florence pacing up and down, becoming more and more agitated but then, all of a sudden, he was there again.

'Come through. She will see you.'

They entered a second hall, this one vaulted, full of shadows and odd shafts of sunlight.

'We just need to cross the courtyard.'

They went along a corridor and an arched gallery and then outside into an internal courtyard surrounded by honey-coloured stone walls. Florence gazed at it in wonder, breathing in the delicious scents of flowering plants.

'Beautiful,' she said.

'That's a fig tree,' he said. 'And over there two orange trees.'

She saw water flowing from three decorative spouts and splashing into a large stone trough.

'They're wood sprites,' he said, seeing her looking. 'The spouts.'

'I love that.' She took a long breath and let it out slowly. 'So,' she said.

'So,' he replied. 'Ready to meet Rosalie?'

She nodded.

They crossed the courtyard and climbed a stone staircase. Eventually the stairs opened onto a vaulted corridor lined with floor-to-ceiling windows on one side and paintings on the other side. Florence smelt beeswax and lemons.

She glanced out of one of the windows and looked across at another sumptuous palace with statues all along its stone balconies.

'My goodness,' she said. 'These houses are all beautiful hidden palaces. You'd never know. From the front they look more forbidding, like fortresses.'

'Wait until you see the view on the other side.'

They went through a hall and then he knocked on a door.

'Thank you, Marie,' he said as a woman wearing a

starched white apron opened the door. 'Marie is Rosalie's housekeeper,' he explained.

'Does my aunt own the whole building or just this apartment?'

'The whole thing.'

'Who lives in the rest?' she asked.

'Nobody at present.'

She was about to reply but inhaled deeply when she saw they had been shown to a balustraded terrace with a view right across the island. Her mind felt sharp and clear but then a woman rose from where she'd been sitting with her back to them, and Florence felt suddenly dizzy. The woman was maybe in her forties, very thin, but there was something startlingly beautiful about her. She had tumbling auburn curls, deep blue eyes, and the same heart-shaped face as Florence herself. Everything Rosalie wore was black. The dress, the shoes, just her jewellery was gold, and the contrast of all that black with her red hair was incredible. Florence froze, unable to move or speak.

'So, you are little Florence, all grown-up?' the woman said. 'I can hardly believe it.'

Florence bit her lip, willing herself not to cry.

'Come here. Let me look at you.'

Florence walked towards her, blinking like a fool. She knew she was going to cry, and she so did not want to.

The woman reached for her, and they stood holding hands but saying nothing. Mr Macmillan and Jack motionless, watching.

'Gerry tells me you have a message from my sister.'

Florence nodded and at last found her voice. 'Yes, I—'

Rosalie shook her head. 'Wait. Marie, could you bring us some tea and cake? I think we all need to sit down and get over the shock of all this. And it's getting a bit warm out here, so we'll make ourselves comfortable inside. Please, follow me.'

They went into a sitting room. Florence couldn't keep her eyes off Rosalie, who now sat down very upright in a hard-backed chair. Florence and Jack chose to sit together on one of two sofas and Mr Macmillan crossed his legs as he settled into a large armchair.

'This was Addison's Darnell's apartment,' Rosalie said. 'He was my husband's uncle and a wonderful man.' She glanced around. 'I still feel him here. Do you ever feel like that, Florence?'

'Like the people who've gone are still around?'

'Yes.'

'I do. I used to feel it most in the Dordogne.'

Rosalie smiled. 'Me too, especially on the river.'

'Oh yes.'

'I think we may have a few things in common, Florence. Well, it was Addison who left this beautiful old palace to me. Bobby had an apartment on the floor below but eventually I moved up here. It was easier once I started work again. Gerry and I are planning our third volume of Addison's pictures and writings. He was a well-known artist, you see.'

'Your aunt is a wonderful collator and editor,' Gerry said. 'In fact, you've only just caught us.'

'Really?'

'We're due to sail for England in a couple of days,' Rosalie said. 'I had hoped to go before this, but my passport . . .'

Gerry laughed. 'Don't you mean your passports?'

'Indeed. Both my passports were out of date. But in the end, we got it sorted and I shall be travelling under my real name once again. Gerry came over from London to help pack up Addison's work.'

Marie brought in a tray of tea things then went back to fetch a plate of chocolate eclairs.

Rosalie poured the tea and handed out the cups and saucers. 'Please take a plate and help yourselves to an eclair or two.'

There was a momentary pause.

'And what about you, Mr Jackson?' Rosalie asked.

'Please call me Jack.'

'Of course. Are you here to accompany Florence?'

'I'm a restoration architect and lending a hand on a project here, but I also came to help Florence find you.'

After they'd eaten the delicious eclairs and were sipping their tea, Florence saw Rosalie take a deep breath as if collecting herself.

'My sister is unwell?' she asked.

'She has incurable cancer.'

Florence saw her aunt's sharp intake of breath.

'She asked me to find you.'

'Why now?'

'I don't know. She first asked in 1944, when I arrived in England from France, but we couldn't travel here till now. I suppose she knew she was ill, though she didn't admit it and I had no idea.' Florence stopped, remembering their argument, the harsh words, but then later the way her mother had told her everything.

Rosalie nodded, clearly moved.

'Of course, that's why she didn't tell me. If she had, I could hardly have left her.'

'And you have a message for me?'

Florence nodded. 'She wants me to tell you how desperately sorry she is for not helping you when you needed her. She said it's the biggest regret of her life.'

A tear slid down Rosalie's cheek and then another. She reached into a pocket for a handkerchief and wiped her face.

A lump formed in Florence's throat.

Rosalie looked at the ground and then up at the ceiling, blinking more tears away. Then she rose to her feet and so did everyone else. 'Where are you staying?'

'In an apartment in Valletta,' Florence said.

'You must stay here next time you come to Malta. We have so much to talk about. I want to know everything, although I hardly know where to begin. I never thought I would see any of my family again.' She paused, clearly finding it hard to speak. 'And I can't thank you enough for finding me.'

'But you could have come back any time.'

Rosalie sighed. 'I didn't feel I could. The circumstances of my leaving were so awful. Anyway, you're here now and I'm delighted.' She held out her arms to Florence and the two women hugged.

'We must go to Claudette. Together. Gerry, can we get

tickets for Florence and Jack on the same sailing we're booked on?'

'We've already booked tickets on a passenger ship sailing in six days' time,' Florence said.

'It would be nicer if we could go together,' Rosalie said.

'I'll see what I can do,' Gerry said. 'It's a cargo ship so there aren't many passenger berths. They sometimes hold back one or two. Failing that we'll have to go separately.'

'I didn't think of asking about cargo ships,' Jack said. 'When does it sail?'

'In three days,' Gerry said. 'It'll take about ten days or so to get to Portsmouth.'

Rosalie kept her eyes fixed on Florence as if not wanting to let her go. 'Of course, you could stay here for the next couple of days if you like.'

'Jack?' Florence said.

'If we can get tickets on the same sailing, I'll need to organise a deputy to oversee the work on the apartment, so it might be better to stay in Valletta.'

'But thank you anyway,' Florence added as she looked back at Rosalie.

Rosalie took her hand. 'Not at all, and all being well, we'll be able to talk all the way to Portsmouth. Don't worry about wasting the money on your other tickets. They'll probably resell them for you. And in any case, I'll be paying for these.'

Florence smiled, feeling light, her heart overflowing with relief and joy at finally having found Claudette's missing sister.

CHAPTER 52

When the ship finally docked in Portsmouth on a grey wintery day, it was so drab after the brilliance of Malta that Florence felt deflated and apprehensive. They'd eaten a hurried breakfast and now she and Jack were standing on the deck watching the dockside scene unfold while waiting for Rosalie and Gerry.

'Do you think they are, you know . . . close?' she whispered.

Jack shrugged. 'Just really good friends, I think.'

'Like us.'

'Not quite,' he said and nibbled her ear.

She slapped him away gently. 'People will see.'

'Do you care?'

'No. But none of that when we see Hélène. I don't want to rub her nose in it.'

'I'm sure your sister will have long got over any attachment she had to me.'

'It's only just over two years, Jack.'

He raised his brows. 'Come on.'

'You don't know Hélène.'

'Will Élise and her daughter be there?'

'Yes, by now I think they will be. Hélène said they would be following on after her.' But Florence wasn't just worrying about seeing her eldest sister, she was also utterly terrified her mother might die before they reached her. Might even have died already.

'Okay,' Jack said, 'looks like we're disembarking now.'

Gerry had helpfully arranged a driver to take the three of them and their luggage to the Cotswolds and he had booked them rooms at a hotel in Stanton, all in the few days before they'd departed Malta. He himself was heading for London.

The journey seemed to take forever and as the car swept into Stanton, Florence recalled her previous visit. Each house and cottage constructed of golden ochre stone flanking the quaint high street, some of the buildings grand, others less so. Of course, it was much colder now, and the wind was icy.

'The entire place looks as if it has been left behind in the past,' Rosalie said. 'A bit like Mdina in that way.'

'That's what I thought too.'

Florence glanced at her aunt, whose thin, beautiful face was giving nothing away but, just like Claudette when she was feeling anxious, Rosalie's hands were twisting in her lap.

'There it is,' Florence said and burst into tears when she saw a tiny girl with long dark wavy hair standing waiting patiently behind the gate. Her heart caught and she couldn't speak. Jack, who was sitting in the front, turned round and squeezed her hand.

'She looks just like Élise,' he said.

Even through her tears Florence could not stop smiling. 'Oh my God, let me out. This is it.'

The car came to a halt and Florence leapt out and raced over the cottage. With eyes the colour of cognac, the little girl gazed up at her aunt. The lump in Florence's throat was back.

'Hello darling,' she managed to say. 'I'm your Auntie Florence.'

'*J'ai deux ans*,' the little girl announced.

'English please, Victoria,' a voice said, and then her sister Élise ran from the door to the gate, swooped the child up and, with her daughter held in one arm, she hugged Florence with the other.

'Maman!' Victoria shouted. 'No squeeze me!'

'Sorry, darling,' Élise said and put her down and her eyes were wet with tears.

Florence felt so moved she was struggling for breath. 'I . . . never thought this day would come.'

They gazed at each other without speaking. At first sight Élise looked just the same, except that her long dark hair was shoulder-length now, and she wasn't wearing her usual wide-legged trousers, jumper, and lace-up boots. The orange dress she wore complemented her eyes, the exact same colour as her daughter's, and when she smiled they lit up and her face looked softer than it ever had before.

Motherhood suits her, Florence thought and smiled back. 'But here we are,' she added. 'Here we bloody well are.'

'Shhh. We don't swear in front of the child.'

Florence laughed at the thought of Élise not swearing.

Jack came round to say hello, kissing Élise on both cheeks in the French style and squeezing her arms. 'Look, I'm going to the hotel to check us all in. I'll see you later.'

'You can stay,' Élise said meaningfully.

'No, this time now is for you women. And a more amazing bunch of women I've never known.'

Élise laughed. 'Always a charmer.'

'See you later.'

Élise glanced at the car. Rosalie was still sitting in the back seat but if the driver was to take Jack to the hotel, unless she went with him, she had to get out now. Florence went round to open the door.

Rosalie, her face blanched of colour, glanced up and swallowed visibly. 'I am very tired. Would it be acceptable if I came to see my sister tomorrow?'

Florence twisted back to Élise. In all the joy of seeing her sister and her niece she'd almost forgotten how sick her mother was.

Élise nodded. 'I'm sure tomorrow will be all right.'

'One thing at a time then,' Rosalie said. 'Today is for you girls. Tomorrow can be for me.'

But the door opened again and a tall athletic-looking woman, with straight light brown hair and strong features stood watching. Hélène's nut-brown eyes were not warm or smiling and she gave no sign of acknowledging

Florence, but briskly said, 'Maman is awake now. I think it might be wiser for Rosalie to see her today.'

Florence's heart started to race. Was her sister not going to greet her at all? She stood awkwardly holding little Victoria's hand. Élise helped Rosalie out of the car and Hélène gave Florence a perfunctory nod then marshalled Rosalie inside.

'Can I come up too?' Florence asked, following them, aware of the tension between Hélène and herself.

Her sister glanced at her, sharply Florence thought, but then she nodded.

'Don't crowd Maman,' Hélène ordered. 'Stay by the door while Rosalie is at her bedside.'

The three of them went upstairs and Hélène asked them to wait on the landing while she spoke to Claudette. Florence gripped her aunt's hand.

'I don't know who is more nervous, you or me,' Rosalie whispered.

'Are you nervous?' Florence asked.

'Terribly. I haven't caught sight of my sister for over twenty years and now she's dying. I long to see her so much I'm shaking.'

They waited anxiously, listening to Hélène murmuring for a while before she softly called to them. Florence followed Rosalie to the open door. They saw Hélène plump up Claudette's pillows then help her sit up. Florence heard Rosalie's sharp intake of breath and fought for her own breath. Ravaged by cancer, Claudette, only in her fifties, looked decades older.

A harsh cry erupted from Claudette as Rosalie entered

the room and then she coughed and couldn't seem to stop. Hélène made soothing sounds and patted her back.

'Hand me that water, Florence,' she said without looking round.

Florence stepped forward and did so and Hélène put the glass to Claudette's lips. Florence couldn't tell if her mother had swallowed any as Hélène soon put the glass back on the bedside table.

Tears sprang to Claudette's eyes as she focused on Rosalie's approach.

Florence stepped back and watched. Some things were impossible to put into words and this moment, as Rosalie sat in a chair beside her sister and took her hand, was one.

'You never wrote,' Claudette said, her voice gravelly, but there was no reproach in her eyes.

'Just the once.'

'More than twenty years,' Claudette said, barely audible. She closed her eyes and Florence took a deep breath while Hélène leant over to check her pulse.

But then, seemingly so close to the brink, Claudette drew herself back and her eyes flew open. 'So, what have you been up to little sister?' she said, then gave a sad little laugh and Florence could see that while Rosalie had been holding on to herself, she now could not stop the tears from falling. After a few moments she too rallied and wiped her eyes.

'Oh, you know, this and that,' she said.

Claudette's laugh was unmistakable, and she stretched her arms out to her sister. As they held each other Florence and Hélène exchanged glances and in that look Florence hoped that her sister might have forgiven her.

When Claudette coughed again, Hélène stepped in. 'I think Maman has had enough excitement for one day.'

Claudette gave her a pleading look.

'Ten minutes more, then,' Hélène said.

'So bossy,' Claudette muttered, and Florence smiled to hear the mother they all knew was still inside her.

Rosalie recited a potted version of her life story ending with where she was living now.

'And you own a palace?'

'Ridiculous, isn't it?'

'Always landed on your feet.'

Then she closed her eyes.

'Come on,' Hélène said. 'We'll see you tomorrow, Rosalie. I'll stay with Maman now.'

She saw them to the front door.

Rosalie patted Hélène's arm and passed her a note. 'Please call the hotel if there are any changes. That's the number.'

Florence was about to kiss Hélène on the cheeks, but her sister stiffened as she neared so she drew back.

As the door closed behind them, she spotted Élise putting a brave face on it, holding Victoria in her arms, both blowing kisses and waving from the sitting room window. Florence gulped back a sob. She could never have imagined this. She and her sisters were already devastated by grief and regret for not having realised about Claudette's illness earlier. For so long Hélène and Élise hadn't been able to travel to visit her because of the chaos in France, although maybe that had been an excuse. Surely if you knew your mother was dying, you'd find a way? They were all thinking it. And now Claudette was clinging on to the slightest shred of life while at the same time knowing there really was nothing left to hold on to at all.

Each day was bringing its own challenges. Seeing her mother had been the first, saying goodbye to her would be next. And only after that would she and Hélène be able to talk.

Rosalie, meanwhile, looked ashen as the taxi carried them away.

When she could speak, she said, 'I would really have liked to have stayed longer.'

'I know. Me too. But Hélène knows what she is doing. At least this way there's a chance you'll be able to talk to Maman again tomorrow.'

'Please let her still be alive tomorrow,' Florence whispered to herself. 'Please.'

CHAPTER 53

In bed at the hotel Jack held Florence in his arms while she sobbed. As day bled into night Florence remained awake, her eyes wide open, feeling the grief beginning to build, weighing her down so that her whole body felt heavy. If only she'd known she could have stayed with Claudette back when she first visited in 1944.

'Try to sleep, sweetheart,' Jack murmured and pulled her close.

She did sleep eventually but a victim of her own disturb-ing thoughts, she tossed and turned. Images of Hélène came and went. Hélène red-faced, Hélène angry, Hélène shouting. Even more painful, she pictured Claudette alive, laughing, making elderflower cham-pagne, full of vitality.

After an hour or so of fitful sleep, Florence woke early. In the half-light she listened to Jack's breathing. Then it changed, grew lighter, and when he woke too, they made love very gently. It seemed important that in the midst of death you had to own the fact that you were alive.

'You're thinking of all the times you spent with your mother?' he asked when it was over, and she lay beside him.

'How did you know?'

'I was like that when my grandmother died. I had to revisit every year going further and further back until there was nowhere left to go.'

'Yes.'

'There's no point fighting the memories even if they make you cry. They come whether you want them or not.'

'Like shadows . . . But she isn't dead yet.'

'No,' Jack said, 'but you are preparing yourself emotionally for what is to come. It's inevitable.'

'I should have looked after her, instead of coming back to Devon.'

'Don't be so hard on yourself. She refused your help. When someone dies, everybody blames themselves.'

'I had a dream last night. I was running and running but couldn't get anywhere.'

'I've had that one.'

'What do you think it means?'

'Maybe you're trying to escape your mother's death?' he suggested.

'I thought that, but I wonder if it really means . . . well I feel like I've got too many things going on my mind, and I can't get away from *them*.'

'You mean Hélène, don't you, on top of what's happening to Claudette?'

Florence sighed. 'She hates me. My sister hates me.'

'Has she said that?'

'No.'

'You're projecting your fear onto her. While she's nursing your mother, it's probably all she's got room for. Imagine how hard it must be for her. Just wait. You'll get a chance to talk. Give her time.'

At the breakfast table they met Rosalie, who didn't look as if she'd slept much either. But at least I do have Jack, Florence thought, while Rosalie is alone.

During the following days they all lived under a cloud of anxiety, tense and on edge, offering each other cautious smiles that quickly vanished behind lines of worry. Rosalie sat with her sister for hours, gently reminiscing when Claudette was awake, but most of the time she simply held her hand, or stroked her paper-thin skin. Florence came and went, as did Élise.

One day they all seemed to arrive in Claudette's room at the exact same time, as if instinct had warned them it wouldn't be long, the air in the room heavy, the atmosphere sombre and sad. Claudette's breathing was irregular and seemed to stop for a few seconds. Florence froze. Could this be it? Then her mother's mouth opened, and she caught a breath. Florence gently stroked her face, cool to the touch, the skin blotchy.

Hélène spoke softly, 'It is all right to let go, Maman,' she said.

Then Florence heard little Victoria singing to herself

as she lay in her cot in the bedroom she was sharing with Élise. Hélène usually slept on a sofa close to their mother's bed.

In the silence of Claudette's room, the words came again in the young child's sweet halting voice.

Alouette, gentille alouette
Alouette, je te plumerai

It was a French song they all recognised. Claudette, who had looked as if she was sleeping, or even unconscious, opened her eyes, and Florence thought she heard her hum a couple of notes and smile in recognition. Then Claudette's breath quickened just for a moment, the muscles of her face sagged, and she looked even paler, emptier, not like herself any more. That was it. She was gone. The final invisible thread that had held her to life had been severed. The moment when life had been there and then was not had finally happened.

Hélène checked Claudette's pulse and then crossed herself.

Florence gasped but held on to her tears.

Élise, who had been standing by the window farthest from her mother's bed, came across and placed Claudette's hands crossed on her chest, then she kissed her forehead.

Hélène sat down on the sofa, head in her hands. Florence longed to comfort her, but Rosalie got there first and she held Hélène, who began to weep. They were such heart-wrenching sobs that, as if by mutual agreement, Élise and Florence left the room. Victoria called out for her mother anxiously so the two sisters got her up, gave her some warm milk, wrapped her up and then took her away from the grieving household for a walk up the hill.

They all wore their hats pulled down low, thick coats buttoned up tight, scarves wrapped around their faces, and heavy boots, but they still felt bitterly cold. Florence didn't know if her eyes were watering because of the icy wind or if it was because she was crying.

'*Mamaaan*,' Victoria complained. '*J'ai froid.*'

'I know, sweetheart, I know. Shall we run? See who gets to the top of the hill first?'

'*Oui.*'

And they ran, swinging the little girl between them.

Over the next few days, ordinary tasks kept them busy. Once the doctor issued the death certificate, Élise contacted the funeral director, who came the same day. She contacted the vicar, too. Hélène seemed to have crumpled, all her energy consumed by making her mother's final weeks comfortable. In France, Hélène's insistence on everyday rituals had held them together. Now she seemed undone. The shopping, cooking and most of the washing-up fell to Florence but she felt as if she was walking on eggshells around her sister. Élise called the vicar, organised the flowers and with Florence's help devised an order of service. Élise and Florence played with Victoria, fed her, kept her relatively happy in a house that was full of sadness and regret. Jack mainly stayed out of the way at the hotel, keeping a broken-hearted Rosalie company.

The news of Claudette's death had circled the village

and people came to the door with condolence cards and bunches of winter flowers from their gardens. Some brought food – cakes and biscuits – and others came with offers of assistance.

'Your mother was a great help during the war,' one older lady said as she handed over a ginger cake. 'We all did our bit for the WI.'

'I'm so glad to hear that,' Florence said. 'And thank you.'

Although crisp and cold, the sun shone on the day of the funeral, the sky so blue it almost hurt, and the church was packed. They held the wake in the village hall because Claudette's cottage was far too small. Towards the end, while Jack took Victoria to the swings, and once people had begun drifting away, Élise took Florence aside.

'Did you know she was so popular here?'

'I knew she was involved in the war effort. I suppose it must have brought the villagers closer together. Something like that might.'

'And, they weren't occupied by the bloody Boche here.'

'It must have made a difference. They were all on the same side. In France we weren't.'

'Have you spoken to Hélène yet?'

'She doesn't seem to want to.'

'No. Maybe not yet but once all this is over, and it nearly is, neither of you will have an excuse not to speak.'

Florence sighed as Rosalie came up to the sisters. 'Well, this sherry is ghastly, isn't it? Coming to the hotel for a decent drink?'

They nodded.

'I'm so glad you found me . . . in time, Florence,' Rosalie added.

While Rosalie went to look for Jack and Victoria, Florence waited for her sisters but after a few moments only Élise turned up, shaking her head. 'Hélène won't come.'

'Where is she?'

'Still standing by the grave. Reading all the cards.'

'You go ahead. I'll talk to her.'

After Élise had gone to join Rosalie, Jack and Victoria, Florence headed to the grave at the back of the church. It was a beautiful location looking out onto cattle grazing in the open countryside.

'Hélène,' she said hesitantly as she drew close. 'Could we talk?'

Her sister looked up and Florence's throat constricted at the sight of the distress in her sister's intelligent eyes.

'What is it?' she asked as gently as she could.

Hélène's eyes suddenly blazed. 'You don't know?'

Florence didn't know what to say. Was her sister talking about Jack?

'Then I'll tell you,' Hélène continued. 'Can you imagine looking after our mother alone, watching her die day after day all on your own?'

'I'm so sorry.'

Hélène didn't seem to hear but gave a sharp little laugh. 'And do you know what she talked about? All that time?'

Florence shook her head.

'You. You and Rosalie. Nothing else. When Élise and

Victoria arrived, she barely looked at her granddaughter. And you just swan around Malta and arrive at the eleventh hour with Jack.'

Florence gasped. 'I wasn't swanning. I was doing what she wanted me to do. She begged me, Hélène, begged me to find Rosalie.'

'How convenient, and now I suppose you want my blessing?'

The bitter wind of the English winter served only to make the atmosphere more strained.

'Please, Hélène. This isn't you. Can't we try to be civilised?'

Hélène snorted disdainfully. 'You didn't care about being civilised when you took what you wanted.'

'It wasn't like that.'

'No?'

'Of course not.'

'How was it then? You knew I loved Jack, Florence, you knew and yet you still did it.'

Florence hung her head. That much was true.

'You thought I was going to say, never mind, *you* have him, little sister. You thought I was going to say that?'

'I'm sorry,' Florence began carefully, needing to choose her words and hating herself for hurting her sister. 'I hoped with the passage of time you'd understand.'

It was awful seeing Hélène's eyes so full of hurt that Florence's heart twisted. Her sister's nerves had clearly been wound terribly tight from the exhausting vigil of looking after Claudette. And now Jack turning up on top of all that must be just one thing too many.

'And, while we're on the subject of being civilised, couldn't you have done more for Claudette?'

'This isn't fair. She asked me to find Rosalie. I told you,' Florence said quietly. 'Doesn't that count for anything?'

'Before. I'm talking about before.'

Florence felt defenceless but stood her ground. 'I offered to stay with her, help her. She told me to go.'

'And you didn't think to tell me she was ill then? I could have done something. Something more than sitting and watching her slowly die.'

Florence kept her voice calm. 'That isn't fair either. I know it must have been awful for you but you're being unreasonable. I told you she wanted me to find Rosalie. I didn't know she was ill. How could I have known? She said she was fine.'

'And it suited you to believe her.'

'I tried.'

'Not hard enough.'

The afternoon slowed, came to a standstill. Florence opened her mouth but nothing would come out. Her eyes watered but she swallowed her misery. Hélène did have a point.

'And now sweet little Florence is going to cry.'

It had been such a long, hard day and now this. Florence gulped back her tears. 'You know what, we have just buried our mother,' she said, trying to speak calmly. 'This is not like you.'

They stared at each other. Florence was shocked by Hélène's cold stare.

Instinct told her to back off but a flash of anger suddenly

made her snap. 'Oh, for Christ's sake,' she muttered. 'When did you become such a bitch?'

'Me?' Hélène said, incredulous.

'Yes. Jack said he wrote to you as soon as we reached England. He explained things. Surely after two years you can't still be angry about this?'

'I never received a letter from Jack,' Hélène said dismissively.

'He sent one. He told me.'

'How cosy.'

'Not at the time, much later he told me. Maybe the letter went astray.'

'If he wrote it.'

'Of course he did.'

'And you believe everything he says.'

'I'm sorry, Hélène. I'm terribly sorry, but Jack and I held back for ages. I thought long and hard. I didn't set out to hurt you. Isn't this about Maman? Not me and Jack at all?'

Her sister remained silent.

'What more can I do?' Florence asked.

Hélène narrowed her eyes. 'You can go back to Devon. That's what. Now I'd like to be left alone to read these cards.'

Florence moved towards her sister and, speaking softly, reached out a hand. 'Jack cared, but he just didn't love you in the way you wanted, Hélène. You're holding on to something that never existed except in your own mind.'

Hélène's eyes hardened. Then with no warning she slapped Florence's face with so much force she staggered back, her cheek and eyes stinging as she stared at her sister.

Shocked, she turned on her heels and stumbled away.

She'd heard about sisters becoming estranged but had never imagined it could ever happen to them. And yet their relationship was in pieces, and it seemed there was nothing she could do or say to put it back together again.

At twilight, Florence sat on the bed with Jack at the hotel. Earlier he had told Rosalie about her friend Charlotte's death and the charm bracelet found on her body. Rosalie had been upset to hear the news and said she'd given her friend the bracelet as a thank you for the loan of her apartment.

'Come to the bar, Florence,' Jack said. 'You look as if you need a drink and Rosalie certainly does. I think she wants to talk.'

But Florence couldn't face people and shook her head.

'Did something more happen?' he asked. 'More than your stumble over a log in the church yard. That was what happened wasn't it?'

'Yes.'

'So there's nothing you want to talk about?'

'No,' she said, unable to admit that Hélène had slapped her face.

'I'll see you later then.' He kissed her, stood up and moved away.

'Wait,' she said as he reached the door. 'Hélène told me she didn't receive a letter from you.'

'Well, I certainly sent one.'

She nodded. 'I told her that.'

'Pity. It might have made all the difference to how she

feels now. But Florence, you really do need to leave the guilt behind.'

'And leave my sister behind too?'

He shook his head. 'No, but life is fleeting, and we have to seize happiness. She will come round. She loves you.'

'You don't understand.'

'Perhaps not, but this isn't doing you any good. I do understand that. Please, Florence, dry your eyes. Come and have a drink.'

'I can't. My skin is red and blotchy. I look a fright.'

He smiled, came back to take her face in his hands and kiss her on the tip of her nose. 'You never look a fright.'

'You go.'

'Are you sure? I can get a message to Rosalie and stay with you instead.'

'No. I'll be all right. Go.' She'd spoken more sharply than she'd intended and felt sorry when he stiffened at her tone. And then he was gone.

Night fell slowly, the darkness creeping around the room, but she didn't switch on the lamps. Didn't want to see her own face in the mirror. She hadn't expected instant forgiveness, but she had hoped to be able to talk, find a way to be sisters again. But nothing could make it better. Jack was hers now and she was his. Would it help to break off their engagement? She doubted it. She remembered how kind Hélène and Élise had been after the rape. How they had protected her, cared for her, enfolded her in the safety of their love. Would it help any of them if she were forced to choose between her sister and the man she loved?

CHAPTER 54

Claudette's will had been read, and now everyone was preparing to leave. She had left the house in France to Élise and her English cottage to Hélène, while Florence was to have her stocks and shares. Before they left for Devon, Rosalie drew Florence aside.

'I don't want to speak out of turn,' Rosalie said, 'but I was wondering if you and Jack already have plans for your wedding?'

'Well . . . no, not really, other than thinking summer might be nice. There will still be rationing, of course, so I'm not quite sure how it will work.'

'There'll be a way.'

'I made gallons of elderflower champagne in June, far more than I meant to and Jack teased me about it.'

'Well, there you are. It's a start.'

'I suppose.'

Rosalie smiled warmly, her face flushing a little as she

said, 'It would give me enormous pleasure if you would allow me to be involved, pay for the wedding, the dress and so on.'

'That's very kind, but, well I'm just taken aback. I thought the whole thing might be a bit make-do-and-mend.'

'We're family. I haven't had a family for such a long time,' she said, and now Rosalie's voice caught. 'Your mother is no longer here to help you, but I am, and I know it's not the same, but I would love to. I'm going to be in England until next August.'

Florence smiled. 'In that case, thank you. Without my sisters here, I'll be glad of any help I can get.'

Élise and Victoria were planning to take the train to Exeter with Florence and Jack to stay until after Christmas before returning to France. Rosalie was coming too. But Hélène, who had been invited, insisted on remaining in Stanton at Claudette's house to see to her effects and arrange the sale of the house to take place once probate was complete. While each of them was choosing one small treasure from the cottage as a reminder of their mother, Florence touched Hélène on the back of her shoulder.

'I could stay too,' she said. 'Let me help you with every-thing here.'

Hélène didn't turn round and just muttered a blunt, 'No, thank you.'

Florence tried another tack. 'You'll be alone for Christmas.'

Hélène shook her head. 'You really think I give a fig?'

'You used to love Christmas.'

Hélène didn't reply, just carried on picking things up and putting them down. Florence hated seeing her sister in so much pain but knew there was nothing she could do. Hélène was the good sister, the helper, the healer. The one to turn to in a crisis. Who was going to help her?

The time Rosalie, Élise and Victoria spent in Devon was bittersweet. Sweet because Florence was enjoying being around her sister and aunt and loving getting to know her small niece, who was turning out to be quite a little terror. They sang songs together, went for walks when it wasn't raining, and played games in front of the fire when it was. Vicky's favourite was 'Ring a Ring o' Roses' especially the *a-tishoo* part when they all had to fall down and roll around the floor. But when Vicky sang *'Alouette, Gentille Alouette'* both Élise and Florence had tears in their eyes.

'How are you feeling about Maman?' Florence asked Élise when Jack and Vicky were out feeding the ducks in the water meadow, and they were alone together in the kitchen.

'I always had mixed feelings about her. You know that.'

'You looked so much like her. But I think your temperament was so different that it scared her.'

'Really?'

'She'd deny it of course.'

'I'm struggling with myself a bit. I feel I should have tried to love her better . . .'

'And on the other hand, maybe *she* should have tried

to love *you* better. Or at least tried to show it more. I'm sure she did love you, really.'

'Maybe. It makes her death hard to come to terms with. Not ever being able to . . . I don't know . . . make things right between us, I suppose. It hurt that she was so uninterested in Victoria.'

Florence reached for her sister's hand.

A little later Florence and Rosalie went for a walk together, up the track, down the hill, and into the woods. It was a cold crisp day with a seamless blue sky. Life had been so busy in Meadowbrook cottage that Florence was glad to have a little time alone with her aunt.

'How are you now?' Florence asked her aunt.

'I'm just thankful I saw my sister again before she died, but I'll always regret the years we spent apart.'

Florence didn't reply, though she couldn't help wondering if she and Hélène were now doomed to repeat history.

'It's very beautiful here,' Rosalie said as she linked arms with Florence, 'and the cottage is gorgeous. I can see why you love it. Jack too. He clearly adores you.'

'I've been so lucky. I loved Jack from the moment I first saw him, looked up to him in fact, but . . . well, it was only when he helped me on the worst day of my life that I began to feel I could never trust another man but him.'

'Do you want to talk about it?'

Florence thought for a moment. She'd come such a long way since that terrible encounter with those two vile men. It was hard to accept that a violation, a rape like that, had really happened to her. But accept it she'd had to, or she would never have been able to love Jack. Maybe she never would accept it completely, but it didn't make her shake and tremble when she thought about it and she no longer felt any shame.

'Maybe another time,' she said.

'Of course.'

There was a pause.

Florence turned to look at Rosalie. 'Your husband, Robert Beresford, do you mind talking about him?'

'My funny, lovable, brave Bobby. I'm *very* happy to talk about him. Great love, if you find it, is one of life's most precious gifts. I had that with him.'

'It must have been terrible when he died.'

'It was . . . but not for one moment did I regret knowing him. It sounds like a cliché, but he really was the love of my life.'

They were both silent. All you could hear were their footsteps and a few birds shifting in the trees.

'Do you think you'll ever marry again?'

'No. I have my life in Mdina, and Gerry and I will get on with the final volume of Addison's work while I'm in London.'

'You're fond of Gerry?'

'Very. He's my best friend. And a best friend is a fine thing indeed. I have other friends in Malta too. Otto – he's a journalist and Tommy-O, a cross-dressing singer, although I see less of him now that he's no longer performing. And of course, after all you've done to find me, we two will be enormous friends as well. And I hope you will come back to Mdina and stay with me.'

Florence smiled. 'I would love that.'

But as she thought about friendship and what it meant, she realised that Hélène and Élise had always been her very best friends and now one of them was not and that made her sadder than she could ever have imagined.

The days soon passed and once Christmas was over Élise and her daughter went back to France and Rosalie left for London. The house had been packed to the rafters with laughter, and tears, but was so quiet now it left Florence feeling low. She put a brave face on it for Jack's sake, because with the unfinished apartment to complete in Malta, in January he'd be going too.

'You could come with me,' he said on their last evening.

She shook her head. 'I'd rather just stay here. I have my job at the manor. I was lucky they agreed to take me back. And I have my writing. After everything, I need to feel settled.'

'I'll only be gone for a few short weeks and when I'm back, we can plan the wedding.'

She smiled. 'Our lovely summer wedding. Actually, Rosalie offered to help and to pay.'

He looked surprised. 'She didn't need to.'

'She really wants to. And isn't it traditional for the bride's family to bear the cost?'

He laughed. 'I suppose it is. Summer still sounds good to you?'

'Absolutely. I'd hate it to be cold and wet.'

He touched her cheek. 'It will work out you know.'

She frowned, unsure, and then realised why he was

saying that. The argument with Hélène. She'd been trying to put it to the back of her mind but had failed miserably. She'd tormented herself over a letter she'd written but when both Jack and Élise had insisted it would be best to leave Hélène alone for now, she had torn it up. But she hated feeling so helpless.

The morning of Jack's departure came round quickly, with a grey sky and the wind and the rain beating hard on their bedroom window.

'Bugger,' he said. 'I was hoping we'd get out for one last walk before I leave.'

'There is something I'd rather do,' she said with a suggestive laugh, then she climbed on top of him and leaning over, kissed him hard on the mouth.

As the winter dragged on, Florence longed to speak to Hélène with love and hear her sister reply in the same way as she used to do. Instead, all she could see was her Hélène's tight, pale face when they'd spoken beside their mother's grave. It had been awful. Her sisters had been the ones who'd loved and accepted her funny little ways. Teased her. Called her their little witch when she spent hours stirring a pot on the stove, her days growing and pickling vegetables, and the moments when, balanced precariously on the table, she reached up to hang herbs to dry from the ceiling hooks. She sifted through layer after layer of happy memories. And terribly sad ones too. Victor's death, Violette's suicide. She missed her sisters with such an ache inside her and tried to nurture the hope that Hélène would come round, accept what had happened, forgive her. But would she even come to the wedding?

Jack wrote by airmail to say he missed her and asked if she was all right.

'I'm fine,' she'd written in her reply, for how could she tell him how she really felt? *I'm bloody lonely and very sad.*

Of course, being married would be an ending of sorts for the sisters, although an ending had already happened when she'd been forced to leave the Dordogne. She began to think more seriously about the wedding because Hélène would not be her only problem. Should she invite her father Friedrich and her half-brother Anton? Both German, they'd hardly be welcome so soon after the war.

The January days stretched out cold and hard, the need she had for forgiveness becoming corrosive. When she should have been happy about her love for Jack, she felt guilty, although Rosalie was coming down for a few days and Florence was looking forward to planning the details of the wedding with her and Gladys.

February was strangely less depressing than January and then towards the end of the month, not long before Jack was due back, Florence realised she had missed a second monthly period. She had assumed the first absence was because of her grief over Claudette's death and despair over Hélène's coldness, but the second? There had to be a different reason for that. She made an appointment with the doctor where she supplied him with a urine sample and then went home. Two weeks the doctor had said, then call me.

It was the longest two weeks of her life. Florence

hugged the possibility to herself, didn't tell a soul what she suspected, and all the time she was thinking of Jack's face when she told him. She saw the first wild snowdrops in the woods and grew excited, then some early daffodils came up in the garden. They'd have to bring the wedding forward of course if . . . if . . . if.

Then early one morning she called the doctor from the telephone box at the crossroads and he spoke in a cheerily brisk voice. 'Congratulations, my dear,' he said. 'I'm assuming your fiancé will be pleased. A bit cart before the horse, of course, but since the war everything is pear-shaped. You'll make a wonderful mother. Come in and see me soon for a physical examination.'

'Well, I'd better get weaving,' she said, 'and thank you. Thank you so much.' Once outside, delirious with excitement, she laughed and laughed, and then as she walked down the track towards Meadowbrook and home, she cried tears of joy.

CHAPTER 55

A few days later she heard the taxi bringing Jack home from the station. She raced down the stairs and outside to the brook, where she ran through the water, grasped him by the arm and as the taxi took off, dragged him indoors.

'Well, I'm delighted you're so pleased to see me, but I have left my bags outside. It is raining.'

'Get them then, go on, get the damn bags. I've got something to tell you. Something important.'

He smiled at her and shook his head in amusement. 'Whatever it is, you look mighty pleased.'

'Go on,' she said, holding her secret tight for just a tiny bit longer.

'Okay. I'll get the bags. I suppose you wouldn't consider putting the kettle on?'

'I've got something better than tea.'

He raised his brow, clearly intrigued. How could men be so stupid? she thought.

When he came back in, she ordered him to put the bags down.

He did so and now he was grinning.

'You've guessed, haven't you?'

'I think so.'

'Well Jack Jackson, you and I are going to have a baby.'

His eyes widened, shining as a multitude of emotions played across his features. Amazement, joy, disbelief. He picked her up and whirled her around, then thought better of it and put her down excessively gently.

'I won't break,' she said with a laugh.

'Oh my darling girl, that is the best news. The very best news.' Eyes brimming with tears, he said, 'I want to shout it to the world. Have you told anyone?'

'Of course not, idiot. I was waiting for you. But I'll be too fat to get married in August. It will have to be April.'

So April it was, and when the morning of the wedding came round, Florence still didn't know at what time Hélène would be arriving. Victoria, who was to be Florence's flower girl, had to be fitted for her dress, so she and Élise had arrived a week before the big day with news that Hélène was planning to follow on. But so far there had been no sign of her. Florence had written to Friedrich telling him about the wedding and the baby. But she'd also had to explain how unwise it would be for him and Anton to come to England with so much bad feeling about the Germans still rumbling on.

I am to be a grandfather, he'd written back, sounding thrilled to bits. *That will be enough for now.*

Now Rosalie entered Florence's bedroom, her eyes shining.

'You have such beautiful blonde hair,' she said. 'I think we should just pin it with a flower at either temple and let it curl naturally to your shoulders. What do you think?'

'Sounds lovely. Do you know where Élise is?'

'Vicky tore her new dress. Élise is mending it while muttering ominously. My, but that little girl is a force of nature.'

Florence laughed. 'Just like her mum.'

Élise would be her matron of honour as bridesmaid seemed the wrong term for someone who was already a mother. Although strictly speaking a matron of honour was a married woman.

'Is Élise happy?' Rosalie asked.

'I suppose so. Why do you ask?'

'Vicky's father's death.'

Florence shuddered at the memory. 'When Victor was executed it was dreadful for all of us but obviously so much worse for her. He was such a brave man and she loved him so much.'

'Love like that and an ending like that doesn't fade.' She paused. 'But we mustn't dwell on sadness today of all days.'

Florence nodded.

'So . . . how are you feeling?'

'I can hardly breathe for excitement. I swear I didn't sleep a wink,' Florence said.

Rosalie smiled. 'Sit, eyes shut and relax while you have the chance.'

Florence did as she was told and sat there quietly, imagining her mother's eyes on her, her cheeks flushed with pride and fussing about something that was not quite right. She laughed out loud.

'Something the matter?'

'Just thinking about Maman. She wouldn't like the bouquet.'

Florence had chosen flowers from an Exeter florist. Daffodils, blossom, and some delicate leaf – so pretty but Claudette would have thought it not nearly grand or elegant enough. Nor would she have approved of the village hall for the reception. The small bouquet had just been delivered to oohs and ahhs from Victoria and was now safely in a jug downstairs where neither Victoria nor the cat could reach it.

Rosalie had stayed at a hotel close to the village hall after spending the day blowing up balloons and arranging greenery and candles. Gladys and Florence had been cooking for days, using anything that grew in their gardens or that either of them had bottled the year before, along with chickens and a ham that Gladys's husband had procured in exchange for some help fixing up an old motorbike. They had no pigs of their own currently ready for slaughter. Rosalie had hired a small band to play dance tunes so everyone was hoping it would be a lovely, happy afternoon.

When her hair was done, Florence stepped into her wedding dress, Rosalie buttoned it up and they both looked in the mirror.

'Darling, you look so beautiful,' Rosalie said.

Florence patted her tummy. 'Thank God it still just fits.'

With a fitted bodice, sweetheart neckline and high waistline which fell into a long very slightly bell-shaped skirt, the dress was simple with lightly padded shoulders and sleeves that came just to Florence's elbows. She had been saving clothing coupons for ages, as had Gladys; they both made their own clothes from whatever they could find so had used very few of them. And Rosalie's friend Gerry had contacts in London who'd agreed to make the dress out of ivory silk from China, as it was too soon after the war to buy silk from Japan or Italy. Florence also had a thirteen-foot net train. Lace would have been nice, but they couldn't run to that.

They had asked guests not to buy presents but to contribute whatever they could in the way of food and drink and to deliver it direct to the village hall before the wedding, which would take place in the church on the other side of the street. Gladys had enrolled an army of helpers to organise the food and drink and to lay the tables. Ronnie and Jack had already sourced all the tables and chairs they needed, and Gladys had been up half the night ironing tablecloths she'd begged and borrowed from all her acquaintances. There were white tablecloths, checked tablecloths, and floral tablecloths, and each table now had a little posy and a candle in the middle. The whole effect was charming and exactly what Florence wanted.

When the bridal music started up Florence sailed down the aisle on the arm of her aunt, followed by Élise in a full-length dress in violet and Victoria dressed in the same colour. When Florence saw Jack smiling at her and blinking nervously her heart did a little flip. She glanced back at the church, full of friends, family, and local people who'd all been invited at Gladys insistence. The entire wedding had been a community effort, so it was only right. But as Florence's eyes swept around the congregation, she still saw no sign of Hélène. She felt herself wobble but Jack took her hand and squeezed it. She smiled and recovered herself.

The ceremony went off without a hitch. When it was over a few photographs were taken outside the church and then everyone hotfooted it over to the village hall. When Florence entered, she paused, and everyone clapped as she glanced at all the smiling faces and the beautifully decorated hall that looked like something from a fairy-tale woodland scene.

Florence saw Henri, Hugo, and Marie grinning at her, and thought of Henri's beautiful wife, Suzanne. That was such a desperately sad story, and she couldn't bear to dwell on it today. But she was amazed and delighted to see her old friends. Nobody had told her they'd be coming but it looked like Élise and Jack had secretly arranged everything. She saw Jack's father Lionel getting quietly sozzled, and Gladys and her husband Ronnie raising their glasses and nodding happily. Grace was there too, looking lovely in cobalt blue with Bruce smiling by her side. Some of Jack's wartime buddies and chaps he'd been at school were wolf-whistling, and many of the locals were clapping as well.

When they took their seats, Rosalie sat on one side of

Florence along with Élise and her daughter, and Jack, his father, Gladys and Ronnie sat on the other side.

'Where's Hélène?' Florence whispered in her sister's ear.

'No idea.'

'She definitely said she'd come?'

Élise nodded.

They drank Florence's elderflower champagne, although others preferred a trip across to the pub to bring back ale. The food was a mixture of potato salads, early green salads, slices of ham and chicken, with vegetables of every shape and size. Some people brought bacon and egg flans – easy to carry – and they were delicious, others brought fresh bread, cheese, or home-made puddings. Florence put her worries about Hélène aside and loved every moment, including the speeches. One of the men Jack had known at school stood up to talk about Jack, which had everyone in hoots of laughter.

'I didn't know he'd been such a naughty schoolboy,' Florence said, sounding horrified, and everyone who knew Jack rolled their eyes and guffawed.

'A terror,' Gladys piped up. 'But he's our terror and we love him.'

Glasses clinked and were filled again.

Then Jack rose to his feet and the room hushed. 'I would like to say a few words about my wife, whom I first met in 1944 during the Nazi occupation of France. She may look as sweet as anything you'll see on these tables, but I would like to tell you she is made of solid steel.'

Florence could feel her cheeks reddening and gazed down at the table, willing herself not to cry.

He went on to tell them about their journey across the mountains but didn't mention why. Didn't speak of her German father.

'We went through a great deal, faced danger together, and I am the luckiest man on earth to be married to this courageous and utterly beautiful woman. She has a wise head on young shoulders. An old soul, I think they say. Anyway . . . she brought me back to life after the loss of my son.' There was a momentary hush, then he raised his glass and his voice almost cracked as he said, 'To my darling wife, Florence.'

With tears in their eyes, everyone repeated the toast and Jack kissed his new bride.

Rosalie spoke briefly and told the story of Florence's determination to find her and when she finished everyone clapped.

Then as the band warmed up, the tables and chairs were cleared to the side and Jack reached out his hand to Florence, his eyes shining. He took her in his arms, and they began a slow waltz to 'All of Me', and she whispered in his ear as he bent towards her. 'Thank you, Jack. I'm so happy.'

'I'm sorry Hélène hasn't arrived yet. I know it means a lot to you.'

She nodded, closed her eyes, and was able to count her blessings as she danced with her husband. *Her husband.*

Then, when the music went more upbeat, several more couples joined the dancing and then more and more until everyone was swing dancing in variations of the jitterbug, even Gladys and Ronnie, which made Florence smile. The band played the music of Glenn Miller, Tommy Dorsey and Benny Goodman, and a female singer joined them to sing the hit songs from the last few years. 'We'll Gather Lilacs', 'I Dream of You', 'The One I Love', and more. Then the dance music started up again, jazzy and fun, but Florence was roasting and told Jack she needed a breath of fresh air.

'I'll come,' he said.

'No, it's fine. I'll go on my own. Dance with somebody else now. Rosalie maybe.' But then she saw Rosalie already on the floor with Gerry. 'Élise then.'

Dodging the dancing couples but having to speak to one or two who congratulated her and told her what a fine man Jack was and how much he deserved some happiness, she finally made her way through the cigarette smoke and the loud voices to the exit. At last! The moment she was outside she took deep breaths of cool air. In the sweet breeze her lungs expanded, and a feeling of calm washed over her. She closed her eyes and let everything drift. She was married. A day that she had hoped for but had thought might never come, had come. She loved Jack. With all her heart, her soul, her body, she loved him. She patted her tummy, a little rounded now but not too obvious if you didn't know. *And I shall love you too, little one. And that is a promise.* When she opened her eyes, she saw birds flying over and heard others singing in the trees. A few clouds drifted by, and she felt something she couldn't quite name. She spotted a couple walking up the road and for just a moment she thought the woman might be Hélène. It wasn't. Her insides twisted with longing. She turned to go back inside but heard her name being called.

'Baudin,' a young lad was saying. 'Telegram for Baudin.'

'Yes,' Florence said, seeing the telegram boy, and with a shiver of anxiety she held out her hand for it. 'That's me.'

She tore open the telegram, saw the words Post Office at the top with the picture of the crown and read.

So sorry. I won't be able to make it after all. I wish you both well. Hélène.

'I tried to deliver it to your house,' the boy was saying. 'Meadowbrook, ain't it? But a neighbour up on the hill said you'd be here getting married like, so I came. Not strictly allowed, mind.'

'No,' she said, her eyes filling with tears. 'You're fine. Thank you.'

Duty done, he backed away, gave her a nod, and hurriedly left.

Florence stood on the pavement not a bit aware of the passers-by who'd stopped to stare and were giving her curious looks, a girl in her wedding dress with tears in her eyes.

'Bad news, love?' one kind soul asked and patted her hand. 'Never mind dear. You just get on and enjoy your day.'

Florence nodded then pressed a hand to her mouth. Hélène really wasn't coming and at that moment Florence understood how deep the rift between them had become.

It seemed impossible. How could she be getting married without her eldest sister?

She turned back towards the hall, and stopped in the doorway where Jack and Élise were talking.

'There was a telegram,' Florence said, fighting back tears again. 'Hélène isn't coming.'

Élise put an arm around her. 'I'm so sorry. Did she say why?'

Florence shook her head and handed Élise the telegram to read for herself. Jack shot her a worried look.

'I'm all right,' she said and took a deep breath. 'I can't let this spoil everything. Come on, let's cut the cake.'

She glanced inside the hall and, seeing the broad smiles on the faces of the people she loved most in the world, apart from Hélène, Florence felt the joy and the sadness at almost at the same.

'Where's Vicky?' she asked.

Élise sighed dramatically. 'With Rosalie, thank God. Our aunt is a miracle worker because I tell you, much more of this behaviour and that little girl will be the death of me. Are small children always this rebellious?'

Florence laughed. 'You were, God help you when she's a teenager.'

Élise frowned for a moment, about to deny it, but then she gave in and laughed too.

'Come on,' Jack said. 'I don't know where it came from, but my father has unearthed some real champagne to have with the cake.'

As she and Jack walked up to the main table, Florence glanced at all the people gathered there and thought over the day. She had married the man she loved, surrounded by all the people she cared about, except for one. She vowed she would do everything she could to rectify things with Hélène – her sister would surely have to forgive her one day, wouldn't she?

'Isn't it amazing?' she said to Jack. 'All this. Life goes on, doesn't it?'

He nodded.

In this post-war time, with life still so grim, rationing still happening, and people suffering from the loss of friends and family, it had been a funny make-do kind of wedding, but even more magical because of that. And seeing the radiant smiling faces, her heart danced, and Florence knew she would never forget the generosity of her friends. Jack's quiet loving presence throughout the day had filled her with such a feeling of intoxication she felt she might simply take off and fly. She laughed at herself. Perhaps she had just drunk too much elderflower champagne.

At the table she closed her eyes briefly, said a prayer for her mother and all her family and then, with her hand on top of Jack's, they cut the first slice of their wonderfully lopsided home-made wedding cake. Jack grinned at her and her heart seemed to explode with possibility and hope. They had survived the war, in France and England, and their whole lives lay before them. Florence couldn't wait to see what would come next. The birth of their child of course, which meant more than she could say. But as she looked down the years all she could see was the love – the love that would see them through – whatever might be heading their way.

AUTHOR'S NOTE

Sadly, I couldn't visit Malta when I needed to because of the pandemic. Instead, I hope I've conjured a convincing Maltese setting, mainly by referring to countless books and sifting through piles of wonderful photographs. I talked to people who know Malta. I watched films, documentaries, and videos on YouTube. I did, however, stay in a beautiful, thatched Devonshire cottage beside a water meadow, and it became the inspiration for Jack's Meadowbrook. I adored the cottage and its setting, and I hope my enthusiasm for it has brought it to life.

ACKNOWLEDGEMENTS

Cheers once again to my fantastic literary agent, Caroline Hardman. I couldn't do this without you. Thanks also to the marvellous team at HarperCollins. I've so loved working with such an enthusiastic bunch of people. It's been a blast. I must own up to putting my husband through the highs, but also the dreadful lows of a writer's life, when everything seems impossible. Thank you, Richard – for the delicious food that gets me through, the not always gracefully received plot suggestions, and for always being there. And, finally, I can't overestimate how grateful I am to everyone who has bought and read this book.

And read on for an exclusive preview
of the next book in the series

Night Train to Marrakech

Coming 2023, and available to pre-order now.

CHAPTER 1

Clemence

Morocco, Kasbah Clemence, July 1966

The mountains had never been a problem. Blinding sunlight. The deepest shadows. Isolation. Snow. All that just felt like a part of who she was now. Of course, people did vanish, but after what had happened in Casablanca, the mountains had never been where *she* felt lost. And here, at night, she was so much closer to the stars. Perched up high, the kasbah had once been a fortress built to withstand attack. Now a sanctuary, it spelt safety for Clemence, and was still firm enough to resist assault, albeit of a possibly different kind.

But one day. One day it would come.

She stood gazing out of her open bedroom window, hoping to catch the subtle changing of the light. These daily rituals kept her steady: exactly as expected, the mist burned off, the high Atlas Mountains began to shine, and the scent of wild herbs drifted into the air.

A perfect day.

She wrapped the turquoise robe around her, fastened its ties, then left the main house and crossed the terrace, pausing for a moment to run her fingertips over the climbing roses and sniff their scent. Blowsy, crimson, and almost at an end, their petals dropped at her touch. *Like blood*, she thought. At the annexe she unlocked the door, slid the bolts, and went inside.

Something was wrong.

She heard the clamour of the birds first then, inhaling sharply, spotted two small copper-coloured butterflies dancing around one of the windows. Overlooking a private courtyard with access to the mountains beyond, the window should not have been open. She glanced around the room, taking in the tray of uneaten breakfast – cooling French coffee, two pieces of freshly baked baguette, butter melting in the early sunlight – and the white robe lying crumpled on the rug. 'Fingers crossed,' she muttered, then ran to the bathroom.

A tap had been left running but no one was there, so she turned the tap off and went to the living room, where she also found no sign of her.

'Madeleine,' she called, aware of the tremble in her voice, but all she could hear in response were the birds.

The woman had bolted.

Then, right then, she felt the panic. As the distant past reared up, her mouth felt dry, the old fear fluttering as if it were one of the butterflies. She dashed outside and called for Ahmed.

'Help me,' she pleaded, and held out her hands to him as he approached. 'She's gone.'

He enclosed her hands in his much larger ones and then let go. 'She can't have gone far, Madam. I carried her breakfast in only half an hour ago. Has she eaten it?'

Clemence shook her head.

'Then she can only have been gone half an hour at most,' he said as they left the terrace.

'Did *you* unlock the window?'

Ahmed nodded. 'She complained about the room being stuffy.'

Her heart sank. 'We have to keep her inside her rooms. She can't be allowed out alone. Not ever. I thought I had explained.'

'You did. But the window is so stiff, I didn't think she'd have the strength to push it wide open.'

'I'll have to install bars. Or a wrought iron screen would at least look better. Assuming we find her.'

'We will.'

But Clemence wasn't so sure. Madeleine could be devious. 'You head down the track,' she said. 'And I'll check the grounds.'

She turned her back and set off to search the entire complex. With few remaining perimeter walls, her kasbah was at the same altitude as the last of the trees, and nothing much grew above it, the mountain sides barren and rocky.

Looking down it was different; looking down it was lush.

Imlil – a collection of little villages – huddled where three rivers merged into one, and the year-long supply of water ensured the terraced hillsides were cultivated. From her vantage point now, she could mainly see the walnut and pine forests, where she walked and collected cones for the fire, and below them, the orchards of apples, quince, almonds, and apricots. She pulled a face at the thought. No one could ever entice her to eat an apricot. Beyond the trees the agricultural land was where villagers grew vegetables, potatoes, and onions, plus alfalfa for feeding a few cows. But there was no chance Madeleine could have walked that far.

The air blowing down from the mountain top was thin and pure and, feeling the cool of it on her cheeks, she glanced up at the rocky slopes. Where had she got to? 'And in a nightdress,' she muttered. '*Pour l'amour de Dieu!*' No wonder she had felt so harried these last few months with Madeleine to look after. Keeping her eyes peeled, she investigated every shrub and every trellis in her garden. This would happen now, just when she wanted to prepare for her granddaughter's arrival. And she had no idea how that was going to turn out. She passed through the bougainvillea-clad pergola, peered behind the rosemary hedge, checked in between the palms, and went back into the private courtyard where the walls were drenched in jasmine. Nothing. No sign of her at all.

She ran towards the steep downward track Ahmed had taken, leading to where she kept her 1950s Hotchkiss jeep close to Imlil. They'd need it if they had to take the two-hour journey to Marrakech. But if they had to climb the high barren mountain peaks and canyons to search, it would have to be on foot. She swivelled round and then round again. *Please, please, let us find her soon.* They had to, for the heat and the mountains were cruel if you didn't know your way. So, so, cruel, and Madeleine did not know her way, and the longer she was out there, the greater the danger. And Clemence could only beg God that if Madeleine began to talk, people would just shrug their shoulders and pay no heed. 'Oh, it's only her,' they'd say. 'The French woman.'

For more information, follow Dinah on Facebook, @DinahJefferiesBooks, or visit her website, www.dinahjefferies.com.

And now, read the first book in the
Daughters of War Trilogy

Daughters of War

'A wonderfully evocative and sensual writer'
Santa Montefiore

'A warm and engrossing tale of passion
and courage. I loved it'
Rachel Hore

Deep in the river valley of the Dordogne, in an old stone
cottage on the edge of a beautiful village, three sisters long
for the end of the war.

Hélène, the eldest, is trying her hardest to steer her family
to safety, even as the Nazi occupation becomes
more threatening.

Élise, the rebel, is determined to help the Resistance,
whatever the cost.

And Florence, the dreamer, just yearns for a world where
France is free.

Then, one dark night, the Allies come knocking for help.
And Hélène knows that she cannot sit on the sidelines any
longer. But secrets from their own mysterious past threaten
to unravel everything they hold most dear . . .

Out now